Extraordinary Acclaim for

Richard Powers and *Prisoner's Dilemma*

"Powers has great novelistic gifts—an ear for speech that expresses character, an intense command of significant realistic details that can easily be assimilated to a larger symbolic pattern, stylistic range and control. . . . In this embarrassment of riches, one senses a writer who learned from both Updike and Pynchon. . . . Richard Powers himself now stands on a high threshold."
—Richard Locke, *The Washington Post Book World*

"An intellectual tour de force, alive with movingly human characters."
—Bruce Allen, *USA Today*

"A marvelous novel, emotionally powerful and intellectually engaging."
—*The Philadelphia Inquirer*

"There is no question after reading *Prisoner's Dilemma* that Richard Powers is a major talent. His voice is unique and his language tricks and verbal games are those of a master. He never strays from the belief that fiction is a willed creation that imposes meaning on the chaos of the real and that art plays a moral role in offering hope and a rallying vision."
—*The Houston Post*

"Powers sparkles throughout this treasure trove of style-become-substance and never misses a beat. His people are real, his situations believable, his book what comedy is supposed to be. Like *Three Farmers on Their Way to a Dance*, it dazzles and satisfies. To read *Prisoner's Dilemma* is to experience a rare, civilized pleasure and to wait eagerly for his next work."
—*The Pittsburgh Press*

BY RICHARD POWERS

Prisoner's Dilemma

Three Farmers on Their
Way to a Dance

PRISONER'S DILEMMA

RICHARD POWERS

Collier Books
Macmillan Publishing Company
New York

Copyright © 1988 by Richard Powers
Published by arrangement with Beech Tree Books, William Morrow and Company, Inc.

Collier Books
Macmillan Publishing Company
866 Third Avenue, New York, NY 10022
Collier Macmillan Canada, Inc.

Grateful acknowledgement is made for permission to reprint lines from the following selections:

From "Burnt Norton" and "Little Gidding" in *Four Quartets* by T. S. Eliot, copyright © 1943 by T. S. Eliot; renewed 1971 by Esme Valerie Eliot. Reprinted by permission of Harcourt Brace Jovanovich, Inc., and Faber and Faber Limited.

From "An Irish Airman Foresees His Death" in *The Collected Poems of William Butler Yeats*; reprinted with permission of Macmillan Publishing Company and A. P. Watt Ltd. Copyright 1919 by Macmillan Publishing Company, renewed 1947 by Bertha Georgie Yeats.

"It's Only a Paper Moon" by Harold Arlen and E. Y. Harburg and B. Rose, copyright 1933 by Warner Bros. Music and Chappell & Co., Inc. Copyright renewed; international copyright secured; All Rights Reserved. Used by permission.

"Der Fuehrer's Face" by Oliver Wallace; copyright 1942 by Southern Music Publishing Company, Inc.; copyright renewed; international copyright secured; All Rights Reserved. Used by permission.

"Chicago, Chicago." Words and music by Fred Fisher; published by Fisher Music Corp. Copyright renewed; international copyright secured; All Rights Reserved. Used by permission.

"The Prisoner's Song." Words and music by Guy Massey. Copyright 1924, Shapiro Bernstein & Co., Inc., New York. Copyright renewed. Used by permission.

From *The Decameron* by Boccaccio, translation by Richard Aldington; copyright © 1930; renewed 1968. Reprinted by permission of Rosica Colin Limited.

"On the Good Ship Lollipop" by Sidney Clare and Richard A. Whiting, copyright 1934, WB Music Corp., copyright renewed. All Rights Reserved. Used by permission.

Library of Congress Cataloging-in-Publication Data
Powers, Richard, 1957–
Prisoner's dilemma / Richard Powers.—1st Collier Books ed.
p.   cm.
ISBN 0-02-036055-X
I. Title.
PS3566.O92P75   1989b   89-7356   CIP
813'.54—dc20

Cover art and design © 1989 by John Craig
First Collier Books Edition 1989

10 9 8 7 6 5 4 3 2 1
Printed in the United States of America

the powers

I am still puzzled as to how far the
individual counts: a lot, I fancy, if he
pushes the right way.

— T . E . LAWRENCE

I bet it's a warrant for my arrest.
Isn't it wonderful?
I'm going to jail.

— GEORGE BAILEY,
It's a Wonderful Life

RIDDLES

Somewhere, my father is teaching us the names of the constellations. We lie in the cold, out in the dark backyard, on our backs against the hard November ground. We children distribute ourselves over his enormous body like so many spare handkerchiefs. He does not feel our weight. My father points a dime-store six-volt flashlight beam at the holes in the enclosing black shell. We lie on the frozen earth while all in front of us spreads the illustrated textbook of winter sky. The six-volt beam creates the one weak warm spot in the entire world.

My father is doing what he does best, doing the only thing he knew how to do in this life. He is quizzing us, plaguing his kids with questions. Where is the belt of Orion? What is the English for Ursa Major? Who knows the story behind the Twins? How big is a magnitude?

He talks to us only in riddles. We climb out of the crib and learn to speak: he warns us about language with "When is a door not a door?" We grow, we discover the neighborhood. He is there, quizzing us on the points of the compass. We fall, we bruise ourselves. He makes the wound a lesson on the capillaries. Tonight we learn, in the great square of Pegasus, how far things are from one another. How alone.

He points his way with the flashlight, although the beam travels only a few feet before it is swallowed up in the general black. Still, my father waves the pointer around the sky map as if the light goes all the way out to the stars themselves. "There," he says to us, to himself, to the empty night. "Up there." We have to follow him, find the picture by telepathy. We are all already expert at second-guessing. The five of us are fluent, native speakers of the condensed sign language, the secret code of family.

We lie all together for once, learning to see Taurus and Leo as if our survival depends on it. "Here; this dim line. Imagine a serpent, a dragon: can you all see Draco?" My older sister says she can, but the rest of us *suspect she is lying. I can see the Dipper, the big one, the obvious one. And I think I can make out the Milky Way. The rest is a blur, a rich, confusing picture book of too many possibilities.*

But even if we can't see the images of myth, all of us, even my little brother, can hear in my father's quizzes the main reason for his taking us out under the winter lights: "If there's one thing the universe excels at, it's empty space." We are out here alone, on a sliver of rock under the black vacuum, with nothing but his riddles for our thin atmosphere. He seems to tell us that the more we know, the less we can be hurt. But he leaves the all-important corollary, the how-to-get-there, up to us, the students, as an exercise.

Impressed with the truth he has just spoken, the one about the place's one prejudice, he gives us a final glimpse of that closet romantic he will keep so perfectly hidden in later years: "For all must into Nothing fall," he recites, the poetry lost on me until I see it in an anthology, decades later, "If it will persist in Being." He recovers quickly, remembers the lesson at hand, and asks, "Why do you think people need to fill the sky with pictures?"

We have a few questions of our own to ask him in return. What are we running from? How do we get back? Why are you leaving us? What happens to students who fail? I have one urgent issue to pick with him before he flicks off the beam. But I have already learned, by example, to keep the real questions for later. I hold my retaliation until too late.

I feel cold, colder than the night's temperature, a cold that carries easily across the following years. Only the sight of my mother in the close glow of kitchen window, the imagined smell of cocoa, blankets, and hot lemon dish soap, keeps me from going stiff and giving in. I pull closer to my father, but something is wrong. He has thought himself into another place. He has already left us. He is no longer warm.

We move, we uproot. We rebuild slowly in a strange place. We tear ourselves up and move again, for reasons only he understands. We strand ourselves, weave between Atlantic and Pacific, a moving target. Once, he tries to console us for the constant repotting by turning it into a geography lesson. "See? Here? Appalachia; that used to be in front of us. It's behind us now. Give me your finger. There. We have shot the Cumberland Gap. Just like Crockett." I care less for Crockett than for the map he's printed on. My father is an arrow saying, "You are Here." I need him to say, just once, clear out, where he is. Instead, he dodges with another riddle. "What's the least number of shades it takes to fill the map so that no two bordering states are the same color?"

From a later year: my father reads to me from one of those thick single-volume encyclopedias that form the backbone of his library. I am older, sixteen, the age of overt rebellion. Now we fight about religion, politics, clothes, hair—everything except the real issue. I finally find the courage to ask him outright why he always hides behind questions. And he answers me by looking up the entry "Riddles," which he thinks I might find informative: "At a critical time, when even a slight thing may decide the issue, solving a riddle correctly may, by a sort of sympathetic magic, help to solve the big problem, may turn the scales the right way." My father, the last generalist, who has always instructed me that one should attempt, hopelessly, to know everything, never once tells me, point blank, why trying to know left him so fiercely alone and lost.

The summer before I go away to school, he takes me out for private counsel. We have never gone out before, the two of us by ourselves. Awkward in the door of the restaurant, he tries, against rules, to seat himself. I am suddenly struck by how odd it is to see my father out in public, with anyone else, at a waiter's mercy. We fumble with menus, and I order something in the middle of the price range. My father claims that nothing looks good and asks for a shot of house dressing in a glass. The waiter withdraws, and my dad, hiding behind the old, sardonic humor, reveals what it is we have come here for him to say. "Don't worry about your major. Don't worry about grades. A gentleman passes with C's. Just try to figure out where history has set you down."

Somewhere my father takes us out in the dark yard. Somewhere he teaches us the names of the stars. "They are not really near each other, you understand. The points in Cetus, the Great Whale, lie hundreds of light years away from one another. They come together into these designs through optical accident." On our backs against the already frozen ground, huddled against his heavy winter coat, we try to make out the words behind his words. We listen for the missing points, for what he fails to say.

The light goes out. We transplant, we tear up again. My father leaves us to ourselves. My mother and sisters rearrange the emptied house. We boys play a last game of catch in the early evening, in spring, in the now-thawing yard. My brother passes; the football parabolas toward me. I reach for it, full extension, and at once understand what the man's real question had been all along. Inside each of us is a script of the greater epic writ little, an atlas of politics so abundant it threatens to fill us full to breaking. My father asks how we might find our way through all of that to a treaty.

My father has fallen away. He is fallen into nothing. For a fossil record he leaves only a few fragmentary tapes, the record of his voice straying over and exploring his one idea, a notion that cut him adrift in the world for a while and failed to show him the way back home. He leaves little else: A favorite chair that holds his impression. A closet of shirts that still wrinkle where he hunched. A few photos. Some freehand lecture notes. And the five of us, of course. The sum total of his lessons.

All of a sudden, as I reach for my brother's pass, I know what the man was all along asking. And I will ask what remains of my family how a person could move through life repeating, every year, the old perennials, the same chestnut riddles, the adored ore, the when-is-a-door-not-a-door? Then I will tell them, straight out, the answer, the treaty: when his mind is an evasive urgency. And ajar.

The first indication that Pop had been seeing something more than heebie-jeebies for all those years came a few weeks before the end, when the old guy leaned over to Artie on the front porch of an autumn evening and said, distinctly, "Calamine." Father and son had come out after dinner to sit together on this side of the screens and see November along. They enjoyed, in silence, one of those nights that hung in the high fifties but could easily go ten degrees either way within the hour. Artie staked out the rocker while his father, as usual, exercised eminent domain over the kapok bed long ago banished to the porch because chez Hobson—a twenty-year repository of everything the family had ever owned—could not take one more cubic foot of crap without spewing it all through every doorway and window.

Silence had gotten them this far, and there seemed to Artie no reason to improve on it. He tried to chalk up his father's mumbled word to an involuntary spasm in the man's cerebral cortex, a first burst of verb salad accompanying the return of autumn. He hoped, for a moment, to hide from it, let the word fall to the ground and add to the November earthworm-stink and humus. But Artie had no place to hide from Pop that the old man himself hadn't shown him. So he put his knuckles to the bridge of his nose, braced his face for what was coming, and asked, "Say what, Dad?"

"You heard me. Calamine. I say what I mean and I mean what I say. I plan my work and work my plan. When the tough get going, the . . ."

"Got you, Pop." Artie preempted quickly, for once Edward Hobson, Sr., was let out of the verbal paddock, he could go all night without denting his capacity for free association. After a quarter century, Artie knew the symptoms. In the man's present condition, it was pointless to ask him straight out just what he meant by the word. Artie tried

1 7

reconstructing: *Calamine, zinc oxide, iodine—nothing in that direction.* Dad's invocation was certainly not a medical request. Dad abhorred all medications. *His* sickness was nothing so trivial or topical as dermatitis, except that in crowds, for the express purpose of publicly shaming any other Hobson with him, he had been known to sing, "It's no sin to shake off your skin and go dancing in your bones."

Artie leaned back in the rocker, farther than safe. He cocked his hands behind his head and again tried to reverse engineer the train of thought behind his father's teaser. *Calamine, Gal o' Mine, Our Gal Sal.* Possibly. Probably. Who could say? In part to forestall the old man from clouding the air with additional clues, Artie announced, "Technicians are working on the problem."

He looked away to the far side of the screens. Under the rustic, ineffectual globes of small-town streetlamps, men of the 19th Precinct, scions of Second Street, used the unseasonably late warm weather to apply a last-minute manicure of preventions to their houses and lawns before the assault of winter. One or two broke from the routines of ownership to throw listless waves in the direction of One-Oh-Three, without expecting any return gesture. Neither father nor son disappointed them.

A snatch of Thanksgiving tune, "All is safely gathered in," flashed through Artie's head, so he sang the line out loud, buying time. Singing made him feel incredibly foolish. He knew a glance at the bed would show his father grinning victory. So he did the only thing possible given the situation. He sang, louder, the next line: "E'er the winter's storms begin."

Artie thought that, with as little as De Kalb, Illinois, had to offer— absolutely nothing except the claim of being the place where barbed wire was invented—there was nevertheless a stretch of fourteen days in fall when no better place on earth existed. Even given the immediate circumstances, he was somehow glad to be here. He paled at the prospect of scrapping his whole semester for nothing—increasingly likely with each new day he spent away from the law-school books. He could not really afford this unplanned trip back home. He had hoped to put the visit off until Thanksgiving, swing out for a few days, share some hormone-injected turkey with the rest of the gene pool, maybe watch a football game with the sibs: engage, for once, in the simple holiday fare the pilgrims intended. But the old refrain had again surfaced, drawing him unwillingly back into the crisis of family: "Your father is not well."

Artie tried to imagine his mother saying, for once, "Your father is *sick*," or even, "Your father is *ill*." But he could not hear her voicing either. The woman had long ago caught from her husband the contagious part of his disease, the part Artie himself had inherited: the hope that everything would still come clean if you only sit still, understate everything, and make yourself as small a target as possible.

"Ah, Ailene," Artie mouthed, almost audibly. He wondered if Mom ever gave up waiting for the miracle cure. He probed her words the way one might test a newly twisted ankle. *Not well.* But Artie did not dwell on his mother's stoic refrain. He had a more immediate test at hand. His father, perpetual high school history teacher, unrepentant grand games master, had issued a challenge: Identify the following. And Artie swore not to budge until he proved more capable of making sense out of fragments than his father was of fragmenting sense.

He stole a look kapok-way, but Dad was waiting for him. Artie never had a very smooth motion to first, and his Dad was the greatest balk detector of all time. "Son?" Pop inquired, fleshing out the word with a sadistic, smart-ass grin. Artie filled with filial hatred, a familiar and quiet disgust at knowing that Pop always had been and would be able to see through the least of the thousand pretensions Artie needed for self-esteem. He'd lived with him too long. Pop had gotten hold of his rhythm. Worse than that: his rhythm *was* Pop's, handed down. And here Artie was, trying to drive past the man who'd taught him how to dribble. Spin, fake, or weave, *he* would be there keeping pace, predictable to himself, smirking, *Who taught you that move?*

"Dad?" Artie mimicked, returning a poor version of his father's grin. There on the kapok, head propped up off the pillow in a crooked arm, stick limbs dangling, a gut that dumped its cargo across the bed, torso decked in ratty corduroys and vintage fifties crew neck: the man was a living denial of social decorum. His face, flushed with challenge, met Artie's in impudent amusement and dare.

"Calamine. Couldn't be simpler. Can we conclude that the much-touted Mr. Memory is stumped?" Dad stumbled on the first syllable, but as soon as he came up to thirty-three and a third, he was almost fine.

Artie forced a laugh and put his thumbnail squarely in the chip of his right incisor. "Don't rush the neurotransmitters," he whistled. His recall tested out in the upper stanines, but that was with objective stuff. With Dad, one could never be sure that the investigation dealt with verifiable fact. Phantom tracers had to be followed down as well. Odds were the word was some allusion to family history. Art considered calling in Eddie Jr. to pinch hit for him; his younger brother coped with nostalgia much better than Artie, although he had lived through less family trivia than anyone. The kid could identify the reference. But Dad hadn't given the problem to little brother. It was all Arthur's, and he'd sit with it until Christmas, if need be.

The trick to bringing something back was to look at something else altogether. So Artie let his attention wander from the emaciated, fat man in the crew neck to the maple leaves piling up on the front lawn. The men of the 19th had long been after the elder Eddie about criminally negligent raking, but Pop stood them off, exercising civil disobedience, the only exercise he got anymore. He refused to ruffle the leafstuff until someone in civil power once again legalized burning. The right to burn leaves, Hobson claimed, was in the Constitution. The Hobsons, he told the precinct, had been burning leaves ever since they came over. He neglected to tell the 19th that the Hobsons came over only seventy years ago, but what the community didn't know about the local opposition couldn't hurt them as much as what they already did.

Artie focused on the leaves, on how each shed piece of maple, in ridiculous tints of flint, cantaloupe, and rose, falling in front of a lamp globe, captured a corona, flapped once to keep aloft longer, preened down the debutante runway, and made that superfluous but all-important coming-out spin. Hair by Austere. Gown by Chlorophyll. Artie concentrated on not concentrating on Pop's secret word as if curing his father, or at least being temporarily rid of him, depended on identifying the allusion.

He was interrupted by sister Rachel, who stuck her head in through the front-room door to check on the Boy Talk. "Okay, Rach," Artie said, drawing her in. "For ten points . . ." He held up an index finger. Attempting to imitate his father's voice, Artie looked at her bluntly and said, "Calamine." But he couldn't keep the questioning out. Dad's voice had had no interrogative. Pop's had been pure command.

Rachel scrunched up the skin below her eyes, thought a moment, then did a search-me, Emmett Kelly look, brows grotesquely up and mouth pulled down to the right. "You two are *both* whacked, as far as I'm concerned." She looked at Eddie Sr., who now lay on his left side, facing the side porch wall, ignoring his kids and taking perverse pleasure in the ellipsis game. Certain that the man couldn't see her, Rach made a motion toward her brother, an inquiring sweep of hands around her eyes. But before Artie could respond with an equally covert gesture, Dad supplied, "Nope. Nothing yet. Your poor father has so far tonight behaved himself perfectly. Give an old guy some time to warm up."

Rachel, herself an in vivo variant on their father's black humor, shook her head in resigned admiration, mildly amused at Pop's once more raking them over the coals. Artie paled, again beaten. He looked at his sister. She shrugged and said, "Calamine, is it? Can't help you, Boy Scout; the tall trees will show you the way." She crossed to her father and sat on the bed next to him. She turned him over like a five-pound sack of turnips, gave him a painful, therapeutic pinch on the deltoids, and asked, "Throw up?"

" 'Throw up?' Is that an inquiry or an order? 'Throw up?' That's exactly the kind of question your mother always asks. These little, two-word interrogations that I'm supposed to answer intelligently. Give it to me with syntax, will you? I can handle it. I'm an educated man, you know."

She jabbed him in the solar plexus and smiled. "Sure y'are, buddy. So's my old man. Have you regurgitated yet this evening, sir? How's that?"

"No, I haven't *regurgitated*. Do you want me to? I can give it the old college try."

"Stop harping on college already. I promise to go back and finish as soon as they start granting degrees in dilettantism."

She rolled him over on his belly again, launching him wallward with an affectionate shove. But Eddie Sr. rolled right back around, saying, "And I promise that as soon as I throw up I'll bring you a sample."

"Gaaa. That's disgusting. Definite lowbrow humor. When did you grow up, the Depression?" But despite her faces and her jabs at the man's midsection, Rachel was, as always, enjoying herself immensely. She was at her best with their father when he was his most boorish. Then she could deride him with lines like the Depression one, hold up his own favorite hobby horses for ridicule.

Nor did she pick only on the sick; she went after Ailene, too, whenever she got the chance. Rach never let her mother forget that day, ages past, when the woman reprimanded four ingenuously foul-mouthed children who had come home full of the joyful discovery of dirty words. Appalled at the naifs, Mother had demanded, "Who do you think I am, one of your alley friends? I'm your mother, you know." Now that the four kids were grown, Ailene could not say the word *potty* without Rachel jumping on her with, "Who do you think you are, one of our alley friends? You're our mother, you know." And their father: their father was their father, as he was tonight again intent on proving.

Rachel folded a pillow over the old man's face and left him where he lay. On her way back inside, she made a point of stepping on her brother's big toe and grinding it into the carpet, grimly warning, "Only you can prevent forest fires." At the door, she turned and said, "You deal with him, Artie. For a change."

"Terrific," replied Artie, who had been dealing with him the only way he knew how. But he was glad at her exit. With Rachel gone, he could think more clearly. Truth was, his sister's burlesque left Artie as queasy as Dad's own. For all her insouciance, Rach could not pinch the word out of the man. It had to be removed by incision. Artie had it almost worked out, that calamine rub. The only thing preventing the recollection was his own reluctance to rebleed. But the alternative to remembering was worse. He turned in the rocker to look at Dad. "We are young," he said.

"Warm," said Eddie Sr.

"We are very young, and all together. Sometime in late summer."

"Very warm," said his dad.

"We haven't moved to Illinois yet. But I think we've left the Brook Street house already."

"Exactly. Getting hot."

"And the kids have something. Some illness. The kids always had something, didn't they? Whoever invented childhood diseases must have been able to retire early." He looked to his father for an encouraging word. But he had already exceeded the usual seldom. The man had returned to the old arm crook and challenging silence.

"It was for *us*. The calamine was for us, wasn't it? Wait a minute. It

---

2 2

wasn't disease. Here it comes. I've got it. Aptos. That summer in California."

It came out of Artie in one piece, the pain of the excision far greater than the pleasure the unrecoverable moment had once given. Intact in front of him, transplanted to the Second Street front porch through a contest of personalities that Artie should have been wise enough not to enter, was the image of a summer from the Hobson past, a seaside vacation from years before.

A summer in a bungalow by the ocean: perhaps the best vacation the family had ever taken together, their only extended trip besides the ongoing one, the one Pop now took them on. They had had the whole summer, and three months to young children is time without end, time stretching endlessly in all directions. Pop patrolled the cottage in a cotton T-shirt and straw hat and any of a number of fifties checkered pairs of shorts: a T-shirted, checker-shorted, four-kidded Crusoe playing camp counselor and lifeguard and quiz master all at once, using any antic, however unforgivable, to soup up and egg on the progeny.

Summer of slate and unseasonable shale, tones and halftones, relentless in their regularity, all the way out to Monterey. Dad paces the captain's walk, hands behind back, bellowing in that unmistakable bass, "Many brave hearts are asleep in the Deep." He orders Eddie Jr., not yet six, "Down to the mess with ye, and back with a grog if y'will, Master Stubb."

"Yie, yie, Cabin."

"And have Mr. Starbuck report above decks." Mr. Starbuck is Artie. But Artie is not around to play. Artie's over bay side, standing over a horseshoe crab, the legs and all the working underparts exposed. He explains to Rachel how he has read somewhere that this thing is a living fossil that has been around since the dawn of life on earth and hasn't changed at all while every other form of life has been steadily improving. "Well, if it's that old, we better not kill it," Rachel says, matter-of-factly. And transcending the ordinary sadism of children, they let it go.

Lily is still active with her paints, and this summer keeps, for the first time ever, an earnest diary: "Today was very foggy. The fog was so thick you could cut it with a knife. (This is a figure of speech.)" Eddie Jr., playing at surf casting, accidentally lands an eighteen-inch striped bass. Had he known there was any chance of his actually catching such a thing, this silvery creature gasping on the beach, he would never have pretended to fish in the first place. It is hard to say whether boy or dying fish blanches more. Mother cleans the animal in the sink for dinner. The family makes the most of things, and eats. Dad explains there is no escaping the food chain. All things turn their trim function on this forgiving earth.

Dad is Ahab, up and down the beach searching for a certain piece of driftwood, while mother, his perfect foil, never leaves her bungalow chair for fear of getting sand in her knitting, the articles of winter practicality she makes merely by clicking sticks through mounds of Canadian wool. At the end of each row, Mom puts down her handiwork and sings a little something herself: "By the sea, by the sea, by the beautiful sea." Only she sings "You and I," instead of "You and me," because of the predicative nominative, which is good grammar.

She goes indoors and hides when Ed takes the kids swimming. Eddie Jr. makes a mighty effort to tell her: "It's not swimming, Mom, it's *body surfing*." And one does it like this: open the chest, breathe deep, then push, push a little more, wait for the back swell, then get out in front, feel the curl breaking a bit, and glide easy and stroke, the whole force of the ocean behind you. Only don't get too far out in front or you will get crunched and crunched bad, tossed over and over into the churning sand, unable to tell which way is safety.

When the whistle blows (the fat man is up on shore, T-shirt, shorts, beaten-up straw hat, roving the terrain like a pro) it means everybody out of the water and count off. One two three four. Four children present and accounted for. The whistle goes off every few minutes; Dad carries it on a lanyard Mom has made for that purpose. When Rachel complains, "Can't you see that we're all here without this numbers thing?" he makes the JDs count by twos, and the next time by threes, and that's education. That's what he does for a living. Eddie Jr. says: "It goes up by four each time! Let's stay out here till we get to googol." And Lily, showing off, says "Googolplex." And they invent names for what numbers come next.

Mr. Starbuck gets taken out to sea in an undertow. He remembers thinking distinctly: "I should have known. The stream of white bubbles is the giveaway." And when being swept out to the Aleutians seems certain, he looks back to shore, and thinks: *This is my family. That's our summer rental cottage on Aptos. We're on vacation. I was born in Saddle Brook, New Jersey. Counting by eights is the hardest. Many brave hearts are asleep in the Deep.* Mom runs down from the bungalow, out of her chair at last, and Dad takes off his T-shirt and hat and runs too. His belly is already a monster, but his legs and arms have not yet reached the extreme emaciation of later years. Just as he is about to surrender and drift, Artie remembers something. He swims *parallel* to shore, instead of toward it, and when he clears the undertow, he is strong enough to crawl back in.

He lies on the beach like that striped bass for a while. But soon Artie jumps up and proudly explains to his mother the parallel-swimming trick that just saved his life. Something he'd read in a science magazine, and it worked just like they said it would.

The morning after an especially rough surf, four sore kids lie bedbound in collective grief greater than any the world has seen since Lily got them all the chicken pox from some kid in the alley. Each has been crunched by breakers many times over, and their sand-pounded sores threaten to fester. Mom yells something supposedly not at Dad about how if Edward won't drive up the coast for medicine, she'll get the Rambler and go herself. Dad tries using the battle-scars line, the one about how "Wounds are the price of freedom." Then he tries "Shake it off," which is psychology, and he gets about 40 percent of Eddie Jr. to come over to this way of thinking. But the older kids tell both parents to be quiet and let them die in peace.

When all four give up on the chance of any salve coming to them in this lifetime, only then does Dad explain to them, whispering at first, then chanting, louder: "The Sea will provide." Something mysterious and convincing in the litany draws the four of them up short for a minute, just listening. "The Sea will provide." He leaves his children and goes down to the beach, combs it far out of sight, and returns triumphantly twenty minutes later, toting a flask washed up from a foreign coast, labelless but watertight, delivered up in the nick of time, drifting in for just such wounds: calamine.

Artie forced his father's one-word chunk of history to the surface. But far from being cathartic, the story of medicine from out of the sea disconcerted him even more this second time around. Nothing appealed to him less this evening than the idea that his life, his father's, the family album, had all been easy once. The interval of lost time came and visited on the front porch, saw the mess it had made, and instantly disowned its offspring.

Artie looked at his father, stripped of whistle, and then at his own thin arms and legs, so unlike the ones that had pulled him out of the undertow. He had accomplished nothing in the intervening years except the steady conversion of early hope into adult confusion, with no indication of how the one had become the other.

Pop mumbled, kapok-muffled. "Good man." He sounded sicker than the three days' symptoms warranted. "Knew you had it packed away." Artie focused on the note of congratulations, ignoring the overtones. He decided that he had accumulated a hefty enough bank balance of contrition through the years to justify his gloating, just this once, over the strength of his memory. Recalling that lost summer, reminded of how his father had always combined just such taunts, pedagogy, and oracular beachcombing to produce balm out of nowhere, Art looked away again onto the silent lawn and let a feeling of All Clear come over him.

Maybe Pop's disease *was* something harmless, after all. It wouldn't be the first missed diagnosis in history. Whatever ailed the old lifeguard, Artie decided, the fellow sharing the porch with him *this* evening was still a good person. His heart filled with a magnanimity toward Dad that ordinarily rarely bothered him, and Artie at once wanted to do something special for the man.

"Come on, big guy. Let's go inside and deal some cards." Among Ailene, Lily, Rachel, and Eddie-boy, they could easily scrape up another partnership. Dad often said he'd made sure to father sufficient children always to be able to make up a table. Bridge allowed him to hold forth on statistics, to comment on the psychology of intimidation, to wheedle Lily or Ailene. And in this way, Artie could test his longstanding hypothesis that nothing administered to his father's perennial illness as well as setting up a dangerous cross-ruff. Nothing restored him to health like going down heroically in Three No Trump.

Artie stood and moved for the door. Lawn and streetlamp, a seaside summer, had taught the two of them all they were going to learn this evening. It was time, Artie felt, to return to the small consolation of family. Art was two steps to the door when he heard something that dropped him in place and overhauled his evening plans. His father was calling his name, but in another man's voice.

"Arthur," he said, and, "Son." He spoke the words sharply, each syllable rising up eerily by spectral fourths. He barely whispered, as if too big a twitch of the vocal cords might pitch him over a ledge that had just opened up underneath him. *Something is happening,* his father's voice telegraphed. *Something I do not want to go through by myself.* At the same time, the tone carried an awful fascination, as if a frightened rare animal had appeared from nowhere in the dark yard, one that Dad wanted Artie to see without scaring.

A salt-pillar glance back over Artie's shoulder confirmed the worst. Pop lay on the displaced mattress, on neither one side nor the other nor even face down as Rachel had left him, but unnaturally on his back, shock-side up, staring up at the ceiling as if reading something there. He clearly saw something, a picture, a scene of terrifying and unnameable wonder, etched on the white boards.

Before Artie could do anything to arrest it, the awful moment was on him. The air turned metallic as he breathed. Time thickened and molded over. Artie's thighs refused to move, and he felt an overwhelming desire to sit down and do nothing, pinned at the bottom of an ocean of atmosphere. He had seen Pop's attacks before, more than once. But this time, the hidden horror in his father's voice blew his composure apart. Artie, from infancy, had a secret terror of sirens at night, of how easily they reduced the givens of the world to nothing. Now, sirens clanging on all sides, his courage crumpled and his equanimity stripped off smoother than steamed wallpaper, with nothing but gaping plaster underneath.

Averting his eyes from the white-wood ceiling, Artie assumed a matter-of-factness he did not feel. He returned to bedside, exhaling a bit of air in the closest motion he allowed himself to breathing. When he felt a small patch of earth resolidify under his feet, he risked a look at his father's face: the man's saucer eyes squeezed into a wince so severe that Art imitated it involuntarily. Dad's hands clenched the rattan bed box, keeping his discarded body from falling farther.

How could Artie have thought a bridge game possible, and only seconds before? He would now be lucky to get the body upstairs and in bed without going to pieces himself. He loosened his father's clamped knuckles, saying, "Okay now, okay," although his father had by now gone under, eyes closed, and could hear nothing. Gradually, Artie started to believe his own attempts at solace. He sat at the foot of the bed and stroked his father's flinty shins. He repeated one more "Okay," which became an "Oh, Dadimo."

He was all at once taken with the urge to sing a refrain of "Many brave hearts are asleep in the Deep," but he was unsure if the joke would be in good taste, even the already-questionable taste he'd inherited from the man in question. He said instead, "The Sea will provide," offering a little crumb of comfort, although his father could no longer hear him. He pinched a row of Dad's hammer toes until they turned red, counting off, as he grabbed each in turn, "Eight, sixteen, twenty-four," and a hesitant "thirty-two." Then he grabbed the man's torso and held on. As the fellow would not be able to feel him for some time, no one would be the wiser.

2

Not surprisingly, the four kids split widely on a diagnosis. Spread over the spectrum as on every other issue, they were not yet, early in November, even unanimous on whether Pop really needed diagnosing. As in all complex matters, the four Hobson baby-boomers, although identical genetic material raised in the same household with militantly unfair equality, swore by four radically different verdicts of what, if anything, was wrong with Pop.

They seemed to agree secretly never to reveal outwardly that they were blood relations, variations on a theme. Sixteen years earlier, when Arthur was only nine, Lily eight, Rachel seven, and Edward, the caboose, just two, Ailene carted all four in the two-toned Ford to a photographer's shop in Teaneck, New Jersey, and came away with a montage of four oval faces in a frame, the kind still rampant in the early sixties. A duplicate print hung in the photographer's shop window for a few seasons, drawing smiles from passersby who thought they could see in each pronounced forehead and high cheekbone an uncanny familial persistence. Among the aunts and uncles, the game was to pick out, from the fourfold photograph, who had whose eyes and whose cheekbones. This favorite holiday talk made Rachel crack the same joke annually from age eight to fourteen: "If I've got Pop's nose, I better give it back before he blows." What passed for sense of humor, at least, they shared congenitally.

But the truly observant, which in the early days included only Mother, soon detected what changing facial bones made undeniable. Nobody had nobody's nose. Out of the blue, each child grabbed a face by mail order, arriving at unique features for no other reason than being the only one of the batch to hit upon a particular chin. Inertial aunts continued to comment on the unmistakability of the strain. But strangers, from the far side of the communion rail on the family's occasional Christmas or

Easter forays into church, looking over the mixed bag of visages, pronounced a glottal "adoption" while choking down the host.

Yet even the garden variety of faces seemed uniform compared to the personalities each staked out, persuaded by Dad's post–Iwo Jima, pre-prefabrication policy of rugged individualism. Rachel let a talent for language die on the vine because big brother Arthur showed the skill before her. She took up sports, retroactively curtailing older sister Lily's perfection of the half gainer. Lily then shifted to an artistic sensitivity, which Artie had given up for his first Lent following puberty. The kids carved out claims on the map of special interests like so many colored wedges driven into blank Antarctica. The loser in this land grab was the latecomer. Eddie Jr., already condemned by name to suffer little-Rickyism without his father's even having the excuse of being Cuban, arrived at adolescence to find no decent interests left, and had to take good-natured ineptness for his identity. The four-ovaled photo now bore only the faint traces of other scripts long since abandoned.

De facto, the kids weren't going to give up their hard-won second, third, and fourth opinions on what ailed Eddie Sr. They had been raised from infancy under the illness's milder forms. They all witnessed identical symptoms: they grew up seeing the sightings, the sick stomachs, the fainting fits. They had heard, for years, their mother's periodic, confidential "Your father is not well," an explanation as inscrutable as the ailment itself. But Lily suffered the hope of periodic remission while Rach hid in good humor, Art kept ironic distance, and little Eddie stuck to fledgling optimism and kidding. Prescription remained a private patent, more individual temperament than observation. The complications of the last two weeks, Pop's sudden and violent relapse into spells after years of relative health, could not trick them into unanimity.

But if the children split on the causes of sickness, they agreed on one shared treatment: no one ever spoke a word of what was going on out loud. By unspoken agreement, they kept mum in public. During one of the rare times that they had touched on what they ought to do about the man's steady deterioration, Lily ended up hurling Rach through a screen window. The boys, pulling their sisters apart, themselves degenerated into a profanity match that they were only able to patch up by mutually agreeing that *neither* woman knew what the hell she was talking about.

They were of the same face once again at least on how to handle the old man among themselves. And so, when he finished counting Dad's hammer toes by eights, Artie calmed down and reminded himself that what had just happened was nothing that he hadn't cleaned up after countless times. He stood up, tested his tendons, and went inside. There he ambushed Eddie Jr., who was seeing how long he could bounce a Ping-Pong ball on a hot skillet before it melted.

Artie grabbed little brother's neck and squeezed. "I need your help transporting someone near and dear to you across state lines, sport." Eddie's face crumpled in fear, which he at once expertly oiled into a look of amused long-suffering. His eyebrows asked, "Again?" although Eddie stayed silent.

The two brothers walked to the porch, arms on each other's shoulders. They surveyed the body, discussing how best to grip it. They had worked together like this the summer before, toting ceramic tile into a trench dug out to the city's main. They lifted their father's bulk up off the bed, one man-child under each armpit. The passage up the stairwell was so cumbersome that the three bodies jammed for a moment and could not twist forward. Little Eddie called out, "Wait. I've seen this one. Laurel and Hardy. *The Piano Movers*, right? What do I win?" He won, for the moment, a maniacally guilty laugh from his brother.

Dad shocked them both by choosing that instant to regain awareness. "Have a little respect for the dead," he said, starting the sentence inaudibly and ending it in full voice. His brisk return to speech so startled his sons that they pulled opposite ways at the turn of the stairs, popping the bottleneck. Dad carried on, "Oh, how sharper than a children's teeth is . . ."

"That's enough," Artie said, covering the man's mouth.

"Cool out, Pop," Eddie Jr. added, gently. "We got you."

Artie had a sudden urge to do violence to both father and brother: squeeze thumbs, wrench arms, throw somebody against the wall. He masked the impulse as he always did—by grinning pleasantly. A dish-breaker at age ten, Artie had since gotten self-control down to a science. At eighteen, he had timed his outbursts carefully for when they would take the opposition off guard and give the best results. At twenty-five, he had paired the physical spasm with the follow-up grin for so long that the desire to hurt father and brother for their inanity melted quickly into the self-defense of goodwill.

The boys got their father undressed and under the covers. Whatever Pop had seen only a few moments before faded back into the domestic landscape, retreated behind the billboards. The old man went down willingly with nothing further to say for himself than, "You guys are the greatest."

"We owe it all to you, Pop," Eddie Jr. said, flicking off the light. Neither son moved to leave. Instead, they sat quietly, one on the floor, the other across the arm of a chair, two aging athletes agreeing to an informal time-out. They gathered themselves in the dark, listening. Soon came the subtle shift in breathing that marked their father's departure into sleep.

"Look at him," Artie said, eyes adjusted to the dark. "He looks just like a boy of ten."

"Twelve, more like," said Eddie Jr.

"Have it your way," Artie grinned. They went back downstairs.

Lily lay in wait below. She'd witnessed the whole proceedings, hiding in her room at the back of the house. Now she emerged to direct them into the kitchen. She gave them both a glass of her specialty: herbal tea of her own devising, a recipe she squirreled away in a spiral notebook under the chapter heading "Sixties Without Shame." Artie took his glass with the grimace reserved for acts of comfort. "We'll only drink this stuff under one condition. You have to play pinochle with us."

Lily agreed reluctantly, although all three knew that attempting the game with her was largely an academic exercise. Every few tricks she had to stop and count suits, tapping her fingers on the table for all to hear. Mid-trick, she would ask, "What's the rank again? Ace, King, Ten?" And Eddie Jr. would have to repeat exasperatedly, "Ace, Ten, King."

Somewhere between table talk and point counting, Lily risked a slow stroll onto forbidden territory. She began confidently enough, as if there were more ways to self-esteem than being able to keep track of what trumps were out. "I remember the first time I ever saw Dad have a spell," she said. "We were still in the Brook Street house. I had just turned eight." She might have been talking about being taken to see her first stage play.

"Seven," corrected Artie, pulling a card from his hand. "*I* was eight." He checked her latest mistake firmly, another Ace-King-Ten.

She scuffed a consonant in silence. "You're wrong, as usual. I was in

Mrs. Buntz's class, and that was third grade, so I was eight. But we'll let it slide. For the sake of pleasant conversation, we'll say seven. Anyway, I was in that upstairs room with the dormers—remember?—getting in my weekly half hour of TV. Do you suppose we were the last children in the Northern Hemisphere to have our TV viewing rationed?"

"Wait a minute," said Artie. Flapped by his sister's patter, he'd misjudged a trick. "That's not the card I meant to pull."

"Laid is played," Eddie Jr. said, keeping his glee as clinical as possible. At the same time, he filed away that old cardsharp's line for use at his high school buddies' next off-color joke-off. Out loud, he added another favorite Hobson card-table adage: "Never send a boy to do a man's job."

"I imagine we were," said Lily, habituated to answering her own question. "I remember the color of the bedspread. The house smelled like pepper steak."

"The house smelled as a pepper steak smells," corrected Artie, revenging himself for his wasted trump.

"The house smelled like pepper steak. The television show was nonfiction, of course. We could watch two nonfiction shows a week, and doubling the allotment always seemed worth having to learn something. A travelogue—somewhere in Asia, I think, although I wouldn't have known Asia from Newark at the time. Five minutes into it Dad came in, which meant that you couldn't enjoy the show anymore because he'd quiz you on everything. 'How far is that country from here? How long would it take an airplane flying five hundred miles an hour to get there?' "

" 'What language do they speak there?' " Eddie Jr. contributed.

" 'Do you know our country's foreign policy in the area?' " Artie said, despite himself.

Lily swelled and picked up speed. "But when they showed footage of this lost temple, for some reason he shut up. I can still see the place, the camera moving over it. Amazing: a ruin, but intact. No human had touched a stone for hundreds of years. A pack of monkeys had taken the place over, colonized it. A temple given up to gibbons. I remember thinking, at age eight, that it looked like the last record of civilization. Then suddenly: bang. Dad went down behind me, flat on his back. I've never been so frightened before or since. I thought . . . God, I don't know. I thought I had killed him, somehow, by what I was thinking."

Artie folded his cards, touched a finger to his eye socket, closed his eyes, and nodded. Lily enjoyed her brother's rare commiseration. She should have left the empathy at that, more than she expected. But wanting one last shot at the topic, and feeling that pushing the point might lead, for once, to partial action, she added, "Do you think it's epilepsy, or something?"

"It's obviously not epilepsy," Artie snapped, retrieving a second miscard from under Eddie's fist, which the kid slammed down to prevent removal. Neither relented, and they ended up tearing a corner off the card.

"But something like it, maybe?" Lily said, retreating into the hypothetical.

"That depends on what you mean by 'something like.' We already know he's got 'something like' epilepsy. It's called a family."

All at once, from his unassuming slouch, Eddie Jr. demanded, "Why the hell doesn't he go see a doctor?"

The outburst surprised the two older children, so long had it been since they thought of that possibility. They exchanged sardonic looks. " 'The human body is a marvelous machine,' " Artie said, in a fair imitation.

" 'It has had a million more years' experience in detection and correction than the boys at the Mayo Clinic,' " completed Lil. Pop's distaste for doctors, his aversion to organized health care, his empirical respect for the mechanism, was one more strange twist of the man's arch rationality.

"Why don't we force him, then?"

Artie took on the task of educating the dewy-eyed. Patient, patronizing, he said, "I don't suppose you remember The Abscess? You were just a log in your father's eye at the time. He came to breakfast one morning looking like he already had a meal stuffed in his right cheek pouch. I'm talking golf ball. And damn him if he wasn't tough enough to pull off a lesson on the *theoretical* approach to pain. The monster didn't even take an *aspirin*. All for our benefit, of course. *I* would have passed out. But he: he just sat there doing this comic bit. 'I wish I had one on the other side, too. I could be Nixon.' Canadian bacon and a hard biscuit, with an entire molar going off like dynamite in the back quarter of his jaw. Two days later, it's gone. Successfully healed through calculated neglect. Return to Normalcy."

Lily took up the slack. "He loves those newspaper exposés about people going into clinics with kidney stones and coming out of surgery on a platter. It's a statistical wager for him: the odds are better if you don't screw with the equilibrium."

There lay the heart of the problem. They had slipped easily into card-table rage against the man's evasiveness, and without changing conversational tones they had ended up somehow adopting the enemy's logic with no one noticing. But Eddie Jr. must have heard the false turn, because he attacked them with a violent burst before he too succumbed to reason. "So what are you saying?" He stood up, flailing. "That we should let him treat passing out the same as a toothache? That just because *he* makes a theory out of suffering, that we have to too?" He stopped long enough to notice Artie waving his fingers at him, a facetious, *down-boy* ripple of digits. Eddie took his seat again, shyly. "I mean, do we gotta wait until he can't object, and then *carry* him into the ER? Great. Then we have to listen to the surgeon say how amazing it is that the guy was still walking around alive for so long."

"What we're saying," Lily explained sympathetically, "is that your father's second-favorite literary passage in the whole world is the bit from *Tristram Shandy*—'I live in a constant endeavour to fence against the infirmities of ill health . . .' "

" '. . . and other evils of life,' " Artie assisted, although Eddie Jr. could have done the same.

" '. . . by mirth.' " Lily delivered the quote intact, despite never having tried to memorize it. Sheer repetition on Pop's part. She smirked, despite herself, remembering his first-favorite speech, Kipling's "If," done at an insanely high speed. *If you can keep your head,* she tested herself, lost to the conversation. *When all about you are losing theirs and blaming it on you.* Yes: she could probably finish that one, too.

Artie didn't think that was what they meant at all. What they were *really* saying was that addressing Dad's illness clinically was not step one. But he thought it wiser not to break up the rare consensus he had with Sis. So he said, "What we're saying is that your father has a considerable jump on us. If we go to him now, he'll laugh. He'll just point out, correctly, that he's been passing out harmlessly for far longer than we've worried what to do about it."

Eddie fiddled with his suits. "Hey, what's with the 'your father' all of a sudden? You two trying to blame him on me now that he's gone whacko?"

Lily, back from mental poetry, countered, "Can you give us one good reason why we shouldn't?" Ten minutes of talk with the boys, and she inevitably picked up their sardonic style. The moment of truth or consequence passed as subtly as it had arrived. No one knew who was on who's side; Pop had confused them again. On one point, though, they were still allied. They had all skirted what they all knew to be the real issue: none had the courage to take on Dad's confidence game head on.

"Damn right we're blaming the relapse on you," Artie chipped in. "After all, don't you think it's more than a little suspicious that Pop should wait to have hallucinations again, after all these years, until the very month you have your . . . hem . . . *majority* thrust upon you?"

Little Eddie was interrupted in his attempt to use the blade edge of the Jack of Diamonds on his brother's jugular by the return of Mother and the missing Rachel. Ailene closed the front door after her and butted it shut repeatedly with her behind. The big oak slab had not closed properly since the early part of the century, and refused to cooperate at this late date. Through the runway leading from the kitchen, the card players saw that both Mother and Sister were red and raw from the night cold.

Artie thought: they slipped out the back way just before the drama broke. He knew that they couldn't have known the fit was coming on, yet their technical innocence irritated him all that much more. He demanded: "Where did you two run to?"

Rachel shuffled kitchenward, left wrist to hip, right arm extended. She grabbed Artie and echoed, "Two-run-too . . . two-one-two . . ." He wrestled out of her dance clinch and asked again. Rach returned his stare, simian fashion. "Art thou thine sister's kipper snack?"

Mother adjudicated, coming down the runway, rubbing her shoulders and burring. She had dropped fifteen pounds after the birth of each child and now nothing stood between the elements and her internal organs. "We were at the Northern Lights. And—" She paused, walked over to the gas stove, and threw open a burner. She placed a kettle over the stove, indulging in the ritual more for the dangerous blue halo of flame than from any real desire for boiling water. "And," she said again, her dramatic pause revealing itself as the fake reticence of a little girl who can't wait to give her news. "They *carded* me." Smug, she skipped over to Eddie and pushed his nose in, making a *smock* sound with her cheeks as she did.

"And you showed him your license?"

"I had to."

Eddie Jr. had long ago become inured to the indignities always meted out on the youngest. He expected his elders to fault him for their still being as capricious and immature as he. But he thought it a particularly ignominious blot on the family name (not that the family name couldn't use another blot here and there to touch it up and restore the symmetry) that his mother, being carded, should dutifully surrender her two forms of ID. "I suppose, Mother dear, that you got up there and fruged, or whatever you young folks are doing this year, with the best of them."

"Don't be ridiculous," Ailene demurred loudly. "I'm no spring chicken, and you know it." *Then why*, the question hung about the kitchen, begging for someone to ask, *did you fail to see through the heartless practical joke on the part of the doorman?*

Casting about for something to sober her, something to sting her back to the hard facts of that evening, Eddie undid the damage to his Irish pug and said, "You two ducked out just in time to miss the show." Instantly he regretted both content and style of delivery. He hated himself when he got snide. "Sorry," he said. "Artie's fault. He's a bad influence on me."

Mom stopped in mid-sashay, searched her children for any sign of willful falsehood, and, finding none, did a distinctly undancelike ball change down the runway and upstairs. Had the Teaneck photographer been present, he might have captured the remaining four in an uncanny second set of ovals—Then and Now—or, more likely, given up the project as stranger than fiction.

Artie got up from the table and shut off Mom's irrelevant gas burner. He poured the steaming kettle water into the sink. When he finally spoke, he kept his head sinkward, addressing the porcelain. "Bedside manner brings out the best in her."

Lily switched alliances in a second. She glared at him, not the universal women's look of sovereign dismissal of men but one tailored expressly for this male. "She has her work," she said, as soft as imaginable, and mimed her mother's exit step into her bedroom at the back of the house.

Artie mumbled a *confusus* of mock Latin just loud enough to hear.

"Mea culpa, mea maxima . . ." In a Catholic, the act might have passed for a blasphemy of contrition, but in a Lutheran it was sheer, scholastic showing off. He fiddled with a faulty washer on the cold faucet, recalling a story his father frequently repeated at table, sometimes varying in the particulars but always fundamentally the same, about how Grandfather, who had died before Artie was born, had come to the Cure. The oldest of the Eddies, Irish by background and temperament, had taken as his bride a Mediterranean woman, one of whose eight personalities (the traditional four better and four worse) imagined that the best way to get a leaky faucet fixed was to appear every fifteen minutes and demand that the huddled immigrant refuse get off the couch and plumb. After a few days of berating, Granddad shouted, "You want that drip fixed? I'll fix the drip for you, forever!" He flew into the kitchen and smashed his fist against the offending pipe. Opening his hand, he was amazed to find a steady stream of blood and bone joining the water dripping into the basin. He vowed on the spot never to allow another drop of alcohol in his house. According to Pop, Granddad had only to remember that color combination—maroon on off-white—to keep his vow. Now, so many years after the reformation, Artie smiled, thinking how simple *that* cure had been compared to what the present generation would need.

He felt Rachel pinch him in the bicep, whispering "Crabs" as she passed behind him and sat down at the table across from Eddie Jr. Little brother sat motionless, head in hands, agonized at causing his mother additional and unneeded grief. Rachel took a pitch pipe out of her pocket, blew a C, and sang, to the tune of "Goodnight, Ladies,"

> *Don't cry, Edski,*
> *Don't cry, Nedski,*
> *Don't cry, Wedski,*
> *We'll let you take the blame.*

Eddie, whose face indeed formed an unwitting, paint-by-numbers version of St. Sebastian, came back to himself. Blushing, he tried to grab the pitch pipe from her hand, but failed. He put his elbow on the table, challenging her to an arm wrestle. Rachel grabbed his palm in both of hers, sprang to her feet, and began to twist his wrist off. When he jerked free, Rach smiled sweetly and said, in her best singsong Why-I-Vote-Every-Four-Years voice, "I win."

Artie, at the touch of his younger sister, felt his static thoughts fall off and leave him temporarily in the clear. Maybe Rach was right: consign Dad to his own muck-making and go on with the work of being well disposed toward the world. He tried to show the other two that he, too, was ready to join back in. He put his voice into treble and warbled, "I thought I told you kids that if you're going to kill each other, to do it in the yard. I just washed . . ." But when he turned from the sink, there in front of him was the object of his mockery, looking shook.

Artie thought for a moment that Dad had taken the long-expected last turn for the worst. But it was just the opposite, and equally incomprehensible. "I thought you kids meant he had a spell when we were out."

"He did. Bad as I've ever seen. Tigers on the ceiling. Eddie and I had to take him upstairs and put him to bed." Artie gestured toward the table for proof that he wasn't lying. Eddie nodded concurrence.

"Then how do you explain that he's all right now?"

"All right?" Artie answered, despite his mother's having spent two dozen years telling him never to answer a question with a question.

"He's sitting up in bed." Ailene shook her head, unable to accept the reprieve. "Happy. Dictating. Working on Hobstown."

HOBSTOWN: 1939

Everything we are at that moment goes into the capsule: a camera, a wall switch, a safety pin. The task, a tough one, is to fit inside a ten-foot, streamlined missile a complete picture of us Americans, circa 1939. Glass and stainless steel, a silver dollar, a toothbrush. A stroke of genius, including that toothbrush—an item so common it might have been overlooked. If people of the future learn everything about us except for toothbrushes, we are lost.

The missile aims at the future. How far in the future? Exactly fifty centuries, five thousand years. Fair officials sink the missile underground, not to be opened until the year 6939. Bud counts backward the same number of years. In 3061 B.C., Egyptians experimented with the plow, Sumerians with wheeled vehicles and writing. Five thousand years is a big leap for a boy of thirteen. But if the first step was big, the next will be bigger. For every thirteen-year-old knows the theme of this year's World's Fair: each year speeds the rate of change. That's why this message in a bottle is so crucial, a note from ourselves to our later selves, when all is forgotten.

The cache includes a tape measure, of course. A can opener. The alphabet in type. Soon Bud sees that fitting all America into the tube would take a tube the size of all America. But thanks to the recent invention of microfilm, we can fit into this space the blueprint for something far larger. On film, we include our favorite magazines, dictionaries, atlases, technical manuals. We slip the Lord's Prayer in three hundred languages between photos of baseball and poker games.

We pack a healthy regimen of news, the same newsreels that supply matinee instruction for boys of thirteen. We choose, from thousands of miles of film, Roosevelt speaking, a Miami fashion show, the bombing of Canton by the Japanese. Bud feels the endeavor take on the air of science and high seriousness. Yet it confuses him, too, about the dominant tense. We make tomorrow's archaeology today. How can that be?

Bud Middleton visits the 1939 New York World's Fair in Flushing Meadow, Queens. He comes with his family from their home in the American Midwest. Dad, Mom, Babs, Bud, and Grandma. The entire twelve-hundred-acre miniature country floors Bud. Its theme, "Building the World of Tomorrow," knocks him over. He begins his tour at the park's Theme Center, with its seven-hundred-foot Trylon needle and two-hundred-foot Perisphere containing the moving platforms, piped symphonies, projected images, and precision models of Democracity, the perfect, planned metropolis. From there he gravitates to the Rotolactor at Borden's Dairy World, missing that it is just Elsie being milked on a merry-go-round. He speeds through the Court of Peace, the gleaming buildings from Greece, Poland, and Czechoslovakia. He cannot afford to dawdle at the League of Nations exhibit in the far corner of the park if he wants to see any fraction of the fifteen hundred exhibits. He catches Planters's "Mr. Peanut and His Family Tree," as well as Ford's "A Thousand Times Neigh," a horse's-eye view of the auto. He waits in line to thrill to the famous General Motors Futurama. He indulges his adolescence for a half hour at the Aquacade, Jungle Land, and Nature's Mistakes pavilions over in the Amusement Zone.

Even getting stuck with his mother at the top of the Life Saver Parachute Drop for three hours, although traumatic, cannot mar the most astonishing, eye-opening vacation of his life. The fair culminates for Bud in the Westinghouse pavilion, with Elektro, the talking, cigarette-smoking robot, and, above all, with the time capsule, that torpedo locked on a target five thousand years off. That this exhibit is his favorite stands to reason, for Bud, Mr. and Mrs. Middleton, Grandma, and even the charming Babs are themselves Westinghouse creations.

The mythical Middleton family is manufactured to serve as model Americans at this model America. In 1939, the family appears in trade books, magazine ads, even a feature-length film put out by Westinghouse promoting the exhibit that in turn promotes the immense and undeniable benefits of Westinghouse's product, the product Bud's dad calls "science's greatest gift to the world of the future."

"But won't the capsule deteriorate in all that time?" Mother asks. But science solves even that. A Westinghouse magic substance called "cupaloy" and a special sealant gas ensure that safety razor and wall switch and one thousand pictures and ten million words will survive their long passage intact.

"What if folks five thousand years from now can't read English?" Bud asks, displaying the practical turn of mind of bright young Americans of 1939. Westinghouse sees to that, including in the capsule an English lexicon with pictures, a Rosetta stone for teaching the language from scratch. They distribute, to countless universities and libraries across the country, microfilmed multilingual instructions and maps for locating and disinterring the capsule if it is ever lost in time. History is a treasure hunt.

Somewhere in Bud's still budding brain he fails to see how any amount of gloss will help creatures from the future reconstruct what the newsreels of Jesse Owens's 1936 Olympic victories mean. He cannot imagine conveying to an alien of five thousand years from now what is obvious to the Middletons: why no time capsule of America in 1939 could be complete without a Mickey Mouse plastic cup. Yet Bud Middleton approves the anthology of objects, especially one final bit of recursion. The capsule contains a newsreel documenting that capsule world in miniature, the World's Fair itself.

For all its elevating vision of the promise of tomorrow, something terribly wrong with the 1939 World's Fair escapes Bud. A tremendous gulf splits it down the middle. It epitomizes all we have done well. It is the abyss of insipidness. It is urgent, high-toned, and aware—the most magnificent civil-engineering project ever, transforming an ash dump into a model of the future. But just down the pastel avenue, shading into the hues of the fair's color-coded "zones," the place degenerates into a nudie show where near-naked girls tussle with octopi. One exhibitor's film, The City, asks of the world we take for granted, "Who built this place? What put us here? And how do we get out again?" Bud has no answer, being just thirteen and himself a creation of that same fair. He has just the degree of insight the fair gives him and no more.

What world do the Middletons return to after their film is over? A world where the family newspaper gives more room to church socials than to the Mine Workers' strike or the collapse of Slovakia. A world where Shirley

Temple, the number-one box-office champion for four years, has just lost her title to Mickey Rooney. The two most popular stars in the most popular medium ever in the world have an average age of fifteen. Bud, at thirteen, with only a few magazine appearances and one second billing in a trade-show feature, is over the hill.

Hollywood, without knowing it, has its most magnificent year ever. Never again will it come close to matching this year's product. Gone With the Wind *takes the Oscar. But it has stiff competition from* Goodbye Mr. Chips, Ninotchka, Stagecoach, The Wizard of Oz, Mr. Smith Goes to Washington, Wuthering Heights, Dark Victory, *and* Juarez. *Even as the movie industry peaks it sickens, although it won't show the symptoms for years. This incredible flowering is not simply escapism from economic hardship. Times have been far harder without producing anywhere near this burgeoning bouquet of other worlds. Movies somehow* replace *the Middletons' lost hold on the real place, now too desperate and absentee to feel.*

Swing is King, a sound that has Bud and Babs almost hysterical with rhythm. "Deep in a Dream" tops Variety's *Hot 15. Television makes its debut at the Fair: Bud stands in front of a camera and does a monologue for his folks. Radio holds an uncontested hammerlock on the Middletons' hearts and minds, the one, oak-cabineted portal through which they catch an astigmatic glimpse of the larger landscape. On September 1, 1939, Mrs. Middleton and Grandma hear an announcer conclude an extended description of Hitler's morning Blitzkrieg into Poland by saying, "We should like to express our appreciation again at this time to . . . the makers of Ivory Soap, sponsors of* Life Can Be Beautiful."

In November, Babs Middleton's copy of Photoplay *runs an article called "Clouds Over Hollywood." It reads:*

The crowds were laughing as they emerged from the premiere of "The Women," gay with the sparkle of watching a gay, sparkling picture, happy with that sense of well-being within the industry which comes from the knowledge that another hit is born. Then, as they reached the street, the newsboys' cries reached their ears.

A stunned moment before the full impact of the news struck home. Bitter silence as realization came. Then a growing murmur of restlessness and fear and heartache for the many strangers within the gates who for so long now had been no longer strangers.

"What of Boyer?" "What of Niven?" "And Richard Greene?"

"Hollywood," Babs reads, an anxious rawness in her throat for Pepe Le Moko, hero of Algiers, *"is face to face with grim reality."*

Across the living room, Mr. Middleton settles into his overstuffed chair with the November 13 issue of Time. *In it, he learns that 1939 has proved the final defeat of appeasement as a credible policy for establishing and enforcing cooperation among nations. Now the world's last hope is Tit for Tat. He reads that Lloyd's of London offers insurance against death and dismemberment from aerial bombing: one pound per one hundred pounds' coverage. He reads a scrap of doggerel currently making the rounds:*

> *Hitler is a gangster,*
> *Daladier's a bore,*
> *Chamberlain's a counterfeit,*
> *And so's the new world war!*

But the piece that slams home, that jumps off the magazine page at him, shouts in great letters, "unprepared." "you unprepared." "Don't let winter catch you unprepared." An advertisement for Quaker State antifreeze. Dad resolves to take action the next day, correct his neglect, and avert what might turn into a family disaster if he leaves it any longer.

Upstairs, Bud struggles with a letter to his friend Ed. "Dear Eastie," he begins. "Seems like forever since we met last spring at the Fair." He stops and chews on his pencil end. He stares into the shedding trees outside his window. When the gleaming pavilions once more reform in front of his eyes, he grows animated and writes quickly. "But that's a bat's blink compared to 5,000 years, huh, buddy?"

Or rather, Ed, in his home in Jersey, stops on a November afternoon and wonders what the Middletons might be up to. He has met them only once, in the Westinghouse film, but their future seems somehow crucial to the boy. He knows, without knowing, that something terribly wrong

---

infects the world of 1939. He learns in school that the world's showdown has supposedly come and gone already, twenty-one years before—averted in the eleventh month of the eleventh day at the eleventh hour. Now he feels what no one admits: that we are about to drift into darkness again. He reads about it, hears about it, waits for it, but neither he nor anyone he knows has the least notion of what to do about it.

But the real crisis of 1939 is not just his helplessness in the face of the coming violence, the final, unthinkable crimes that will end up, as always, harmless in history books. Little Eddie's great terror is that his life is more benign and beneficent than ever. An unimaginable gap opens between the place people make to live in and the place springing up all around them and despite them. Enjoying life like everyone else might actually make things worse. The possible no longer keeps pace with the necessary. Little no longer divides cleanly into Big. Eddie Hobson no longer has anything to do with events. He is too small to be the only one to fall out and say no. That is the subterranean evil rising from the sidewalk cracks behind him as he pedals down the street. What can Edward Hobson do, being just thirteen and himself a child of the darkward drift? He is just a beginner in his own life. He is only as insightful as the world that made him. He can't be expected to sew up the rift running right down the middle of his paper-routed world. But to live through his remaining days, he must.

The sun shines crisply if weakly on his autumn afternoons. The wind creates its allaying breezes. Light glances off grass lots and squints under bridges. All is the same as in any other year, except the balance between livable, awful, and real.

Something sinister sits open on the Hobson coffee table. In an ad in the May 15 issue of Life, Grandma Middleton stands in front of a model of the time capsule and regrets, "It's too bad Westinghouse couldn't put in all those other electrical devices that make our lives so much more pleasant." "Yes," says her daughter, Bud's mother. "Like refrigerators, irons, toasters and vacuum cleaners. If they don't have those things 5000 years from now I certainly wouldn't want to be living then." Her grammar reflects the current confusion over the dominant tense, what light is about to go out, what the capsule must urgently preserve.

Edward Hobson, in northern suburban Jersey, pure product of this *year's World's Fair, goes to a matinee of that other Oz: Oz. The show begins with this year's Academy Award–winning cartoon, Disney's Ugly Duckling. Then a newsreel, one that did not make the Westinghouse time capsule, on the first decimation of Europe and Asia. A big leap to make, even for a boy of thirteen.*

3

The local crisis passed, as Lily knew it would. As always, Hobson's crisis was that there was no crisis, and so nothing the rest of them could do. Hearing of Dad's instant return to health, Lily watched the others pump their lips like astonished aquarium fish, then dissolve a few minutes later, spread into the house's corners to rule over independent, empty countries.

Later, she sat by candlelight in her room, putting her hand to the draft where the window sash had long ago warped. Dad fixed the wood once, but it warped again. The flaw was now part of her room, like the sagging bookshelves and the cozily threadbare rug. The imperfections made things bearable. Lily put her hand against the cold, glass skin standing between herself and November. Her family did not suspect the expense their mute calls for help caused her. She alone saw the emergency afoot.

She had always underwritten the negligence of others through private deficit spending, abiding her sister's cute obtuseness, suffering Artie's indignities in private, and putting Little Eddie's ignorance on tab. She spoke the family code, cracked the required caustic jokes, but all the while watched out for them without their knowing. But tonight, Lily felt her outlay reach a debit ceiling.

When her mother and sister had asked her along for Ladies' Night, Lily had affected a mock shuffle and palsied palm. "You girls go dancing, and don't worry about me."

Rachel had jumped all over her, saying, "Look, Sister. You've been nursing some serious old-maid qualities over the last couple of annums."

Lily had spit back, "Old maid? I've earned it. Come talk to me when you've been where I've been."

At the quarter-century mark, she'd been through the mill twice already. Her father was borderline certifiable, her mother a martyr. She herself was divorced, careerless, and without prospects in either. Worst, she had three siblings incapable of facing the coming disaster. Nor was she herself ready to go after the man. Not just yet.

She lifted the stereo needle gingerly onto an old favorite LP, an early-seventies vocal group whose combination of African and Elizabethan harmonies always made her feel as if there *were* some possibility of new air that everyone had overlooked. The sound of the familiar tunes always made it seem that something was about to happen, something simple and wonderful. But after two tracks, the chordal formula sounded dated and precious. Without warning, she had to go for a walk, get out of the house's residual static. She killed the phono, stubbed out what remained of a burned-down joss stick, went to the front-hall closet, got her winter coat, put it on, thought better of it, and replaced it with her lighter autumn one. Then she set off through the front door her mother had butted shut just two hours before. Three steps into the lawn, she concluded that Precinct 19 was right in their legal battle with her father: some Hobson had better do something about all those unraked leaves. So she lay down and rolled in them.

When she at last stood up, she picked off leaves, leaving a few oranges in strategic points for perverse good measure. Then she followed the front walk out to the street. Turning to survey the family plot, she grew grateful for one thing: whatever indignities her family made her endure, they had never once graced their parade of exchanged houses with one of those horse-tether replicas topped by a miniature coach-and-four announcing "The Hobsons'," or worse, "The Hobson's."

For in reality, it never came down to the plural or the bastard plural possessive. It was always *the* Hobson. The man turned the We and They of their endless bridge scorecards into You and You and You and You. *He's upstairs working on Hobstown.* Lily wandered away from One-Oh-Three toward town along Second Street's unnecessarily rustic cobblestones. She reminded herself that there was, in fact, no such place as Hobstown: an Erewhon, an Emerald City of her father's devising. The place she had to navigate was De Kalb, Illinois, a corn town sixty-five miles due west of Chicago, Birthplace of Barbed Wire.

Pop always insisted that one's only hope of salvation lay in finding out where history dropped you down. Yet the same man, trapped in phantoms, lived for Hobstown, a makeshift, escapist fantasy, as far as she could make out. She had her own, of course. She lived for names, and the names of places. The disaster of her own marriage lay in her having chosen Wayne Leeds not for any redeeming or damning qualities in the man himself but for the delicious alliteration that matrimony worked on her: Lily Leeds. It came off the tongue with poetic perfection, and who could help but honor such an offer?

But Lily Leeds—perfect sound, perfect name—had led, after only ten months and ultimate violence, back here, imperfect place, imperfect town. In the end, she had nothing to show for the escapade but broken furniture, no remedy for the mistake except to come home to Hotel Hobson, a bed and board whose rates required putting up with a father's black humor as he slowly did away with himself, erased himself for good from this place. Her father had lost his hold on Here. He could no longer calm her, as he had when she was young, with "Don't be afraid. I'm Here, and so are you."

All she could do was embrace this flat, pragmatic state, layered north to south like a seasonal parfait, where three hundred miles along any road, roads that cut across county lines in compound scars, advanced or reversed by half a month the degree that next season's temperature had homesteaded the area. Last week was still intact a short drive south of her, December some seven hundred miles north, rolling down on her at a fixed rate.

And in spring, May rolled north from Cairo at the state's southernmost tip. Then she watched farmers plant their thousand-acre maws, betting on when the best weather would break. Green systematically erased the state's black cipher in a northward wave, spring's parfait-fuse. De Kalb waited under snow blankets with a practiced patience until, in just weeks, the place denied it had ever been white once. Another month brought the double insult of 90 percent humidity and 100 degrees.

Lily walked north, rushing December by several seconds, concluding that The Hobsons and one false Leeds were the only flesh west of the Fox River that did not make a living off the land. They were neither harvesters nor harvester-hybrid developers nor even, anymore, teachers of harvesters-to-be. They alone neither toiled nor spun, sowed, or reaped. They were stranded without practical skills, beached on the blessed black fields, impounded forever at Fifth and Main with no means of getting out.

Though outwardly they showed no mark. They lived in a house identical to the dozens she now passed. De Kalb's standard model: a white, wooden A-frame with pitched roof and screen porch added two years before the War for Democracy. Once her favorite joke was to tell anyone who gave her a lift home, "That's my house. The white one with the pitched roof, up there on the right." Can't miss it. She thought it funny, like saying that Granddad's grave in the photo of Flanders was the white stone cross with the dates on it. She rarely made the joke anymore.

Their home, like all others, wore its garland of meters, meting out trickles of electricity, water, gas. The spin of dials marked the only evidence of change, the only proof that something inside the house had indeed altered from yesterday. Their door, like its neighbors', already wore a winter wreath of Indian corn and gourds, products of the world's richest earth. Mother, a genius of protective coloration, made their doorway blend in, hiding the fact that theirs marked the den of another species.

From a hundred gourded doors in a few more hours, the air stinking of leaves and the sky taking on the color of a conch, interchangeable widows in slippers and gowns would put their hands to the cold stoop to retrieve the morning news. Her family would be waking, too. But safely back in bed, Lily would beg off breakfast, already having completed her effort for this day.

She passed a Pentacostal barn whose sandwich board announced Sunday's Special: BRICKS OF RELIGION. Across the way lay the town's sole memorial, a garden-variety monument to the homegrown war dead. Twisted committee logic selected for the marker one of the agents of massacre: a tank of the Ardennes variety. She passed the town's second-greatest claim to historical fame: the only place in North America where two state highways and a railroad track intersected. On the far side of the tracks, she loitered for the expected late freight, to hear the rich sixth chords it always issued. When the train tooled by on timetable, she identified the chord out loud: "Andrews Sisters." Her father had formed her knowledge of music, as of so much else.

The town looked more movie-proppish than ever at this late hour. The row of retail outlets one block deep along either side of the main drag held no interest for her. She hooked left, picking up her trail.

Although she had not chosen the place, the family blamed her for their still being here. They lay the responsibility, under the guise of good humor, squarely on her: if Lily had not chosen to attend the local land-grant college just after the family's arrival, De Kalb would have been just another four-year whistle-stop like all the others. This joke was especially cruel, as the choice wasn't hers. Lily had intended to follow Artie's lead in attending an Eastern public university, Dad's school, the "family's school," as Pop ironically called it. "The university that the Hobsons have always attended." Dad and Artie were the only two Hobsons who'd ever gone on to school.

But Lily capitulated, giving up her choice at the last minute, the day before she was to fly back East. She was about to travel in two directions: forward into adulthood, and back to the place of her girlhood, the place she had loved before the Hobsons had started their long life of wagons west. For the first time, she savored that delicious smorgasbord of possibilities that life becomes when trimming down worldly possessions to two suitcases.

When Ailene walked in on her during the bag-pack, Lily motioned to the wardrobe that had not made the final cut and asked giddily, "Oh, Mother! Who was it wore this chartreuse, and those floppy collars? Certainly *I* never had such taste."

Ailene sat down quietly, extinguishing her daughter's excitement. Lily felt a wave of shame at delighting in something her mother had never done. But that was not the problem. Ailene, who had never dreamed of trying the same trick on Artie when it had been his turn to go, remarked offhandedly, "If only you weren't starting off to school *just now*."

Lily instantly understood the tacit code: the man on the kapok, whose condition that summer had once again flared. Lily stopped in mid suitcase-stuff and knew that her careful, curatorial job of packing was irrelevant, that she would never leave. At that moment she glimpsed her adult role—always accommodating, seldom appreciated. Without protest, she changed her plans.

The culprit responsible for the episodes timed them with the same heavy-handed burlesque behind the old joke about the family's school, Hobson U. Her father lived in vignettes and thought in maxims. Lily recalled Dad's favorite pedagogical aphorism, fired off when any of his charges committed a hasty conclusion: "All Indians walk in single file. At least the one I saw did." A oneliner if ever there was one. No generalizations can be trusted. Least of all this one.

The precise mix of meanings Dad injected into each of these gags contained so many unrelated and conflicting ingredients that Lily had long ago given up trying to pin him down. He kidded and ridiculed; he was deadly earnest. He got to the heart of the urgency, only to slide off into sarcasm. He threw away lines that distilled everything he knew. And when survival itself was at issue, Dad uncorked a cliché that meant nothing and everything all at once. His voice showed that he knew he couldn't get away with it. Yet he always did. "We always let him," Lily said out loud to the empty street. "At least the We I saw did."

So when her mother stopped her short with "just now," Lily unpacked her bag and enrolled in the town's normal college, one of those institutions that damns itself to mediocrity by adding a compass point to its name. She chose to study special education. But her undeclared major was campus radicalism, a field retreating from its high-water mark of the previous decade. Everyone had some alternative to things as they are, some escape from everyday limbo. Lily's was to live in a year when raw history scraped open the surface of things and made it seem that something else could happen.

This demure woman, who for twenty years had spent all her waking hours with a paint box, on her first Philosophy of Education take-home final declared that "making even one colored mark on a blank piece of newsprint should be an act of moral revolt." More than a revolt: an appeal for grace. All human beings were due a full accounting, but they had to ask for it. Art was a way of asking. That, at least, was what she had had in mind when, totally in the dark at eighteen, she settled on special education with emphasis on fine arts. To teach the wordless another kind of speech, a way of articulating and demanding: that, she felt sure, was certainly worth studying. Eighteen, just Edski's age. And now still no farther along than he.

She did well her first year at school. But within a year she made the staggering discovery that "developmentally disabled" and "emotionally impaired" were simply euphemisms for what almost everybody, both within the profession and without, still thought of as retards. Certainly no one bought her belief that it was sufficient to get her charges to make colored marks on paper. "Well intentioned, but misguided" was the way one professor evaluated her classroom technique. *Mainstreaming* was the byword of the day. The borderline nonnormals were turned loose into public life, the moderates attended to, and the severes pharmaceutically maintained. But by the time Lily made this discovery, she was committed. Her father's daughter, she could not stop halfway. All she could do was finish the degree and watercolor for her own sanity, between educational colloquia.

The allure of collegiate unrest also proved disappointing. Things had grown so comparatively calm by the early seventies that one scarcely remembered the war was still going on. Her generation had waited for her to arrive to deny that anything needed protesting. More than one cafeteria debate she had incited ended with the enemy insisting that activists were only kidding themselves. The prevailing argument was that the present had achieved a permanent state of militarization, so why bitch about a magnesium brush fire?

This was, Lily knew, the Voting Fallacy that the Hobson had once given his kids as topic for a table debate. No matter which candidate I like, the fallacy goes, *my* vote itself will not alter the outcome. *My* scrap of litter is not the problem; it's the mountain already made by the other three and a half billion. Or: one air-conditioner more or less will not rescue or deplete the doomed ozone layer. So why should *I* swelter for a virtuous but impotent ideal?

Lily knew that the argument led to more air-conditioners, but it sounded so unimpeachable, she could not penetrate it and point out the error. Activism, when sufficient of her friends refused it credence, *did* seem irrelevant. It was only viable if everybody agreed it was. But doing nothing was complicity. She might have asked Dad to reveal the fallacy, the flaw in the logic. But during her first year, Dad was in no shape for dialectics. She would not have gone to him anyway; that would have involved admitting that she had missed the point of the lesson the first time around.

Yet there were still enough of the dispossessed hanging around in Liberal Arts programs for Lily to take arms against the Voting Fallacy and pull off one final piece of resistance, one last act of articulation. In the spring of 1972, when talk of an impending peace pact was everywhere in the air, Lily and a commando gang of underclassmen prepared, under cover of the night, a reminder that the president, even at that threshold moment, was mining North Vietnamese harbors.

With a hydrogen canister commandeered from Chemistry, some string and party balloons obtained over the counter, and a handful of stones dug out of an unwitting accomplice's backyard, the covert band went about their protest. Just before sunrise, they set up the gas canister alongside the lagoon in the middle of campus and began inflating. Except for one lunatic who waved his cigarette around and made jokes about the Hindenburg, everything went smoothly. Filling each balloon with hydrogen and gluing it to a stone, the special-forces unit sank each sphere to the bottom of the pond. Asleep in the deep. By eight o'clock that morning, early classgoers saw something remarkable: colored balls, one by one struggling up from the surface of the water and drifting up into the air, each with the word *Haiphong* written on it in a deliberate if not to say artistic hand.

But all that activism now seemed so many years ago. Lily looked off to her left, where two of the college's taller buildings shot up out of the vacancy of fields. The fields were harvested now, brought in like clean linen off the line. The campus had reverted to the days of an MBA for the boys and an MRS for the girls. Since the mock harbor-mining, she too had done her bit to build up equity in the status quo. She'd tried the tie that binds, and after its dissolution, moved back home. Those more assimilated of her classmates had simply figured it out before her: in the wider conflagration, what could one objection work? Not very much, she now suspected. Best bury your talent these days in the ground, where, if it failed to cumulate or compound, it was at least, in Minuteman lingo, a hard target.

Yet the woman who had mined the Haiphong harbor that sat in the lagoon that lay on the campus that taught the town that barbed wire built still could not reconcile herself to the *here* in all this here. Ludicrous, that her family should end up where they were—the only ones for miles who couldn't say what roguing and winter wheat were. She wished as she walked that what troubled her father had been as straightforward and unexotic as cerebral malaria or dissociative schizophrenia. If only he had chosen jaundice, a disease with clinical rationale. The only predictable pattern to Eddie Sr.'s illness was that after the initial, frenetic fit-period passed, usually in ten days, he would pull himself together, deny that anything out of the ordinary had happened, go back to work on his pet urban-development project, and then get the urge to take a lower paying, more obscure job farther west, deeper in the interior.

Dad island-hopped from Jersey to Philly to Cinci to De Kalb, carting along wife and kids for no better reason than that anyplace else was one leg up on here. Lily had always believed her father's job changes—clearly successive demotions in the eyes of the NEA if not in his—were separate from the rest of his sickness. His spells had cost him a job or two, but she had never before suspected cause and effect. Yet tonight, the wandering and the fits seemed cut from whole cloth, two aspects of the same trip, one from which, the unconsulted specialists were sure to concur, he was unlikely to return.

The folks had started out on the East Coast, and in twenty years' searching for a healing climate had exhausted every spot up to the Mississippi. Each major illness announced a move. The pattern would have left De Kalb behind long ago, as soon as Dad was well enough to move. But Ailene had come and watched Lily pack, saying, "If only you weren't leaving just *now*." And then, "because Lily's in school here," they had bought the house. The white one, with the pitched roof. Can't miss it. She had stayed for *their* sake, and they blamed the place on her. It was not her fault that the Hobsons were always in the middle of a "just now." It occurred to her that they were once again in a "just now" just now.

But at that moment Lily could no longer consider Dad's migration. She had arrived at the place she was after. A house: not white; no pitched roof. Alone among all structures in that insular, white-wood town, it partook of an exaltation of lacework, a swell of rotundas, a badinage of balustrades, bricks, ironwork, and bayed glass. She had come to the home of a Master Elwood, who, with a Master Glidden some hundred years before, had had the barbed inspiration and invented the wire. The three-story brick mansion, like all palatial monstrosities, had devolved upon the public, becoming that least historical, most unthreatening of status quo structures, a museum.

She moved past the servants' quarters, outfitted with display cases of early wire prototypes, barb-stamping machines, and legal documents.

She crossed to the carriage stables, peeking in on their restored surreys, coaches, and horse-drawn sleighs. The side windows of the big house, dimly lit by gas burners, revealed the inner allure of a music room, a library, and a parlor full of foot-high porcelain Limoges figures. Lily did not stop for any of these seductions. Her goal lay at the back of the property, on the outer edge of the now bare woods. Tucked away in the shadow of the estate was the first of two houses that Elwood had built his daughter. The second, a honeymoon mansion, stood downtown, now the lodge for one of those Animal Clubs where men get together to wear funny hats and tell dirty jokes over dinner. This first house, still on father's property, had been built for the girl when she was only a child. Everything about it—doors, windows, alcoves, gingerbreading—had been painstakingly scaled to half-size.

The doll's palace was lit, as Lily knew it would be; whoever took care of the property could not resist the look of a little house lit against the late-autumn woods. Night after night, the caretaker damned the expense and set the tableau. Lily kept out of the pool of light the little windows cast. Working her way behind the tiny two-decker, she lifted the back-door latch and crawled in. She barely fit in the diminutive rooms with their half-sized furniture. She sat down, monstrously filling the downstairs, crowding up against a table set for tea. She took up one hemi-demitasse, then tipped it over to see where it had been made. She had come to the only bearable place in town to think in secret. Now she found that she could think, and devastatingly clearly, but not about the topic she had come here to work out. Lily had come to the dollhouse to devise a plan, a course of action for helping her father. Now, filling three rooms with her giant body, she felt that he was not the one most in need of healing.

She had left open the door of the tiny house. Its frame cut a rectangular gash into the pitch-black woods. She looked into the shortened frame and, unable to slow her thoughts down, she began to spook herself. She felt the half-sized door would suddenly fill with a hideous, escaped night figure whispering, "I am here, and so are you." Quickly, she filled her mind with her family's birthdays, the color and make of the family car, the titles of popular tunes. She forced her eyes away from the door, now less afraid of a night visitor than of the frame opening onto nothing at all. "All daughters," she said out loud to the half-scale tea party, "come to the same end." Calming a little, she laughed at her frayed nerves. She hiked her skirt to the cold November night, and tried to remember the agenda. After long silence, she spoke again. "At least the one I saw did."

4

Rachel, at her traditional Saturday morning crack of dawn, prepared breakfast while the others slept. Despite the events of the evening before, she remained vintage Rach, setting the breakfast table in grand George III style, mirroring both that monarch's opulence and his senile dementia. Widened by two leaves, the family Formica looked the algorithm of elegance. She covered it with heavy linen and six full settings of the best bone china, a wedding present that hadn't been out of the hutch for thirty years. Six plates, platelets, saucers, cups, and bowls: layout for a wedding or a wake.

She flanked each place with a contingent of mint silver which she chose for its baroque complexity, compiling an anthology so varied and arcane that the typical Hobson—raised on simple cutter, holder, and digger—could only guess at their functions and hope to make it through the meal by sticking to the standard rule of working from the outside in. She spent minutes folding napkins of the same heavy linen and embroidered trim, propping them up like boat prows at each place head. She filled six massive brandy snifters with incandescent orange juice. And in the center of each place setting, alone on the pristine bone china, sat the punchline to this expanse of porcelain and filigree: a showcased, solitary, red multivitamin.

A long setup for a short gag. But she delivered that elaborate parody deadpan. Rachel's world view—although she would have called it that only in farce—was simple. As long as she was condemned to a culture that mandated magnets on the refrigerator, she would be a blessed saint of refrigerator magnets. She lived in a land where folks in thirty-second spots on national TV made love to their clothes because they'd been washed in the right sauce. So be it: she'd prewash and fabric-soften with the best of them.

She sang the praise of science, those white-coated fellows who tamed Premenstrual Syndrome by turning it into an acronym and rendered roughage a topic of polite party conversation. She wondered out loud in Laundromats how Granny ever ran her drier without anticling squares, and, getting no response from startled strangers, would add, "The static buildup back then must have been lethal." She saved herself with simple silliness. All one could do against the ludicrous was love it.

In short, Rachel, stuck in an America trapped between William Cullen and Anita Bryant, between the twin possibilities of Dr. and Jimmy Doolittle, got along by out-outraging outrage. She never laughed at her own ironies, never gave away how much of the routine was earnest and how much joke. So long as the status approximated the quo, she knew that the only way to live in what was fast becoming a global pillage was to take cover and defer to the damage the other guy was doing to the place. She talked daily to her consumer products, believing that if she kept as much faith as a mustard seed in the dialogue, one day the mustard would, as advertised, say something back.

She styled herself as her older sister's corrective. She shared none of Lily's nostalgia for the lost-encounter culture, none of what she called the woman's sense of tragic relief. Rach, in her slot, had followed Lily, putting in a tour at the local land-grant. But she quit after two semesters, exclaiming in mock horror, "They want you to *know* things when you get out of there." She spoke of higher education in the tones reserved for the seven warning signals of cancer. For a year after dropping out, she wore a homemade button that read: THIS MIND INTENTIONALLY LEFT BLANK.

Despite her goofball truancy, Dad had not disowned her, as he had threatened to do if any of the kids didn't finish college. She never gave him the opportunity. Reviving a grade-school propensity for figures, she scored higher on the actuarial exams than most CPAs and was swept up by a megalithic, conglomerate numerics firm secretly run by the Trilateral Commission. Plunked down in a lake-front skyscraper in Chicago, she dealt all day in the mathematics of futures. She calculated to eight significant digits how likely an individual was to die over a given period of years. She never thought to apply the secret formula to her father.

Neither father nor employers approved of her method—a private, black-magical system of symbolic manipulation. But neither could fault her, because the numbers kept coming out quickly and correctly. While she did not deal in scholarly math so much as in brute arithmetic, Rachel nevertheless met Dad's long harped-on insistence that the kids somehow promote the world's knowledge.

She had a knack for sliding past Dad's morass. She got along famously with the man, far better than any of the other kids. He cut her no favors, but she evaded his caustic fire. She fought back with an artless "Quit being *stupit*," or "Hey, you're *hurting* me." Her secret was that *she* was not her parts. Dad could no more fluster her than could hunger or distress. The first she distanced with "My stomach is ravenous," the second with "My mind just felt something awful." *She* was just along for the ride.

Rach got along with everybody who wasn't certifiable and three quarters of those who were. She had as hilarious a time at the Farmers' Market as she did on Rush Street. She alone of the kids did not look on De Kalb as the gulag: "Sure, it's a little behind the times. But so's Colonial Williamsburg, and people pay big bucks to visit *there*." Nevertheless, she teased her folks, saying she would not do the hour drive out through the corn belt any more than she had to: "You guys are great fun, but after six or so round trips a year, the actuarial odds of being taken out of commission on the East-West Tollway by some boozer in a Mazda become absolutely unacceptable."

She had driven out this weekend partly because of Eddie Jr.'s eighteenth birthday and partly to try to weasel Eddie Sr. out of his newest decline. She had a third motive, kept secret. She thought, everyone else being in and the holidays just a couple of months off, that she might coax the nuclear family into a few renditions of "The First Noel." Not even the Hobson Tabernacle's occasional polychords nor the crass contemporary incarnations of midwinter—magnet figures infiltrating the manger crèche—could kill in her an unrepentant addiction to Christmas-carol harmonies.

She put the finishing touches on her extravagant table-setting joke when Eddie Jr., the second one up, rolled in. In flannels, he looked untimely ripped from dreamland. He gravitated to the table and took in the profusion. He blinked, saying groggily, "Sorry. Must have wakened at the wrong stop." Rach played nonchalant. He tried again. "Look at all this stuff. We having a garage sale?"

Eddie sat down and amused himself by chasing the little red pill around on his plate with his knife. Rachel maneuvered in front of him and yanked his face up by the chin. She narrowed her eyes and clenched her teeth until her head shook with full-scale muscle tremors. She hissed, "Don't you ever, ever, ever, ever . . ." repeating the word with increasing savagery until Eddie at last backed down and laughed. She dusted her hands of him with one more wrist-arabesque, and went back to cracking eggs into a saucepan.

"So what's for break," Eddie asked. "Fast?"

Rachel jabbed her kitchen knife toward his posh table setting, indicating juice and vitamin. "What you see is what you get."

Eddie resumed batting the tiny thiamine puck around his plate, knocking off delinquently when their mother came into the room. Ailene Hobson, née Kobceck, was dressed in a pale-yellow wrapper that in *Our Miss Brooks*'s era might have passed for a housecoat. She went to the stove and autonomically flicked on a gas halo. But Rach anticipated her.

"Café, madame?"

Mom took the proffered mug, surprised. "When did you learn how to make coffee?"

"Learn? What I know about java could fit on Juan Valdez's green card."

Her mother mumbled thanks and drifted aimlessly around the room. Coffee thus ready at hand, Ailene's entire morning ritual dissolved. Dazed by her efficient daughter, Ailene lit a cigarette in the superfluous gas flame and left the flame burning for reassurance. Rachel had already been out to the store and back, snagging the breakfast groceries, now spread all over the counter. Seeing them, Ailene went to her purse, perpetually wedged between the refrigerator and a cutting board, and fished out a ten-dollar bill that she tried to give to her daughter. "Here," she said. "To help defray the cost." Rachel took the bill, rolled it up, and hung it out of her nostril. Her mother grabbed the money back, tsking her disgust. "Ish," she said. "You don't know where that's been."

"I can well imagine," Rach said.

Rejected but not rebuffed, Ailene tried to give the money randomly to the nearest alternate child. But Eddie Jr. declared that he would hold out for a twenty or nothing at all. Mother stuffed the note back into her purse, ammunition for a later date. She idled for a moment, then began tearing the price labels off the newly purchased breakfast goods.

"What are you doing?" asked Rachel.

Ailene fluttered her hands. "I'm just removing the little . . ."

"*Why?*" Rachel demanded. Getting no answer, Rachel steered her mother by the shoulders, coffee mug in hand, to the place next to Eddie Jr. Ailene put on her facetious face of good behavior, sitting obediently as if she, after all the years of dishing it out, had become at the end the disciplined child.

Mom was an enigma to Eddie Jr., the force that kept the house together through a miscellany of arcane formulas such as, "One out, one in, and one on." He had gone from the adoration of childhood to the polite bafflement of late teens without feeling the seam. But this morning he understood her nervous habits implicitly. "So how's Pop?" he asked, recommencing vitamin field hockey after the brief delay of game.

He failed to ask the point blankly enough, and she looked up, brightening. "Except for his annual fall bronchitis, fine." She had served too long as press secretary to unlock herself now, even to the man's son. "He got up at about three this morning and went into the study. More dictation, I assume."

Although Dad looked like a big-bellied Bob Hope with hair and without the nose, little Eddie could not help imagining him with Mussolini's chin whenever the topic touched upon the man's late-night habits. The Great Dictator. In Hobstown, at least, they got the trains to run on time.

Artie shuffled in silently, sliding into an empty place. He took in Rach's rococo prank and smiled weakly. Then he plunked his vitamin into the juice glass, swirling the concoction vigorously. Only when he was sure the pill had dissolved did he sip the mixture. For the ten or so days following his first hearing that Dad had once more taken ill, Artie invariably found he could not swallow anything more substantial than creamed corn.

Ailene, still searching for something to do, upbraided him. "Arthur, you look like you slept in those clothes."

"Well, Mom, there's a good reason for that. Left my jammies in Chitown."

"And go put something on your feet."

"What do you mean 'and,' Mom? And no, Mom. I don't want to just yet."

"You'll catch cold," insisted Ailene.

"Are you suggesting that a pair of socks will provide an antiseptic layer between me and viruses? Why do the little suckers always go for the feet?"

"Because that's all the farther they can reach," explained Eddie. "The floor-dwelling viruses anyway. Now the wall kind can bail onto just about anyplace on your body. They ambush you from above. Then there's the tree dwellers. They can only attach to wet hair."

Mom was an easy substitute, especially when the boys ganged up. Artie silenced his brother by presenting him with a spiral-bound book of multiple-choice questions, a preparation aid for yet another in an endless queue of exams that he had been taking, as he often put it, "since kingdom kong." He sincerely and, he knew, naïvely believed that if he could just get over the next battery of tests, the next hurdle, he'd be in the clear. Eddie, also a seasoned veteran, made the obligatory round of Legal jokes about how Rachel was making torts for breakfast and began quizzing. After a few rounds of when-in-doubt-go-with-B, Artie broke off the review. He asked, "What's up with Lil?" addressing the question to the cabinets under the sink.

"She's . . ." Eddie Jr. replied, searching his memory for "asleep in the Deep" but forcing the ancient quantity into deeper and deeper hiding. He settled instead for, "She's still in the rack."

Artie challenged his mother. "Pop was up and working when you went upstairs? And he stayed in one piece all night? No relapse?" Ailene simultaneously shook her head and nodded, master of the self-contradicting signal. "No vomiting?" Ailene made another no, gravely. "How about temperature? Not febrile?" On Mom's third denial, Artie said, "I just don't get it. He's got more severe symptoms than ever and he's coming out of them faster than ever."

By way of explanation, Mom crumpled. The brave-soldier shoulders came forward and her voice collapsed. "Get him into a clinic, at least." Her throat constricted as if she needed to spit. "He'll talk to you, Artie. You can trap him."

Artie made a sound like a stifled hiccup. The kids had been all over this the night before, and tacitly for many nights before that. Mom knew all the arguments, and each kid knew that she knew that they knew. The stink of mutual knowledge filled the kitchen, as fat and acrid as Rachel's bacon grease. No one said a word. At last, the silence flushed her out.

"Or why don't *you* go see a physician when you go back to Chicago, and tell him about your father, and see what he thinks?" Her voice returned to normal. Her suggestion might at first glance have passed for a realistic compromise.

Artie answered jocosely, more for his brother and sister than for Ailene. "Sure, Mom. 'Doc, it's like this. There's this guy. Well, actually he's my father, believe it or not. He's having these hallucinations, only he doesn't want to come talk to you himself, because he's afraid you might think he's bonkers.' They'd put *me* away. *I* don't need Bellevue, Ma; I've already got University of Chicago Law."

Eddie Jr., positioned to see down the kitchen runway, cut off his mother's reply by announcing, "Yo! Here comes the man of the hour." And there was Dad, as little as life, trapped in his swollen body, framed in the doorway.

"I've just had the most marvelous idea," he said on cue, in showman's voice. "You guys are always egging me on to make a buck, ragging me about living up to my earning power." None of them had ever once mentioned money to the man. "How's this: I'm going to put up a booth just to the side of all the other toll booths out on the East-West and charge five cents *less* than the others. It'll corner the market. The American entrepreneurial tradition. As an initial promotion, I'll even give out discount coupons for the return trip."

A grand entrance; Dad again in peak form. It was once more impossible for any of them to insist on the facts. Artie snorted. Eddie Jr. toyed with his place setting and managed a deferential grin. Rachel shook an eggy spatula at him, and Mom morosely kissed him good morning.

In the morning light, Pop looked as hearty and hale as in the family-scrapbook photos. Artie recalled a page of three snapshots: a swimmer; a wrestler in attack crouch; and a cocky, slender man in uniform. They were from when Dad was just Artie's age—a beautiful, gravity-defying gymnast, a scrapper. And seeing Dad's clean factual break, his full departure from the past, Artie felt his intestines contract as he sailed over a crest that dropped off sharply.

Big Eddie swaggered in, signing his own full bill of health. "My work goes on trippingly, if anyone cares. I've finally busted out of a bottleneck that's been holding up the show for years. At last I have an angle on how to bring the thing I know best into the modern world. Without offending the authorities, that is." He looked around magisterially—quizmaster, king of the heap until someone said otherwise. He took his chair at what he managed to make look like the head of the round table and breathed in deeply. "I knew that taking the . . ." His malicious eyes belied a sheepish mouth. "The *early retirement* was a great idea."

As even the most Pollyannaish among them now admitted, the latest "retirement" had been forced on Dad some months back when he passed into near coma in front of a class of high school American history students. Again the kitchen filled with the stale air of mutual knowledge. "Get a load of this guy," Rachel said, somehow immune. "Jeez. I don't have to take this. Lemme out of here."

"What's all this, then?" Dad asked, indicating the sumptuous table setting. At last Ailene noticed what her child had done with her mint-condition treasures. She screamed softly, as if bitten. She leapt to her feet and grabbed two bowls to return them to the hutch before she realized the deed was done and sat down again, sadly.

Had Dad come downstairs obviously ill, Artie, as oldest son, might have beseeched the rest: *We can stop this guy, stand up to his retirement jokes, force him to face facts.* But with Pop the picture of health, their combined strength counted for nothing. Had Artie appealed to solidarity now, he knew what the others would say: *That Artie. Always exaggerating. Why fight the man when he is feeling so good?* Their own perpetual hope prevented action.

The man routed them into themselves. Reduced to one on one, Rachel was the only person who stood an even chance against him. She squeezed open his jaws and stuck the penultimate vitamin in, sending OJ in after it. Then she slammed his mouth shut and kissed him. "Would you care to see our dessert menu?"

Unflustered, Pop primped his place setting until it met his satisfaction. With a few deft origami folds, he transformed his linen table napkin into the protruding cups of a brassière, which he promptly held up to his chest to the delight of Eddie Jr. and the cultivated indifference of everyone else. When Rachel began to sling her carefully prepared slop, a much-guarded recipe midway between scrambled eggs and hash browns, he called out,

"Hey! Wait a minute. We're not going to start eating without number-two child present, are we? Count off." And he made the closest sound to a whistle that his partial plate allowed.

From some distant recess of the house Lily's disembodied voice called, "Start already. Leave me be."

Hostile enough in tone, Lily's outburst, chiming in on cue, so compromised her that it curled Dad's lips. "You heard the woman," he said. Each Hobson started in as instructed, without any face giving away its private reasons. Artie, eggs in hand, ate along with the rest, trying unsuccessfully to remember the source of the old adage he had read somewhere, confirmed so clearly in this silent, common consensus, that each of us is truly alone.

As he had done for every family meal over the last twenty years, Eddie Sr. put forward something for the tribe to consider while digesting. These instructional sessions had grown more intense over the years and seemed to peak whenever he was between jobs. "So what's the topic for this morning's meal?" he asked, simulating democracy.

Artie suggested, "How about multiple choice Q and A about corporate litigation?" Dad overruled him, as expected.

Suppressing that outburst, Dad began, "I've been doing a little reading on a puzzle called The Prisoner's Dilemma. The modern form of the paradox comes from a guy at the Rand Corporation, 1951, a year wedged between a couple of dates that ought to go off like bells in your brains. But we won't examine the historical milieu just yet." He nibbled on a bacon end, pretending to take food. "Here's the gist of the problem, in my personal version. Two men are summoned into Joe McCarthy's office . . ."

Rachel groaned. "Not this again. We've done witch hunts." They had all heard Pop speak many times of his bout with collective policing, his minor brush with martyrdom in front of committee years before.

"No, no. You misunderstand. The questioner is not the villain in this one. We can make it anything. Let's make it two countries exchanging . . ."

"Make it two men and McCarthy, and get it over with," Rachel said.

"Two guys are up in Senator Smoking Joe McCarthy's office, sometime in the early 1950s. The gentlemen are both prominent public servants. The senator says, 'Fellas, we know that you are both Reds. I've got plenty of evidence for an indictment, but not enough to guarantee the conviction you deserve. Let's make a deal. If either of you comes forward with the dope on the other, the man who talks will go free and the other will fry. If neither of you spills the goods on the other, you'll still suffer public humiliation at the very least.' "

"What happens if they both squeal?" Eddie Jr. interrupted, drawn into the game despite the situation.

"Good question, number-two son. That's important. If they both rat on each other, their double crosses partly invalidate the other's testimony. But they still lose more than they would compared to shared silence. Let's say mutual incriminations will hurt them more than if they both say nothing, but that in undercutting each other, they prevent the unopposed squealer from leading them to electrocution." Dad looked frustrated at articulating a very simple situation. "Here. Let me draw it for you."

He jumped up from the table and looted a pen from Ailene's purse. Ripping off a sheet of paper towel, he drew a few quick lines, adding some all-caps block printing. Dad never wrote in cursive or lowercase. "As you can see, I've been brushing up on the numbers racket." He dropped the finished product in the center of the table:

| | | HIM | |
		KEEP QUIET	SQUEAL
KEEP QUIET		I GET 2 YEARS HE GETS 2 YRS	I GET CHAIR HE GOES FREE
ME			
SQUEAL		I GO FREE HE GETS CHAIR	I GET 10 YEARS HE GETS 10 YRS

Artie reached for the sheet, looking it over cursorily. "I can see what's coming," he said.

"It's amazing what law school can salvage from undergraduate liberal-arts training," Pop noted.

Ailene put down her fork but declined the sheet when Artie offered it to her. "I for one don't see where there's any paradox. It's obviously in their best interests to keep quiet. That way, neither of them will end up in bigger trouble. The two men simply have to trust each other, not be intimidated, and realize that they're in the same boat and would end up worse off if they start naming names."

"That's exactly what they do realize, for about two seconds. *They're in the same boat*, as the lady says. They make eye contact, and it occurs to them both that as long as they hang together they can't hang separately. Then the senator puts them into separate rooms, going back and forth between them and asking, 'Well, how about it now?' No rubber hoses, you understand. This is America; it's all done with logic."

Rach grabbed the paper from Artie's grip. She looked it over quickly and spun it in little Eddie's direction. Hearing the man weave his special breed of silence, Lily came quietly out of her room and sat herself in the last empty place. She took Dad's drawing from Eddie and held it in front of her as she sipped orange juice, grimacing.

Dad, with expert timing, let them each have a look before going on. "Then each guy starts to reason, 'The other guy can do one of two things. Suppose the other guy says nothing. Then I can save myself two years, two good years of my life, by talking, getting off free rather than being publicly humiliated. On the other hand, what if he talks? Then if I stay silent, I go to the chair. But I can preempt my opponent by delivering the goods first. Ten years, while stiff, still beats high voltage. Whether the other guy talks or not, I can improve my payoff by talking.' "

"And since they both reason that way," Artie said, as if co-inventor, "they end up with five times the jail term."

A dry silence followed. "I've got it," interjected Rachel, rising to her feet and slamming the table with her fist. "They say, 'Joe, if you do this to us, we'll tell everybody about what you do with that Errol Flynn.' "

Ignoring big sister's routine outburst, Eddie Jr. handled the summing up. "So the point is, when reasoning separately, they drag themselves down. But what about reasoning from above?"

"Good man. I like that. *Reasoning from above*." Dad sat triumphantly at table, gratified by the response from his brood. "But how can they get there? *What does it mean?*"

Ailene ignored his question, even more distressingly hypothetical than the original problem. "Never mind *above*. They're both in it. They both know what they need to do."

"But they can't be sure the other can be trusted," Lily added, catching up to where she could doublethink the old man.

Ailene was now near tears over the apparently abstract problem. "Where's the flaw, then? Which way *should* they reason?"

Dad explained, "There is no flaw, dear. And there is no *should* in reasoning. There's only practical outcome."

"And so, folks," said Rachel, voice-over style. "Yer dandruff you do and dandruff you don't."

"Now for some variations," Dad persisted. "Airplane hijacking with hostages. Price wars at the fuel pump. Food hoarding. Bank runs. Industrial poisoning. Amatory jealousy. Divorce proceedings, for that matter. The arms race. Double-parking. Anyone want to take a stab at how they're all related?" An average breakfast-table question, at home, Saturday morning with the Hobsons.

Just then Artie, who had gotten the now dog-eared paper towel back and was juggling the numbers for any mathematical escape trick he might have overlooked, flashed onto a little reasoning from above of his own. He thought: *Good Christ. Ten minutes ago the topic was how to save the man's life. Now it's game theory.* Artie held the epiphany in his hand for a fraction of a second. His father's miniature classroom was a prisoner's matrix all its own. Dad diverted them from addressing the real catastrophe by drawing them into this game of defection and cooperation. They had to play his dilemma if he was to play theirs. Pop trapped each Hobson in an inverted payoff matrix where the promise of a phantom premium, the threat of being left holding the bag, drove each to be the first to defect and the last to come clean. Artie saw the circling antagonists caught in the need to cut a deal but not knowing how to reach it. Dad *himself* had become this contest between "he" and "I," an agile, evasive mind trying to outdance the slow process of his disease, whatever it was.

And the island of mutual collaboration that logic and good judgment kept unattainable, the ability to step out from the unassuming and familiar breakfast nook of the last family in these parts choosing to eat at home, left Artie powerless to defy reason, set aside decorum, and say, "Listen, old man. You are patently and dangerously ill. You've spent the last few days with something haywire in your cells. You've killed the last several years nursing an antisocial obsession. You've lived the last few decades chased by God knows what. And you must now, against your will and for the greater good, pack yourself off to whatever sanatorium will take you, to purge the symptoms for one weekend at least, to do what all our combined anguish cannot do for you."

Before Artie had power to say behold, Pop's breakfast-table robustness made it seem that perhaps his dizzies were, after all, only a persistent virus. Artie watched the man conduct his class and thought that maybe the family *should* consider itself lucky that Pop felt better than last night. The big stink, the showdown, could wait, in any case, until the family was not all together, steeped in a harmless word game where reasoning from above was so much more difficult than the harmless and more acceptable solution to the dilemma: stay still and preserve diplomatic relations. And reasoning this way, Artie walked away from resolution.

The next minute, Dad, sensing that the magic web was weakening, the entangling dilemma in danger of being outflanked, held up a ringmaster's hand and in familiar carnival huckster's voice announced, "Friends, for your listening alarm and delight . . ." He sprang from his seat and fiddled with the ancient tube receiver that kept court on the top of the refrigerator. The radio looked to have been last tuned in for the Bay of Pigs flash. Dad tweaked a variable capacitor and the device squealed the ethereal, high-frequency audio-graffiti that is second language to anyone born in this century. Ghostly tracers of disembodied banshee bands blared out along the dial, asserted themselves temporarily on center stage, grew garbled, then died off just as suddenly in the shift of frequencies.

At last, in a recess of the radio band where citizens ordinarily never ventured, the man found what he looked for. As if nothing had changed since the days when women were virtuous and men were tenors, dulcet Rudy Vallee, CVL (Certified Vagabond Lover), amplitude modulated but still unbowed, filled up the breakfast room too brightly for this hour of the second week of Daylight Savings Time, releasing the prisoners from their McCarthian matrix with a nifty number from Dr. Vallee's Musical Hospital: "Spread a little music wherever you go, and nothing can ever go wrong," replete with Helen Kane's boop-boop-de-doop.

The family issued a collective groan. Lily stood, whined a muffled "I hate you," and stamped out, punctuating her exit with an offstage slam of bedroom door. Eddie Sr. threw his hands out to the side in a mock objection. "What did *I* do? What's wrong with a little old-time religion?" But they were not panning Rudy, criminally optimistic as he was. It was Eddie the others howled down, Eddie and his thirty-year claim to the psychical ability, which he himself never attempted to explain, to sense, anywhere and in any circumstance, whenever any radio signal carried any popular tune from the years between 1939 and 1946. The kids had, on a few occasions, gone to great efforts to set up controlled experiments to disprove the talent, to show it up as a hoax. But to date, Dad had repeatedly stymied the positivist strain that he himself attempted to nurture in them. Eddie Jr. had, the year before, even tried to persuade the old man to be his high school science-fair project, claiming it would get him into Carbondale at least, if not Stockholm.

Dubbed by Rachel the Glenn Miller Tiller, Dad's gift was incontrovertible. Every time he turned the radio on it would be Harry James or Benny Goodman or Les Brown and His Band of Renown. Worse, Pop never dropped in on the middle of a tune but always on the very opening bars. Sometimes, for a special splash, he fiddled with the dial before turning the set on, and then he'd land right on the target with a Midway Island precision.

The effect of Mr. Vallee, Artie suspected, was exactly what the big guy had intended: the school session immediately ended, the students heading off to whatever private work called them, while the invalid instructor slipped out of the conversation's back door without further interrogation. Rach attended to dishes, puffing on her pitch pipe, Toy of the Week. Mom went upstairs. No further sound issued from Lily's room. Eddie Jr. pushed back his chair, strode for the runway, and put his shoulder into Artie's gut in simulated slow motion, saying "Pigskin" as he spun off-tackle and fly-patterned for the front door.

"In a minute," said Artie, clamping down on his escaping father's shoulder. "Just a second, sir. There's something we've got to talk about."

Dad interrupted him with the same hand wave of *voilà* he'd used to introduce his radio act. "I think I can anticipate what you are about to say," he said, pulling back the sleeve of his cotton T-shirt as he spoke. On what would have been the fleshy part of anyone's armpit whose flesh hadn't dropped off the limbs and slid into the belly was a round, cherry ring. Too surprised to do anything else, Artie reached forward and touched the spot gingerly.

"Did you know that that old children's game about pockets of posies and ashes was really a medieval invocation to ward off infection? Seems the rings and the rosies were, in historical fact, buboes." Artie could only stare at the sore, a gap of many centuries separating him from the man who had raised it. Choosing between the bad taste of going forward and the impossibility of going back, Dad pressed the issue, explaining, "Plague, you see. All fall down."

THE DOMINANT TENSE

Sometime during those last few weeks, my father and I watched the late show together. We used to do that two or three times a year whenever I was home. Movies let us sit in the same room without having to talk about anything. He would lie on the couch, I would slouch in a chair next to him, and we'd turn the set down low in the dark so as not to keep anyone else up.

Our last late show together was a completely expendable forties musical called Orchestra Wives. I've since looked the film up, reading that it starred George Montgomery, Ann Rutherford, Cesar Romero, and the Nicholas Brothers, among others. My father named the performers, lying on the couch announcing the cast as they made their black-and-white entrances and exits in the dark. But the names meant nothing to me, and, along with the film's plot, I instantly forgot them.

As far as I remember, the story concerns the wives of a big band's members being bitchy to Ms. Rutherford, the newest swing-time bride. Themselves neglected, they apply group cruelty to the woman my dad called "Andy Hardy's eternal Polly." In the end, as mandated by the motion-picture code, everyone learns the value of compassion. Just how the healing fiction works its trick I've forgotten too.

For the film was truly forgettable in all respects except one. Its music was the finest of the era. The story was an excuse to get Glenn Miller's orchestra in front of a camera for the second and last time. Not long after, Miller was shot down in the English Channel without a tiller. But behind the silly escapist plot and despite real life's less than compassionate ending, Miller and men are there, preserved on film, making that great sound with those freewheeling, dangerously abundant reeds and brasses.

Although I failed to understand at the time, my father lay in the dark, involved in the stupid vehicle, evidently moved. Of course, he saw all sorts of phantoms in the thing that I could not. He said he'd been sixteen when he first saw the show, a confession I discounted, as I was the eternal sixteen-year-old to his perpetual forty-seven. When a tune began he would arch his eyebrows and sing along, neither ironic nor nostalgic but absolutely deadpan archival, to "Serenade in Blue," "At Last," or "I've Got a Gal in Kalamazoo."

As with 99⁴⁴/₁₀₀ percent of American films made during wartime, the movie's hidden message was a simple, contemporary variant of the advice given dutiful newly married Victorian women: "Close your eyes and think of England." Hollywood's meal ticket: give the forbidden appetite fantastic, rebellious slack. Then draw it back, fifth reel, into sacrifice and the public good. I'm not sure how it happens. In times of crisis something clicks, and suddenly vested self-interests vanish. Or at least that's the myth of the wartime feature, one that's always been good box office.

I guess at all this: I have never lived through a popular war effort, except via the late show. But every morale film I've ever seen has a curious way of giving and taking away simultaneously. Like Betty Grable on the lockers of GIs: nothing satisfies like the unavailable. I hear my father sing: "Get a load of those Gobs, doing their jobs, keeping the sea lanes free." I see him at sixteen: after two hours in the matinee, returning to daylight in a world where the apocalyptic battle, untouchable, remote, and final, required that everyone play team ball. A world where women sacrificed stockings with delicious pleasure; men, gasoline.

Nodding off in the dark, I pretended Dad's interest in the film was only clinical. He had a weakness for the dated artifact: the Shirley Temple single, the Mademoiselle issue of March 1942—"What's New?" I filed the film away with those. Besides, I never sat where I could see his face. We watched the story, groaned, and then sat through the news. We groaned again at the headlines, and then we said good-night.

Much later I was shocked to discover how much my father, the archrationalist, loved this movie. Most old movies for that matter, escapist time-wasters included. I never once saw him go to the theater. But at home, at night, he used to ask me deferentially, "Want to see what's on?" I should have been tipped off by his knowing all the lines and each of the actors' names.

But I didn't catch on until too late. Astonishingly, the professional educator, friendless, intent on discovering what was really going on, still

---

loved the fables of moral fallen women and criminal moguls with hearts of gold. He fell victim to the cheapest narrative tricks. Until the end, he was a secret fan of the possibility of another place, the other person's story. I always thought that intellect and sentiment formed the horns of an exclusive either-or. They do not. My father had them both in doses that he, as well as the rest of us, paid for healthily.

My father at sixteen, too old to be precocious any longer, spent 1942 pent up in the Palisades, attending high school and moonlighting as a singing waiter at a showboat-turned-restaurant moored on the Hudson. I picture him reading a newspaper headline, BRITISH COVENTRATE COLOGNE, or poring over an account of the Bataan Death March, understanding, in theory, that the old world was dead. Not that apocalypse touched home. The nearest the war came in the first two years, he once confessed to me, was when the FBI picked up a half dozen German saboteurs that an enemy sub had dropped off on Fire Island.

Between innings on weekend ball fields, he exchanged stories of how Japs used GI skulls for shaving dishes or broke teeth and snapped off fingers for gold inlays and rings. I see the young man in his two-year holding pattern, pacing his cage, agonizingly delayed, frantically waiting to graduate, come of age, and contribute. For the world was entering its last unquestioned holy cause. The outcome was far from certain: the ball fields he lolled on might soon be run by Krauts. So he agonized, ached for eighteen. Even at his age, he did not delude himself that one more pimpled kid would tip the outcome. But more certain than the rightness of the cause was that win or lose, those who had not contributed would be beneath contempt.

I'm sure there was only a fine line between his laudable desire to help save Europe and his self-interest in securing the same official papers that gave his homely older brother free rein with what were then referred to, without irony or infringement, as dames. My grandparents, to his shame, would not let Pop enlist illegally. And no one could do preparatory sit-ups all day long. So he was forced to get through each day by killing time, which in northern Jersey required a substantial amount of social diversion.

One afternoon between school and waiting on tables, he caught a matinee of Orchestra Wives and was duly impressed by the film, if not by its philosophical underpinning. I am sure that even that first time, the dramatic tension of Orchestra Wives took second place to the glorious Big

Band chords. He adored the music from the opening bars and immediately incorporated "I've Got a Gal in Kalamazoo" into the showboat's after-dinner set, a novelty number where the waiters strummed tennis rackets as if they were ukes.

The movie, coupled with Holiday Inn, Babes on Broadway, Yankee Doodle Dandy, and the other big-budget escapist enterprises Dad went to see that year, more than Doolittle's Tokyo raid or the battle of the Coral Sea, affected who he became, and, by relation, me. The universal point of all these tales was that the best a fellow could do to fight the terrible vicissitudes of the Big Picture was to stay home and mind the local store. In particular, a man could move the world if he were happily married. And the trick to a happy marriage was to do one's homework beforehand, before one's condition had been permanently altared.

So Dad, at sixteen, found an outlet for the frustrated energy stirred up in him by the world's burning. Years later, he elaborated for us at dinner his deadly earnest decision to do the legwork and locate the perfect girl. Too much was at stake in the early forties to settle for what was near to hand. However, since Kalamazoo was a shade too far for overnighters, Dad limited his first research forays for the ideal spouse to the greater New York metropolitan area. He concentrated around north suburban Jersey, fertile ground. Somewhere in the tens of thousands of girls his age, he felt sure to find one who combined the best parts of city girl and ingenuous hick, a woman both debutante and bespectacled wallflower—brilliant, bookish, industrious, but who could sing with a swing. All things abundant, but in moderation.

Yet to my father, all things in moderation always included moderation itself. It was not sufficient for his mate-to-be merely to maintain the Joan Leslie look while avoiding a criminal record. His woman had to shine. At sixteen, held to the sidelines in the hour of greatest urgency, he devised criteria severe enough to screen Supreme Court nominees. Starting the search at sixteen, he figured he'd have plenty of time to do it right. In Pop's mind, marriage, like birth, death, and world war, only came along once in a lifetime.

The first gal who looked good enough on paper, accumulating a sterling GPA, amassing the obligatory public-service points, and even garnering, at the tender age of fifteen, the distinction of Passaic Meat Packers' Union Junior Princess, fell from the running when Dad discovered that her crazy

Greek father lived only for his obsessive dream of stealing the Elgin Marbles back from the British Museum. A second beauty, so his story usually went, took the disqualifying demerit because of a harmless pathology that drove her, every time she got a hundred yards away from her house, back to the front door to check if she'd locked it. As Dad told us, he calculated how many minutes of their life would be lost to this habit over forty years, and quietly shook her hand good-bye. By this time in the recitation, Dad would always have us in hysterics. To finish us off, he'd wind up with the tale of still another young lady who went into File 13 because, although she knew everything there was to know about matrix manipulation and made a dynamite peach melba to boot, she thought that Cervantes was a Mexican mariachi band.

Despite his later facetious retelling, the boy he'd been was really out there, digging. The old guy in embryo, the child's research grew increasingly rigorous and took him farther and farther afield. Passaic, Paterson, and beyond: still nothing panned out. Saturday nights he tried the time-tested, dance-marathon, trial-by-erotica method, but always came away empty. Pop grew older, more sophisticated in the art of the stakeout. Turning seventeen, he escalated his efforts. Dad became adept at sifting information—the Library Municipal Room, City Hall, even the public-school system's records. Somewhere his wife waited for him to discover her. He had to check everywhere.

As time passed and his less fastidious classmates pinned and unpinned, engaged and disengaged themselves many times over, my old man began to suspect that he was a victim of his own search techniques. He liked to speak of his dark night of doubt: maybe there simply weren't any girls of marriageable age that could meet selection standards as stringent as his. But once having started out on the path of talent scouting, he doomed himself to sticking to it. For if he settled now for second best, he could never hope to respect, for life, a woman whom he deliberately avoided measuring against surrendered standards. In his entrapment by perfectionism, he never changed.

Why a lower-middle-class teenager couldn't content himself with the simple cycle of dating and mating, of love–marriage–baby-carriage, that satisfied everybody else is as much a mystery to me as it was to him. Granted my grandfather, a hard-drinking latter-day economic immigrant who managed to squeak in just before the country slammed its doors shut *and sealed the Ellis Islands, had cultivated a modicum of Irish morality in the boy. But Dad's father's idea of a clean and ordered world required only that the boy maintain rulered sideburns and hang his pressed pair of Sunday pants upside down in big wooden cuff-clamps. The fastidiousness that the old Irishman meant to instill in his progeny degraded in Dad, who thought it sufficient to hang his trousers upside down by their cuffs from dresser drawers, only to resurface cruelly in me, a man who single-handedly subsidizes the dry-cleaning industry.*

In place of this shed clothes-conscientiousness, Dad had a rage to order that his immigrant father, as well as his assimilated children, never quite understood. For even though he rose no higher than deplorable in father's and son's hierarchies of good grooming, Pop contracted a far more lethal strain of the efficiency disease. The search for the perfect spouse was one symptom. He was infected with the need to squeeze the full, appropriate use from every item in his life. The need helped kill him.

He told us where he had first been exposed to the virus. He'd caught it three years before Orchestra Wives, the year his voice changed, 1939, out in Flushing Meadow at the New York World's Fair. The place was a septic hotbed of the Progress disease, and Pop contracted it at once. Several visits to the Fair, an unprecedented celebration of technological progress and utility built around the theme of "Building the World of Tomorrow," changed the boy profoundly in a way that rippled down a causal chain and never stopped.

The etiology was even more specific. Of the more than fifteen hundred exhibits, one in particular did him in. At thirteen, he did not understand the earth-moving events behind the premature closing of the Czech pavilion. In the amusements and side shows, he was already too sophisticated to have more than passing interest. He stopped at Westinghouse long enough to chat and share a cigarette with the robot Elektro. The time capsule fascinated him, but he did not then have the patience for the past that circumstance would later force on him. He would come back to the buried metal message later, dig it up from an all but lost printed map.

But the pavilion that utterly floored him at the time, completely overhauled his life and therefore mine, was General Motors's Futurama. Three times that year he stood for hours on the sinuous entrance ramp, waiting among a crowd of tens of thousands for his glimpse of the astonishing city of 1960. He fidgeted through the preshow in the darkened auditorium, then climbed into his self-powered conveyor chair, leaned back beside the speaker, and listened to the recorded voice narrate a synchronized tour of the wonders opening up in front of him. He spun past the thirty-six-thousand-square-foot model of futuristic landscapes, farms where plants grew under individual globes, power factories that doubled as recreation areas, impeccable suburbs, logical industrial parks, and, finally, the staggering city center itself, a vision beyond even the recorded narrator's ability to describe. "Unbelievable?" I can still hear him mimic the voice-over. "Remember, this is the world of 1960."

Pop described how each time, at the end of the ride, he would stand up from his chair, still under the spell of the model, and leave the pavilion, only to find himself outside in a full-scale version of the panorama's final scene: a typical intersection of 1960, a life-size implementation of the model, a large-as-fact creation of the miniature replica working out the simulated future he had just witnessed. That, he often explained, first fired his forming mind: the exhibit's last prediction fleshed out in the full-scale world.

I can feel the rush of arrival that passed through him each time he stepped into Futurama's final chapter. This glimpse of perfection only twenty-one years off remade the teenager in its own image. Overnight, he grew obsessed with bringing this future world about. He made himself into a mobile sieve, extracting order from disorder, decreasing entropy by directing things to their proper place. He never stopped believing, as far as I know, that if he followed his own miniature exhibit through to the end, he would eventually come onto the last, life-size display, out in the open air.

This Futurama-induced administrative competence stranded the boy in singing-waiterdom while the future of the real place was being decided. Bricked in, the urge demanded a hundred other outlets, ultimately driving him to Passaic for the spouse research on weekends, not to find the most desirable mate but the most appropriate.

Dad probably should have been an engineer, the only line of work that fit his temperament. The job might have given him that illusion of slow improvement that could have saved him. He would have become one, too, *if it hadn't been for the detour that history arranged for him. He wanted me to take up the work he never did, but on that hope I could not deliver. My product has to be another.*

Some months after Futurama closed, when he heard the news about the miracle at Dunkirk, Pop thrilled to it as only a suitor of progress could. He cheered not so much the escape itself—light technology throwing mud in the Nazi's eyes by evacuating a third of a million soldiers in fishing boats. He was electrified by the delicious sense of the episode being managed efficiently, meetly, and effectively.

If the other major evacuation of the war, the one Roosevelt authorized on February 20, 1942, failed to give him the same sense of engineering perfection, it was because he never heard it happening. Like most wartime Americans aside from those imprisoned, the boy probably would have approved of the internment of a hundred thousand of his fellow citizens, Americans of Japanese Ancestry. Since he had never met any AJAs, Dad thought them as mythical as Assyrians coming down like wolves on the fold. At sixteen, the efficiency of our country's reverse Dunkirk would probably have interested him more than the morality or defensibility of the matter. Had Dad heard of the mass imprisonment, coming from a matinee of Orchestra Wives, it might have seemed no more real than the pictures of Nazi concentration camps that year distributed to boys on bubble-gum cards, reading "Don't let this happen here."

By the time we sat in the dark and watched that ludicrous film together a third of a century later, most of his issues had already been decided. Dad had settled on a life where all his emotional possessions were small, light, or easy to give away. He had already planned the details of his own break, even as he called out the movie's cast of players to me.

I have long since forgotten what the film was all about. All I can recall now is sitting in that room, in front of the faint, gray glow of the tube, wondering where my father was escaping to. I was still sidetracked on second-guessing, in the progress of his health, the covert message he meant to send to himself, to us, to the runaway and untouchable world. I overlooked the principal point: I should have seen that whatever Dad thought his illness represented, he was really sick. He was going through an actual hell of tortured and poisoned cells. I should have addressed the illness first and not waited to discover what it stood for.

It's obvious, in retrospect, what I should have done. I should have gone over to the couch and issued a soft but impatient order: "All right, old man. Tell me what's the matter." I ought to have made clear to him that it no longer mattered what happened then. I should have given my one, obvious reason why he should stick around, here, now, healed. Back in the present.

But I had no idea of what the present was. All the headlines agreed that the old place was dead. But what at that moment struggled to replace it was anyone's guess. I should have forced my father to return to the local urgencies of this place, this year. But I could not tell him how to find his way back to them. I had no more sense of '78 than he had had of '42, on the rumor-filled ball fields at sixteen. I was not even sure the trade-off was fair.

Thinking of that evening, I am filled with revisions. I allowed my father to lose me in the dominant tense. I looked at the man lying prostrate on the couch, jaundiced, debilitated, crazy with fever, a sardonic smile holding down the terminal gut-retch welling up in him. But all I could see was the boy of sixteen, the one he had told me of, involved in the enterprise of screening the files for his potential helpmate. I saw him attending school, perfecting his evening waiter's act, memorizing Miller's serenades, dabbling at lifting the long ball, wading through the whole mid-teen High Lutheran cycle of devotion, apostasy, and disgust, breezing through algebra on his way to an engineering career, alternately too serious and too irreverent for a boy his age, and, most of all, agonizingly waiting for his eighteenth birthday to enlist, but in the meantime daily wearing, even when it clashed with his civvies or his waiter's duck-tail suit, a bright blue-and-white pin, obtained three years before at the General Motors Futurama exhibit highlighting the world of 1960, that bore the inscription "I Have Seen the Future."

5

Eddie Jr. thought it the classic routine. Artie snapped him the pigskin and trotted leisurely, like the geezer pushing thirty that he was, up Second Street. Eddie waved him downfield with the universally recognized quarterback's hand motion for a big-play bomb: deep, deep, deeper. Then, when the sucker was incredibly, ridiculously deep, and it became obvious even to Artie that nobody in hell could possibly chuck a football that far, Eddie Jr. reversed his hand motion and waved big brother back in. Artie did all that he could do to save face in the situation: he grinned sheepishly, *I've been had.* He yelled "Asshole" into the crisp, bowl-game air, scrambling to reverse his fly pattern as if wise to the joke from the beginning.

"You talkin' to me?" little Eddie yelled, upfield. *"I'm* an asshole? What a terrible, terrible thing to call your baby brother. I may be an asshole, but at least I'm not the one doing the scatter pattern." This small blow was no retaliation for the dozen years of sadism that Arthur and the girls had enjoyed at his expense. Eddie was too nice a fellow to retaliate. Even his anger was benevolent. Nevertheless, the comeback gratified him, and for the next few passes, he took a little something off his return spirals, as apology.

They lobbed the ball to one another with an earnest relaxation, as if this were not the big game but only the warm-up. Artie threw for precision—the ICBM guided all the way from Vladivostock to the neighborhood junior high school, landing after twenty thousand miles in the third aisle of the faculty parking lot. Eddie preferred the wild but flashy hot-dog pass—the flee-flicker, Statue of Liberty, double-reverse, play-action fake. His were heat-seekers, or TOWs, not the most reliable missiles in the world but undeniably novel technology. The brothers shuttled the ball back and forth in the expectant daylight, Artie for accuracy, Eddie imitating the dramatic vees of last month's departing geese. They did not throw hard. The air was now cold enough, however, that even relaxing one's spine required work.

A handful of flamboyant goal-line heroics later, Eddie Jr. collapsed to earth, using the pigskin as a pillow. Artie, his yearly autumn anxiety once more welling up in him—*you're wasting time; you'll die in school as the world unfolds out here*—lay next to his brother, uncushioned on the iron ground. "I think," began Eddie, in confidential burlesque, "I know what's wrong with your father."

Artie did not turn his head. "Great. But it's *your* father we're trying to diagnose, buddy."

"Know how he always sort of curls up when it comes on, cringes all of a sudden, like?" Eddie's speech, whenever he tried to sound serious, grew awkwardly casual, returning by reverse evolution to the embryonic speech of his grandmother, a rich, weird branch of Lower Manhattan, Southern European English. Her inflections slopped back out of the melting pot to claim him. He recalled her telling of how eighty years earlier she had caught a wild turkey in the prairies of what was now only a half hour out of downtown Hoboken. "Flinching," Eddie continued, a victim of diction. "You've seen it: like he's bracing for something. And then—watch him next time. Always this upwards sweep of the eyes."

"I've seen it," said Artie, quietly. "So what are you suggesting? The Henny Penny syndrome?"

"In a manner of speaking, my man. À la 1978. Put it together, mofo. What's on the news these days, almost every night?"

"Basketball scores?"

"Besides that, you overeducated nit. 'Scientists fire retros, wrestle to stabilize Skylab. Details at ten.' "

Artie tried to imagine Pop obsessed with the idea that an artificial moon, out-of-control, threatening to crash any month now, had his name on it. He imagined Dad, periodically tearing his family out from their established bunker and insisting they remain moving targets, lately growing convinced of a terrible destiny, a celestial downward arc that, no matter how he wound his path across the map, would soon swoop down for the final interception. SPACECRAFT BITES MAN. Despite going a ways toward explaining Pop's secondary symptoms, his brother's interpretation was too far on the tabloid side, even for Dad.

"Where'd you get that idea, the supermarket check-out line? I thought I told you to stop reading newspapers that carry alien-invasion stories as their main headlines." He tried unsuccessfully to pull the football out from under his brother's stout neck.

"Ha! I suppose you want me to start reading that New York liberal rag of yours, now that I've grown up? How can you trust a paper that hasn't covered sports adequately since sculling went out of fashion? No way, palomino. And I think you ought to quit denying the obvious. Your dad's bracing himself for falling space stations."

"But what about the high fever? And the vomiting?" Only after making these objections did Artie realize their ridiculousness. He had once more been utterly duped. Things had gotten so far out of hand that he had forgotten that his brother's suggestion had been facetious. Dad had, after all, been dosing out since long before Sputnik. Eddie Jr. had tricked him into taking a second downfield hand wave seriously. Artie thought of how he used to run riot over the kid. Once he could have gotten him to believe anything. But something had turned for the worse between the two of them in the last few years. Artie confronted the awful possibility that under the stress of current events, he had somehow become the gullible one.

Eddie enjoyed the advantage. "Yeah. You're right. What about the vomiting? I mean, if *I* were about to be hit with NASA's finest, I'd want it to be on a full stomach." When his older brother did not reply, Eddie added, contritely and sadly, "Joke, Artie," too late to unscrape the wound.

Artie stayed in his vacuum of sound, committing himself no further to little bro's truce than the ambiguous gesture of pinching the bridge of his nose. He conceded that Edski was funny. The kid had a natural punchline, as with so much else. Even when pretending acerbity, Eddie was nicer and kinder than was safe. His little brother would swallow his phlegm sooner than offend anyone by spitting. But certain facts about the littlest Hobson had by now made themselves apparent to Artie. Artie felt that the kid, in coming of age, had reneged on an understanding, had become a questionable quantity. One could not, for instance, send him to the store with a twenty-dollar bill and expect to retrieve full face value on the remaining change. Eddie would come back with coins of varying denominations spread over his person and would spend weeks pulling singles out of hitherto undiscovered pockets, remarking in surprise, "Hey, check this out! I'm loaded."

Each time Artie headed back to U. of C. Law to knock out another semester, he hoped that upon his next return his brother would at last demonstrate competence. But Eddie Jr. remained the same—cheerfully inept. Coupled with his proven unreliability, linked to it in a way that Artie couldn't put his finger on, was Eddie's alarming propensity for making friends, a practice the male Hobsons had scrupulously avoided for centuries. Soon it would be Thanksgiving, and through the startled house would pass sundry craigs and barbaras and kellys and bobs, each of whom Eddie would take pains to introduce to the family, optimistically beginning, "You all remember . . ." knowing full well that nobody did.

Artie lay perfectly still, feeling each breath, staving off hypothermia through sheer will. He thought back to the last time he had felt any urge to bring an acquaintance over to the house. It couldn't have been later than third grade. He had discovered early on the effect of his father's erratic illness on his friends. Easier not to bring outsiders by, easier to stay just outside the arms' length of intimacy. But his little brother had somehow achieved membership in that envious class that Artie had long since banished himself from. His own flesh and blood had become a joiner—the very class that had persecuted Artie throughout school for having to base his image on intellect rather than social confidence. Little Eddie had arrived in the islands of the well liked, a place as mysterious to Artie as his father's mythic town. His brother and he had inexplicably ended up in opposing camps.

Aside from last night's glimmer of a calamined summer on the Pacific, Artie's memory of his own childhood was far less powerful than his recall of encyclopedia facts. His first vivid recollection of being driven out of the safe haven of simplicity was of one winter day when his father explained a joke that precocious Artie had read in a book that lay beyond his six years: "A: There's a man at the door with a package marked C.O.D. B: Sounds fishy to me." Typically, Pop explained the punchline recursively, saying the joke *itself* sounded fishy to him. Only after little Artie wailed in protest did Dad explain the play on words and the obsolete cultural practice of cash on delivery.

Artie recalled Dad proceeding to free-associate on fish names, telling his son, with the utmost urgency and solemnity, what he claimed was the world's longest palindrome: "Doc, note, I dissent; a fast never prevents a fatness: I diet on cod." And closing his eyes on the frozen-over front-yard football field, Artie could still summon the precise look of mysterious intensity filling the man's face as he turned to his firstborn and said, "What'll you give me if I say it backward?" From that moment, the boy's relations with the outside world carried the complication of two directions.

Artie suspected the trauma that scattered his early memories beyond regrouping and the trauma that instructed him with childlike sensitivity not to bring friends over to the house were the same. Making this connection, Artie understood that his folks, who in their Jersey heyday had been the epicenter for the Mid-Atlantic Charter of the Drop-in-for-Cocktails-Unannounced League, must have been compelled by the same decorum to make *their* steady decline out of sight. They became once-a-monthers at the Other Guys' place. At last they achieved their current status, quarantined in Fortress Second Street, One-Oh-Three. Society itself had not outgrown the spontaneous visit, as Artie had for some time vaguely concluded. The Hobsons alone had something solicitors shunned and arbiters avoided.

Yet somehow Eddie Jr. had escaped, immune. With his easy grace—a trait lurking recessive in the Hobson genotype for generations—he made friends broadly and indiscriminately. Peers of both sexes genuinely liked him and, most remarkable to Artie, found nothing unusual in him or his old man. No doubt little Eddie (this particularly filled Arthur with horror) even joked away his dad's pathology with these perfect strangers as he had just tried to do with his brother. Artie would have winced thinking about it; but not wanting to give Eddie any cause to think that he too had the first stages of Skylab sickness, he froze his face into a slate of pleasantry.

Granted the girls had had their friends as well. Lily had even taken the extreme, although temporary, step of marrying outside the family. But none of those developments alarmed Artie so much as Eddie Jr.'s defection. His sisters were different, in a way that Artie would not dare to articulate to anyone of his own stratum. They were not true Hobsons, but had the name only on extended loan. He kept this distinction to himself, knowing he could never explain his sexist medievalism to the enlightened organic fascists of his law-school class. Nor could he hope to convince his contemporaries that such a lack was not a failing but a freedom. Hobson's Choice was one asset he would have gladly come out from under.

Eddie, oblivious to all his brother mulled over, kept at the wisecracks. Adopting a falsetto, he said, "The Skylab is falling, the Skylab is falling." When Artie looked over and smiled sweetly, Little Brother, understanding that he had transgressed worse by trying to appease, shifted back down ottava. He asked, "Well what do *you* think it is, really?" The boys—those saddled with the liability of a lasting last name—began hashing out the fine points of what had until then been a politely avoided division of opinion.

As his joke indicated, Eddie came down squarely in the Your-Father-Is-Ill-of-His-Own-Accord camp. What ailed Eddie Sr., as far as his namesake made out, was part and parcel of the fellow himself. "Tell you what, Artie. I'll grant the man is clearly in the middle of a medical catastrophe. But when *hasn't* he been? Sick for as long as we've known him, anyway. He makes sure the fits get a little more devastating every year. It's a tradition. Otherwise, it wouldn't be Pop. Can you imagine him completely well?" He spun the football on end in the palm of his hand, adopting the tone of a play-by-play. "Pop wants to be on this road. Nobody's put him on it. Hell, Pop built the road himself. Pop *is* the road, no?" It wasn't clear whom he was convincing. "Maybe Granny toilet-trained him with glaring lights and loud noises. That's it. And now he's gotta have it undone by analysis, has to cure himself by one of them . . . what's it called, Artie?"

"Catharsis?" Artie suggested, unpersuaded.

"Yeah, one of them catheters," Eddie smiled. First, he'd cure his brother. Then they could talk about Dad. The whole unintelligible complex of symptoms seemed to Eddie easier to parody as an absurd infant trauma than to assault medically. Parody, at least, kept *them* uninfected. To Eddie, the art of the wince and blackout didn't hinge on anything; it was simply the only way Dad could absorb the massive accidents that the Big Picture dealt the Little. And to Eddie Jr., nothing could be crazier or less called for. He himself saw the everyday more as a reprieve than a punishment. Even the words to state his case against Dad lay half a step beyond his active vocabulary. "*Pop* won't let Pop alone. Passing out is just his way of dealing with himself. Oh, I don't know . . . you know? Know what I mean, bean?" He asked the question as a way of peacemaking, pretending the issues were still open. He knew without Artie's ever having spoken a word to that effect that they came from as far across opposing sides of the tracks as imaginable. But he wanted badly to agree.

Artie responded in litigant's form, watered down so that Little Eddie wouldn't take to travesty. "Disagree. The way I see it, Pop's disorder must be somatic. Lumps in the neck and armpits, for instance, are not your typical hysterical symptoms. We have to assume the disorder is real until it's proven invented." And suddenly, he remembered a night last summer, passing the bathroom door, hearing the man lurching his soft bowel up into the toilet. He felt a sympathetic cloud of nausea that made all negotiation for recovery pointless and repellent. At the remembered sound of his father's pulpy, mulched insides hitting water, the sickness became real.

He sat up. "What we need to do, since the fool is afraid of a walk-in clinic, is to get a copy of a Merck Manual or a Stedman's dictionary and work up a differential diagnosis as systematically as possible. Otherwise, we're reduced to guesswork. And the man *wants* to keep us guessing." He did not look at his brother. He put his hands out in front of him to receive the football, and Eddie, without looking, lobbed it to him.

"So what do you want us to do? Traipse up to the librarian at De Kalb Public? 'We think our Pop's buying the farm. Got any helpful printed matter?' " Eddie giggled, then sobered quickly. "Artie, if it were something *real*, the guy would have been dead years ago." Eddie Jr. declined to follow up his point. For most of his eighteen years, he had lived for his brother's occasional, affectionate nod. But now, when it mattered, he could not bring himself to concede to Big Brother's plan. "You make it sound like we have to stop him this week or never. Christ, Artie, what's waiting another month or two to see what happens?" Eddie himself rejected this even as he said it. "We probably missed our last chance to help him five years back."

Artie did not admit that he'd been waiting for Eddie to turn eighteen so that it could at last be the two of them against one. Here, on their backs, on the hard ground, Artie saw that it would never be two against one. It would always remain mixed singles.

To assure himself that he had not yet conceded the issue, Artie suggested an assortment of possible pathologies. Meantime, Eddie tossed the football straight up in the air, difficult from a prone position, snaring it one-handed. Artie would say, "Parasitic infection," the ball would go whoosh, and Eddie would do his Raymond Berry. Then Artie would say, "No, stool's normal, as far as anybody can tell." He'd say, "Brain lesions," the ball would go whoosh, and so it went. By the time Artie proposed leukemia, Eddie had accumulated an amazing four hundred–plus yards on shoestring catches, enough for the record books.

Each might have forgiven Dad his illness had either held the other's point of view. Eddie, hopelessly well adjusted, relied on himself as a model and assumed that everybody was equally capable of happiness. If miserable, they wanted to be. The wince was the wincer's responsibility. Physical illness would have been okay by him. If Pop's *cells* brought on his spells, then that would have been rotten luck, deserving sympathy.

Artie, on the other hand, would have forgiven Dad so trivial a thing as neurosis. But as he ticked off possible culprits—hypoglycemia, blood clots, Korsakoff's syndrome, organic dissolution—he grew increasingly resentful of anyone who would stoop to intractable disease. To Artie, blame had less to do with sufferer's guilt than survivors' inconvenience.

Although producing a lengthy list, Artie's heart wasn't in the diagnosis. Instead, he found himself marveling at the physics of Eddie's tossed football. He was appalled at how such a thing could go straight up and still come straight down to Eddie, despite the earth having spun out from underneath it in the interim. He knew it had something to do with inertia, that there was an m_1 times m_2 divided by r or r^2 term in there somewhere. It seemed impossible and morally wrong, nevertheless.

Artie recalled the Butterfly Effect, that model of random motion describing how a butterfly flapping its wings in Peking propagates an unpredictable chain reaction of air currents, ultimately altering tomorrow's weather in Duluth. He played Name That Disease, I've Got a Symptom, but all the while more intent on imagining the storms Eddie's harmlessly tossed ball would generate on the far side of the globe.

In order to get the proper vantage on this rippling storm, Artie projected his view upward in the air, looking back down on the two overage and too-large boys. At first he could create nothing more dramatic than the famous crane shot at the train depot from *Gone With the Wind*, the one that prompted some die-hard reb at the Atlanta premiere to remark, "If we'd had that many soldiers we'd have *won* the war." But gradually he managed a larger pullback, a grander dollying away, a logarithmic jumping out, until, in very few steps, he could no longer see the butterfly, Duluth, Peking, or even the space between.

He collapsed telescopically back to planet surface when a voice, unmistakably his mother's, broke in on their reserved frequency. "I'm not disturbing you, am I?"

Ailene always unintentionally disturbed her children doubly by prefacing her disturbances with the genuine hope that she wasn't about to be any bother. She doubled each interruption by interleaving every remark with the plea, "I don't want to take up your time." When the children were growing up, things had been very different. Mother had been far from deferential, seeming sometimes not to know the limits of maternal indignation. Her spit-moistened thumb, rubbed across churchgoing faces to lift off the dirt of too much playground, frequently lifted off tender skin and raised welts instead. But now the woman overacquiesced to her children, embarrassed at once having had to break them in.

Like Lily, Mom kept a girl's paint box in long-term storage at the bottom of the clothes closet. She was that peculiar late-century creature, the unwitting ironist. Born in one of those Oak Hill Park Forest Elm Grove places on Chicago's North Shore, she had fled to the East Coast to escape the life of dental hygienist that every intelligent, midwestern, not-yet-married urban woman was forced into. Instead, she had collided with Pop outside Paramus. They married, and the man inexorably and against her will edged her back to within sixty miles of the nest she had tried to flee. While she had not yet ended up cleaning teeth eight hours a day, her present emergency employment left her perilously close. Her inability to escape her destiny infused her actions with a certain fatalism. She knew that if her husband's death did not intervene, she would inevitably have to take up residency in some division or subdivision or supersubdivision in Maple Vale Creek Crest Ridge and even at her advanced age be made to don the little white uniform and clean teeth until she died. "I don't want to . . . I know you two are . . ." Mom began.

Eddie sprang to his feet and, with a mock growl of "Get to the point, you mom, you," shook her by the shoulders. Recalling from some long-lost quarter the ancient phrase "knock the stuffing out of you," he realized where he had gotten this very gesture, and was shocked to notice how much the woman who had formerly dished it out had shrunk into the woman who now took her own punishment with a polite grin.

"Your father," she began, her grin broadening, "has said that he'll go to the hospital."

"He *what?*" Eddie yelped, then cut his mother off when she tried to answer. "How in the hell did you get him to do that?"

"I just asked him," she said, and waited to be told that she had done good. But Eddie, while approving the results, knew that the method used to get them was terribly wrong. Thinking for two, he looked down quickly at his brother. But Artie lay on the ground, waiting for this brief disturbance to disappear in order to get on with the diagnosis–football-chucking game. At last Artie flashed a curious look, one that didn't get a lot of airplay in his increasingly lean face as of late. The look hung about the bushy area where his massive eyebrows ran into and merged with each other. Eddie recognized his brother's look as the failed attempt to sidestep Hope: the old damned if Do, doomed if Don't.

1940-41

He is without doubt one of the most universally recognized figures in the world. Millions who couldn't pick Stalin or Einstein or Chiang Kai-shek or Picasso out of a police lineup know his face. His acclaim is unmatched in recent memory. He is loved more broadly by more strangers than almost anyone who has ever lived, reaching this pinnacle of adoration by remaining an honorable and nice guy, with no personality flaws to speak of. Strangest of all, he has enjoyed this astonishing recognition for his whole life, which in 1940 is just over twelve years old.

Anyone who has not witnessed it cannot imagine his popularity. But everyone alive has witnessed it. His simple, trustworthy face and figure appear everywhere. Even those exceptional few who have never heard him speak, have never seen his characteristic walk or smile or wave, still own some pennant or article of clothing with his picture on it. His image crops up several times a day without attracting notice. Most countries on the planet carry accounts of his adventures and exploits in the daily newspapers.

His appeal is nonpartisan and ecumenical, uniting the most disparate men. Eleanor Roosevelt says her husband rarely plans an evening off without requesting his appearance at the White House. The same was true of King George V and the Royal Palace. Hirohito, too, is a great admirer. African tribes refuse to purchase bars of soap without his imprint. He is the toast of intellectuals, the wonder of the working class, the favorite of children.

He has traveled the globe, pursuing adventures in far-flung places from the South Seas to the Sahara. He has labored at countless professions: explorer, inventor, magician, detective, cowboy, convict, castaway, trucker, tailor, sailor, whaler. He masters every sport. He speaks a dozen languages effortlessly. He is already in Tussaud's wax museum.

9 7

He is, in short, a world phenomenon. And no one can quite say why.
His stepfather attempts, unsuccessfully, to explain:

Everybody's tried to figure it out. So far as I know, nobody has. He's a
pretty nice fellow who never does anybody any harm, who gets into scraps
through no fault of his own, but always manages to come up grinning.

This hardly accounts for the gent's hypnotic hold on the mind of the
collective world. More plausible, if unpleasant, is the explanation of the
last few years, of 1940. The air of an old planet even now fills with new
names: Blitzkrieg, Radar, Dachau. His immense popularity must come
from our learning, in a few years, how to ignore things that would have
frozen previous generations with total horror. In a world already lost, he
is simply the finest provider of escape from the confusing, opaque,
overwhelming, paralyzing, deadly serious, irreversible, and appalling
times. He alone, free from the killing machine of current events, is
untouched by the mass-murderous political impasse. That is why he's
welcome everywhere. That's why we put his mug into the time capsule. As
an enthusiast declares in an open fan letter, "Let there be one God, one
Caesar, one Lincoln, one Napoleon, one Mickey Mouse."

The man behind the mouse is not half so well known. Disney supplies
the world-renowned, high-pitched squeak, but his own speaking voice goes
unnoticed at the other end of a phone. His picture appears in hundreds of
magazines and newspapers and newsreels, but always in the company of
his creation. Without Mickey by his side, countless unsuspecting admirers
for whom he has made the present tenable pass him in the street.

One photo of Walt, appearing in a popular magazine six years earlier,
is remarkable for Mickey's conspicuous absence. It shows Disney, not in
some Never-Never Land but cocked behind a desk, dictating one of his
famous Silly Symphonies into a black bullhorn. This is his method of
creation. An idea strikes: it goes into the electronic dictation machine. The
recording device, his alter existence, is the secret land where he creates the
alternate worlds that give the public safe haven.

But these other worlds, cartoon realities synchronized to music, already
make unfortunate brushes with reality. The most popular and successful of
the Silly Symphonies, The Three Little Pigs, *with its hit song of 1933,*
"Who's Afraid of the Big Bad Wolf?" coincides with Hitler's appointment

---

as German chancellor and the establishment of the Third Reich. Then there is Disney's greatest gamble: For four years, he pits the prestige and economic resources of his studio in a make-or-break effort, a ninety-minute fairy tale. When Snow White at last appears in the year of the Anschluss, the war in Manchuria, and the Sudetenland crisis, it breaks all box-office records. But its story—a heroine poisoned by a wicked witch's apple and resurrected by a prince with the aid of seven small allies—is construed as a thinly veiled political allegory in America's raging isolationist debate.

No matter what inspirations Disney spits into the black bullhorn, they emerge infected by outside events. This is nowhere truer than in his second great gamble, 1940's Fantasia. The film, wedding images to classical music, is one of the screen's towering achievements, among the most innovative since sound. As never before, Disney combines real figures with painted ones; they talk and respond to one another within the same frame. The dramatic high point of the film, Mussorgsky's "Night on Bald Mountain," animates the final assault of the forces of Evil, only to give way to the apotheosis of Good in the guise of Schubert's "Ave Maria."

But the public, in the guise of young Eddie Hobson, trained by the sparkling futures of World's Fairs, never doubts the outcome of this Manichaean showdown. Eddie is far more excited about Mickey's feature debut. Although Fantasia draws mixed reviews and falls far short of Snow White at the box office, Mickey's role in the film increases his popularity, if such a thing is possible. For young Hobson, the film's highlight comes when Mickey pulls on Stokowski's tuxedo tails, so neatly does the meeting refute all distinction between event and invention.

Later in the film, Mickey has his narrative moment as Dukas's "Sorcerer's Apprentice." Left alone by his master, who departs with prohibitions and grave warnings, Mickey cannot resist the temptation to don the Hat of Power and use it for the most harmless task in the world: to help carry water. He animates a broom, a neat, recursive trick, to do the toting for him. He falls asleep and dreams of great might. He wakes to find the broomstick flooding the study. Grabbing an ax, he splits the broom in two. But the splinters leap up, each mindlessly pursuing the task he set them on but cannot stop.

If Little Eddie is too innocent to see the contemporary allegory, he still squirms in his seat at the classical dilemma. Each attempt to stop a porter starts two more. Mickey can't give up and drown, but his *intervention only aggravates the crisis. Fortunately for the mouse, master returns in the nick of time, rescuing the hero of millions and saving his movie career.*

Disney, in 1941, develops broomstick problems of his own. He runs his empire as a benevolent dictator, in both bullhorn sense and otherwise. He demands of his employees the loyalty oath invented by his colleague Sam Goldwyn: "I want you to tell me the truth, even if it costs you your job." Protest over Disney's tyranny and his insistence on naturalistic drawing results in a mass resignation from his studios, the biggest group walkout in Hollywood history. The manufacturing of enchantment becomes especially tricky under the threat of complete business collapse. The only thing that saves Disney from ruin is the miraculous invention animating the single vote.

How much can one vote count? That depends on what's being voted. If it's the one vote that gets the Draft Act out of joint committee and back onto the Congress's floor, then one tally means everything—the beginning of the end of isolationist settlements, after a battle unforgettable for anyone who has witnessed it. The Great Debate polarizes the nation. It comes up as frequently and violently as ball scores. The country in 1940 is still willing to confront the subtleties of idealism. The isolationists, among them many powerful single votes including senators and congressmen, Lindbergh, Robert McCormick, and the popular rabble-rousing radio priest, Father Coughlin, stand firm in the long tradition of American moral noninvolvement. But the one vote that keeps the Draft Act alive through a storm of controversy is on the other hand a small enough margin to convince the Japanese that a surprise attack might go unanswered. Pacifism and nonconfrontation actually help draw us into war.

The power of the lone vote depends on the perils of the issue. This year, the perils are your basic all or nothing: does the beautiful heroine come back to life and triumph over the witch's poison? Does "Ave Maria" have the last word over "Bald Mountain"? Do we drown faster by standing aside or by picking up the ax? Does the world-famous mouse succeed in preserving a place where mass deportation and extermination do not and cannot happen? The issue being voted is the only issue there is. How much does one vote count?

If it's Chamberlain's vote, returning after the debacle of Munich, waving the signed paper around as proof: not much. But if the vote is Von Braun's—a future colleague of Disney in a collaborative film enterprise called Man in Space, whose Hollywood biopic will be called I Aim for the Stars but who is currently working on reel one, "First, I Hit London"—one vote erases many. How much does one vote count? To the young Eddie Hobson, that depends on how the other guy votes. And those results are still out.

When Secretary of War Henry Stimson at last dips his hand into the same bin used to pull draft numbers for the war to end all War, and when the World's Fair's "World of Tomorrow" is dismantled to convert the area into a recruiting camp, the era of one vote comes to an end. The scale of things shoots off the top of the graph. The power of the local voice to tip the curve now seems miniscule, insignificant. Unless, of course, the local voice is larger than life.

Although Admiral Yamamoto himself votes against the move, he plans and executes Japan's successful attack on Pearl Harbor. We are once more unanimously at war. A majority of the American electorate doesn't realize that it's not going to be Teddy Roosevelt or even the romance of Pershing this time. But both legislatures vote unanimously for the declaration with one holdout, Montana's Jeanette Rankin, the first congresswoman ever, who in a previous act of conscience also voted against our going into the First One. The opposing vote costs her her job. The vote is a remarkable enough "beacon," as the high school texts call such things, that when the great film finally gets under way, someone suggests devoting ten words of voice-over to this woman's action.

Rankin says that she just wanted to show that a good democracy doesn't always vote unanimously to go to war. But her one vote aside, the tally is unanimous: 82–0 in the Senate and 288–1 in the House for throwing our combined weight into the fray. Roosevelt allocates some number with a lot of zeros after it—50 billion, if memory serves—for guns, and since everybody has been without butter for some time, he gets much the sum he's after.

What happened out at Hawaii was bad. But the common Joe reading the daily papers doesn't know nearly how bad: pretty much the whole Pacific fleet, counting the other bases bombed that same day. The simple explanation for this ignorance is that the average Joe's newspapers don't carry the full story, don't mention specific losses. The phrase making the rounds is "voluntary censorship." To coordinate the voluntary, the government establishes an Office of Censorship twelve days after the Hawaii attack, to provide a second line of defense should the newshounds fail to cooperate or should one reporter, fearing that another might break ranks and scoop him, leak a story preemptively. Information becomes the nation's most valuable and protected commodity, and we can no longer afford to entrust it to individual hands.

How much does one vote count? It depends on who's voting. One vote can be a doozy if it's one Caesar, one Lincoln, one Napoleon, or one God. No sooner has the Great Debate over isolationism and neutrality faded forever and given way to the consolidated war effort than Disney gets a call from Henry L. Stimson, the secretary in charge of coordinating that effort. Stimson recruits the Disney studios into a crucial and unique role in the national mobilization. The request saves Disney from his labor strike and unites his new outfit in a common cause.

The man who has combined live action and fanciful imagination, who taught the two to co-exist peacefully in the same frame, is, in short, drafted. Stimson lets Disney know that he must now turn out, by the mile, morale raisers, training films, and propaganda. These cartoons, infused with a deadly new seriousness, will be instrumental in winning the most important theater of the campaign: the battle already called the Home Front.

And why not? The penchant for wishful thinking does not wither in front of a firing squad. Spring fashions do not stop permutating just because of sneak attacks. Perhaps they should. But even on the staging grounds for the final battlefield, the mind needs another place. The troops themselves, most just eighteen, are the first to admit that they need a decent Silly Symphony to see them through.

The word animation derives from Latin meaning life, spirit, breath, courage. We will need these exact quantities in good measure if we are to survive. Besides, we have long ago lost our ability to know whether facts beat belief or the other way around. What the newsreels from Europe could not bring home, Welles brought on with radio fantasy. If transparent fiction is more frightening than fact, it must certainly have more power to delight. And the side that comes through this final fight still loving the *exhausted, ruined world, the side with more delight, will be the winning side.*

Eddie Hobson learns of the news that will change his life one afternoon at the matinee, late in December of 1941. Pearl Harbor has weeks before sealed his fate. The outcome is terminally uncertain. But that day, he hears the awesome power of a single vote enlist. Mickey Mouse goes to War.

Dinner was a disaster. Everyone arrived at table euphoric with the news but determined to say nothing to jinx the turn of events. Even Dad was in good humor. He did not look like someone who'd just agreed to surrender himself to the authorities. His topic of discussion that evening was The Drunk and the Lamppost, also called The Random Walk. Dad said it illustrated Brownian motion among other things. "Set a drunk up against a lamppost. Assume he walks a random number of steps and then turns a random angle, continuing in this manner. Where will he end up?"

"Farther and farther from his starting position, in a random direction," said Eddie Jr., trying his hardest to please.

"Back, eventually, at the lamppost," said Artie, having read it.

"The rehab clinic," said Rach, in her helpful deadpan. This crack precipitated the blowup. Lily, a piece of pepper steak in her mouth, began to choke. Eddie Jr., thinking her laughter a vaudeville take, began to laugh with her. When Lily went on gagging, Artie, finally thinking quickly, jumped up and whacked her on the back. Out came the offending piece of gristle. Lily jumped up just as quickly, smacking Artie back for hitting so hard. When she recovered, she turned on Little Eddie, saying, "And damn you, too, you little sycophant."

Focusing her full anger on her sister, she narrowed her eyes and dropped to staccato. "Do you *ever* stop to consider what your punchlines cost? What we *all* pay to keep you in chuckles?" She threw her napkin down and slammed off, barricading herself in her room.

Artie sat back down in silence. Little Eddie looked as if he had just cut himself shaving. Rach sat upright, eyes and mouth wide. The bottom of her face puffed out as if it had been slugged. "Somebody tell me what I said."

"She thinks," Dad explained, eye-twinkle only a little subdued, "that you were insulting me."

Ailene quietly folded her linen napkin and placed her silver perfectly at the side of her plate. She stood up demurely. "And you were." Then she too disappeared, upstairs.

Rach shook her head, still stunned. "Remind me to take my next vacation in Wisconsin." She went to the front hall, put on her coat, and left for the Northern Lights.

A minute passed as the dust settled. Artie grinned weakly, stood, and said, "Gotta study. I leave you gentlemen to your own devices."

The two Eddies sat together, pushing food around on untouched plates. After a long silence, Little asked Big: "So tell me. Where *does* that drunk end up?"

Hours later, the house closed up for the night, Rach returned from the neighborhood bar and knocked on Lily's door. Her sister's "Come in" sounded almost cheerful. Nothing had happened: that was the way Lily meant to play it. Rach went into the room and sat on the antique armchair. She grinned, the kind that doesn't know if it helps or hurts. At last, Rach asked forgiveness the only way she knew how. "Let's play something."

"What?" Lily asked pleasantly.

Rach looked around the room. Her glance settled on Lily's ancient Olympia typewriter. She hoisted it up onto the spool table between them, rolled a sheet of scrap paper into it, and began typing.

```
New game. First I type two lines on this sheet of paper and give
it to you. Then you have to continue from wherever I leave

off? What do I win for guessing that? I suppose there are more
rules than just that. If there's anything I've learned from your

darling games over the years, dearest sister, it's that they are
marvelously unencumbered (pretty posh phrase for one who's never

been able to tell the difference between posh and purple) with any
sense of purpose. Why are we playing this game anyway? Can't you just come out and

gimme that. Rule 1 is that you have to stop after EXACTLY two
lines, and no fair going over from now on. Rule 2 is that there
```

is no Rule 2. How are we going to know which lines are yours and
which mine? I mean years from now. Of course there's my impec-

unious way of handling the ''e'' key. Is ''impecunious'' a word?
Like I was saying before I was so rudely interrupted, I've never

been able to differentiate between mere whim and what the rest of
the world commonly agrees on as reality. You never answered my

simpering. Nor do I intend to. The fact that we ARE playing
ought to indicate the futility of hankering over why. After all,

Not that question. The one about how we'll be able to tell who's
who. Shouldn't we start each line with an ''L'' or an ''R''? That way

we raise the possibility of our ''L'' not knowing what our ''R'' is
doing. Nope. It's better without the IDs, because years from

I disagree, Rach. Let's do it playscript style. Otherwise, we're
just going to run into one another, create a conflict of identi

Rule 3 is that you can't break off the last person's thoughts and
start something different. You have to make a smooth transition

from one thing to the next. How's that? Now will you answer me?
Ten years from now I'll want to know whether this is me asking you

or you, me? What's the difference? We can avoid the problem all
together by keeping the ''I''s out from here on. Rule 4: No ''I''s.

''All right,'' said her considerably less flighty older sister, wise
beyond her years. Yet still something tugged at her, and she

would have rectified (potty joke) the problem if not for a nervous
if not to say apprehensive colon, thus: If you make one more

rational protest, you'll what? Brain the poor woman? If there's
no more ''I''s than ''you''s have to go too, ok? Let's do the

whole thing in third person,'' agreed the always fairminded Rachel. But
the new rule rapidly bored her, and seeing as how it was her game,

little sister thought clearly and carefully before making any
sudden and potentially disastrous moves (didn't she?) and decided

that Rule 5 was that Rules 1-4 would only apply if, when, and
where I want them to apply. Got it, Lady? Hey wait gimme help

Now what kind of rules would they be, if the rules keep changing?
Two can play at that game. This is my typewriter, remember.

Okayokayokayokay. So they repealed Amendment 5, for Lily at
least. Now both sisters had exactly what each one needed. Rules

for the self-controlled, and anarchy for the animal. By this
time, however, Lily was getting into it, and wanted to see just

how far the sisters could sustain a thought without any barriers
between them. They had, until this moment, been circling around

the issue that was on both of their minds, if ''mind'' could be used
to describe what stuff was in the younger one's brain case. But

just as they thought they had fallen into lockstep, the women
discovered each other way off on opposite sides of the lamppost.

Why do you always have to do that? Saw the real issue coming,
didn't you, and thought you'd jump ship. I quit.

No pouting, now. That one violated the pronoun rule. Also, the
tacit rule about finishing a stanza all the way to the end, even

steven. Getting that out of her system, Rach was ready to come to
terms with the issue. Again they asked one another, ''What IS the

best way for those two mutual felons of Dad's to stay out of the
hoosegow? That one does interest me, though I wouldn't in a mil-

lion years let the poor guy know it? Of course not. You don't
think his problem is at all related to his daughter taking it on

herself to torture him? Not bloody likely. He loves it. Now
stick to the point. How do those guys keep from ratting on each

other? Search me. Seems to me a clear cut case of trust begets
trust, lack of trust begets lack of trust. Pass me the truffles,

Tess. The curry Carrie. Gosh, fellas, she's funny and pert too.
So why is it so bloody hard to get out of the Hymen League?

Believe me, you're better off as is. Treat men as if they were
walking encumbrances, if you want what's best for you. Take me,

please. Come off it, girl. So you marry a guy who threatens to
hang himself to get your attention. That's going to leave any-

body WHO'S BEEN THROUGH IT a little shaken, yes. Gimme a cig.
Gratias. It struck me at the time that if I were a recessive car-

rier of dad's disease, with wayne-o as batty as wall stucko, that
you two'd probably have produced an exceptionally strange brood.

Stucco has two ''c''s. Unless we're talking about my condition,
which seems to contain that ''k''. And who'd ever heard of ''two'd''?

Try not to leave me high and dry, on a new line. It's not as fun
when you have to start out a new couplet from scratch. The thrill

is gone. Hey, look back a couple lines. What do you think you've
been doing to me? Brood. Lamppost. League. Take the log out of

the lion's paw. OR is that the Monkey's Paw. Nobody's Paw but
mine. I want a Gee just like the Gaw that married dear old Maw.

You did it again. Just for that I'm going to end my next three
with periods. Why am I playing this with you if you won't cooper-

Well, sis, I wish I could tell ya'. But I'm afraid that's a
question that everybody is just going to have to answer for

me. Now look. As usual, we've degenerated. This is no better
than trying to hold a conversation with you. I preferred it

in third person,'' she said. The nimble-witted Rachel agreed.
Once again in lockstep, the dialectic duo of sibling synonyms

forged ahead into research on Pa's prisoner problem. Lily
remarked that the knot became trivial if each knew what the

other meant to do ahead of time. ''True,'' remarked her genetic
alter-egg. ''But they don't.'' Was she being laconic, or just

coy? The world would never know. For as in a flash, it dawned on
both women that what they were really discussing, what really
concerned them was their

Alert alert alert: Rule 1 violation in sector A-7. All rule-
police report immediately. If we let this go unpunished, then

Rach, quit it. I'm really scared. What if he's going in too
late? I'm not sure I still want to know what's wrong with him.

He is in no more danger now than he has always been. All we can
ever do for him is stick around. But no sooner did Rach say this

than the girls' mother loomed up in the doorway, an imposing figure from a bygone era. With finger to mouth, she made it plain

that the incessant type-clacking of the dutiful daughters would
wake said Dad from his much needed healing sleep. ''You can

"You can keep typing," Ailene said. "Just type quietly." Both daughters, products of the woman, knew that this meant "Quit typing." Yet because they were enjoying a rare moment of mutual accord, neither wanted to break off negotiations just yet.

"New game," Rachel demanded. "Get the Ouija." Lily stood on a chair and rooted around in the back of the closet's top shelf. Neither had played with the beaten-up occult object for years. Lily brought the equipment down and dusted it off. They darkened the room and placed the board between them on their laps like seasoned mediums.

They slid the heart-shaped pointer around the board, loosening up. Rachel commenced the questioning. "Oh, murky spirits from beyond the pale—it is 'pale,' isn't it?"

"Just ask the question," Lily hissed.

"That's what I thought. But wait: what's 'veil'? Veil has something to do with this spiritual racket too. Painted veil, and so on."

"Get serious, will you? They won't show up if they think you're goofing off."

"All right. Oh, mighty spirits from beyond the Snail, to whom do we have the pleasure of speaking?" Their four hands lurched into low gear, and the device haltingly traced out:

R-A-G-E R-A-G-E RAGE IN DU PAGE

"Glad you could stop by, Mr. Rage," Rachel said. "How *are* things in Dupage?" The Ouija sputtered and spelled:

THIS IS NNY GHT NOT A GAME

Rachel giggled at the garbled spelling. "Well, it's no picnic for us either."

Lily shoved her sister with her wrists and took charge of the interrogation. "Spirit, what can you tell us about where you are?"

WHAT LIKE WHAT INSTANCE

The answer, however uncommunicative, excited Lily. "Tell us a little bit about what it's like, there, on the other side."

IMPOUNDABLE IMPONDER

"Imponderable, Spirit? Is that what you mean?"

Rachel cut off any answer. "Yeah, yeah. Heard that one before. You don't have to lecture *us* on life's little imponderables. You want imponderables? How about telling me why I'm the first person since Victorian fiction who has to address her boyfriends as 'Mr.' "

"That's your own fault, woman. Stop going out with your married bosses." Lily hushed her sister's comeback as the board resumed.

NOPCH COLD NOVEMBER NO POR

"Spirit? November?" Lily looked at her little sister. "This is getting spooky, Rachel."

"Oh, pish. There is no way in hell this little piece of plastic crap can know diddly. Spirit, is Lily pushing the weejee, or what?"

N-O Y-E-S

Their interlocked hands battled for control of the pointer, and Lily's lost. She crossed her arms. "Quit pushing. Play right, or that's it."

I AM PLAYING RIGHT SIS

Pouting, Lily again linked little fingers. She commanded, "Spirit, can you tell us about our household?"

SIS GIX ARE

The answer took two full minutes and much shuttling. "Great," Rachel snorted. "That makes a whole load of sense, you insubstantial lump of ethereal . . ."

Lily interrupted. "No! Don't you get it? He means there are six of us."

"Terrific. *I* could have told you that. Woulda gotten all the words right, too. And wait a minute. How do you know it's a man?"

"Spirit, are you a man or a woman?"

CLAUDIA

As the name spelled out, Rachel giggled. "Claudia? Not *the* Claudia from my sixth-grade intramural field-hockey team?" The Ouija spun around several times before spelling:

NOCKEY

"That's funny. I was certain it was called hockey, with an *h*." Rach looped the pointer across the board in figure eights.

"Will you grow up?" Lily snickered, despite herself. "This could be interesting, if you'd just behave for ten seconds. Claudia, we're trying to find out what is wrong with our father. He's . . . he's sick and getting worse."

HAS HE PHYS

Lily sat up, startled. "No, he hasn't been to a physician, if that's what you're asking. He only today agreed to an exam. For our sakes. *He* doesn't think it's serious. But I guarantee you, it is." The board shuddered and the women's hands defined twin compasses.

SEE SEES THINKS

Each letter heightened Lily's agitation. "That's right!" She shouted in a whisper. "He has some kind of hallucinations."

EYES EYESORE

"Naw, not an eyesore," Rachel objected. "Not the prettiest thing in the world, granted. But he's not that ugly." Her tone turned to righteous indignation. "We know he sees things, clot. Tell us what."

Sure enough, they looked up to see Dad himself halfway inside the doorframe. "Poisoning my household with instruments of the Devil, I see."

Ailene, behind him in the kitchen, protested that she had asked the girls to knock off hours ago. "But they're too inconsiderate to think of anyone else but themselves."

"Who isn't?" Dad asked, joining his daughters.

As the soft glow from the kitchen spilled into the room, Rachel turned to her sister and asked, "What does that do to Claudia? Doesn't she die if light gets on the board while she's talking?" She screwed up her face, trying to remember her Black Magic.

"She's already dead," Lily laughed, self-conscious. Dad sat next to them, forming a small circle. He gave the Ouija a look between revulsion and ridicule.

"The one value I try to instill in you two over the years—*the single burden* I place on you—is to try to be a little skeptical, a tiny bit rational about what you believe. And look at the two of you. *Just look at you.*" He snorted good-naturedly, enjoying cornering the cabal. Lily looked down and toyed with her nicotined nails. Her hands shook, a fight-or-flight mechanism. She scaled up for the inevitable confrontation when Rachel came to her rescue.

"But Meester Ed, jew shood haf seeen theese women Clodeene. She come to tell us all abowed was wrong weeth jew."

Lily looked at her sister, dumbfounded, unable to believe that the woman could talk to Pop like that to his face. She herself would no more have mentioned Pop's illness in his presence than ask an amputee if he needed a hand. The man would have taken her apart, laughing all the way. Lily had been condemned to circumspection by her mother's example, and could never understand how Rachel had escaped to become the Mrs. Simpson of family propriety.

Ordinarily, she would have kept her head down out of the crossfire. But tonight, she composed herself sufficiently to follow her sister's lead. "We were asking it all sorts of questions, really." Lily kept her voice as blasé as possible, given her adrenaline level.

"Theese woman say jew be seeing the ah-beese," Rachel said, unrepentant. She traced out a wild pantomime of letters across the board with the plastic heart. "She toll us, from b'yon de grave, 'ask jew jewselves.' "

Dad aped back, greatly amused. "She said that, did she? Now *there* is something worth looking into. Let's give this another try, shall we? Mind if I sit in on a session?"

Lily certainly did mind. But Rule 0 was never scrap with the old guy unless you were ready to go all the way to the brink with him. She was not ready for brinksmanship tonight, so she cleared a little space for him at the magic message board.

"What's the theory behind this piece of malignant machinery?"

Lily scowled, and linked the man's fingers with hers. "There's no *theory* behind it, Dad. Only *ghosts*. Just keep your fingers on the pointer as lightly as possible. And ask it what you want to know."

Rachel began once again. "Hola, Claudia? Come in, Claudia. Claudia, this is Mission Control. Do you copy? Over." Slowly, the board returned to life under new management.

N-N-N CLAUDIA NIX NOT

"You're not Claudia?" Lily sounded disappointed. "Who are you then, Spirit. Where did Claudia go?"

MMQX YYT XKKX

The board failed to reach consensus under its six hands, partly because Rachel was laughing so hard. "Oh, I remember him. The little guy, from the Superman comic books. If he says his name backwards, he's got to go back to the fifth dimension." Pop remembered the same comics, the caped hero of the world's crisis decade who everyone hoped might arrest the rapid deterioration of real events. Suddenly, the needle swung smoothly and quickly over the letters, spelling:

I LIKE YOU RACH

By the time the note came clear, Rachel was ready to fight. "All right. Which one of you did that?" Lily and Pop denied everything. "Well just cut it out, all right? This isn't a game, you know." She rabbit-punched them both for good measure.

Pop took his turn at framing a question. With great seriousness, he asked, "Spirit, is there a God, and can he show two forms of ID?" The pointer reeled, insulted.

ELO AB TWO AND MORE HORATIO

The answer delighted him. "Well-read creature we're dealing with, here. Can you do the 'hollow crown' soliloquy from Richard II?" The letters began:

UNEASY LIES

then stopped as suddenly as they started. Pop grinned accusingly at both daughters. "We'll give you partial credit for that one."

Rachel said, "You think we're *pushing*, don't you? Huh? All right, then. We'll see who's controlling this thing. Board, what's playing in Hobstown these days?"

NOW PLAYING IS NOW PLAYING

"Get to the point, will you?" Rachel shot a look at both the board and Pop.

COME TO TOWN AND SEE

Rachel slapped the Ouija. "Bratty kid. Okay, let's ask this thing another way." She shot a look at both blood relations, testing them. "Are we ready for tonight's Big Question?"

Lily said, "Ready," but did not sound it.

Pop said, without flinching, "Ready here, boss."

Rachel paused, then backed down. "Go on, Lil. It's all yours."

Lily gave her sister a withering look. She took a breath and addressed the linked hands: "Spirit, can you give us some idea about what it is that Dad sees? What brings on the spells? And are the, you know, vomiting and fever and sores all part of the same thing?"

Rachel, her courage back, added, "What she means is, WHAT HELL WRONG OUR POP?"

THERE IS MORE

All held their shared breath, but the board stopped. Finally Lily could stand it no longer. "Yes? Go on. More what?"

MORE TO ANY THAN ANY SUSPECTS.

7

Ailene sat in her kitchen listening to the séance scratchings long after the mediums went to bed. She sat alone at the table that perpetually doubled for meals and cards. No one told her what messages had arrived from beyond the grave, and she didn't inquire. Some things she saw no advantage in asking. Near the top of her rules of thumb was her deep belief that people made things more complex than they were. *People* meant, for Ailene, her children. Her husband.

She went to the sink and fetched a damp rag, then ran it over the spotless table. Back at the sink, she wrenched it out and spread it over the faucet. She drifted to the radio on top of the refrigerator and turned it on, aired it out, tuned to no station in particular. Calmed by the background sounds, she sat down.

She was not born suspecting complexity. But, then, she was not born married to Ed Hobson. She had attained simplicity over the years as a counterweight to the man, to keep their marriage near the American complexity median. When Ed turned the breakfast table on its ear with noxious, logical knots like the prisoner's problem, it fell to her to insist that, with the right rules of thumb, the problem vanished. That was her expected line. That was her.

But the simpler a counter she grew to Ed, the more he disappeared in curlicues. No one would have given his breakfast-table bind another thought if they didn't know the man like their own breathing. His mind was a maze, an overly ornate metaphor. Everyone knew at once that his latest thought game spoke for him. Him and them. Just the way he'd drawn it on the paper towel. It fell to Ailene to show the simplicity underpinning the riddle.

She suspected, alone in the kitchen, sitting in the dusk of the forty-watt range light, that the way out of the paper-towel prison, *her* way out, the way Ed could not find, was merely for each man to say to himself and no other, "I must choose not to compromise *myself*, as if no one else is implicated in the deal." Forget the complex consequences; damn the other guy's doublethinking. If Ailene had learned anything by living a life attending to the needs of others, it was that the two in the trap could only *escape* conviction *through* conviction. So simple: they had to do what they thought was right, no matter where it led.

There was a time, years back, when she troubled herself over those *Teach Yourself the Great Thinkers* series. But as far as she could make out, Kant's Categorical Imperative, which she perpetually saw paraphrased in those books as "Each of us must act in the way that we expect everyone else to act," sounded to her suspiciously like the Golden Rule, handed down to her as "Do unto others as you would have others do unto you." The only difference was in the fancy packaging. You needed an advanced degree to appreciate the former, whereas *everybody* learned the latter in first-year Sunday School.

Because of this difference, the Golden Rule inspired Ailene while Kant's dictum filled her with shame. Kant helped mirror her favorite regret: her never attending college. When Ed was not holding forth at dinner, she sometimes sneaked in the story of how, just four days before she graduated valedictorian of her high school, she was asked by the school guidance counselor, a not-so-closet alcoholic, what university she would attend the following fall. Explaining that she had no means to get through college, she was shocked to see the fellow pull from its shelf, far too late to be of any help, a massive tome that had not been touched in any semester in recent memory: a two-thousand-page index of grants, fellowships, scholarships, and awards.

That massive book became her life's icon. It stood for all blocked opportunities and missed chances, the "what ifs" of dashed hope, those matters of concealed occasion that were common knowledge to everyone else on this earth. Yet late at night, the same thick volume reversed its role and comforted her. Because the cash prizes of this life came bound and maintained in a handy reference work cross-indexed by place, amount, and designation, she slept well, knowing that even though she stopped short of where she might have gone, her children didn't have to. Salvation was simple and indexed. Answers were alphabetical. All we had to do was look.

Reminded of lists and indexes, she stood and crossed to the pristine counter. She fiddled for a moment in the accumulation of depleted pens, calendar pages, and phantom match covers scrawled with forever unidentifiable phone numbers that nested between stove and refrigerator. She passed through the pile twice, forgetting what she was looking for. She came away with a pencil and tablet of gummed note paper. She sat back down and considered the blank page. No, she reaffirmed; four more years of higher education would only have confused her, obscured what she already knew, the only thing she needed to remember, whether she called it Kant or canticle: do what was best for the common good. She touched the pencil tip to the paper, freezing there for a full minute before sweeping:

1 doz eggs

Her script was perfect, an exact replica of those cursive loops from third-grade writing texts that most children never got closer to than rough approximation. As she wrote, she decided that the additional diploma, the superfluous degree, would have left her worse for the weathering. She had seen what upper-level sociology and psych courses had done to her husband. She had met, dated, and married an overgrown boy who returned to school after the service an idealist, seeking technical skills that would let him contribute to a better postwar world. He went into college an altruist but came out an educated man, his golden imperative hopelessly tarnished, complicated beyond recovery by that collegiate puzzle called the Tragedy of the Commons. As she had it paraphrased from Ed, the question ran: when the world grows too small to support everyone, who will let their livestock starve so that the others will have enough common grazing ground? Survival favors the self-interested. And so, educated, we all perish together, protecting our private claims.

Outwardly Ailene proclaimed her inadequacy, her lack of education. But inwardly she knew that four years of self-sacrifice and debt would only have taught her that Do Unto Others didn't go nearly far enough toward prescribing *who*, exactly, could do how much of the grazing. Nor would additional letters after her name have led to a solution. Once started, the attempt to salvage simplicity would have led her, as it had Ed, into the province of the eternal postgraduate, or worse. So Ailene, shame notwithstanding, happily avoided throwing bad knowledge after good. Not quite happily, but steady of hand, she wrote:

1 gal milk

As an afterthought, an eye to family health, she soured her nose and added, in parentheses: skimmed. She had much too much native intelligence to live in naïve bliss. Since she could not have the degree without the attendant confusion, she asked only for a small, peopled garden in some tillable spot of the globe, governed by mutual respect and free from competing interests. She designed her household toward this end. On husband and children she bestowed unledgered, endless acts of affection—soaking undergarments in bleach, washing up after them, drawing up shopping lists, stocking the larder. All this she did without complaint, never doubting that her family would, in their own time and manner, repay her invested trust and return the favors when needed. Tonight they were needed.

She *was* those simple acts of trust. Things would be simple if only we let them. Back when she and Edward still socialized, she had enjoyed being the ingenue at gatherings of that small circle of high school teachers they had been so tight with once. The clique enjoyed having Ailene around: she made them feel sophisticated and subtle in comparison. She knew her part, and early on mastered the little-appreciated social art of saying only the extremely self-evident. While all the circle struggled to deliver clever or controversial points of view, she spoke so far beneath contradiction that others dropped in their tracks with stunned smiles. For that they loved her.

But her socializing days were history. She tried not to think of the night it had all started to unravel, and in rapid fire added to her growing list:

3 lb gr beef
head lettuce
brocc
oj
small sack potato

She broke off violently and exhaled. She tore off the note she'd been nursing and flipped it over. Listlessly she traced out three ovals, then wrote:

I should have started a diary thirty years ago, back in the fifties. Now I can't even remember what happened when.

But she had no difficulty remembering *what* had happened the night Ed first collapsed in public. It was at a teachers' Christmas party in the North Jersey high school district where Ed had taught history for the first seven years of his career. Ailene had never seen anything like it happen before to anyone, let alone the man she tailored her life around. He had not, back then, developed the practiced, insouciant air with which he managed later fits. He even went so far, in this first public crash, to point, scared witless, at whatever had ambushed his retinas. Obviously not the average passing-out, nor benign enough to ignore.

But that's what she tried to do, at first. Ed crumpled onto a chaise lounge, streaming word-salad as if truly schizophrenic. He had been doing this tremendous baritone imitation of Sinatra, "A Sinner Kissed an Angel," and all at once he was elsewhere. Somebody thought he'd hit his head on a nearby shelf, knocking himself down. Another bystander insisted he'd gone into the fit first and slammed his head only afterward.

Ailene stood in the center of the room, thinking it was all a joke. When there was no punchline, she tried the old trick of stating the self-evident for all she was worth: "My husband has fainted." It didn't work this time. For Eddie, although far from conscious, had not fainted. He was simply intent on that steady word stream, trying to attract the other partygoers toward something that seemed to lie not next to the divan, nor on the wall of the room, nor in the yard outside. The sight he tried to ward off lay far away.

Ailene insisted the fit was just too much booze on an empty stomach, but that wouldn't wash either. His colleagues had long revered Ed Hobson as every schoolteacher's drinking mentor. No matter how much he drank, he never got smashed beyond reciting Kipling's "If," teary-eyed, in booming bass, but unslurred. One woman in social studies said she'd seen this before. It was a stroke, and if they didn't get an ambulance here within three minutes the man would end up mute or limping for the rest of his life, if he lived. But Eddie, reemerging on cue, refused to let anyone call an ambulance. The more his friends protested, the more violent he became.

From the vantage of her belated, one-page diary, Ailene saw that this refusal to treat the thing, Ed's rejection of the socially prescribed treatment and not the illness itself, had lost them their visiting privileges, their niche among the others. She wrote:

> First he got sick. Then he turned down the amenities. That's when he got in trouble. That brought on the tribunal. That's when we started to move.

During the remainder of the school year Ed's fellow teachers showed what they thought of the incident: the man was mentally ill, and contagiously, judging by the sudden drop in invitations Eddie and Ailene received. At the end of the term, Eddie collected his fifth straight Outstanding Teacher Award, which he left on the assistant principal's desk just prior to their leaving town on what, from then forward, he euphemistically called mutual consent.

Ailene replayed in her mind the family's slow descent into gypsyhood. She found the sequence impossible to recover, mainly because her own relations with her husband had remained unchanged throughout. The only complaint she allowed herself—and only at her lowest moments, never outside the breakfast circle—was the cheerfully stoic, "After all, I've signed the papers." This meant she felt legally bound never to develop a muscle tick's difference in her feelings toward Eddie from those she had had the day they drew up the marriage contract. Looking over the perfect script of her chronology, she found that keeping her part of the bargain had always come easier than the outside might have suspected. She felt a wave of shame at how she had blossomed on the compost of Eddie's decline.

Her husband's trail of crises brought out the best in her. She had learned, under fire, to issue the quick cover-up and invent the ingenious excuse. His suffering required her; she filled a need. Even his later illness, domestic and familiar, gave Ailene that whiff of forbidden tragedy, her one graspable proof that things did happen now and again in a daily canvas that otherwise insisted experience exists only far away—the Middle East, Asia, or Washington, D.C. His were the only headlines she believed. Newspapers announcing PRES BLOCKADES REDS or SAIGON CHAOS AS EMBASSY TOPPLES had an unnatural urgency, as wholly implausible to her as JESSICA TELLS TED SHE HAS BEEN MARRIED BEFORE or LIZ BEARS ALIEN'S BABY. Without Ed, she had no front page, no news: only warehouse clearance circulars and advice columns.

She understood, without benefit of college degree, that the price extracted for the model life, the one she was supposed to strive for, was anesthesia. Ordinary blessedness required that the occasional incident—burglary, car accident, or siren—never came closer than a block or two away. She felt how easily she might have become that dutiful mother who troops her kids in single file, stands them in front of the once-in-a-lifetime neighborhood blaze, and pretends to teach them, "See? This is what you get when you play with matches." But her husband's constant, low-grade emergency showed her how such women's children always hear them lying. Kids know otherwise; the lesson of every other day is that matches cannot harm them, nor the one-in-a-million bolt from the blue. Blessed children already sense the steady, blank lay of the terrain. They mouth, "Sure Mom," the Good Fairy, their faces baked in the neighbor's blaze, all the while shaking their heads No Chance, as if death by fire were theater.

No, Eddie had for years been her only current event, and for that she was almost grateful. She loved the threatening thrill that unemployment brought twice every decade. She cared little for security or money, and could have made do on occasional ten-dollar gift certificates from friends. She gladly traded steady income for a cause. Ed's expulsion required of those nearest him only that they sacrifice small amenities—security, comfort, a life in common with the rest of the precinct—in order to regain the lost capacity to know *and* feel. And as much as she hated to see the least anxiety shade her children's faces, this continuous domestic disaster, at least, gave them something tangible. Crisis, at least, was real.

She never spoke of her great, unpublished discovery. His worsening bouts denied interpretation. *He* coughed up solid mass and remarked, clinically, "Ah! Blood." *He* was upstairs disintegrating. There was no lesson. If Hobson's sickness was Ailene's one harbor, *his* refuge refused her altogether. She took the pencil tip out of her mouth and wiped it dry. She added to her shopping diary:

> Just around then, he started Hobstown. Or maybe just before. I should have written it down as it happened. I can't remember sequence anymore.

She tried to imagine the project that had taken him over, the one hobby he still enjoyed. She knew little about the place, but linked it with the disastrous Christmas party that night so long ago. First one had happened, then the other. And ever since, her husband periodically removed himself from here to build this other place, the last monastic in the age of community. Every move he made was a Protestant's bid for Blessed Saint of Indifference. And Hobstown was his hermitage, reliquary, shrine, his chapel to the virtues of doing without.

Three decades back, when she had just gotten used to marriage, her husband produced a pair of pinking shears, a bridal-shower gift from a girlfriend Ailene had long lost track of, and relieved her of her hard-won credit cards with a few deft snips. Not that Eddie questioned her least expense. She, if anyone, pulled the pursestrings. Every cent of cash he had he gave her willingly. He simply could not live under the umbrella of credit, owning the unpaid for. Ailene, with a sense of wonder that grew daily, found she had married the last man in America who couldn't owe money. That was *his* golden rule: no one deserved to draw on what wasn't there to begin with. Everything that Edward practiced, the table talk, the pedagogical riddles, the banter, the bluster, the evasive employment pattern, even the passing out: everything preached one and the same thing. Hobstown was the only sovereign state ever to practice the principle of complete self-sufficiency: sacrifice everything, pare it away until all that's left is the unencumbered mystery of getting along with, for, and by yourself.

The only thing she knew for certain about her husband's endless sessions with the tape machine was that her favorite rule of thumb about things being simpler than people made them out simply did not apply. And if it didn't apply to her husband's model town, it did not apply to him. And if not to him, then her own home could burn down at any moment, sacrificed to the bonfire of complexity.

She put the possibility out of her mind. She had narrowly escaped that danger. For today, things had changed. The tapes, the evasion, would be put away. Soon, his sickness would become material, hard stuff under the touch, properly attended to. Soon the doctor would hold up in front of her the unintelligible film collage of X-ray grays and point out, "Here. This spot here is wrong." Soon the violation of his sick chest would become harsh and definite, stark contrast to the regular and newsless days.

For today, Eddie had vowed to take the cure, go public. Perhaps no treatment, at this late a date, could interfere with or improve the course of the disease. But the tests, medications, and prognoses themselves, each a narrative with pacing, drama, character, and denouement, were worth their weight in secondary symptoms to Ailene. Soon she would have a word for what was wrong with Edward. She would have the experts' *name*, the name in the medical manuals. And then she could translate the agreed-on term into Hobson dialect. The Hobsons, who had their own words for everything, their private language, a tongue that excluded eavesdroppers, defined club membership, condemned one another to intimacy, would soon have to accommodate a new term.

Years before, when the world still smelled of well-floured hands, Ailene had compromised with the kids. Wanting to squeeze the most use out of the few hours allotted them between their release from school and consignment to dinner, they refused to keep to the backyard and insisted on ranging the neighborhood. Her working agreement with them extended the Hobson grammar: three shrill blows on a metal drill whistle, rescued from Ed's lifeguard stint at Aptos, meant they had five minutes to get back, scrub, and be seated at table. She could still recall the sound: six P.M. on a summer's evening, *brrilll* three times from the back stoop, and through every plate-glass front room on the street, in each neighborhood child's heart in no matter how distant a sandlot or park, most of all in the blood of the children to

whom the whistle dictated, there registered the idea she now wrote
down:

The Hobsons are speaking to themselves.

What this whistle no longer obliged in her children, Ailene could
reclaim by Latinizing the disease. A new word could call them in and
remind them: *blood*. The old mystery of sacrifice and connection needed
a name. They had learned the watchword *sacrifice* from the man. Could
they not now teach him new vocabulary?

She carefully inverted the pencil and touched the eraser to the paper.
After a last look, she rubbed until the whole brief history she had written
that evening dispersed, returning the sheet to its white simplicity. She
flipped the paper over and looked at the other list, the groceries: her way
back to the golden rule.

Ailene stood up, walked over to the refrigerator, and attached her
shopping list to it with a free magnet. She opened the fridge, which
Edward, stubborn thirties holdover, still insisted on calling the Ice Box.
Inside, she thumbed the dial down from 7 to 6. The machine lumbered
to a halt, cut down in its freon prime. She straightened and switched off
the radio, which had drifted just wide of the nondescript station she had
set it to. For the last few minutes, it had sprayed a fine mist of static into
the room without her hearing. Then she walked stoveward and flicked off
the range fan which had been going since dinner, drawing off the
suspended fats and airy colloids and storing them, inoculated, in internal
hidden reservoir.

Silence sprang up, thunderous silence, stripped of the background
tracks that had accompanied her evening. In the audible silence, Ailene
committed to memory today's date. Today, Eddie had made a historic
concession.

She left the forty-watt bulb on over the sink, in the event that her
children might wander down at night. Children needed something to see
by, as a rule of thumb. After one last worldly inspection, she gave the
kitchen a final salute before taking the trip upstairs.

Safe in the bedroom, she moved silently in the dark, so not to wake
the invalid. She went to the back of the closet where all the important
papers hid, extricating a folder marked "Keep." She read, by closet light,

behind closed door, Eddie's trail of long untouched insurance documents, to see if any still applied. For he had given her the green light. Her trust had been returned with trust. Tonight, they had arrived at a place she had never, for three decades of marriage, doubted. Every reef connected underneath. Tonight, she had news. Ailene knew her husband's every spell was elaborate Hobson lingo for "Nurse me." And now she would.

SPRING. 1942

Eddie Hobson's local urgency scrapes up against the Big Picture in February 1942, two months after the Japs bomb Pearl Harbor and we enter the war. The collision of inside and out begins unnoticeably. The world around him mobilizes, but Eddie's life is unchanged. He goes to silly matinees. He dances the Lindy and the Big Apple. He sings his sixteen-year-old waiter's heart out on the Hudson. Sings with a swing.

He joins scrap metal, paper, and rubber drives. He turns in used toothpaste tubes. He lives his life around his parents' ration stamps. He polices his neighbors' minor violations of home-front thrift by repeating the popular refrain, "Don't you know there's a war on?" But in America, the one untouched, enchanted island in a world submerged in bloodletting, the war is not always obvious. Only the occasional State Department telegrams to newly minted gold-star mothers affirm it. And in early 1942, these have not yet begun to come home in earnest.

Consumer hardships aside, the biggest impact of the war in '42 is the awakening of American exuberance, the delight in the fight. Neighborhoods take to the conflict with violent enthusiasm, aggressive confidence that shocks the world. The country's spring cleaning, dusting away musty isolationism, rumbles its dormant strength, announces the arrival of its hour. It celebrates its jazz-age boundlessness, its Copeland fifths performed by backwoods brass choirs. These things waited for the attack. Now they break loose.

Its very cigarette packages go to war. Its March of '42 fashion magazines ask "What's New?" The answer is Elizabeth Arden sporting service cap and monkey wrench, a two-page cartoon spread on the consequences of drafting women, and a buyer's guide to refrigerators, although no new refrigerators can be had at any price. "Our charming young model goes *backstage at the Imperial Theatre to sell a Defense Bond to Danny Kaye. . . . For this big moment, she chooses a two piece faille suit in a new high shade. . . . $19.95."* We join this epochal shoot-out, but on our terms.

We wake up. We will buy this victory. Boys will win it with scrap drives. Myrna Loy will win it by sassing Hitler. Thomas Hart Benton already paints the victory celebration, complete with dusty fiddles. We're flexing in Motor City on the armaments line. Flexing at Hollywood and Vine and on the family farm. For the first time it's okay, even fun, to be coarse—coarse Oakie, coarse Rocky Mountain, coarse Lower East Side. Coarse will come out of this conflict leading the world. And everyone else on the block will have to learn to play by our rules. The rules of the Empire State spire, Iowa Corn Boil, Appalachian Spring, Broadway Boogie Woogie.

The Depression is finally sealed. The Dust Bowl becomes Ma Joad, who in turn becomes Jane Darwell. Two months after the sneak attack, it seems as if we were itching for it, daring the enemy to do it. Now we set out on a global enterprise, ebullient, charged with energy. The war is not about civilian bombing, torture, deportation, people hiding in shelters or burned out of foxholes. The war is about righting wrong with unprecedented industrial production, Tit for Tat.

But before we can fully celebrate our strength, we must address the fact that the Arizona has gone down, and the Oklahoma, with at least fourteen other ships sunk or badly damaged at Pearl alone. We have no navy to speak of between our coast and the Japs. That's enough to turn what is still called national sentiment toward defense at any cost. In February 1942, our national exhilaration explodes against the Japanese, all Japanese, even Japanese of our nationality. A spontaneous outcry, both among administrative higher-ups and ordinary, government-issue citizens, insists our national interests are threatened by those eighth-of-a-million Japanese Americans living up and down our now unprotected West Coast.

This untested element, sitting on the vulnerable Pacific rim, might take the opportunity to do guerrilla work or reconnaissance for the Imperial Army. Then again, they might remain forever as blameless as they are at this moment. But national sentiment, the disgrace of peace-with-honor sympathies, and the stakes involved in guessing wrong, make it impossible, so goes public reasoning, to gamble on good behavior and lose.

How endangered is California? Could we really be attacked? What threat these AJAs—Americans of Japanese Ancestry—really represent is never spelled out. But the general alarm centers on the possibility of beacons from church steeples, and the like. FDR puts through a proposal in mid-January: all aliens must register with the U.S. government.

On February 20, 1942, Dr. Win-the-War writes another prescription, stronger but just as silently mandated. Roosevelt approves of a plan to round up more than one hundred thousand of these Japanese Americans—two thirds of them American citizens. They are forcibly removed from their homes and shipped inland for safe internment. The government builds concentration camps in Colorado, Montana, Utah. There is no other good name for these prison villages, surrounded by barbed wire and manned by armed guards. They are built for the express purpose of imprisoning our internal enemy.

By rough calculation, 90 percent of all Americans of Japanese extract are rounded up. This includes not just issei, or foreign-born Japanese nationals, but also more than 60,000 nisei, first-generation American citizens empowered with every constitutional right enjoyed by the FBI agents who come to arrest them. Altogether, more than 112,000 civilians are herded off to the camps and kept there for the next three and a half years.

Among their number are UCLA graduates to whom kanji is Greek, whose idea of preserving their heritage is wearing a kimono to the costume party following the Bruins' homecoming game. Fathers, mothers, and little children end up on opposite sides of wire fences. Some are kept in animal stalls until space opens up in the permanent camps. Students at Hollywood High, sons and daughters of directors and starlets, come to class one morning to find that their buddies, sons and daughters of studio executives and scriptwriters, are mysteriously absent.

The emergency-evacuation project is smoothly and adeptly administered. People who have committed no crime and who are not charged with any must sell everything they own at fire-sale prices, strip down to two suitcases, and hop flatbed trucks to relocation centers. People are arrested in evening dress, coats and ties, work aprons and blue collars. Many are *issued prisoners' clothing: denim with stenciled numbers. Each receives an internee's record they must keep with them: name, roundup date, and places of internment. Some sheets are on government stationery printed with the message, "KEEP FREEDOM IN YOUR FUTURE WITH U.S. SAVINGS BONDS."*

It's a messy business. Earl Warren, making a brief stop as California attorney general on his way to the U.S. Supreme Court ten years later, adamantly backs the roundup. Some suggest he's pressured by protectionist interests, eager to remove the Japanese small businessman from the land of free competition. Maybe he is, maybe he isn't. Can we afford to take a chance and see? Once sabotage is done, it's too late to admit mistakes. When, two days after Roosevelt's approval of the internment, a Jap sub shells a Santa Barbara oil refinery, opposition to the idea collapses. A few fire balloons explode on the Oregon coast, making the move seem increasingly prescient, albeit ugly and indiscriminate. Better alive and compromised, say most, than virtuous and overrun.

But when weeks go by and no more attacks against the mainland materialize, no one thinks about the matter again until too late. Nobody takes up arms to oppose the measure. The arms have already been taken up in other operations, other countries. Besides, what can anybody say? To oppose what everyone else deems a necessary evil is to be a collaborationist.

The mass imprisonment is one small and mostly overlooked step in the largest and fastest mobilization the world has ever seen. One sacrifice in a time of nationwide sacrifice. Everybody does his or her bit, however indirect, for the collective cause. Some people are shot out of the sky, some people work the USO, some people go to camps. Housewives save fat and Ford converts to manufacturing aircraft. Old men go back to work; women smelt iron and build ships. Girls raise victory cabbage. Boys who do nothing but dim lights and keep their lips sealed contribute to the fight.

All industries, even the frivolous, do their part. Hollywood enlists en masse. One fifth of Tinsel Town dons uniform. Some see actual combat. Others do the invaluable work of spelling out the ethos. Several hundred of the movies' most talented are recruited by the Signal Corps for their own film unit. The pictures they make fuel, define, and sustain this national awakening.

Disney already has ideas for any number of films: morale raisers,

cartoons conscripting Mickey, Donald, and the gang into the war effort.
They can put Minnie to work raising yams in a victory garden, if that's
what it will take to win the vast showdown. His studio is occupied by an
antiaircraft unit for eight months until the panic over impending invasion
dies down. (In case of air raid, goes the L.A. joke, go directly to RKO: they
haven't had a hit in years.)

When he gets the call from Stimson, Disney promises to turn his studio
into one of the most powerful weapons for winning the home front. More
than a third of his prewar personnel are conscripted, but are returned when
the importance of their work is made clear to the local draft board. The
unofficial slogan circling the animation office runs: "They also serve who
only can the bait."

After several secret sessions in D.C., impassioned presentations by the
government, Walt flies back to L.A. and enters a flurry of production. His
staff puts a hundred short subjects into the pipeline. Among the first are
twenty films teaching spotters how to identify enemy airplanes. Next
comes a trailer called The Winged Scourge, *with a cameo by those seven*
model citizens, Snow White's dwarves. The film is not about the Luftwaffe
but about how the average foot soldier can guard against malaria. There's
also Chicken Little, *an anti-Nazi condemnation of mass hysteria, and*
The New Spirit, *in which everybody's favorite, irascible duck learns to pay*
his income tax so that the country can stay solvent long enough to
purchase the triumph. Nobody uses the term propaganda, *but that's what*
the films are.

Technically, Disney's great achievement of these months commences
with Victory Through Air Power, *begun in the spring of '42. The work is*
a tour de force, combining live action and animation, of extreme tactical
and strategic value, produced by the team that created Bambi, five years
in the making. Victory is done in a little over eight months, even though
its script is rewritten throughout production as its predictions come true
and become outdated. The finished product so impresses Churchill that he
asks FDR, at the Quebec conference, why the latter has never seen it.
Roosevelt has no answer, so a special print is flown up by fighter plane
from New York. The president is so excited by Disney's aircraft choreog-
raphy that he forces the Joint Chiefs to see it. Only this way do the Allies
ensure adequate air protection for the Normandy invasions in June of '44.

But in these early days, the crowning burst of animate ingenuity comes when Walt gets the studio composer Oliver Wallace to write him a burlesque tune which his artists turn into an animated nightmare where Donald Duck finds himself forced to work in a Nazi munitions factory. Der Führer's Face, *performed by the musician/comedian Spike Jones, instantly becomes one of the era's runaway hits:*

> When der Führer says, "We is the Master Race,"
> We Heil! (phhht) Heil! (phhht) right in DER FÜHRER'S FACE.

The song is a Bavarian beer-hall polka done in phony accents, a bit of impudent silliness in the face of the terminally horrible, only conceivable in America. Punctuating the "Heils" with raspberries is so enchantingly insulting, such a triumph of the average, irreverent schmuck over the titanic forces behind the crucible of history, that the ditty takes the world by storm. The lyrics are translated into a dozen languages, and a film print is smuggled onto the Continent through the underground, where it contributes to the ground-swell support of the resistance. Der Führer's Face wins the Disney studios 1942's Academy Award for best animated short subject. It's in the record books. Mrs. Miniver, with Greer Garson hiding in the cellar from the London Blitz, wins for best feature, and it's not clear which is the more naturalistic presentation of this unthinkable war.

Disney and company achieve an admirable wartime production record, and their enormously popular films become indispensable. In their own small way, the animators help win the war Over Here. But Walt, tireless overachiever, wonders if his effort has gone anywhere far enough. The daily papers show us pitched in an apocalyptic battle, Manichaean. Ultimate Good against ultimate Evil. For the first time, Disney considers just what we are up against. Cartoons may not be enough to win it. Even feature-length, big-budget, narrative animations—the art form Disney almost single-handedly invented—may be of only limited effectiveness in democracy's arsenal.

One night, as Disney strolls down Hollywood Boulevard's blacked-out Walk of Fame, it comes to him: the studio, the country, the cause of freedom, need something more. Disney's team must initiate a venture far beyond any yet undertaken, one that will motivate by words and pictures, appealing at once to heart and head. Disney must create a film falling both squarely in this world and far, far outside it, a tough-as-steel fairy tale that will, for the first time, bring home to the GI and the Rosie Riveters and the Joint Chiefs as well as the shiftless teenagers in suburban Jersey just where they are in Time, just how urgent, critical, real, and present the present is, just how central each of them is to the larger picture. Only one person in 1942 is capable of bringing moonlight into a chamber, of enchanting history, taming it, and leading it up the front stoop of America. That person is Disney.

Like a V-1 going off inside his head, the title for this extraordinary venture comes to him: You Are the War. But that's as far as he gets. For the first time in his creative life, inspiration fails him. He knows what the story must be, but he cannot form the storyboard. Walt spends a restless, long night. The next morning, he convenes an emergency wartime meeting of the Disney brain trust.

This is the band of geniuses who set tutued hippos dancing to Ponchielli, who created a wicked witch so terrifying that Radio City Music Hall had to reupholster all its dampened seats after Snow White's record-breaking run. These are the artists who made Mickey's exploits the most famous ongoing narrative of modern times. Disney strides into the boardroom where his crew sits. But before he can make his pitch and tell his creative henchmen about his brief glimmer, their need to find a way to reunite little and big, he notices something wrong.

"Where are Tom and Ralph?" he asks, irritated at being held up by the two empty spots. The rest of the board look down at the table top. They give no answer.

Disney thinks for a minute that the truants might have been drafted, but all his personnel have been returned at Department of War insistence. He would certainly know if they'd enlisted. Disney has a fleeting vision, cartoon-style, of the two men suffering the long-feared first strike of Japanese aerial bombardment. And then: the Japanese. All at once the father of the single-cel technique and the multiplane camera comes back to the here in all this here, suddenly understanding where Ralph Sato and Tom Ishi have disappeared to. The Chicken Little syndrome is not restricted to the enemy, the other side. You are the war.

He looks up, startled. Momentarily, around the table, his brain trust shimmers and dissolves into the animated characters that are the studio's bread and butter. They segue into a cartoon tribunal, a jury of peers. To his right, Mickey folds his white kid-gloved hands pensively in front of him, Minnie taps her tail tip on the table. Smoke comes out of Donald's ears. The dumb dawg Goofy just looks plain heartbroken. The scene fades and Disney once more finds himself looking at his idea people, in the same despondent postures.

"Why are you looking at me?" Disney shouts. "I didn't give the order." Nobody accuses anybody, but Disney, feeling their palpable helplessness, gets up and storms out of the room. He goes straight to his office and locks himself in, refusing to answer knocks or intercom buzzes. He does not come out that entire day, and he is still locked inside when the last of the staff leaves late that evening.

His door is still closed when they come back the following day. A worried junior executive—a new hire whose task is simply to look after the boss and attend to his needs—puts his eye to the keyhole but sees nothing. He puts his ear to the door and hears a truly remarkable sound. Disney is there, all right. But speaking German.

It might be nothing, but the aide realizes it might also be the war's most nefarious act of defection since Quisling. His boss could be in that locked room with a wireless, relaying secret morale information to the Nazis. He can go to no one at the studio to relate his findings, as anyone might be in on the ring. Realizing without a second thought that his duty to country far outweighs any oath of fealty to employer, the aide goes straight to the CO of the antiaircraft unit still quartered at the studio.

Two GIs proceed directly to Disney's office and knock down the door. Disney looks up from behind his desk, for all the world the identical picture that had appeared in Fortune a few years before. He is talking into a black horned dictaphone, in the language of Göring and Goebbels. The soldiers confiscate the machine and take Disney under custody. Their CO listens to the tape. There is nothing on the machine except the same line, repeated over and over again a hundred times:

gleich im Rücken der Planke, gleich dahinter, ists *wirklich*.

Decent Americans, no one in the AA unit speaks a word of Kraut. Repeated over and over like this, the German phrase does take on the tone of a traitorous Mayday. Disney laughs, and asks to be escorted back to his study. There, still under guard, he produces an en face edition of Rilke's

Duino Elegies. "But just in back of the billboard, just behind it, everything is real."

He explains that he gets his best ideas by extended meditations on such lines of poetry. Everybody has a good laugh. The soldiers apologize. Disney takes the aide out to dinner, rewards him for his unmeditated patriotism with some Series E bonds, and fires him.

For he has had a remarkable idea while in his intensive seclusion. One of his best. He has had the first inklings of a way not only to produce You Are the War—the apotheosis of the art of live action and animation—but also to free his imprisoned men and as many other compatriots as he can bring out. It occurs to Disney during his bout with the dictaphone that victory at that price is no victory. If, after the war, in a world finally made free, he is praised as the maker of Der Führer's Face and Victory Through Air Power, it will count as nothing if he is also remembered as the private citizen who looked the other way at the crucial moment, who did not see his countrymen disappearing.

Walt Disney gets on the horn and rings Washington. He makes an appointment with the secretary of war. He has an idea to run past Stimson, an idea on how to bring history into the American living room. An idea that will bring home, at least to one singing waiter, the war, the terrible urgency of the present, just behind the board. Bring it home forever.

8

The next morning, Artie sat alone on the front porch, on his traditional chair next to the empty kapok bed, filling it in his mind. A handful of minutes after ten in the morning, the sun was so weak, the air so pastel, they compelled one to look after oneself. Artie did exactly that.

He looked out on the lawn, at the once-startling oranges and ambers that had become chilled, drab brown in just hours. He thought, quietly and hidden, that something was about to happen, something important, the denouement of things long in the works. He felt that a secret, unexpected compartment in an old and favorite toy was about to spring open at his press. He wondered how people could live with dim anticipations of life-shaking events and not be destroyed by them. But before he could get an answer, a voice from behind him interrupted his thoughts. "There's more to any of us . . ."

Artie, unable to help himself, completed the tag to one of Dad's favorite maxims, "Than any of us suspects." But he did not turn around to face his father. He knew, coming out here to think, that eventually the man would follow. He had expected the aphorism; he had already thought it to himself several times that morning without being aware of it. He did not know what the saying meant. Like the man and all his sayings, it was always expected but never fully delivered.

Dad slid into the horizontal on the bed in front of Artie, as if no time at all had passed since they had sat here two evenings before. Eddie Sr. had been doing his Sunday morning reading. He recited for Artie's benefit an old Eastern seaboard tongue twister, the "Drunken Saylor," which he had just found in a dictionary of American folklore.

Amidst the mists and coldest frosts,
With barest wrists and stoutest boasts,
He thrusts his fists against the posts
And still insists he sees the ghosts.

Father challenged son to a speed match. They tossed the twisty syllables back and forth until they fell. Artie couldn't say the quatrain as fast as Dad, who had obviously practiced before dropping in.

9

At Sunday lunch, Dad forced the family to agree to two conditions before he would be checked out by a legitimate physician. The first was that the hospital be Hines, the enormous Veterans Administration facility near Maywood in Chicago. "The Old Soldiers' Home," as Eddie Sr. fondly called it, was the only place he would surrender to without a fight. Dad's two-year tour of duty toward the war's end, although confined to the continental U.S., qualified him for VA medical coverage. "I consider it ignominious for our nation's ex-servicemen to deteriorate in any hospital except one designed, built, and run by government agency," he announced over sandwiches while no one listened. Truth was, after losing his latest teaching job he had no other insurance.

Second, Pop stipulated that the family not commit him until after Thanksgiving. He insisted they spend the holiday at home, as usual. Before they made him check in, the family had to give him one last afternoon in downtown Chicago, to see the Christmas windows on State Street. Granted, the midwestern display never matched that of Fifth Avenue, on which Eddie had been raised, a working-class Jersey kid whipped into a frenzy by deeply imprinted four-part hymn tunes, intoxicated by the end-of-year stink of pine tar, wet woolies, and smoky paraffin, and thrilled by the ruinously expensive, ice-cold taxi ride over the George Washington Bridge at dawn. "I'm not expecting much from Second City, but it's No Go without Christmas windows."

If the holiday dioramas at Field's and Carson's weren't as magnificent or carried fewer moving porcelain parts as those On The Avenue, if they were less successful in revealing, from out of the folds of mundane activity, that buried, ancient order of another time—the announcement of a miraculous birth just at our hour's crisis, a globe of angels pouring from the sky to announce the news—if Chicago's Christmas getup lacked magical transcendence, an afternoon in the Loop during the post-Thanksgiving shopping rush still offered a whiff of the ineffable. Just being downtown, taking in the miniature living displays, steeping in the annual imprint of capacitance-triggered frost-blue point lights synaptically blinker-linked to that passage, as familiar as breathing, beginning, "And it came to pass," anticipating that brilliant tenor suspension against the three moving lines of the Glorias in "Angels We Have Heard On High," might be enough to call up the old, street-wise *gratias tibi*, to shed mental habits as first virgin snow once again redeemed the city curb-soot that would soon deflower it.

Pop talked of flying everybody to New York for a window-hopping weekend, but funds wouldn't permit it, even if he had been working. Practical impediment had not stopped his chattering about the pipe dream, however. Lily had. As he carried on about the superiority of Fifth Avenue's windows to those of State Street, Lily simply reminded him of the story he had often told them of how his mother, with her very last breath, lamented that the art of making the ice cream she had enjoyed as a girl had been forever lost. Lily repeated, with perverse enjoyment, Pop's own conclusion. "It wasn't the flavor, but Grandma's taste buds that were buried in time." Dad smiled wanly at being brought into line. Swearing he would not go to his end ignobly, he said State Street would do for his last outing at liberty.

Thus constrained, Dad's momentous concession to medical science meant that life on the home front, until after Thanksgiving, would remain Illness As Usual. None of the five ancillary Hobsons cared for these two conditions, but they had to accept them. Pop had them over a barrel. They could play on his terms or not at all.

For her part, Lily did not protest the imposed delay. She had long ago saturated her heart with the boom-and-bust cycle of hope she foolishly held for her father's perpetual battle with phantoms. She met Pop's promise to undergo tests with a pretense of cynical pessimism, one that would allow her to keep the next few weeks on a fairly even keel. But after the meal broke up, she hid out with a calendar and counted the days. Rach shrugged at the announcement and its conditions. After lunch, she sneaked up on the fat man as he reclined on his trademark kapok mattress on the now-freezing front porch and put him in a headlock. She threatened, "Ok, buddski. You get any thoughts a backin' outta dis, and weese pincha you earlobes off."

Eddie Jr., hearing Pop's invented postponements, breathed deeply, swallowed hard, and then "shook it off," as his father had taught him to do since boyhood. He promptly spent the afternoon exchanging sports scores over the telephone with a dozen friends. Artie, skeptical, still intent on a diagnosis, alarmed himself and aggravated the situation unduly by discovering that Dad showed a "positive Romberg's sign," meaning the man collapsed spontaneously when asked to stand, look straight forward, and close both eyes. How long the condition had existed or just what if anything it meant neither Artie nor anyone else in the family had the slightest idea. Ailene, who after her first breakthrough had thought he would be in the hospital and partly cured by the following week, was quietly decimated by her husband's delays. But she agreed to them without outward sign.

That evening before departure, Rachel made the family rounds, smacking everybody good-bye. "Back to the old nosebleed," she said, as always at the end of a visit, alluding to her upper-altitude office in the Standard Oil building on the Lakeshore. She was about to pull the same joke on her mother when stopped short by the Mayday in the woman's face. Rach sobered and, in the tone reserved for private times between the two, said, "It goes without saying . . ." Unable to complete the sentence without contradiction, she laughed. "I'll be back in, at least for T-Day, Mrs. I've got the full four days then." Anything else would be brutal, pointless, or untrue, so Rach consoled her mother with actuarial figures on hospital recoveries and hit her up for a favorite Christmas cookie recipe.

Artie spent the evening convincing himself that he could not hang around any longer either. He, on the other hand, did not make the long rounds of good-bye. Instead, he waited until the last moment and then asked Rach for a lift back. "If I leave with you tonight, I won't have to deal with The Dog. Bus exhaust always nauseates me." Rach checked the bottom of his shoes and only then cleared him for boarding.

To kill the minutes before departure, Art and Eddie Jr. played a last round of chucking the pigskin. "I can't believe you're leaving," Eddie said, good-naturedly. Artie knew his brother meant the line as a harmless rib. But the insinuation so infuriated him that, overcompensating, he underthrew his brother's perfect buttonhook.

"School, Eddie-boy." He squeezed his vocal cords into joviality. "Got to pass de ol' Bar X-am so I'll be able to get you off all those DWIs you will doubtless rack up." His brother returned a weak smile, as technically convincing as a film performance by one of those countless, interchangeable jocks-turned-celluloid stars. Artie's anger, which he had for days managed to spread in a thin residue over the neighborhood, reversed directions and concentrated until he could appease it only with a preemptive strike against Eddie; either Eddie. Artie was sorry that he had attempted to leave the boy an escape through affected cheer.

"What the hell do you expect?" he asked, keeping his voice hidden below the first rose-tints of rage. "If I hang around any longer I'll flunk out. What would I accomplish by staying here? What do you propose I do? Help you drag him up to bed every night?" Working this outlash to the surface, Artie felt his fury just as suddenly shut off like an overheated thermostat. He saw a delicious irony in his inability to raise anything more than a politely underplayed anger. After all, he, of all the children, had been the only dish breaker as a kid.

Little Eddie, feeling how close they were to a full-scale blowout, fell into his patented strategy for undoing the tension he had inadvertently made. "I can't believe you're leaving." He subscribed to the principle that if you said something often enough, you would eventually make the accidentally injured party laugh. "I can't . . . I ca-ca . . . I just can't believe . . . You can't be . . ." All punches walk in a single line. It always worked for *him*, anyway.

Artie knew what the kid was up to, and part of him thawed. After a dozen drunken Eddie-iterations of the offending phrase, the boys exchanged wry looks: no need for escalations here. Artie backed down from his docket. He ran looser, flicked with a little more flair. But just as Artie started to enjoy himself, the surprise prowess of his body, and the bite of the air, a sharp spiral bullet pass from Eddie caught him on the jaw and took a chunk out of his face. The pass came in so treacherously that Artie didn't even have time to put up his hands. He crumpled to the grass, the freezing ground. Eddie ran over to him, streaming, "Sorry. Oh Jesus, I'm sorry, it was an accident, sorry, accident, acci . . ." At the same time, Artie objected furiously, "No, no. It's nothing. My fault. I wasn't paying . . . I was having too good a . . ."

Eddie brought Big Brother inside and propped him up underneath an ice pack. Artie, peaceful now that he had earned his Purple Heart, chose the nursing moment to deliver up his belated birthday present to Eddie. Eddie Jr.'s eighteenth, the ostensible reason they had gathered here for the weekend, had been all but forgotten, upstaged by the Invalid's latest and greatest return from remission.

Artie went to the bottom of his bureau and brought forth the peace offering. Little Eddie recognized his brother's gift at once, something he had for years coveted: a set of World War II photographs of enemy warplanes replete with performance statistics and markings, still packed in the army-issue box stamped "Secret" that Eddie Sr. had received in the service. Pop had passed the photos on to his firstborn, with solemn instructions to learn the silhouettes by heart. "The WEFT method: Wings, Engine, Fuselage, Tail. Every man must do his part," the man had said, giving it the same intonation as he always gave to "There's more to us than any of us suspects," or "The Sea will provide."

"Oh, Artie. You don't have to. Maybe you want to hold on to these, in case . . ."

Artie overrode Eddie's protests and objections of unworthiness. "Take them. You've wanted them for years. I've memorized them long ago. Just don't tell Dad that I'm reneging on surveillance duty, okay?"

He had enclosed a card, which Eddie now read: "Congrats on surviving Basic. Never thought you'd make it this far." A brotherly allusion to "Chain of Command," the game Dad had always used to get them to make their beds, take baths, practice musical instruments, do homework, and stay in line. Eddie was the Buck Private, Artie the Sergeant, and Pop the General, liable to make surprise spot inspections at any time. When the boys complained, asking when they would be able to get out of boot camp, Pop always responded, "You don't get out of Basic until you're eighteen." This gift, Eddie Jr. understood, was his promotional papers, from Artie to the next in command.

Before the visit broke up, Lily surprised everyone by dragging out the camera that had been hanging in the back of her closet, filmless, for the last few years. She documented Rachel and Artie's departure, a photo opportunity unremarkable in the extreme. In this way, she maintained the longstanding Hobson family-snapshot tradition of feast or famine. Their photo album alternated between drought and glut. They would add no new pictures for years. Then someone would shoot a dozen exposures of five people hanging around the front door, giving a misleading significance to a moment whose importance, if any, was soon forgotten.

Such was the present: four photographs of a confused group milling around the front door. "Well," Ailene said, summing up everyone's feelings. She could think of nothing more appropriate to say, and left it at that.

"Welp," agreed Rachel, smacking her lips and nodding. "Yer got that right. You . . . sure . . . got that right." Eddie Jr. giggled. Provoked into hilarity, he reached out a hand as if to shake Arthur's good-bye, but instead kept going and rammed him in the solar plexus. Suddenly, Lily couldn't stand the false festivities another second. She put her hands to her ears and beat a retreat to her room. There she reshelved the camera and put a forgotten vocal group from the sixties on the grinder, blotting out the noises from the outside.

Eddie Sr., however, was in rare form. Filling the silence created by Lily's quick exit, he stood in the doorway and told, by way of a send-off, about a recent article he'd come across: a marvelous gorilla who had been taught to speak sign language. "Most attempts at animal communication," Dad explained, "on examination, rely on cuing and conditioning. But what sets this guy apart is that he's been filmed flipping through a picture book and signing *to himself*." Artie, Rach, Ailene, and little Eddie, unable to connect Pop's monologue with the situation yet certain of a link, however Byzantine, looked on in horrified fascination, not daring to stop him or anticipate what topic he would jump to next.

Seeing he had garnered a modest success with the ape, Dad turned his attention to the angels. "You might also be interested to hear that engineers at Hughes Research Lab have succeeded in answering a timeless metaphysical question by microengraving one hundred thousand gold-deposit angels on the head of a pin. Unfortunately, the pin subsequently squirted out of the technician's tweezers and is now lost forever in a crack in the laboratory floor." And he began to free-associate completely, launching into a Robert Service travesty, "The Pin on the Laboratory Floor."

He would eventually have found a way around to Kipling's "If," had

Rachel not blurted out, "Hey, hey, hey. Wait justa, will ya? Haven't we forgotten something here? Nobody's going *anywhere* until . . ." She dug the ever-present pitch pipe out of her coat pocket, tooted it, and began singing the crystalline soprano strain, "Lo, how a rose e'er blooming . . ."

To hear the full four-part treatment was, after all, one of her chief incentives for coming home this weekend. Now she was determined to collect the pleasure, even in the closing minutes of the trip. The others didn't make it in on the down beat, but three of four parts made the glorious hemiola at the end of the first strain. By the end of the second, even Lily had derailed her record player and crept shyly back out of her room to double her mother on alto. The boys, tenors true, doubled the other interior line, while Eddie Sr. supported the beefy bass part with so precise and clear an intonation that his kids once again felt he might have made a career out of singing-waiterdom, now atrophied. Pop's musical ear left only the legendary Miller Tiller as its fossil record. Had he made a living making melodies instead of teaching, more than one of them now thought, everything might have turned out differently.

Whatever the truth in that, by verse two Rach had her full chorale. The passing harmonies confirmed her belief that, if one avoided their attendant misery, no folks more deserved her love than these. This fact welled up in her ears as they glided into that deceptive modulation just before the last cadence without anyone either accidentally repeating the dominant or giving away the transcendence by telegraphing the surprise chord.

All at once, the flash that each had tried so hard to evade was there, intact: a moment of tender visiting hovering over them as the tenors slid down that narrow half-step to the F sharp. They all felt it, momentarily. And each knew the others received a momentary hold on the instant, too. All six stood looking into a place before irony, before wit, before anxiety, before evasion. Surfaces dispersed, and in the still point underneath, they saw what was so terribly obvious to all of them, despite their long gainsaying: how hopelessly each cared what happened to the other. The care shouted out uninvited between them, like a candidate's criminal record. They had no choice but to tune their chord to it. They stood startled, flushed into that snare, aware for once of the connection between them that could reach down at leisure and destroy them. Caught in glorious chord, in facts gathered from each other's faces, they all felt the fissure—fragile, dangerous, and beautiful—close up and leave them in the incurable call back to tonic. The rose I have in mind.

The tune stopped, and so did the room. When the spell broke, they again exchanged counterpoint good-byes all around. Parents and children traded the pointed, pointless trivialities of leave-taking: "Drive carefully. Don't kill yourself." "Okay, Ma, we won't." Once more, fainter, briefer this time, a trace of the first visit came back: this is the last such time.

All was indirection; they lapsed back into Hobsonspeak. Everything spoken stood for something else, with one exception. For when Dad grabbed Artie's hand with his own insistent grip, he raised his eyebrows in a new intellectual challenge. Rather than echo anything so trivial as "Take care," he said, "Dr. Harold Wolff, of Cornell."

The remark startled Artie, coming without context or gloss. He hadn't a clue to what Dad meant. But Artie had cut his teeth on just such ellipses. With Dad, the out-of-context challenge was standard fare, meat and potatoes. "What field is he in?" Artie called back, thinking on his feet, as Rach dragged him out the door. But Dad just lifted his brows again, shrugged, and waved, already fading back into the well-wishing crowd.

Artie and Rachel boarded Mr. Nader, a Ford Pinto complete with exploding gas tank, which she had chosen for perversely unactuarial reasons, and tooled down Second Street. Slowly, there descended on the severed family something like the dull thud following a failed simile. The homebound four reconnoitered at the door one full measure longer than required. Then the ranks broke into a rout.

Late that night, Eddie Jr., looking for Dad in all the shamelessly optimistic places, saving the only likely one for last, found him racked out on the porch, stretched on the kapok, not sleeping yet but fortunately not tranced-out either. "Damn it, Pop. What the hell are you doing out here? It's witch-titty cold out. Or didn't you notice?"

"Is that any way to talk to your father? Did I raise you to be a potty mouth? That's witch-*breasty* cold, boy."

Eddie Jr. threw a blanket over his father and dropped into the side chair, filling in for the departed Artie. He thought, with only a little remorse, of what a relief it would be for Pop to kick off *right now*, die of something unexpected, say, exposure or pneumonia. Yet Little Eddie found himself admiring the guy for his obstinate jocularity under stress. Dad's comic curiosity in the face of everything struck Eddie as the only form of dignity possible these days. But as the look of familiar whimsy shaded his dad's face, it seemed, in the shadows, to tip toward vicious. Perhaps Artie was right: Dad's good nature was not good-natured, his bluff not just bluff. Eddie looked again at Dad's face, but could not longer see anything in the diminished streetlamp glow. He thought how he was now eighteen and would have to start being more discriminating.

He picked up both of Dad's discarded socks—the man was *trying* to get pneumonia—and juggled them along with a pewter ashtray, exercising the athletic grace that he alone of all Hobsons commanded. The three unbalanced objects stayed aloft best when he focused not on them but on the scar on his father's exposed ankle, a wartime wound marking where part of a B-17 fuselage had pinned Dadimo to a dolly.

"Fire with fire," Eddie Jr. said suddenly, the juggled items not even wavering. "As ye give, so shall ye get. And verse-vica, you scratch my back, I'll scratch yours."

He might have been falling benignly into randomness. But Dad needed no grace notes for explanation. He answered his son without missing a beat. "Interesting position. But it won't get you out. You mean each prisoner should retaliate with what the other guy does the turn before? Is that right?"

Eddie Jr., implementing the policy for himself, said nothing, juggling in the dark. Dad continued. "Tit for Tat. God knows it's an honorable attempt at stabilizing. In fact, it's the strategy of choice in the best textbooks. And it's the option with the greatest chance of success with prisoners who are simple and good enough to assume the other guy is also simple and good." Here Dad gave Eddie Jr. a look that could, in the dark, pass for heartbroken fondness. The quick, covert glance betrayed Dad's secret favorite among his children, this simple foreigner whom the world would soon methodically dismantle. The look said: I care for you most *because* you don't know what you're up against. Eddie Jr., eyes on his orbits, did not notice. "But practically speaking," Dad continued, "the policy collapses in at least two cases."

One sock circumnavigated the juggled loop, followed by the pewter, then the other sock. The smooth motion was Eddie Jr.'s nod to continue.

"At first thought, cooperating with cooperation and betraying betrayal seems to stabilize the situation and stick it to old Senator Joe. But this strategy requires that the dilemma occur not just once, but repeatedly. It doesn't help the one-shot event at all; you need retrials to make your policy known to the other guy. Retaliation won't enforce anything if there's no tomorrow. That's breakdown number one." Eddie Jr. bobbled the pewter, but kept on. So did Dad.

"Let's say we agree to exchange hostages at remote drop-off points every Monday night. It's the same bind as the McCarthy model, only it happens regularly. Mutual cooperation is still better than mutual back-stabbing, but there's still a premium paid for being the *only* one to rat. Now we can test your Tit for Tat. You both play fair for a few weeks. Then, the other guy tries the rewarding double cross. You pay him back the next week with a taste of his own medicine. If he cooperates, you reward him in spades. What we used to call the Old Testament law. As soon as the pattern reveals itself, it should be clear that nobody's going to get away with anything much. The game has been greatly simplified. He knows you'll seek retribution if he tries anything. And you're both lulled into a false security.

"False, because one Monday night, there's an accident. He's late with the delivery. You think he's defected. You pay him back the following week, while he plays fair. Angry, *he* plays Tit for Tat in week three, and you fall into a game of perpetual revenge." Outside, cars scythed up and down Second Street. Houses lined the cut, preparing private glows as an Arctic air mass rolled in from Canada. "Besides," Dad added, "any week might be the last. So there's always that additional incentive to take a chance, rat, and cash in."

Dad looked at the boy with real concern, wishing to keep him from harm. But he set his jaw and kept on, intent on disabusing him, hurting him, if need be, to keep him from greater injury. "There's an even bigger problem. True. In a world of independent vested interests, you need some threat to prevent the other guy from threatening you. But please tell me what threat is big enough to check the force we are *really* up against? PREZ SEZ HE WILL NOT BLINK FIRST. How do you retaliate against something that size, little man?"

One of Eddie Jr.'s air-bound socks caught on the tip of the pewter ashtray. The unstable amalgam flew out of orbit, and the kid was left pumping his hands in empty air. He put his hands in his lap. After a proprietary pause telling Dad that the diatribe had not gone undigested, he smiled and repeated, simply, "Fire with fire. With a little space for forgiveness."

Dad propped himself up on one arm, an action requiring visible sacrifice and agony. He leaned over to little Eddie, all pedagogy wiped from his face. A rippling irritation softened and broke over him from north of the diaphragm. He put his chin to his clavicle. Perhaps the convulsion was just gas spasms; perhaps it was part of the larger disease. Or perhaps Dad was the victim of a different, unmanageable concern, something the prisoner matrix, the threat of retaliation, kept him from saying outright. Perhaps Dad knew the feeling that had him by the throat but, for the boy's sake, did not name it. The culprit could only have been love: he could not have *helped* but love anyone capable of such irrational kindness. He *had* to love anyone of his blood who was the equal of keeping to that shameless ideal. And what he felt for Little Eddie Dad admitted only indirectly, saying, "Good man," punctuating the confession with a nervous, under-the-breath swallow.

But his implication was lost on the boy when a pair of headlights swung into the drive. The two Eddies froze in their separate tracks and turned toward the beam, caught criminals, or animals dazed in the pool of light. *Mere interrogation turns innocent actions into complicity*, thought Ed Jr., a mnemonic for something he had forgotten, probably from a quiz session in Artie's law books. He recalled the one that went, "On Old Olympus's Towering Top, a Fat-Assed German Viewed a Hawk," a mnemonic for the eight cranial nerves. Artie taught him that one, too, and he was grateful. He'd completely forgotten the cranial nerves themselves, but he held on to the memory-jogging device as if it were itself the catechism. The same with Mere Interrogation, as the beam in the driveway caught father and son holding the bag.

"Gotta head, Pop. That's my ride." Eddie Jr. stood, spun, and flipped a twenty-foot jumper with the remaining sock, which came down gently over the war wound on Dad's shin. With one smooth motion Eddie lifted a coat off the rack near the door and fell into the front yard. He was almost to the waiting car full of friends when his father called him back once more. Eddie Jr., protesting, returned, compelled by something in the old bellow, the old "Sea will provide" chantey.

"Where you off to, little man?"

"Oh . . . just out. Friends from school. You know us kids, Pop. It's always something. Hormones."

"Should I wait up?" asked Dad, tasting the irony, a pernicious smile at his lips.

"I'll be back by Thanksgiving at the latest. Don't you worry about that. You're not getting away with nothing." Eddie turned again to the car, toward society and mutual support. But once more, perhaps for the last time, Pop called him back, this time with a whisper.

Eddie Jr. came back, obedient but complaining. He stopped, shocked, when the beam of the headlights caught his father's red-rimmed and swollen eyes. All the while they had been sitting here, shooting the abstract shit, sardonically debating one another, Pop had been crying.

"Son, I happened to read, only this morning, that native North Americans broke the necks of their dying."

TIT FOR TAT

My father spoke to us only in favorite sayings, a stable of workhorses saddled up to fit any occasion. The common ones are still with me, as familiar as the alphabet. We could never be sure just what fresh derangement he might squeeze out of the overused maxims, what foreign situation he might wedge them into. He let them mean everything and its opposite. All we knew in advance was that whenever the world threatened to do us in, whenever we most needed him to assure us that life could still be reinvented, he would instead resort to one favorite saying or another. For the longest time, I assumed that all fathers did. After all, as everybody knew, all Indians walked in single file.

I now know that he thought such familiarities would be more useful to us in the long run than mere care. Looking back, I see how he wanted us to love his mysterious homilies the way he loved them. He meant them to substitute for him, the distant fellow lost in an abstraction. But we couldn't and they didn't. Not at the time. I did not even understand what they meant, what the man was all along announcing, or what he was up against until after he was dead.

My father's real imprisonment hid in those single-file Indians, in "There's more to any of us than any suspects," and in a few others. Alongside those two, he favored "Take all that you want, but eat all that you take," a metaphor, by turns, for the need for foresight, the indivisibility of means and ends, and the impossibility of true satisfaction. Then there was the paradoxical "We sometimes need coaxing to act on our own." Whenever he resorted to this one, I would throw back "Tell us how free we are, Pop. Tell me how free I am."

The phrase of his that most haunted me when I was young, that seemed the most beautiful and inscrutable, that came closest to pulling me beyond the barricade into the cell where he wasted away, was "If you bail out the tide with a twopenny pail, then you and the moon can remove a great deal." As mysterious and poetic as the ubiquitous couplet was, I never once guessed until the repetitions ended that Pop's enemy was necessity, and what, if anything, the private citizen could do to spite it.

I recall his most urgent one: I would break an anniversary vase, or my sister would despair over headlines, or our mother would go to pieces at the old man's latest raging fever, and he would say, from his half-coma, "Suppose the world were already lost." Suppose it is, because it is. I never took this advice, I never bothered to suppose while he was still living, because I always thought he used this most crucial of all his phrases as a way to evade the camp of conscience we are all thrown into. Just the opposite. "Suppose the world were already lost." Somehow Dad understood that forsaking everything was the only chance we had of saving what we cared for.

But the aphorism that blew the man open for me, the phrase that gave me a foot into the barred gate, burned into my memory through Pop's thousand reiterations, was "Fate is the stuff we stick in the time capsule." His favorite variant was "This place is how we got here." While he lived, saying it every chance he got, all the line ever did was annoy me. But when, days after he left for good, I heard him repeat it one last time, I finally understood that he had been begging history's pardon.

God knows, he'd given us his capsule's inventory often enough. I still hear him tell the whole family, assembled at dinner, how in the spring of 1944, a shopgirl in Saddle River Township, New Jersey, had her first look at history. He described her periodic sweep past the drugstore's magazine racks, doing her bit, in the words of the trade, to reduce shrinkage, waging hopeless war against deterioration of store stock, preserving margin from shopkeepers' plagues. He had seen her countless times, on untouched afternoons, patrolling the magazine section to chase away those star-struck, fact-starved, and surreptitious browsers who even today, when current events can be had for free, sneak all the news that fits into a few-minute cram.

On that afternoon's rounds, the shopgirl found, according to Dad's version, two half-pints who pealed out of the store at her approach and a debutante who, caught red-handed in a brief fantasy of discovery in a soda shoppe in Southern Cal, guiltily slid closed the book of Life and moved on to Cosmetics. But in addition to these three regulars, she came across something she had not bargained for: a boy-man, just old enough for the service, looking over a weekly picture magazine and weeping.

I can no more imagine my father crying than I can imagine how saving toothpaste tubes could defeat the Nazis. But the boy with the picture magazine was my father, the same man who had to assume the world was lost to love it. My mistake, repeated each time my father told the story, was never connecting the two. The shopgirl had a similar problem. Not knowing how else to respond, and washed in guilt as if she were the cause of the crisis, she offered, "It's okay, mister," although she knew it was not okay, either with Management or with the diminutive Mister she meant to comfort.

Choked speechless, the boy showed her, by explanation, the magazine he illegally browsed. She looked obediently, but could not make out which of the stories on the proffered page caused him to break down. I have since looked up a copy of the same magazine spread. I can see her eliminating the pictorial on a nationwide scrap-rubber drive as devoid of intrinsic emotion. Similarly, a brief photo-biography of a one-armed major-league ballplayer, although fascinating, lacked the necessary pathos to reduce even a fan to tears. Down on the lower left of page 17, a detailed account of the immense jump in the cost of living, while disturbing, could not have brought on such anguish.

Process of elimination left only one picture on the two-page spread that could account for the fellow's public sorrow. She studied the holdout, a two-inch-by-two-inch grainy black-and-white snapshot of the body of a young Army Air Corps pilot being removed from the wreckage of a fluke accident near Brownsville, Texas.

She quizzed the boy with compassion, seeing his face for the first time. It crossed her mind to tell him that, although against the rules, he could browse as long as he liked. A miniature oral seizure told her he was trying to say something. She listened, leaning closer, and thought she made out the phrase "My brother." My uncle. I imagine she fought off an urge to touch his arm; not wanting to intrude on his grief even to look at him, she glanced back down at the glossy page.

And then something happened to her that she doubtless regretted daily for all of the thirty-odd years that followed. She lost her presence of mind and, at the urging of the weekly news magazine, whose home-front function was to turn disaster into something bearable and diverting, asked, "Is it really your brother? He's really dead, then?" With a horrible noise, half sob and all laugh, an inhuman sound that both she and I can still hear in late century, the boy turned from the magazine rack and was gone.

I can trace this Jersey shopgirl, call her Sarah, easier than I can follow what happened to my father. She grew, acquired a college degree, married, had four children, and retired somewhere outside Orlando, Florida. Yet throughout the course of her long and varied life, concealing this incident from those nearest her, never speaking of it over dinner, she could not understand how she could love some perfect stranger more than her successful husband and flawless children, how she could care for someone she didn't even know, someone she had met for all of three minutes, someone already lost, how she could still remember, daily, down in the suburbs outside Orlando, her once having stumbled across a boy-man who broke all the rules and openly cried his loss, despite the magazine rack being clearly posted NO BROWSING.

About Sarah, I speculate. The boy's story I have firsthand. A few months later, graduating from high school, my father spent the evening of his qualifying birthday in a bedroll outside his neighborhood selective-service office. Dad passed the medical and psych exams without incident. But he came up short, or rather too tall by inches, to make his intended field of service. At six foot one, he was just over the maximum height for both his first choice, pilot, and second choice, gunner. His board laughed good-naturedly, and told him to swallow his bad luck. "Shake it off," they supposedly said, although the words sound more like his than theirs. "Some guys has got fallen arches, some's too tall. The war's winding up anyway."

Pop's ensuing comic monologue, in which he claimed that he was really very short for his height and swore that he would stoop and wear shoulder weights for the duration, left the draft-board officers unwilling to bend the rules in this instance. They asked him why he was so hot to fly, and he told them the familiar motive, the solution even heads of state could not improve on: fire with fire. Revenge.

They had more than enough applicants for the combat flight positions, and with the war in its transitional stage, the time needed to train greenhorns for such demanding jobs was prohibitive. But seeing that this kid was more than usually desperate to contribute to the fly-boys' war, *they offered him a bit part as an airplane and engine mechanic. I have the papers spread in front of me: Job Spec 747. Within the year, they guaranteed, he'd never want to see a plane again, inside or out.*

Thus Pop discovered that practical history had no salve left in it for the local soul. For that, the griever must make another place. He spent two and a half months in Air Corps Basic, Job Spec 521, thirteen weeks in Amarillo Mechanics School, and an additional six weeks in Transition Airplane and Engine Mechanics, learning how to "Examine portions of aircraft such as wings, fuselage, stabilizers, flight control surfaces, propeller and landing gear for evidence of wear or damage and correct such defects by appropriate maintenance." He worked mainly on B-29 Superfortresses, a plane he often described to us with clinical interest.

"What did you do in the War, you ask?" he would answer, although we never asked. He'd get that wry, dry, sardonic smile, and say, "Prophylactic surgery." But even preventing a thousand Brownsvilles could not undo this one. I suppose that was why Dad rapidly won a reputation for being the guy you could always ("had to" sounds closer to the truth) send in for the potentially dangerous scut work—the jammed bomb payloads, the inflammable fuel ruptures.

Dad always described his tour of duty as a Johnny-come-lately's domestic Bataan Death March. As the war rolled into its final months and enemy resistance collapsed without his lifting a weapon, Pop and his paperwork moved from Stateside air base to air base, throughout the South and Southwest, rolling up the increasingly obsolete runways. He joked to us ad nauseum that whenever the Joint Chiefs wanted to close up a base, they called him in. On the strength of this sterling service record and mocking his notorious love of photoplay, his buddies called him the Leo Gorcey of airplane mechanics, the seventh Dead End Kid.

Flight mechanics kept him too busy to consider the hopelessness of his situation. I imagine Dad longed for civilian life, not for ordinary reasons but for the chance to suffer something, make some sacrifice, help pay for Victory out of his own pocket, if only indirectly, by toughing out the hundred national rationings and shortages—rubber, shoes, or gas. But R and R worsened the condition. He asked that his leave be cut; the higher-ups told him special arrangements couldn't be swung. If they let him have less leave, others would want to take up the slack. And yet, for reasons reason understood, he hated more than anything to return to Jersey for a weekend, where in the front window of my grandparents' railroad apartment hung that indicting chunk of star-shaped precious metal announcing: We Gave. My father's son, I feel him sliced down the middle with Sunday's pork roast, seared by his parents' casual words, trapped by the epochal events he could get no closer to than his safe place under the fuselage, resting on his brother's laurels.

On one such unwanted home leave, while suffering through a particularly lightweight matinee of Busby Berkeleyesque fluff in which two hundred blond, curvaceous hoofers tapped out the logical necessity of the current geopolitical situation in a brilliant piece of choreography involving spiked heels that discharged low-caliber weapons at Hitler silhouettes when kicked out to the proper angle, Dad, in an early exit to the lobby, collided with my mother. The escapist cineadventure horrified him because he alone of the Allied War Effort did not want to escape from stresses so much as he wanted to escape into them. But by both accounts, when their eyes met, she over jujubes and he over a Lucky Strike Red—because "Lucky Strike Green has gone to war"—they re-created a life-sized enactment of what had earlier taken place between hero and leading lady in the first reel. Silently, without introductions, they accompanied each other out to the street and into the sunshine.

They used to re-create the dialogue that followed, playing it for us in tandem. Sometimes they disagreed slightly over a minor turn of phrase. But overall, they agreed remarkably. Over the years they hammered out a compromise of what had transpired in their first conversation. Both loved to playact their courtship for us. This touring repertoire was the only public romance they ever performed. Fate is what you put in the time capsule. Here is how we got there.

They exchanged names and thumbnail biographies. Mom confessed that she hadn't cared for the film either. She explained to him as they walked that she ordinarily worked days, for a company that put the homo *in homo milk. She had only gone to the afternoon show because her boss, although not a dentist, nevertheless weighing in very close to one by wearing a white smock all day long, had threatened her with an enforced week's vacation with pay if she didn't take the afternoon off. "He thinks I work too hard," she explained shyly.*

"Don't have that problem with my current employer," Eddie joked,

indicating the uniform. "But they make me take the vacation anyway."
Something in their body odors smelled of mutual sacrifice, and they found
themselves linking fingers almost without thinking. Mother would do it
again, years later, stroking Dad's knuckles in remembered protection.
After another silence, he raised their knotted hands to his face, kissed the
back of her wrist, and smiled with the resigned sadness and gratitude of
one finishing the last chapter of a book. I re-create that smile on his face,
a police artist's composite.

They walked side by side along a row of shops, looking, pointing,
swinging hands, but not saying much. Finally Dad, looking away from
this unknown woman, said, "That movie . . ." alluding to the escapist
morale musical they had just escaped. "That war . . ." making the same
bizarre and untenable equation the film itself had just tried to make. "I
lost a brother to that war." An act of courage just to say it, let alone repeat
it for years. His voice filled with horror at anyone trying to film the
incomprehensible present with song and dance.

His wife-to-be bowed her head and looked away herself. She said
something, an "I did too" that carried away on the wind down an
east/west cross street, taking a forty-year detour.

After some blocks, he drew near her and asked, "Does this tune mean
anything to you?" He whistled a few bars of "Moonlight Serenade." She
nodded, swiftly and succinctly, a glow filling her eyes. She squeezed his
hand, and he squeezed back. Then he asked "How about this one?" And
he began "A Mighty Fortress."

Mother looked down at the sidewalk and nodded more slowly. "Yes, but
I've never heard it whistled before." Her confusion was so sincere, her
answer so earnest, that they both suddenly broke out laughing at the
sound. Their laughter took them, like falling, the most natural movement
in the world, into each other's arms for that promissory kiss everyone can
make only once in life without perjury. They drew apart, laughter quieted,
needing further assurance.

They were still joined at the hands. They walked for blocks, through
residential neighborhoods, retail strips, warehouses, empty lots. They
looked in the windows of every structure they passed, exercising the
eminent domain of those marginally happier than the median. After
twenty minutes, Dad at last asked, "Well, what about children, then?"

And my mother, in the most quietly assured voice she would ever muster for him, answered, "Oh, the more the better, of course. A dozen."

The PFC clapped his hands and opened his throat. "Yes! A dozen. A baker's dozen." Then he fell circumspect. A minute later, he added confidentially, "They really are the only sure form of protection, you know." He could not have meant us.

The next day, Sunday, the libraries and civic offices were closed. By eleven A.M. Monday, however, my father had all the institutional cross-references about the stranger that he needed. He appeared cap in hand at her place of employ and asked her out to lunch. How he'd gotten her work address he never revealed and she never discovered. Over deli cuts and funny stories about the service, he popped the question. Years later, he told us that he never had any anxieties about her refusing.

And on account of the uniform, his high cheekbones, her general commitment to national duty, or some deep disaffection with social mores, she did not disappoint him. She cabled back to Oak Hill River Park Forest Grove, more to impart information than to seek her folks' approval. Days later, the two children edged into the office of the justice of the peace and signed the pact just before Dad headed back down South to close up the rest of the Army Air Corps' shop. It was, they both agreed later, a regulation wartime wedding.

When she found out how her husband-to-be had spent Monday morning, Mom took a deep and lasting offense. She could not decide which pained her more: her future husband taking it on himself to research her, or his being too hurried to do as comprehensive a job on her as on all the previous candidates. She passed the test after only one morning of record-digging, calling into question the thoroughness of his job.

She never dropped word of it to any of us, not even to that unacknowledged child who was her secret favorite. Over the years she listened smilingly as Dad told her children how he had looked up her files and passed her in rigorous inspection. She helped him reenact the whirlwind courtship over our faked protests of indifference. But I'm sure it ruined her, although she never said the first word. There was more to our mother than any of us suspected.

The pain that pinned her down through the man's extended self-excision walked clearly across her face like schoolchildren behind a crossing guard.

She had thought, wrongly, that their afternoon walk was itself the audition, not needing the proof of public papers. She had believed, naïvely, that he had no need to double-check. It had seemed to her that for a few hours, they two alone of everyone on earth had experienced simple trust and mutual goodwill. She had imagined them holding back the tide of 1944 between them, unassisted, with a twopenny pail. But he reminded her, cruelly and daily, just by turning into the man he did, that nothing came to pass without the aid of the complicitous moon.

Dad, too, felt the scars of their courtship. Not its bluntness or brevity, but something altogether different. Failing to break himself of his fondness for movies, it irked him that they had met at the cinema, at a morale booster that had insulted them both as well as the memories of their spent brothers. As he saw it, they had both shot the afternoon escaping the horror of the world conflagration, hiding inside the confines of a darkened theater. They had tried to lose their own survivors' guilt in an afternoon of Ruritania or Shangri-La. They had been no better than the thousands of gold-star mothers who weekly tried to win back their own murdered children through blissful oblivion at Judge Hardy's. It convinced him of a permanent flaw, both in their marriage and in the capacity of the human mind to recover from annihilation too easily, that while they had found no consolation in the two-hour world, they had discovered one another in a motion-picture lobby.

Much later my father discovered the value of escapism in standing ground against the real. By that time, most of the censuring gold-star mothers were dead themselves. Their losses, debits carried over in public accounting, had been posted so long ago that they were struck from the active book, transferred to the dead ledger. Those who remained, when they thought of the war years at all, remembered that trick with the cigarette Bette Davis always did better than they did Dieppe.

Tara stands out, sharper than Tora. We revive, rebuild, resew our wardrobe like the feisty little Brit girl making that green dress from the draperies. The Blitz becomes its fictional victim, Mrs. Miniver, trapped in a bomb shelter, reading Alice in Wonderland to the kids. Whatever the long-term consequences, we preserve "Night and Day" over "Night and Fog." And even the casualties themselves wouldn't have it any other way.

Besides, as Dad himself learned firsthand in the months immediately *following his own overnight, cinematic marriage, most of the history we can ever hope to get comes in newsreels. And movies could conspire toward worse things than escape. In a world already lost, we must sometimes pack our keepsakes, keep our heads down, and create a magic kingdom of maxims. My father has disappeared into one, leaving me here. Sometimes we need coaxing to act on our own.*

10

"I've got a great idea," Rachel said, behind the wheel of Mr. Nader, the Pinto deathtrap. She and Artie tooled their way east on Route 5 back to Chicago, still on the forsaken side of Aurora. They had forty minutes of late evening left, not enough to get them home. "Why don't *you* reach over with your left foot and control the accelerator. Then *I* should be able to handle everything else pretty easily."

"I've got a better idea," Artie answered drily. "Why don't *you* just drive like everybody else and get *me* back to Hyde Park without killing me. Then *I'll* give *you* a little brotherly peck on the cheek as a reward."

"Jeez Louise. Or as the Espanich say, Heezoo Flooizoo. What's happened to you, buddy? You're just no fun anymore. Know that? Absolutely no fun."

Artie smiled beatifically and nestled deeper into Mr. Nader's passenger seat. His sister continued to berate him in a variety of dialects and portmanteaus. Listening to her was like watching a French farce: he was amused without really knowing what was going on. Rachel alone had the capacity to turn the East-West Tollway into something more than the world's most expensive, desolate, opaque, and eventless tour from nowhere to nowhere through nowhere. Artie's job, on the other hand, in his self-appointed role as acrid older brother, was to provide, less out of fear for his own safety than from a private need for symmetry, a counterweight to her idiocy.

At home, he never hesitated to add his own modest humor to the runaway routine. But alone with Rach, he had to be straight man. Any other combination fouled up her bravura performances. Besides, when Rachel drove, *someone* had to watch the road and keep everyone alive.

Adopting a tragic mask at the rebuff, Sis pulled an old gag that shattered Artie's outward, straight-man composure. Ostensibly driving, she yawned, flopped down on his shoulder, drooped her eyes, and said, "Wake me up when we get to Oak Brook." He lunged for the wheel and jerked them back on the road. Part of Artie knew, even as he overreacted, that her stunt presented no real danger. Theirs was the only car for three counties, and the shoulder, perfectly smooth, black midwestern soil, the richest soil in the country, lay as level and firmly packed as the road itself. Fields, safely gathered in, spread as far as they could see in all directions, an endless, flat landing zone in any crisis.

Nevertheless, Artie countered his sister, ethos for ethos. Completing the rescue, he scowled Wagnerianly and shot back, "Great Scots, woman. You'll get us all Kilts."

Rachel, giggling, battered his soft underbelly with both hands; he had no choice but to hold the wheel and steer, under attack, for a hundred yards. He protested, stentorian, "Your mother has told you and told you: play around, and somebody's gonna get hurt."

The Pinto veered out of the lane as Artie tried simultaneously to pilot the car and defend himself against this congenial maniac. They were the only motion, the One Thing Wrong in an otherwise eventless picture. Amid the subtle smells of end-of-year manure and nitrates, wrapped in the minimalist architecture of the straight row, bare box, and spare headland, they could have disappeared into flatness, agrarian Judge Craters, and never be heard from again. Or missed, for that matter. Rachel punched him with an abandon inviting disaster. Artie panicked and shouted, "Quit. Grow up, woman. Snap out of it. Take the wheel back. Now." They played driverless chicken for fifty feet until she surrendered and took the wheel, grinning meekly.

Despite his faked protocol, Artie had the awful thought: *We have sprung ourselves, flown off. The rest of our flock are snared back in barb city while we, careless, escape across county lines out of eminent domain. Because our father is back home dying, life has never felt fuller. Never more immediate or real.*

But the crime was too terrible for him to take credit for, so he blamed it on his sister. "Your mom has told you and told you, but *you* know better, don't you?" The car jerked dangerously and his words, stripped of the game, sounded harsher than intended. He startled himself with the bitterness that slipped in. Rachel drew up abruptly, tipped off by the tenor in his tenor. She did not take offense easily. Ordinarily, only a solid slug could bruise her. But her brother's sudden turnaround caught her squarely in the face. Her eyes puffed up in rare, hurt questioning, and even Artie's overeager compensatory attempt to tickle her could not shrink the swelling.

As usual when he mucked things up, Artie's gums let him know. His body parts were emotional seismographs, recording pens spiking at the least flare-up of bad conscience. Gums and colon were most sensitive to offense. Then came lower back. He had twice been unfaithful to the first and still most important love of his life, a blameless, Nordic thinking man's woman named Fran, and both bouts left Artie prostrate with what he had been convinced were slipped disks. Now his gums clamped down on broken razor blades. Not because another man's creeping virus made him bless his own clean lungs for being. That much was not his fault. His gums screamed because he did not allow this equally blameless woman the same way out.

After a minute of silent treatment, he figured out a way of bringing her around. "I've got a great idea," he said, slipping his foot over the transmission hump onto the accelerator. Immediately Rachel brightened. Free forgiveness was Rach's greatest weakness. Incapable of bearing a grudge, all she needed was that the other fellow play today's game. She pulled her right foot up Indian-style onto the seat and flashed him a look of complicity: if we both say so, it must be all right to break free from the sickroom, to tear back the curtains and breathe.

Artie's gums still ached, so he accelerated, flooring it. Rach's giggles became horselaughs. When Artie did not ease up, her horselaugh became swearing. He turned a deaf ear, saying, "Come on. New game. Particle accelerator." Out of the expanse of nowhere, from its hiding place in the pastel November evening, came the inevitable siren and flashing lights.

Artie surrendered the pedal, letting kid sister pull the car over for the arrest. Grinning hysterically, Rachel cursed him, hacked at him, laughed, and choked on her spittle. "*You bastard*. Bass-tard. You did this to me. I'll finish you. You'll never co-pilot again!"

Artie talked over her harangue. "It never fails to amaze me how the police can do that. Every time. Absolutely nothing for miles that they can hide behind. Nada. Guaranteed safe. Then whammo. Prison record. That's the problem with radar. You invent it for a good cause—to go after the Krauts. But you never know when it's going to bounce back and be used against you."

Before the policeman could saunter up to the side of the car, Rachel rolled down the window and called back to him, "Officer, here's your man. He made me do it. Let me explain. Here's your culprit right here." With an involuntary twitch toward his holster, the cop carried on with his may-I-see-your-license spiel. Protesting innocence, Rachel dug out her two forms of ID. The officer took them back to his squad car to check her numbers against a nationwide data base of criminal offenders. Encountering the unexpected, a woman of heretofore complete civil innocence, the protector in blue faltered a moment as he came back to the Pinto, unwilling to cast the first blot on her blank slate.

Artie seized the instant of hesitation. He infused his voice with such authority and confidentiality that for a moment he convinced even himself of the counterfeit. "Officer, I wonder if you couldn't make an allowance for first offense and circumstances. You see, we've just found out that our father, back in De Kalb . . . has a teratoma."

The cop swayed again, and the day would have been won if Rachel had not chosen that precise moment to start snickering. Realizing the setup, the officer changed demeanor swiftly and mercilessly. He slipped a toothpick into his mouth, becoming a Kane County avenging angel, rescuing both the law and his own authority from two shameless punks who would stoop to invent an old man's illness to get out of a ticket. He intimidated them as if they were delinquent schoolchildren, making them answer degrading questions: "Know what happens to people who drive seventy-five? I don't like to scrape scum off of the pavement. Is that clear? *Answer me.*"

Suppressing their giggles, the two Hobsons could not give the desired response. "No. I mean, yes. Right, Artie? Yes." Furious, the cop asked if they wanted him to double the fine then and there. Artie nodded his U. of Chicago law-school litigant's nod.

"You do that, sir. Be sure to write your name and badge number at the top. See you in court, friend. Love your shoes, by the way."

Eighty bucks later, Rach, shaving her big brother's sideburns with her Moving Violation, announced, "You're going to pay for this, buddy. As God is my witness, I'll never eat turnips again until you do."

"Me? I should pay? You're the one who blew it. We had that sucker.

He was about to *apologize* for pulling us over. Bought the entire prognosis. Then you have to go and lose it."

"Gimme that. Who perpetrated this crime, I ax you?"

"Who was driving the car?"

"Who had the hammer down to the floor?"

"Whose idea was the little recreation in the first place?"

"And what the hell's a teratoma anyway?"

Artie shrugged, and they broke into hysterical fits. When one stopped, the other's laughter set them off again. At last, collecting himself, Artie said he'd represent her in traffic court. "We might get the money back if you want to go through the hassle of appeal." Just as suddenly, his hilarity disappeared. He reached that crest of fullness where everything seemed charged, poignant, rich, comic, strange, remarkable, and worth doing. In another minute, he would stare down the escarpment on the other side. Shook back to a sense of their wider catastrophe, Artie clammed up completely, stranded in accusing silence.

But Rachel, bringing him this far, would not let the facts come between them. "Appeal, *schlemiel.* You might as well kiss the eighty bucks good-bye right now, friendo bendo. One way or another I'll get it from you. I'll turn my brothers loose on you. I won't sleep until justice is done."

"Hey, just pay it, okay? You've made it into the Fortune Five Hundred. You're on the take. You've got a lucrative job, one of Chicago's young up and coming. You can swing a bloody speeding ticket, I should think. You'd be a disgrace to your class if you couldn't."

"Oh, yeah?" She couldn't keep a broad smirk of retaliatory delight off her face. Nothing matched Artie when he got indignant. "What do you know about the Fortune Five Hundred? You probably think it's a road race." She had him where she wanted him: squarely behind a noble cause. Artie for Artie's sake. "And what do you mean, 'disgrace to my class'? What class is that, may I ask?"

"Upwardly mobile Boho." He had to grab the wheel again as Rach went into further fits. Art understood that she did not find the punchline half as funny as she found his righteous indignation. It even amused him to see her eyes water and her brows pinch together as she let loose. He decided that as long as he had her cackling, he would go on a roll, make up for the lost weekend at the folks' with a spate of inspired nonsense.

"Don't be so American, woman. Your conditioning has left you *absolutemente* boozjh-wa-zee. You sound like June Allyson, know that?"

"Who dat?"

"Christ, I don't know. Ask yer old man, while you can. That's not the point. The point is . . ."

"What's the point, Artie?" She rotted with laughter.

"The point is, you'd be a goddamn disgrace to the revolution—and don't you dare ask 'What revolution is that?'—if you weren't capable of taking one of these meaningless little speeding-ticket numbers and . . ."

He waved her citation and rolled down the window. Rach flailed at his arms with her free hand, screaming, "No, Artie, no. Pull-eeze don't. I'll be your friend for life. I'll be like a sister to you. I'll never, never make fun of you again for as long as . . ."

"If you weren't capable," Artie reiterated, "of taking one of these and chucking it out the window onto the lone and level interstate stretching far away." The scrap of colored triplicate danced in the rearview mirror and disappeared. "There. Simple. Paid in full! Vanished. It has, in the face of Eternity, become somebody else's problem."

Rach groaned a five-syllable "Why." The word took several seconds, resembling those primal air-raid drills that used to get a lot of network time when she was a child. "I don't believe you did that. I'm gonna open my eyes and everything's going to be back to normal. You know what you've done? You've ruined me. I'm going to have to defect. I'll never be able to get auto insurance again." But in short order, she got into the swing of incendiarism. She began singing the Union Label song and speaking with a goatee. She couldn't help herself. She was simply built that way. She could feel no anxiety that didn't shed as easily as late November leaves. "But Artie, eesent trowing dot teeket joos a leetle beet ee-lee-gal?"

"Damn straight. And that's just civil disobedience act number one. This is the start of a whole new life of political statement for me. The Monk of the Midway turns activist guerrilla. First, a hunger strike until they cut the zip code down to four digits. Then, I'll mastermind a boycott of all eight-hundred number ads on TV. And if society still refuses to respond: window-bomb all retail outlets that refuse to turn the Muzak down to livable levels. Don't want to resort to violence, but if they force my hand . . ."

Artie rarely talked silliness except on the road. And only to Rach, as a general rule. Rachel applauded his last political proposal. "I'm glad to hear that somebody else whom I vaguely respect is hip to Audio Creep. They'll probably Muzak the libraries in another five years. My friends think I'm off the wall. But I swear the stuff is being cranked up, *poco a poco.*"

Artie agreed. "You know how to explain that, don't you? Habituation. They set the sound to level three. After a few years, everybody's ears adjust to where they don't register level three anymore. And so, if the magic narcolepsy's gonna keep doing its stuff, they've got to nudge it up another decibel level, to volume four. Then everybody habituates to level four, and on it goes. I think I'll call it the Law of Increasing Dosages. Credit you with co-discovery." He broke into an overly authentic rendition of "Will the Circle Be Unbroken," bobbling the tune somewhere on the "by-and-bys."

Rach supplied descant. Getting through the chorus, she returned to the thread. "My favorite joke these days is to go into stores with a bunch of friends. Doesn't even matter what kind of store anymore; they've all got it. Then right in the middle of the conversation, go, 'Shhhh. I'm trying to *listen.*'"

Artie added, "You know, the most pernicious part of piped music is how it puts you into unconscious dance steps: One-*two*, one-*two*. Your walk turns into a samba." But it dawned on him that the *most* pernicious thing about Muzak was that any complaints they made about it remained ineffective, clichéd, and *themselves* background noise. He saw that social critique, this late in society's collective game, had become ordinary, established, acceptable.

"Who are we kidding?" he explained out loud. "Why bitch? Muzak; traffic cops. The fiendishly clever *they* invented them so that we don't catch on to overpopulation, test-ban treaties, and poisoned water. Even if we could get to the real issue, acid rain or whatever, nobody really expects that even collectively, which is impossible, we can fix things. Here we are, whining about something of absolutely no significance. Our only common culture is complaint. Antisocial small talk. Complaint is the last tool society leaves us for feeling we belong."

"Yer whacked," Rachel countered. "At least we bitch and moan. My friends don't even mind the Muzak. They don't even *hear* it. If they did, if we put ten million people on the White House steps, don't you think they'd pass a law?"

"Oh, Rach. Say it ain't so. *You*, defending activism? You sound like your sister. Lily's a perfect case in point. She's just like the rest of us. Sure, she made the marches for a few years. But that was just her ticket to a happy despair. Her niche in the world."

"So how do you explain the kid?"

Artie smiled. "*Good* question." Eddie Jr. alone remained free of the antieverything infection. A generational difference lay hidden in the few years that separated the first three of them from the youngest. Artie remembered the scene of a few months back, when Lily had tried forcibly to restrain the then-still-minor from obeying the law and registering for the reinstated draft. Ironic turnaround from how things had been when he was a kid.

"The way I see it, you, me, and Lil grew up postwar, in the mirage of prosperity. All the high expectations floating around must have wrecked us for any chance at real satisfaction. Now Edski, showing up after all the appliances arrived and the all the hope vanished: he's got no reason to believe that anybody deserves anything better. So he's genuinely happy, gripeless."

They both knew who was next in line for analysis. But neither brought him up, surrendering to late-century anesthesia rather than face, however briefly, the heart of Dad's dilemma. And that, they half-saw, *was* Dad's dilemma. Why was it so impossible, these days, to experience anything, to look out the window and *feel*? Because the question itself was already self-conscious. Because the basic four-chambered heart and the standard two-chambered brain were not designed to live in the kind of place they had made of the world. Because the only things left outside the window were unknowably huge and removed, in which the old animal legs of progress, long out of control, lopped off by the scythe, still kicked as if galvanized in the harvested, empty fields. Because to get downtown by nightfall, they had no choice but to take the prescribed anodynes and keep to the wheel.

They reached emergency. Not knowing how else to back away, Artie turned on the radio and fiddled with it, getting one of the proliferate Chicago Ignore-Me stations. He lowered the volume appropriately, snapping his fingers and humming "Strangers in the Night," although that was not the song playing. He looked over at Rachel, his face a perfect cipher, and asked, "What were you saying? I couldn't hear you without background." Rach, with nothing to lose but her new criminal record, rabbit-punched him while Artie kept her car on the road.

"It's yer dad's fault, you know," she sighed at last. "I mean, Discontent as an art form."

"Oh, unquestionably." Artie no longer noticed their mutual habit, initially humorous, of democratizing blame by rendering the old man a "yer." The gag made unwitting third parties think they were only half-siblings. Artie looked away from her. "And rightly so, don't you think? You couldn't respect the man if his great act of social protest took some banal form, say, alcoholism, or heart disease. No; he brought us up believing that the ordinary is our enemy, and we've got to fight it in style. Extraordinarily."

"Maybe. But nobody ever killed themselves with eccentricity." The patented silliness slid from her face. She was, for the first time in a while, speaking from need, not just skipping stones. "Artie?" She sounded frightened. "Where do you go with 'Westward Ho' when you *get* West? You know, he could have stayed in Jersey, if he was just going to come out here and fall apart. Nothing wrong with Jersey, except that 'The Garden State' is a clear violation of truth in advertising. Or Pennsylvania? Philly? Philly's perfect for falling apart in. Plenty of people fall apart in Philly. Or Ohio? Goddamned Birthplace of Presidents?"

A scratch of phlegm tore off on the last word. If anyone else in the world had started to choke on Artie, he could have handled it. But for *Rach* to go to pieces: so impossible, so out of character, that Artie felt his neck flash cold. He could not manage this, not here, not Rachel. But the only thing he could think of to avert a collapse was limp, agreeing sympathy. "You're right. There's such a thing as carrying this fixation for elbowroom too far. I mean, look around . . ."

They both did. Outside, the last, sourceless light scattered across vacancy, running unopposed all the way to the horizon. Another stunted sob came from Rach's throat and she burst a laugh. She looked, eyes liquid, at her brother, unable to add to the unmitigated Illinois landscape with anything so small as words. They were surrounded by an endless, fenceless detention camp of openness where nothing—not rage, not native contrary, not even their father's final illness—could ruffle this

Euclidean perfection. To stop the car, pull over, and protest to the fields that they were being cheated would be the absurd mismatch of scale of antimissile demonstrators attacking hardened silos with dime-store hatchets. Artie wondered for a minute if he would have to slap his sister's face.

Rach spoke deliberately, a flat matter-of-factness fighting for control of her voice. "What happens when Eddie goes off to school? Pop's gonna drag Mom up to the Northwest Territories. Somewhere north of the Arctic Circle. I'm *serious*, Artie. He's going to. And we'll be reduced to one phone call from them a year, at Christmas, on a surplus field radiotelephone."

The image was so ludicrous that they both laughed nervously. Artie flicked off the drizzling radio. He knew that Rach knew that what Pop might do *after* Eddie went to school would probably never be of concern. He needed to keep her talking, but could not get back to the cutups in one swoop. So he stuck with what had soothed her a little: the truth. "*I'm* worried that Pop has only agreed to Hines in order to make a party out of the whole thing. It's not real sickness to him yet. The most that he's giving us is, you know—'Let's go see about My War Wound.' "

"Old forgotten soldier?" Rach interpreted. "So goddamned what? Let him pretend he's the sacrificial lamb, so long as he gets the tests done."

Trying to keep her intact, he embittered her instead. She misunderstood: Artie meant to fault Dad for his *happy* martyrdom, how the man tossed off the insult of daily life as if it were nothing more dangerous than a stale practical joke. Artie meant to condemn Pop for reading the newspaper accounts of contemporary madness out loud, shaking his head and saying, "Can you believe this place? Ya gotta love it." He wanted to say that Pop's show of high spirits and appetite—the flip quips, sardonic dismissals—hid a dark and secret bruise, something clearly and terribly wrong that Hines couldn't treat. But Rach misread him because Artie had not said as much. And he had not said as much because that would have revealed that Artie knew as much from personal experience. He too sat in state at the breakfast table, reading aloud from *The New York Times* and *The De Kalb Chronicle* alike the latest installments of national and local insanities, smiling and shaking his head over toxic spills, government double-dealings, bank-underworld liaisons, the countless, felonious, five-finger exercises committed in the name of freedom and sovereignty. Artie himself had supplied Pop with details for Hobstown, that imaginary tumor that had grown out of the daily press for years now. Artie could not give the old, cheerful soldier any solution more tenable than Eddie Sr.'s own chuckling desolation. But Artie would never give such perversity, however much he himself resorted to it, his *Good Housekeeping* seal. That was what he had meant to tell Rachel. But she had misunderstood.

However much he had botched things so far, he had to keep talking. Something. Anything. Let Rach know he was just across the seat from her. He changed the topic, burying what he could not hope to tell her even in perfect circumstances. "Ever hear of a Dr. Wolff, of Cornell? Harold, I think the first name is. Harry, maybe?"

"No." Rachel sensed current underneath, and let it run. "Why?"

Artie should have remembered sooner that nothing consoles better than a mystery. "It's probably nothing," he said. "A name Dad called after me on our way out. I'm supposed to be detective, see? Figure out what *he* has figured out about what nobody can figure out."

"Taken to crying Wolff, has he?" Rachel slid back into form. Her voice was once more Rach's voice. Artie felt safety return, and for the next twenty miles, the two kicked around the enigma. The world became pitch dark. After the toll plaza at Oak Brook, they underwent the gradual escalation of nothing into vacancy, vacancy into sparsity, sparsity into FOR LEASE signs, lease signs into industrial parks, parks into complexes, complexes into conglomerates into skyscrapers and finally into the Sears Tower. Winding along the inbound Eisenhower into the Dan Ryan, "Damn Ryan" in Rachel's private vocabulary, they picked up traffic until they were bumper to bumper. They began to breathe easier in the anonymity of overcrowding. Artie co-piloted Rach into Hyde Park and up to his old brownstone off Cottage Grove. She had taken him there scores of times and should have been able to locate the building herself, even in the dark. But she never could. Each time, he patiently marveled over how any townee, even an adopted one, familiar as she was with the Chicago grid system, could still lose herself amid all the indelible logic.

"North Sider," he razzed her. "Coming up?" Artie's sudden invitation surprised them both. Normally, after a weekend of Hobson's choices, he couldn't wait to sequester himself with the law books. Maybe he'd habituated to companionship; maybe he was afraid to leave Rach alone so soon. Whatever the reason, he asked her, curtly, not to take off right away.

Rach tipped her head at him, quizzically, the way a parakeet sometimes will. Only she kept tilting, through 180 degrees, until she sat completely twisted in the driver's seat, craned all the way upside down, head to the cushion, looking at him as he dangled one foot on the curb. Vintage Rachel, returned fully from the tremor moment. "Say that again."

"Coming up?"

"God. From this angle, it looks as if your mouth is in your forehead."

Losing his patience, he grabbed his rucksack, assembled his stuff, and closed the car door in disgust. He had done all that he could for her in the car, and now that she felt better, she fell back into sight gags. He completed the send-off brusquely and was halfway up the walk when Rachel rolled down the passenger window and called him back.

"Artie." He knew, because she used his real name and not some coinage, that he was in for a dressing down. He dragged back to the car, wronged but nevertheless cooperative. He thought, somehow, that she was about to speak directly to the issue, the thing that, in the drive back through the open fields, they had avoided touching on. He knew, by the tone of her voice, that the subject was *friction*, was *fishing*, or *forgiveness*; something fricative.

She would call him out, he thought. Implore him to forgive the old man. Tell him not to hold it against the guy for both falling ill and then evading the differential diagnosis. But Artie wasn't ready to forgive. He couldn't do that yet, even for his favorite Rach of all Raches.

But he had guessed entirely wrong about his sister's scolding. He had guessed wrong about everything. He had guessed wrong in the car, in thinking that *he* had to hold *her* together. "Artie," she said gently. "I'll see you soon. Go easy on yourself, okay?"

FALL, 1942

By fall of 1942, the roundup of AJAns is historical fact. The press does not cover it, but letters slip out of the evacuation zone describing the great rumblings up and down the West Coast. The rumblings explode in molten silence and quickly cease, leaving no record but an extinct and hollow cone. Whole neighborhoods vanish. Prisoners write of flying the Stars and Stripes above their fish crates and orange bins, with no success. Others describe birth certificates and citizenship papers masking-taped to the picture window next to the hard-earned front-porch swing. Nothing turns the trick. Everyone of tainted descent is interned, "relocated" in the official idiom, brought to camps deep in the interior where they cannot harm tenuous national security. In a few weeks, information from the camps dries up. Letters come through cut to ribbons, jumping right from the Dear to the Sincerely. Getting no replies, many interned nisei give up writing.

Years later, history books carry a famous photo with a Library of Congress credit showing "Wanto Co.," that small fruits-and-vegetables market just across the street, a huge printed sign posted across it reading I AM AN AMERICAN. The shop is empty, the inside dark. The cause is already lost. A stunning image, the moment just after shame; the photo arrives too late for any remedy. For all its anguished power, the photo becomes a dated artifact, something that happened to the other fellow. More recent tragedies take us worlds farther into error.

People are herded out of dance halls, football games, weddings. They're allowed to collect things—a toothbrush, change of underwear, only what they can carry. Businessmen must sell off their assets for 5 percent of real value. Families are split up and loaded onto livestock trucks, driven to barbed-wire barracks where they spend the next four years. Some camps have unfinished, communal toilets, where a perpetual, overwhelming stench lingers on everything. People sleep in converted animal stalls. Children attend camp schools, where they study the founding fathers and recite the Preamble under the aegis of armed sentries.

Many die along the way, die of shame in the four-year transit. Even to assimilated American descendants, shame is worse than death. Overnight, the program kills an entire way of life. Now we are all victims of precaution, prisoners of conscience, losing our tune in a world at battle pitch.

In the middle of his legwork for the war effort, Disney stops in full stride. Months after the accomplished fact, he sees what has been going on around him. He cannot figure how the authorities yielded so readily to public frenzy over saboteurs and spies. He speculates on the role of protectionist interests, racism, and partisan politics in the mass arrests. He wonders whether any fight against might can ever be won without sacrifice of principle, or whether the forces of efficacy can only be beaten efficaciously. Nothing makes any sense to him except that two members of his brain trust have been imprisoned for nothing. The only thing he knows for sure is that his fellow countrymen wouldn't be in jail without everybody else looking the other way.

The morning before he flies out to sell his cinematic brainstorm to D.C., Disney sits at his drawing board and wrestles up a pen and ink cel of the Mouse. "What do you say to fighting fire with fire?" he mumbles to the image. With a few deft strokes, he blows a talk bubble above Mickey's head reading, "That makes a big fire, Walt." Disney puts his pens down and sighs. He knows the size of the blaze we are up against. He has heard Murrow's London broadcasts. He has seen what the Imperial Navy accomplished in the Philippines. He knows about roundups far more hideously evil than the local one. Terminally evil. And other than retaliation he cannot think of a weapon large enough to put this fire out.

He exhales, stands slowly, and slinks to his writing desk. Ashamed, he unwinds the speaker cone of his dictaphone and turns on the machine. After an appalling pause in which he can think of nothing, he speaks into the horn:

Ariston hudor.

Smiling to himself because he doesn't know which side of this latest catastrophe the Greeks are on, but certain that he can't afford to risk another house arrest, he translates:

Water is best.

This is the secret blueprint Disney brings out to Capitol Hill for his tête-à-tête with the Powers That Be. A government Douglas DC-3 wings him into Washington. Disney knows that not even his world-famous Mouse has sufficient leverage to charge into Henry Stimson's office and call the secretary of war onto the carpet. He cannot demand, point-blank, the release of his friends. Not with a war on, anyway. But he has another plan, more powerful than frontal assault.

Stimson, the man who, blindfolded, stuck his hand into the vat of paper scraps to start the Selective Service, roundly considered one of the best public servants this country has produced, drummed out of his own party upon his appointment to FDR's cabinet for speaking softly and grinding a big Axis, greets Disney from behind a mahogany cruiser, shuffling through four-color maps of the world. The secretary stands and delivers the obligatory accolades: he has seen and loved the first rushes of Victory Through Air Power. *Walt thanks him graciously, giving him a Mickey watch and autographed cartoon photos.*

They get down to business. Disney, armed with sketches and storyboards, presents his idea for the feature-length, revolutionary motion picture You Are the War. *More articulate and charming than ever, he sells the plan for all he's worth. He claims this unprecedented wedding of cartoon fantasy with grim live action will provide the boost to home-front morale that will break the back of the Axis. The picture will show contemporary America its own front stoop, awaken it to the fact that it alone, and not High Commands and secret conferences, determines what is past, passing, and to come. "Think* Fantasia," *Disney urges, "only set in Aunt Edith's Victory Garden in Smith Center, Kansas." Disney will show, using every fabulous technique in the book he himself has written, that no fairy tale ever told can match the here and now for sheer mystery, urgency, and power.*

Stimson is hooked from the start. He raises one halfhearted fear about the scope of the proposed scheme: timid members of Congress might object that the material would better serve our literal soldiers overseas. Disney reassures him. He urges Stimson to think imaginatively about the long-term benefits of such an epic ode to the national spirit, payoffs that will outlast wartime. He promises that he will school recalcitrant legislators on the necessity of thinking historically. He's sure he can persuade any objectors by pointing out that we could not have won the first war without Chaplin, Mary Pickford, and Irving Berlin. If we don't answer Triumph of the Will at once, theirs may. This is Democracy's testing hour; he, Disney, the reigning, preeminent statesman of American values, must be allowed to pull all the stops for his cinematic slap in the face of totalitarianism.

Out from the top drawer comes Stimson's checkbook. The secretary fills in the payee and signs it. He pauses at the amount, giving Disney a significant look: what do you need? Disney looks him back, stating a figure higher than he expects to get, a staggering budget by 1942 standards. If Stimson turns down the number, he'll be softer on the next point. But Stimson fills in the figure without flinching and says, "I assume that's just a first installment." Disney begins to get an inkling of the real power lurking underneath the currently popular contradiction in terms, Arsenal of Democracy.

Stimson hands over the check and tells Disney to make something for all of us, something that will last. He turns his back on Walt and goes to his window, looking out on the Lincoln Memorial. A sweep of his hand indicates the panorama of classical revival buildings. But these marbles have always made Disney nervous, as if one look in the other direction would reveal an enormous pillared stadium filled with Vienna Choir boys. He demurs, saying that his film must be about the median fellow, the American's American, the butcher, baker, fruit-and-vegetable vendor, who masterminds history without even knowing it: You are the war.

Stimson nods his head abstractedly. "Perhaps. But no jingoism. Film it for the future, so that a national switch in enemies will make no difference." Disney is taken aback. Stimson sees the dismay and patiently delivers political-science lecture number one: the ins and outs of adversarial relations. "Don't be too concerned with this little scrap we're having with the Germans. Or even the Japanese, for that matter. They are only today's enemies. This too will pass. The director of Mission to Moscow, for instance, as blamelessly patriotic as he is now, will find himself embarrassed in a few years."

Walt gets a quick glimpse of the divvied-up postwar world. He asks Stimson point-blank if it's the Russians, our allies, that we're really after. The secretary of war just grins sadly and shakes his head no. Disney has seen that grin before. He places it with a rush: I'll huff and I'll puff and I'll blow your house down. What only now occurs to the animator of The Führer's Face is that the civilized world stands on the threshold of liberty, the cutting edge of the age of universal justification in the name of necessity. And he cannot believe what he sees over that threshold.

Stimson stares out over the memorial parkway, exercising the statesman's prerogative of holding conversations with his back turned. He muses about the New York World's Fair of '39, waxing nostalgic, wishing it were still possible for Disney to retrieve and film another world like that one. He speaks of Flushing Meadow as if it took place three centuries and not three years ago. The man who got his start busting trusts for Teddy Roosevelt stands gazing upon a new and unfamiliar landscape. He watches the old one roll down the Potomac out to the ocean. He falls silent. "History," Secretary Stimson finally says, turning to Disney, "is servitude." He implies that this year's alignment—the Japs and Germans as the incarnation of evil, China and Russia as the heroes—is irrelevant, a deliberate and misleading bill of goods come the inevitable 180-degree reversal just a few years down the pike. What will the war films of thirty years hence look like, when half our market is in Germany and Japan? "Make something that will last," the secretary reiterates.

Stimson gazes out on a world where it has become irrelevant whether or not detachments of Japs on Pacific islands really knock out American teeth for their gold inlays or play ringtoss with brains and bayonets. Irrelevant who, exactly, pulls the severed tendons of a dissected Jew's hand, making it wave hello for the recording scientific camera. A subterranean current of darkness has made its way to the surface of daily life and can no longer be pushed back down. He describes, wordlessly, how national states must now take up the game, learn it, formalize it with power politics and covert operations. We have given birth to the world of the permanent threat.

This much Disney understands the Cabinet man to say. But he cannot tell if Stimson, the man who more than anyone else has his finger on the present's pulse, implies that the battle is already lost, or if he is pleading with Disney, the Mouse, and the power of enchantment as if they were the world's last chance. He does know, however, that this ambivalence will make the secretary no more agreeable to his next request. For Disney has come here with much more than a blank check in mind.

"Mr. Secretary," he interrupts the other's reverie. "For this project, I'll need a staff." He tells Stimson how his own studio is booked solid with government work for the next three years. No problem, says the other. Hire what you need; the bankroll is here. Disney explains the difficulty. He needs sets, costumes, actors, artists, writers, construction engineers, technicians. For a project this size, Disney says he'll need ten thousand bodies.

It's Stimson's turn to be taken aback. "Where can we find those numbers in wartime?" Walt glides over to the colored maps on Stimson's desk. He finds North America, locates the Southwest. He puts his finger down on a small town that was not on the map before February of this year.

The implication sinks in. Stimson raises his head and looks at Disney, comprehending, sympathetic. But across his face is the grisly certitude that there is no countering the enemy's concentration camps without camps of our own. The only answer to runaway fire is to raise the risk of irreversible conflagration. "I'm sorry, Walt. We can't do that. Even for you." We must have the courage of our convicts if we want to win.

Disney wastes no time arguing the ethics of the point. Instead, he smiles like a man about to pull a larger-than-life rodent out of his hat. He informs Stimson that if he can't get the ten thousand bodies out, he will publicly demand to be arrested. Stimson suddenly recalls the well-known but hitherto conveniently overlooked fact that Walt Disney's grandfather was the offspring of a geisha girl and a midshipman on Matthew Perry's ship Susquehanna. Disney is, in short, an American of Japanese Ancestry living in that sensitive national security area, Hollywood. The Cabinet minister and his administration are handcuffed by their own pronouncement. They cannot incarcerate the man who brought another world to the screen, a world in every way superior to our own. The public would not abide it; they would throw the war. But the law is the law. If Disney holds a press conference and the Feds make an exception by not taking him into custody, the whole infrastructure of the roundup will crumble into embarrassing and indefensible double standards. The situation is what is known in political science as a hot potato.

Stimson is trapped into meeting Disney's terms. He agrees to release, gradually and without press, ten thousand inmates into Disney's private custody. They will be issued special exemptions reserved for sensitive projects. Work papers. Walking papers. Stimson insists that Disney must not shoot the project anywhere on the Pacific rim. They must be kept out of urban areas, under parole, inland, as hidden as possible.

Walt has anticipated that, already selecting a secret tract deep in the interior for the filming. For practical as well as emblematic reasons, he plans the shoot for the weighted center of the nation's population, equidistant from every average you he will eulogize. That, by 1942 calculations, puts the set not far from the town of Disney's birth, hidden in covert and invisible fields of corn.

The interview finishes. Disney takes Stimson's hand, strides from the office, and reboards the DC-3. He flies from Washington straight to that new jail out near Bonneville Flats, Utah, where his two employees are held. Walt scrambles down the improvised exit ramp onto the desert runway, flashing his startled welcoming committee his disarming trade-mark grin. He finds Tom Ishi and Ralph Sato, his fellow nisei, who greet him courteously but listlessly. He is astonished at their transformation. Well fed, well clothed, well treated, his friends are nevertheless little more than walking broken spirits, a condition familiar in prisoners of war.

Walt takes a guided tour of the camp, ending up at the bunkhouse Sato and Ishi share with five other captives—two businessmen, a lawyer, an engineer, and a junior-college president, Americans who have fallen through the wartime cracks and are lost. He huddles his seven fellow passengers together in the bunkhouse and presents them with a what if: suppose they could prove to their wardens that they are a national resource and not a liability. Suppose that even those of enemy extract can prove to be as good Americans as the next duck. He eases them humanely into the escape plan that will spring them all from jail. But not too abruptly, or their hearts might ossify.

Slowly Disney unfolds it to them: they can enjoy special exemption, walk away from this place, but only if they agree to partake in a massive escapist and propaganda project on a scale larger than anyone has ever *dreamed possible. The film must do more than merely prove the patriotism of the AJAns who put it together. It must reveal the spirit of the nation itself, contribute to the common defense, promote the general welfare. Every shot, camera angle, and inked image must celebrate the American, showing in an immediate, visceral, and irrefutable way why he and nobody else is destined to win this one. If, calling on both real and imagined pictures, they can tell a story that convinces enough people of the inevitable victory, then the inevitable will follow.*

The vote in the bunkhouse is unanimous, Jeanette Rankin's theory of democracies notwithstanding. Anything, even conscription into working on the most shamelessly naïve and flag-waving cartoon imaginable, is better than spending another night of unearned humiliation. They ratify their allegiance to the project by taking the nicknames Dopey, Sleepy, Happy, Grumpy, Doc, Doc II, and Doc III, because none of them, including Walt, can for the life of him remember all of those other dwarves' names.

Over the next weeks, Disney demonstrates his genius for administration. He and the dwarves scour the one hundred thousand prisoners and assemble a crew possessing extraordinary and varied creative skills. Countless brainstorming sessions later, the newly formed nisei corporation has in place all the logistics for the transfer of these ten thousand to the planned midwestern location. With an unlimited budget, the Acquisitions Committee buys a vast maw of farmland at wartime prices. They purchase the ideal spot, a historical emptiness nestled in an impossible expanse of cornfields: the birthplace of barbed wire.

Advance construction crews move out, appropriating an old barbed-wire magnate's mansion for use as HQ. They construct living quarters, dining hall, even a small auditorium for screenings and meetings. In the first week of December 1942, they stage the groundbreaking. A bank of documentary cameras catch the moment when Disney paces out the area by foot. The film is developed and sent to Washington. Then the Steering Committee freezes all further construction until they have a better sense of what they're doing.

For truth is, neither Disney nor his associates Ishi and Sato nor the other five dwarves nor any of the ten thousand extended support personnel, only a handful of whom have ever worked on a movie shoot before, has any real film script in mind. The project has been from the beginning nothing more than airy nothingness with an urgent motive. Disney, from the day he was caught reading Rilke into his recorder, has decided that he would first free as many compatriots as possible, and then figure out the specifics of freeing the wider audience of millions. He has appropriated a considerable government sum to make something only marginally more planned than home movies.

Inside the enclave, however, the atmosphere is one of joyful carnival. A plaster cast of Mickey rises larger than life over the new village: black-tailed, white-gloved, hollow-irised, hemisphere-eared. For the time being, the scriptless prisoners of war enjoy the estate privileges of Lords of Misrule. All the while, a steady stream of newcomers trickles through the gate. Many drop and kiss the frozen ground, although it is the same ground they have just escaped from, and in many ways the same compound.

The only thing they do have, aside from Stimson's mammoth check, is a vast, flat, empty, infinitely pliable, blank slate of land cordoned off with wire. They can make of it anything they choose. At groundbreaking, Disney delivers an inspiring address to the small cadre of still-assembling ranks. He tells them to look at this evacuated place and imagine it filled with the perfect world. *Think one step beyond verisimilitude. Do not stop at the goal of creating a replica "just like real life," but imagine a finished product that fleshes out real life and improves on it.*

He promises that what tech engineers cannot build, what cameramen cannot capture in the lens, artists, under Disney's supervision, will paint right on the emulsion with animating pens. Trust to imagination, keep good faith, and technical matters will attend to themselves. Disney, ever the American Pragmatist, wraps up his speech resoundingly: "Soon, we will get to work, make in this blank place a two-hour adventure that will change the way people look at their part in the big picture. We can't see the finished shape yet, but we'll discover what we're after as we go along. If we love our material, we can make a picture that will hasten the advent of the camp-free world."

Disney steps down from the makeshift podium to tumultuous applause. He discovers, to his surprise, that he has set out on the rickety, impossible, and enormously suspect enterprise of making a populist epic. In the next few days, he manufactures busywork for the cast of thousands: orders for a dozen sets, three sound stages, developing rooms, offices. He does not hope for great results, but he must start producing something tangible.

What comes of the collective camp spirit surprises even Disney. By the first thaws of 1943, the set begins to blossom with inspiration. A band of houses appears, forming a filmable Main Street. Not far away, three newly released generations of artisans revive Oriental papier-mâché technique and raise a convincing model of the snow-capped Rockies. Painters create whole Manhattans out of muslin backdrops. Others, without instruction, do what they know how. Some sew, some script; others orchestrate, hang lights, or practice handling cameras. Disney marvels at what can come about when ten thousand voices hash out their community rules with no vested interests except results.

Disney himself makes great progress in focusing the film. Most important, he finds the film's hero. For once it is not Ike, Marshall, Walter Pidgeon, or any of those iconic soldiers. For the hero of this most ambitious Disney epic yet, Walt will pluck an average face right out of the theater audience. The hero of this prodigious, unprecedented undertaking will be the Man Behind the Man Behind the Gun.

A returning burst of the old inspiration that has been bottled up ever since he first caught a glimpse of the film tells Disney who the lead must be. Taking an inadvertent tip from the nostalgic Stimson, he will return to Flushing Meadow. What happens when a wide-eyed boy wakes from a dream of progress to find himself the king of swing-shift swing time? What happens when, from behind the billboard announcing Coral Sea and El Alamein, he suddenly emerges, colossally real, as persistent as the sixth in an Andrews Sisters chord? Walt will find that boy, the one who stood in '39 marveling at the missile to the future. He will track down Bud Middleton to his position in the home-front line. The boy, nearing draftable age, will be the film's star, the force leading the way to that promised, future world.

The kid ought to be easy enough to find. He's worked in Hollywood. He's a natural in front of the camera. All Bud needs to do to emblemize Americans is be himself. To stand for everything there is, he must simply do what he has always done: be Bud Middleton, in the here and now. The boy's story will certainly fill five reels, especially with Mickey as co-star. "After all," Disney says, resorting to a favorite phrase, "there's more to any dwarf than any of us suspects."

By the time Disney takes off for Hollywood to track the boy down, the movie set has been christened. Someone invents a sobriquet that catches on like cholera. Although they know it is a little fulsome, the nisei cannot resist calling the burgeoning magic kingdom World World. One group of craftsmen creates a pastel banner to hang over the movie set's main gate. For text, they reject the first proposal, WORK WILL SET YOU FREE, in favor of the far superior:

IT AIN'T NECESSARILY SO

Disney stands under this gate with his right-hand man, taking leave of the community and vowing not to come back without the movie's hero-to-be. He and Sato look back on a flurry of activity spreading irrepressibly over the former cipher of land. "All this motion, all this doing," Sato exclaims. "My God! We are actually going to pull this thing off." He meets Disney's glance, and falls silent. Very quietly, he asks, "We're really sprung, then? It's really up to us?"

All Disney can answer is, "Tell me how free we are, Ralph. You tell me."

‖

"Buffalo gals won't you come out tonight . . ."

Eddie, Jr. had left Pop beached on the front porch, abandoned his mother and Lily to the shipwrecked house, and let Artie and Rach drift out of town on Illinois 5. He had felt no qualms about making his own emergency exit in the company of friends. Pop had promised to turn himself in in a couple of weeks. Eddie Jr. could do nothing between now and then but give in to November at eighteen.

And that came as easily to him as the answers in the back of an algebra book. At the end of the evening, warm in the belly of his friends, Eddie paired off with the prettiest, a junior named Sarah. He had talked her into seeing the second showing of *Fantasia* at the Egyptian, De Kalb's 1930s Deco revival theater. Now he walked her back home, singing in two-part harmony, "And dance by the light of the moo-oon!"

The duet, flush with possibilities, hung on the deserted street. Eddie grabbed Sarah around her willowy waist on the cadence. "God, that was great. I had no idea you could sing. You sound just like Donna Reed." Sarah, lovely in the limpid darkness, looked puzzled. "Donna Reed. *You* know. From *It's a Wonderful Life*." Astonished at not yet ringing the bell, he added, "Tell me you don't know it! Impossible. It's on a hundred times every Christmas. What were you, born yesterday?" And answering her mumbled, tentative rejoinder, "No, that's Judy Holliday, nit."

Eddie shook her lightly by still unknown shoulders, scolding her in pantomime. "Know what my pop'll say when he finds out his flesh and blood spent the evening with a woman who confused Donna Reed with Judy Holliday? 'Out of this house! You're no son of mine.' "

In fact, the only response Dad ever made regarding any of the girlfriends Eddie brought home was the sad, cryptic chant, "Girls, girls, girls." Once he had said, confidentially, "Remember, son. Forty million

Frenchmen *can* be wrong. Would you trust an appraisal of the fairer sex from the folks who gave you the Maginot Line?" That was the closest the two had ever come to discussing romantic love.

Sarah lifted her head to him and said, "I'm sorry. I haven't seen very many of the classics."

Eddie, hearing only her eyes, slipped his hand down into Sarah's floppy jacket pockets and played there. "Who said anything about *seeing* them? I haven't *seen* three quarters of the old films I talk about. You just have to *know* about them, is all."

"So how is it that you know all about them?"

"Blame it on my folks. They raised me on old-movie references."

"Just a slave to your upbringing, I suppose," Sarah said archly. Eddie felt convinced of his suspicion that she was somewhat smarter than he, and infinitely more cultured. She played the cello, for God's sake. He had to step lightly or he'd end up in deep mischief. The kind of over-his-head treading for dear life that he lived for.

"I was *raised* to blame myself on my being raised that way. How's that?" Sarah gave a sophisticated "Ha!" but drooped her shoulder toward his at the same time. Eddie supposed that indicated the answer was just fine.

"Funny you should ask, though. About my upbringing. I was designed by committee. Sins of the fathers, and all. Nature versus nurture is one of my dad's favorite debates. But *my* father, he never comes down on one side or the other. He asked us once whether a person raised in solitary confinement can know what it means to get lonely."

"Your *father* asked you that?"

"Yeah. Over hot oatmeal, as I remember."

"Really! He sounds remarkable."

"Uh, that's the polite name. Look, I had better warn you about my family right now. They aren't the Cleavers." Eddie looked at her sidelong and said, "That's Ward and June, for those of you just back from the rococo."

Sarah shoved him and pulled his hands out of her pockets. "Enjoy the man," she ordered. "Mine just talks about what's wrong with the car. What about the rest of your family? Are they nature or nurture?"

Eddie dropped into the tones of dramatic voice-over. "The close-to-the-chest older brother. The testy, ex-radical big sis. Sis number two, everybody's favorite flake. The patient, long-suffering mom. All lost in orbit around the master of ceremonies. You tell me. Now that I think about it, we might make a halfway decent sitcom after all."

She drew close again, and Eddie thought that nothing on this earth came close to the first feel of the waist of an unknown quantity. She had an easy grace, this stranger, a way of holding gingerly to his belt loop that made her seem unafraid of the consequences of knowing another person. He felt a rush of anticipation, doubled because he knew that she encouraged it.

For some months, seeing her in the halls, he had assumed that she was standoffish, that she liked cellos better than boys. And so he had fixed himself on her. Two weeks before, they had caught one another making a mutual appraisal. The three-second glance proved how bendable the social circles of late adolescence still were. Each strained to find some 'mutual overlap of friends, and at last hit on some contrived entree for breaking into the other's crowd. And here was the same imaginary girl, made real in a few unbelievable days, teasing him on a late walk back home. Her pretending that he was half as interesting as she could only be early flirtation and a trick of the amber streetlight.

Eddie decided that before he dropped her off he would up the uncertain ante, answer her easy style. He started to steer them back to simple teases, but surprised himself by saying, "Pop's off to the hospital in a couple weeks."

"Oh? I'm sorry to hear that." She didn't bristle at the mention of illness. Eddie felt a sudden hurry to admire her, before life knocked her out for being perfect. "What's wrong?"

He even liked her wording, how she left off the *with him*. "We don't know what's wrong, really. Vertigo virus. The shimmies. Who knows? That's part of the problem. That's the *subject* of the Cleavers' misadventure this week."

"Don't be a curmudgeon. It's not becoming. Not if the man's not feeling well."

"Who you calling a curmudgeon?" She poked him in the sternum. "Oh, yeah? What's it mean?" She gave him the dictionary definition. "Damn it, that was on the SAT. If you'd have told me that three months ago, I'd be going to the college of my choice next year. Well, a couple of decades of jaycee never hurt anybody, huh?"

"Three months ago, you didn't know I existed. Maybe you should have gotten *Laura* to tell you what *curmudgeon* meant."

"How do *you* know who I was going out with three months ago? Anyway, I swear to you that *Laurie*, as she is called by the general public, was just a passing physical insanity."

"She's a strumpet, that's what."

"What's a *strumpet*, pray tell? Who was that strumpet I saw you with last night?" Eddie could not keep his voice from resembling the old man's. "That was no strumpet, that was my curmudgeon."

"Don't push your luck. What about Barbara, then?"

"Barbara? Barbara Simms? You jest. I wasn't going out with her. We were just childhood curmudgeons. All right, we *talked* about rubbing our bacons together. Once. In the interests of Science. But that's as far as it went."

Sarah tucked her lower lip under her top teeth and pushed him again. "You are unbelievably crude, Hobson. 'Bacons.' I'd walk home alone if Rabelais hadn't used the same phrase."

Eddie assumed Rabelais was a passing indiscretion of Sarah's. Her Barbara Simms. "Who wants to know all these names from my sordid past, anyway?"

"I do," she said obstinately. And the kid fell in love.

"Listen. I want you to know, you have a terrific alto. Beats Donna Reed, I swear. We have to get married and form an act. I know you have a vote in the matter, but listen. We could take it on the road. Take it to Europe. Do Italy. Hop over to the Vatican and see the famous Medulla Oblongata."

Sarah laughed and corrected his anatomy. Then she lowered her eyes and hinted, "I've studied a little Italian, you know. On my own. It helps when reading scores."

"That's okay. I'll marry you anyway. We don't have to tell anyone that you know things." He had heard her excruciating maybe; *I wouldn't mind Italy; I don't mind you.* There was nothing to do but maybe her back.

The banter exasperated her. She withdrew her fingers from his and cast his hand away. "There's no way I'm going to marry you, Hobson. You are a proven unreliable quantity."

They walked in silence the length of three houses. The night air was cold, but not cold enough for either of them to know it. Near the horizon, just outside of town, sat the hunger moon. "If you bail out the tide with a twopenny pail," Eddie said quietly, to the motionless air.

"Then you and the moon can do a great deal." Eddie looked at her in astonishment. He did not dare ask where she had heard the phrase. He had always considered it Dad's private stock, and the discovery that it was known to this beauty alarmed him with possibility. Sarah saw the quick look come across his face. Their hands fumbled back and knit together, static-charged hair to winter wool.

"Know what my mother says?" Eddie asked, not believing that he was going to make this detail public. "She says, 'I would never dream of leaving your father. I signed the papers, didn't I?' How do you explain somebody like that?"

Sarah tucked her chin into her jacket collar. "That's who she is, I suppose. But I bet her feelings are the real contract."

He could not help himself from cupping both hands over her knit cap, behind her ears. "Well, if that's how you really feel about the matter, could we just live in sin, then? I'll move out to Harvard or Yale, or wherever you end up. Huh? Pretty please?"

She laughed out loud. "Oh, all right. If you insist."

The cadence of their step changed. Eddie tried wordlessly to get her to avoid stepping on the sidewalk cracks, still visible through a first dusting of snow. After a silence that any other girl would have surely deflated, he asked, "What do you think of children?"

Sarah's face modulated to seriousness. Not oppressive seriousness, not brooding agitation or the end of enjoyment, but a richly textured, nuanced, sonata seriousness, the slow weighing of possibilities hidden in a minor key. "I don't think . . ." she began. "I'm not sure this is the best world to bring children into."

Eddie dropped a beat. He had heard the notion before. Pop had put it forward once to the older kids when they broke into their twenties: Suppose there was a final crisis in the world and the outcome of everything was uncertain? Would any decent parent risk an infant to a world turned upside down? On the other hand, what good do we do by not enlisting new children? Now, suppose the crisis is too many children. Suppose the world is already lost. . . .

Eddie, Jr. had ignored the what-if when Pop had brought it up. Dad had a way of manufacturing sounds that weren't there. If the world were tearing at its seams, wouldn't the air fill with riot horns and sirens? Only now, curling the ends of this girl's hair, Eddie Jr. understood that they would never get such advance warning. Sirens come only with returning order. All they would ever hear would be a questionable hush. If someone as jaunty, full-spirited, and *seventeen* as this woman felt the touch of the child-forsaken world, maybe the place was upon them.

"We'll discuss this later, my little chickadee," he said, tapping imaginary cigar ash onto the snow. "Change of subject. Let me tell you a joke. There's this famous Broadway impresario—that's the right word, isn't it?—who wants to stage the greatest *Hamlet* either side of the Atlantic. They put out the word for auditions. 'Looking for greatest Hamlet ever,' They listen to hundreds of guys. Famous, not so famous, good, great, unbelievable. But nobody rises to the heights of perfection this impresario has in mind. Then this little guy comes down from Washington Heights, paunch, receding hairline, shuffling, just off the boat. "I vant to audition Hemlick." The impresario groans, but lets the *schlemiel* do his thing, because nobody else has been quite good enough either.

"So the guy gets up on stage and after a short silence says, 'Thrift'—pretty good, eh? 'Thrift.' Didn't think I knew anything about Willie the S, dija? Thought I was a big dumb jock, dinja?"

"Just tell the story," she said, putting her hands in her pockets, refusing to take them out until he got on with it.

"You curmudgeon, you. So anyway, he says, 'Thrift, Horatio.' His voice fills the theater, and the dust from his clothes falls off, his paunch recedes, and he is in another world. He transports everyone with that one word. He goes on: 'Assume a virtue if you have it not.' He holds up this skull, says how he kissed it once when it still had lips."

"Hobson, you counterfeit. You really *know* that play, don't you?"

"No way. But I've got this joke down pat. Now please. By the end of the speech, the impresario is weeping. The other auditioners are weeping. The guy sweeping the back of the theater is weeping. The little man on stage has them all in a place where the skull is somebody *they* knew." Sarah took hold of his arm and slowed his walk.

"Then the man stops, turns back into a little *shlep*, and comes down off the stage. There's this moment of silence, and the impresario says, 'That was the most astonishing, moving Hamlet I have ever heard. How did you do that? What kind of man are you? Where in God's name did you get that power?' And the *zhlub* shrugs and says, 'That's ecting.' "

Sarah laughed melodically, but not at the punchline. "I don't get it, Eddie."

"Come on, woman. 'Ecting,' you see. E-c-t . . . Immigrant's accent. You see, if he can talk like Hamlet, if he can fly away, change the place, then why does he . . ?"

She covered her mouth and doubled up. "It's not funny, Eddie. It doesn't make any sense."

"What do you mean, not funny? You just don't get it. You eggheads have no sense of humor. Come to think of it, I don't really get it either. Thought *you* might be able to explain it to *me*. Blame it on my brother. He told it to me. Maybe you should marry my brother. He's an egghead too." She shook her head rapidly and gathered a handful of his shirt fabric into her face. She said something Eddie couldn't catch. "Know something? You are a terrifically good-looking human bean. Don't scrunch your nose up like that. It'll leave little lines."

They turned at random onto Locust. Eddie no longer knew where they were heading. He considered asking Sarah about the Drunk and the Lamppost. They peered into low-lit living rooms, intimate domestic scenes that were fair game from street level, each holding the secret of how to get by but revealing nothing. They slowed again, as if only faint streetlamps, the hollow moon, chill air, sidewalk cracks, the smell of a cold front rushing down a street already folded and put away for the night, only this collected instant, could lead them to the specific weight and exactness of the world. They had fallen upon the legendary *there*, or as close as they could push to it, and all life after tonight would amount to trying to re-create *this* moment.

At last Eddie broke the spell. "One thing I have to ask you. If you ever *do* marry somebody, if you *do* decide that it's okay to bring children into this world, don't name them after their parents. You know: Junior. What can you do then, besides join Order of the Arrow, or some other Elk-induced, paramilitary, junior chamber of . . ?"

Sarah listened to him trail off. She thought for a minute that they were going to stop under a shed maple, but they did not. When the chance was lost, she said, "Thanks for talking me into that movie. I'd read a lot about it, but none of my long-hair friends would ever deign to go near it."

"No kidding. You mean you've never seen that film before? One of my favorites. Classic animation. 1940. Happens to be one of the few old-timers I *have* seen."

"Admit it. You've seen them all."

"Have *not*. But this one I love. My favorite part's when that little rodent goes up and pulls on the old guy's tuxedo tails. I always want the maestro to turn around and go, 'Eeeek, plague.' "

She hit him again, and her grace brought them back to innocence. They compared favorite parts. She liked the Bach best, although she felt that the transcription was a little heavy-handed and inauthentic. Eddie liked the little colored horses with wings.

"And speakin' of rats and plagues and all," Eddie said, alluding to Mickey and Stokowski, "I learned something unbelievable this weekend. From Big Brother again. Did you know that 'Ring around the Rosie' was first played by little kids during the Black Death? It's all about those lumpy sores and how they had to burn the bodies and all."

"Yes, I remember reading that somewhere."

"It's not fair. You can't be attractive and know everything, too. Make up your mind and specialize, like everyone else." Sarah declared that her specialty tonight was Donna Reed. So they took it again, from the top, with feeling. "Buffalo gals won't you come out tonight, come out tonight, come out tonight. Buffalo gals won't you come out tonight. And . . . dance . . . by . . . the light . . . of the moo-ooon."

"God, you're beautiful."

"Let's not be blasphemous, now."

"What? I didn't say nothing. I said, *Gob*, not *God*. 'Gob, you're beautiful.' I've got a great idea. How about you and I . . ?" He took her elbow and pointed to her mouth, then to his, waving his index finger back and forth between the two, inquiringly. She nodded almost imperceptibly, and they kissed a tentative exploration.

Eddie felt that it was almost impossible to be less than an inch from the face of another without wanting to shout love like a signed confession. But somehow he did not. He said instead, "Mmm. Oh! That was perfect. Now *that's* ecting."

Sarah looked off shyly. Facing away, she said, "You wouldn't be kissing relative strangers while keeping a certain Barbara Simms sequestered off on the side, somewhere?"

"I don't know. What does *sequestered* mean?"

"How about *duplicity?* Know that one?"

"Duplicity. Dee-you-pee-el-I-cee-I-tee-why. Uh, that's when the half note gets the beat, right?"

She mugged a look of long-suffering. "Men."

"You've got me all wrong. No kidding. I'm really a shy kind of fellow. 'Thrift, thrift.' I stand helpless in the express lines behind those people who try to sneak in with thirteen items. I want to tell them off, but I can't get up the nerve. See . . ." He faced her, taking both her hands in front of him. "I'm really emotionally scarred, underneath. There was this traumatic incident when I was two, when I tried to cut an English muffin with a knife, and my mother came howling out of the next room, screaming, 'Fork!' I've been virtually spineless ever since."

She took his arm, patted him gently on the back. "Maladjusted, are you? Poor boy. Tell me, what was the greatest embarrassment of your life?"

"Hmm. Tough one. Let's see. There was the time in Sunday School, when we were saying the Lord's Prayer just prior to heading off for the work week, and we got to the big finish—kingdom, power, glory for everandever—and I just kept going on with the Hobson evening version, 'God bless Mommy and Daddy and Lily and . . .' An unfortunate solo that my peers did not soon let me forget. How about yours?"

"Well," she grinned a sheepish, demure, but absolutely fetching overbite smile that made Eddie squeeze her shoulders in appreciation. "Last summer, when I went to Red Fox Music Camp on full scholarship, I stepped off the bus in front of the entire music faculty and my suitcase exploded and all my clothes came bursting out."

"Oh, Jesus. How indiscreet. Come on. You can do better than that. Let's talk real embarrassment. You know Paulie Kogan, the stocky guy with the wire rims? Last year, we were supposed to do weight training for some stupid jock thing or another, and he comes to me and says, 'Eddie, don't pick me up tonight. I'm leaving town on a family thing.' 'Oh, what's up?' I ask. 'My dad's dead,' he says. And before I know what I'm saying—stupid, middle-class, knee-jerk—I say, 'Oh, I hope he gets better soon.' You wanted embarrassment." They fell silent; stupid, middle-class, knee-jerk silence. Sarah sensed it wasn't *Paulie's* dad that stopped them in place.

Eddie, brave as the recollection was, kept back the real contenders for the title, the public incidents involving Pop and his proclivity that he might consider telling this woman after he got to know her better. Like in another twenty years. He assumed a virtue, and continued comically. "My life is one continual embarrassment, really. Confusing Lerner and Loewe with Leopold and Loeb. You know, pronouncing *epitome* like it looks. I hate being at the mercy of words. Gonna hafta learn a few one of these days."

Sarah stopped. She pulled Eddie to her, and returned the previous favor. To cover her awkwardness when they drew apart, she said, "We ought to do this walk again in the spring, don't you think? I love it when it's rained lightly while you are in the theater, and when you come out, everything smells of earthworms and something about to happen."

Eddie matched her voice, enthusiasm for enthusiasm. "I know. How the air fills with spore cases. You know, how when it rains, water trickles off of tree branches and lands on those bungalow-looking structures? Here's a couple." He produced an imaginary sample. "They grow up around the tree trunks, and then the water force makes them release this powder into the air."

It was, he was suddenly aware, not one's standard high school dialogue. But something about Sarah made him trust her without being able to help himself. Anything else would be that word: *duplicity*. "Here's one. Go ahead; tap it. The spores are in your hair; let me help." He held her strands up to the light. "These are among your more serious fungi. They aren't ones to dance around in fairy rings to *The Nutcracker Suite*, for instance. And look, see how the water pulls itself into spheres on the surface of the leaves? And underground . . ." He overturned a rock, revealing nothing but the frozen ground.

"Bugs!" Sarah exclaimed, a cry of complete fascination. Eddie was astonished at her response. They had somehow jumped together into the same lost place. But since she had proved herself perfect in every other way, he took this additional sympathy in stride.

"Sure. The night's when they really come out. More beetle activity per square leafstuff at night than anyone imagines." It was below freezing, and crouched on the ground, they could not help but start to feel it. She was on her knees beside him, peering intently. He put his arm lightly around her, gratefully. "Not too many of them this far north, this time of year. November's tough on the food chain."

"What else?" she said. He had seen that look before, a genuine interest in whatever there was to learn. The discovery of the complex world under the rock, making the world above it almost livable.

"I think," Eddie said, standing and unfolding himself slowly, "that if I hadn't already made a complete botch of my future, that I would have liked to make a living doing this, what we were just playing at doing. Digging around in the leaves, studying bugs."

"An entomologist!"

"I'm pretty good at sketching with a pencil, and I can look at things for hours without blinking. I just like to watch life. Maybe see something nobody else has yet."

"Good Lord, boy. You talk like the chance is gone. Do it, if you love it."

"Naw, it's too late already. Don't have the grades. And I'm not so good at the studies part. You know, turning it into a science, with math and all. My sister Rach got all the math genes. She didn't even have to study it. The formulas were just there, intact." He fell silent. Then he began to walk in circles, animated again. "But think of all these combinations, under our feet. The size of it. The possibilities." Sarah stared at him with a look of incredulity, which he misunderstood. "Sorry. I get that way as the night goes on. As the saying goes, 'That's . . .' "

"Don't say it!" She sounded violent.

"How did you know what I was going to say?" Eddie joked. But he had upset whatever she had been feeling about him. They strolled again, turning by accident almost to the front of the Hobson house before he noticed. "Hey! Look where we are." The soul of Second Street. "How did we wind up here? I thought the gentleman was supposed to walk the lady home." Sarah made a joke about the Equal Rights Amendment that Eddie didn't understand and was afraid to ask about.

"Well, I'd ask you in," he apologized, "but I'm afraid my motorcycle-gang–intelligentsia family would work you over." She was the first friend he could remember being reluctant to take inside.

"I'd love to meet them, actually."

"Well," he waffled. "There's just the four of us. The party's over. My older brother and sister have jumped ship. Chitown. The remaining three would probably grill you until you confessed."

"Don't be so down on your family."

"I'm *not* down on them. They just never know what to make of my friends." After an awkward pause, Eddie added, "Want to sit in the yard for a while? We can dig up grubs, or something."

Sarah nodded eagerly. She smoothed her skirts and began to settle into the cold front lawn. Eddie shot a nervous glance front-porchward. "No, the backyard; it's better. Darker. We've got a swing rigged up, too."

As they skirted the side corner of the porch, they ran right into the cameo Eddie had dreaded. Pop's face, as drained of blood as the Mariner's, loomed up through the dark storm windows, disembodied. Sarah let out a sharp, frightened shout. "Wave to him," Eddie said, taking her by the hand. "Humor him." When they reached the backyard, he put on his most deferential face and said, "That's my dad," hoping to ease the situation by stating the obvious.

It didn't work. Sarah was absolutely peaked, as white as the apparition itself. "Oh, Eddie. He's sick. What's wrong with him?"

"I told you, I don't *know* what's wrong with him." And to joke away his having spoken more curtly than intended, he added, "We're running forbidden scientific experiments on him. Don't tell anybody, all right?"

Sarah sat on the tree swing and Eddie pushed her gently. They talked the quick, idle, expendable talk used to gloss over sudden shocks. He commented that they hadn't mentioned Top 40 all night, and that she was a disgrace to her age group. She thanked him. Then, bearing out that very observation, she returned becomingly to the matter. "Tell me everything you think you can about your father."

He caught her at the apogee and held her waist until she released herself with the kind of brushing kiss one might give after two decades of shared uncertainty. "What do you want to know about him?" Eddie began. "He cleans his teeth with strips of cellophane from Lucky Strike cigarettes. And when Mom's not around, he tells me shocking—what's the word for when the first letter of every word . . . ?"

"Acronym?"

"Yeah. He invents shocking meanings for the L.S./M.F.T. acronyms on those cigarette packs. He's . . . well let's see . . . he was in the army. But then, so was everybody's dad. During the war. *The* war. Is this what you want to hear?"

"Tell me everything that you think I should know."

"His brother got killed in some freak airplane crash. Stateside, was the weird thing about it. One of the central events of his life, as far as I can make out. With him every day, since."

"Is he morbid?"

"What do you mean: does he get schnockered once a year religiously on the date? Not really. No death shrines. No; it just sort of left him with this freak sense of humor."

"Black humor?"

"Coal dust. He's funny, all right, only . . . only everything's fair game. A kind of sarcasm, but not sarcastic. He jokes the way people hug at fiftieth-year reunions: too much back-slapping, when what everybody really wants to do is kiss all those shattered faces and weep. He parodies everything. He never repeats the standard jokes. Dad would never do a one-liner for the one-liner's sake. 'All jokes walk in one line . . .' "

"Eddie?"

"Nothing. Just free-associating. He likes catchphrases. Pop is capable of saying, in the same breath, with the same degree of seriousness and importance, both 'There is more to any of us than any of us suspects' and 'The secret of happiness consists in not eating grapes just after you've brushed your teeth.' He is totally maudlin underneath. A sentimentalist who refuses to put himself at the mercy of caring what happens to other people."

Sarah sat on the now-still swing, her legs underneath her. She pulled her mouth to the side in an urbane twist. "You wouldn't have picked up any of that, now would you?"

"Me? How can you say that?" His irony proved the simple and unequivocal if self-attacking fact: *No Hobsons can be trusted.* "He wants to know everything. He reads everything, and then he gets talkative about it all, and drags everybody down into the facts with him. Funny. It's exactly the opposite with my brother, Artie. The two of them read a lot of the same books and everything. But the more Artie learns, the quieter he gets."

"And what about Number Three?"

"You talking about *moi?*" *Suppose this girl were already lost.* The terrifying thought shot up his backbone, and Eddie hunched over. "I say live all you can. You make things worse for everybody if you don't."

Whether she agreed or simply did not want to disabuse his simplicity, Sarah stayed silent. Eddie began talking faster, without looking at the woman he was swinging. "It's like Pop never made the compromises everybody else makes in growing up. He hit the age of twenty and looked around, you know, 'These people are *off the wall,*' and decided to regress to what the white-bread company calls the formative years. You know, try it all over again from the top. For instance, he's got this hobby . . ." Eddie trailed off and tried to push the swing. But Sarah would not lift her feet from the earth where they dragged.

"No. Tell me. Don't be embarrassed. My father plays with model trains."

"Really? Does he? Well, I suppose you could call Pop's thing a model-train set. A surreal monstrosity of a model train. He plans this . . . You wouldn't get it. I don't get it. He plays at city planner, on the sly. Cheaper than golf, see? And you don't need an opponent."

Eddie put his hand inside her open collar and tentatively, almost frightenedly, rested it on her deltoids. "What can I say? The man's my dad." She touched her hand to his, not to arrest his forward progress but to give him the powerless gesture of comfort. And to direct him to the right place.

Eddie talked into the black air. "They say if you want to see how the son is going to turn out, look at the dad. That means if you marry me— and I intend to make your life miserable until you do, and probably after as well—I'll be decked out on the porch in thirty years, like the Big Guy. My belly will be out to here, and my arms and legs will be this little around. And off to the vets' hospital. Sound attractive?" He understood that he had gone beyond the repartee with which she could live. His words had become ugly. There was no taking them back.

"But why are we talking to one another about our *folks?* We're supposed to be talking about how pretty your nose is." He touched the part in question. "Like it makes any difference what the folks are up to.

We're supposed to give them something to drool about. What a great time the kids must be having, so young and all."

She laughed, both at how he talked and at the new force with which he suddenly swung her. "Too high, Eddie."

"High? You haven't *seen* high yet. We need to achieve antigravity." She closed her eyes and kept still. The look of bravery that then crossed her face made him call out, "Know what? I'm crazy about you."

She opened her eyes wide and just looked. But she had the presence of mind to taunt, "What about Miss Simms?"

"Oh, I'm crazy about her, too."

All sophistication vanished, and she was once again seventeen. "Jerk! Play nice. That's not fair."

"Of course it's fair. Don't you think it's better, the more people you care for? And I'm crazy about those hippos and those twinky horses with wings, and the mouse, and the foreign guy with the music stick, too." He teased her mercilessly, until he found her on the edge of tears. "No, friend. It's you. As of tonight." She brightened. "Still, people are really okay by me," Eddie pursued. "Doesn't matter what kind of roof they put up to keep themselves dry, I guess. I defy you to come up with somebody I can't get along with."

"What about . . .?" She cast a furtive glance toward the white wood house.

"What about wh . . . ? *Jesus*. My family? I *love* my family. Whatever made you think . . . ?" She looked so hurt at his volume, so genuinely wronged, that he remembered the words that had, naturally, led her to that conclusion. "Oh, *that*," he said, eyes appeasing. "That's *ecting*."

Standing behind her, he put his hand deeper into her shirt. It fit nicely. She struggled up against him, to move his fingers to the right place. Feigning a bout of propriety, she said, "Those are my breasts, young man."

"I *figured* as much."

"Would Donna Reed do this?"

"No, Donna never let ol' Jimmy do this. Not without certification, anyway."

And they began to learn about one another in the nimbus of the back-porch light. When the world once more seemed to need speaking about, Eddie said, "Peaceful here. The backyard. A good month, November. Not so cold as you'd expect. I like it. And you?" Without waiting for a reply, he began to sing, "Won't you come out? Won't you? And? Dance?"

12

My dear Mrs. Swallow, you marvelous creature of habit:

You are my last certainty. I wake each morning to your daily ritual. I know by heart how you crack open the front door, a litmus test to see what century it is outside today. You haul out your body's bulk slowly on swollen ankles and close the door behind you. Your key slides the bolt shut so that even I can hear it. Then remarkable instinct takes over. Arthritic bird claws jab at the door handle, jerk it violently, testing its ability to withstand foreign invasion, baffling in advance the burglar's every alternative. Mrs. Swallow, I am glad you don't know how easily bolts buckle, panes pop out under the persuasion of jeweler saw and putty.

You head up the walk, take the first main right and you are off: Power Company, Phone, or Water—some public utility where you've worked since the war. But total security eludes you. Every other day you turn back after a block, something triggering the fear that this morning you forgot to check the door. You return to the stoop, execute a final handle-jerk. ''I thought so,'' you think; ''But one must be sure.'' Locks against alternatives, as if they could keep the outside out. As if every lock could not be beaten. You lose confidence in your current deadbolt. You put on a stronger one, test it. You walk to work, stop, double-back, test it again. All a dare, an invitation to escalate. New preventions lead to better burglars.

What drives you? Was your house robbed decades ago? Mrs. S, apocalypse cannot strike a town this size twice. Your trauma is an inside job. Two competing camps split the world down the middle: those who believe precautions keep crime at bay, and those who see that Mrs. Swallow's

burglary takes place daily. Sorry to say, you must
include in the second your neighbor,

Lily Hobson Leeds

Dear Mrs. Swallow,

Sorry to end so abruptly, but I did not sleep last
night and needed to close my eyes. I'm afraid I'm back
to naps again before noon. I did not mean to judge your
little ritual, no more predictable or pitiful than my
own. Mrs. Swallow's burglars. Mrs. Swallow: the bulk,
massive ankles, probing birdclaws and darting eyes,
whose concern for the nest steals her liberty, whose
self-protection cuts worse than snares.

Species-instinct, or true habit? On certain days,
your obsession takes you by the brain stem; you come
back twice or more, surrendering to extended handle-
wrenchings, a bird-mechanism gone wrong, the swallow
smacking suicidally into an expanse of plate glass,
thinking it the promised opening to spacious places.
But if I ever woke in mid-morning to total silence: I
feel the panic just imagining it. Only your audible
insistence that outside forces threaten you reassures
me that none has yet carried out the threat. You are a
comfort to me, wrenching the handle, protecting private
interests, interests that keep you under house arrest.

You head out each morning for your post, to hover over
switches, pipelines, or huge parfaits of trickled
power. Or maybe your line is customer complaints.
That's it: you work in Service, answering the accusa-
tions of injured parties. You staff a window: Insults
and Injuries. All complaints left on your desk at day's
end you get to take home.

Back in the unentered house, you line them up on your
mantelpiece, scatter them across endtables: other
people's injuries, the heirlooms you surrender your
peace to protect. Someone tried to take them from you
once. Now, each morning, it grows harder to leave them.
Knickknacks, bric-a-brac, your near brushes with others
accumulate through your rooms. Proof that you have
lived. Please add to the stockpile of entrapping stuff

these thoughts from your admiring neighbor, lost at home for much the same reason.

Lily L.

Mrs. Swallow,

One more shot at this, my own obsessive handle testing, an exercise that will never go farther than this back room of my parents' house, even should I myself ever again get it together to fly the coop, which each day seems less and less likely.

My father is fond of saying that only habit can break habits. Only I'm not sure that <u>habit</u> is behind your self-protection racket. Habits cannot batter so hard as your behavior. Habits must have results to keep them from extinguishing. Yours is no habitual flinch. It comes from deeper in the nerves than learning.

I know from experience what threat you test your door against. You claw, shove, dare the latch to give way, not from fear of strangers but from need. You could no more skip your door-check than you could stop breathing. You could not live without this routine. It orders your remaining days, lends them a motive they would be pointless without. You do not really fear a burglary. What could thieves do against you? Toast the break-in with coffee from crocheted tins? Violate your photo albums? No, the one you really fear is the officer of the law, making his preventative rounds. What if <u>he</u> checks your door for your own safety, only to discover to his bitter disappointment that you have let the neighborhood down, fallen slack on the one job expected of you: the job of living by common precaution? This officer, whose duty is your peace of mind, becomes your daily, if well-meaning warden. Meanwhile the true thief, never far from the scent of security, hearing your desperate door-shaking from her post in the window next door, thinks: ''Such measures! Here at last is something worth stealing.''

Your thief is here. The house next to yours threatens the whole neighborhood. Not fire or flood: nothing covered by the standard policies. The whole town is terrorized by my father's loving either/ors. I steal

205

the sounds of your predictable routine, your banging
and clattering. Your door—test is the noise that keeps
me moving. If I did not have you, my only sound would be
the total silence that means he has come downstairs and
collapsed on the front room floor.

How do you still hold out? I see you as a child,
stepping down the same stoop in seersucker, a century
ago last May. Look through your diaries and imagined
letters. Wasn't there a day when the fullness of wonder
slapped your hands, rebuked you for wanting too much?
How did you survive the spring? You have cut and dried
the old bouquets, wedged them away in your house. Your
claws bang the door on the vanished garden behind it.
You lock and bolt the warehouse of faded spices,
preserving your remnant of May.

I see you in your hair—bobbed youth, running with a
crowd like the one I ran with, demanding new rules in
the neighborhood. Your ears ache from the urgings of the
popular press, the war to end all War. My crowd's was a
different jungle deadlock: ''We had to destroy that
village in order to save it.'' What did you say at
twenty, to the charm of paradox? Did you already give in
to the madness of testing locks? I did not, not yet. I
took up the challenge to sanity, the call for conviction. I can't bring back that exact shade of those words
now. Old formulas, embarrassing, dated, naive.

I see you at the moment of choice: resist or be lost.
My crowd, for our part, resisted. We made resistance
into a game. I became a marvel of Magic Markers and
posterboard. You had a different call to arms. While you
kept the home fires burning, we lit up the town hall
steps with draft cards. You see, we thought the future
would be what enough people agreed it should be. And we
were sure that belief was all the agreement we needed.

Your movement, like mine, must have breathed for that
much—awaited return to safety when extraordinary measures would no longer be needed. Our cause was the day
when our cause could disappear. I hoped each protest
march would succeed and be the last. How did your fight
against so obviously evil an enemy turn into ours, born
in the best of intentions, one sunny day deciding it had
no power to stop the next escalation short of resorting
to the virtuous letter bomb?

Our movement splintered in two. Half said that it was better to play fair and get beat; to stay clean-handed, or destroy our own goal. The other said that dead and virtuous was still dead. I had to choose: go under with the ideal, or throw it away on pragmatics. Worse: what if we won? We could only free our hostages by jailing just as many jailors. The best we could hope for was a pointless exchange.

And from that day forward, my resistance trickled away. My involvement vanished into a vague policy of personal prevention. Once, I had felt compelled to clean up the world; now it seemed enough for me merely not to litter. Only whoever touched the piece of trash last was responsible. Is that what you came to, too, Mrs. Swallow? Knowing that all you could do to quiet the howling is to keep silent?

I see you at forty, discovering the bind, and from that day deciding that the best you could hope for was indefinite postponement. That it sufficed for you yourself not to make things go wrong. And that is as far as you have gotten. You pull your door behind you with historic obsession. Ten yards down the street, you double back, wondering, ''Have I remembered, or was that yesterday?'' And in following prevention to the letter, you exempt yourself from active guilt. ''I took all precaution, and the world robbed me anyway.''

I watch you for evidence of the last phase coming on. Soon, we will surrender even our small acts of prevention, reduced to feathering our own swallow-nests. At last, you will give up your routine, lie in bed, think that it is enough to pray your burglars away. But we will both be, at the end, criminally negligent, criminally apart. In stopping no crime, we will be guilty. From active to passive to self-protective: we are stuck, at the doorknob, between effective and correct, stepping into the trap in order to defuse it.

That is why I write you unpostable letters late in the day, a day I should have spent looking for work, or an apartment, or at very least, a replacement husband. I, unlike yourself, was not born into widowhood, but had to earn it. I was married once upon a time. You may find that a little hard to swallow. I did it to a fellow named Wayne Leeds, for my own unnaming. No one pressured me into believing that good girls marry. I did it perversely, to set back the revolution.

The whole thing lasted about ten months. Four months after we'd moved into our first home, still in the sunny honeymoon, Wayne—o took offense at something I did or failed to do. I've tried daily to remember the issue, but to this minute it eludes me. After my sin of omission, Wayne changed. He began a campaign to elicit from me the magic words that would clear things: an apology perhaps, or a retraction. I would have given it gladly, had I any idea what he was after. But he wouldn't tell, and it was no good asking. I had to divine it myself or it wouldn't be valid.

He thought I refused to confess the magic words to spite him. But I swear this once I wasn't being willful. I simply could not read the man or what he needed. Nothing I did would wash; yet, Wayne—o insisted that something I should do would help, if I only cared for him as much as I cared for myself. One day he took to breaking things. Monday, my guitar. Tuesday, my Rubaiyat. After several days of attrition I was down to subsistence, and I decided to break the contract.

But leaving wasn't the secret word Wayne was waiting for. Just the reverse. If he wasn't over the edge before, my threatened departure pushed him over. He went through an outline of textbook reactions. First he feigned delight. Then he took to pleading. Then he went into the basement and came up with ten feet of rope. He set it on the coffee table, which I owned with some shame. When I couldn't figure out his gesture, he erupted in rage. Before I could stop him he was out in the yard, tying the hank to a tree branch. It was raining heavily, very dark. I couldn't make him out. I stood on the porch waving a six—volt light, not daring to come a step closer. Wayne positioned himself to give me the best view, but it was just too dark. All I could make out was a shadowy figure darting in and out of the globe of my six—volt. Then he stopped and after a moment of silence said, ''You think I won't do it, don't you?'' But I honestly didn't know what he was threatening. ''You think I won't? I'll do it. Just try me.''

Then I understood, and every scrap of admiration or mystery that the poor male had ever commanded in me dissolved, and I just didn't care what path he took. He put me up there in the branches instead of him. Or I had beat him to it. I shut off the six-volt, went back into the house, and began looking up bus schedules out of town.

For several minutes he stood in the dark rain, yelling, ''You think I won't? You just leave, and try me.'' I'm surprised the neighbors never called the police. Families all up and down our block must have huddled in their living rooms, listening to the cries of this mad boy seep through their storm windows and insulation. In a few minutes Wayne stopped. He reappeared in the house, the rope coiled neatly around his arm. He went down in the basement and put the coil back where it belonged. When he returned, he was more than civil. He even helped me with my bags. And he's stayed that way ever since—the annual Christmas cards, the occasional phone call, always so dignified.

But when I see my ex-husband now, or hear from him, no matter how self-possessed, I see him in that moment when the trapdoor opened under both of us. He is not a person, but an infantile need. And he knows that I see him that way. Given a chance, I'd make another try to live with him in peace. But every boy carries a variation on hanging himself in the backyard branches, in the rain. At least the one I saw did. I love nobody. I feel I am on the verge of loving everybody. Then I step outside my room. And he is waiting there.

Mrs. Swallow, pull the latch, bang it, twist it left and right, but never suspect that we lock our burglars <u>inside</u>. He is here, that boy, hiding where I have come to escape him, playing a more sophisticated version of the same rope trick. My father, blacking out, seeing things. He brushes his teeth and his gums bleed. ''You think I won't do it, don't you?'' He spends long hours late at night, inventing a protest, an alternative history, all the details tailored to suit him alone. My father lives in this place, his third spot between the effective and the right. But in the boy in him, written on his heart, is a trapdoor, a rope, a tree, out in the darkening backyard.

If he had a stroke, who would I go to, my brothers and sister gone, and my mother in pieces? Who would come

stop him if he set the house on fire, or took to breaking
things? No one, no one at all, up and down this
evacuated, silent and A—framed street except the
neighbors. You, Mrs. Swallow. I am condemned to come to
you. There is no one else. You must lend me your answer
to being alive, the force that keeps you here in one
piece long after you should have gone home. You must
teach me that love for the trap that keeps you rattling
the locks, refusing to quit resisting, to give up the
senseless ritual as lost.

You must tell me how to care for the man, instruct me
in that stupid, repetitive checking. A care indifferent
to the consequences. Compassion unconcerned with
whether it is effective or correct, a routine, like
laundry or trash. You must give me your trick, or I will
steal it.

As it is, I barely have the strength to evade another
day of Classifieds. Someone is out in the dark backyard,
swinging. Tonight, it is just my little brother and his
newest charmer. Pop's off in Hobstown, gum—bleeding, or
passing out. Mother is abiding. Across the way, you read
by kitchen light, browsing a hardware catalog for
security supplements. You prepare for bed, slip under
the covers, certain of today's lesson. In another
minute, you are in that place where there is no fight
between right and efficacy.

But you will only be there an instant before you bolt
upright. You have forgotten to check. But it will be too
late. Someone will see your oversight of locks. The
long—feared burglar will have broken in. Running up to
your bedroom in the dark, breaking your heirlooms all
the way, she will burst in upon you, shouting fire,
shouting help me, shouting save the man, shouting do not
be afraid, it's only your neighbor.

1943

In a suburban London movie theater in the spring of 1943, Alan Turing sees a matinee of Disney's masterpiece, Snow White and the Seven Dwarves, the first feature-length animation. Turing, at the tender age of thirty-one, has already been as instrumental in saving England and the entire Allied war effort as any other single human. Without firing a shot, he keeps his green island afloat in the blood-dimmed tide of Nazi bombers and submarines. He gives civilization this second chance by tapping into the mind's miraculous ability to model and simulate. In the apocalyptic game, where victory goes not to the side that can wage the most violence but to the one that second-guesses better, Turing has discovered a way to find out what the other side's murderous millions are about to do.

He steps from the darkened theater into the blinding light of midday. Still savoring the film, though this was not his first viewing of it, he lets his eyes adjust to the grainy light of the wartime street before heading back to his office, a nineteenth-century estate named Bletchley Park, fifty miles from London. From this headquarters, Turing and a cadre of mathematical brains provide the steady stream of hypotheses needed to crack the German Enigma Machine code. Out of the gibberish of infinite decipherings, Bletchley Park strains the sole meaningful reading. Thus able to put her ear to the channel and clearly hear the Enemy's next step, Britain's casualties plummet and her inflicted toll soars. We now know Them as well as they know themselves. So long as Turing and Company continue to corner Information, the world's crucial commodity, their side will come out the victor.

Behind his desk, a sheet of numbers in front of him, Turing replays, in mental images, the scene from Snow White that terrifies him far more than any petty attempt by Aryans to set fire to his city: the Wicked Witch, *preparing the lethal apple intended for Snow, invoking, "Dip the apple in the brew, let the sleeping death seep through." The imaginary image appalls the young man. He knows, firsthand, the power of animation over live action. For the skill that has given him the upper hand over the minions of evil is his ability to create a similar alternate world, to play a similar game of mathematical What If, to forge a crucible of numeric Maybe where real life can be smelted out and purified. The world must first be saved or lost on paper. That's why the Witch threatens more than Hitler.*

In his code-cracker's office after the matinee, Turing senses the real terror lurking behind the billboard. Far from springing the forces of good from this lime-tree bower their prison, the success of Bletchley Park in cracking the Enigma code lands the Allies in a greater dilemma. Turing supplies High Command with advance warning on all manner of dangers: he foretells the bombing of Coventry, with its consummate cathedral. He announces the threat to flights carrying Churchill and Leslie Howard. High Command must choose: save the cathedral and tip off German Intelligence that their code is broken, or do nothing and preserve their Informational edge. Seated over his tabular data, Turing sees the double cut of that edge. It is our only hope for survival, yet we cannot play it for fear of losing it. Every loss we foresee but do not prevent is partly on our own hands.

Eleven years later, in 1954, publicly humiliated, Alan Turing will kill himself by eating a cyanide-painted apple just like the Wicked Witch prepared for Snow White. The act will be Turing's terminal testimony to the frailty of the line dividing mental imagery and life as lived. Disney will read the account of his handiwork in the trade press. The next year, the father of animation will commemorate the father of simulation by building a fantastic kingdom for the consumer of fantasy, a live-in monument to our ability to cross over from the unlivable emptiness of Here into a smaller world.

On the same day that Turing returns from Snow White to the business of saving the Free World, on the other side of the Atlantic, safe inside an enclave of barbed wire, Disney's paroled planning committee finishes the final edit of a humorous short subject documenting the completion of the studio and set for You Are the War. The teaser runs only twelve minutes and is intended for Disney's private amusement, to show him what the community now has in hand for the still unscripted project.

The sole existing print catches up with Disney in New York, where he has flown in search of the ingenuous time traveler, Bud Middleton, whose ability to portray the quintessential American boy is the make-or-break element in Disney's grand plan. Walt receives the single spool with excitement. He closes himself off in a private projection room and threads it up. He is much amused by the hand-lettered title on the opening frames: The Furious Phase. Next come the credits: "By Grumpy, Dopey, Happy, Snisei, Doc, Doc, and Doc. And introducing . . ." A great pullback shot of the entire crew wipes into white, newsreel-style headlines: ". . . a Cast of Thousands!" The last shot of the credits, although meant to be funny, closes up Disney's throat with a sorrow beyond telling. It is an intercut of the old footage of Snow, making her surprising discovery: "Why, you're little men!"

An overdub of the theme music from Bambi trills while the camera pans across the enormous, living ordinance survey map of unsuspecting, frozen midwestern cornfields. A voice-over, perfect parody of a forties documentary narrator, quavers about how a band of home-front soldiers, at the insistence of their country, have lucked upon the ideal geography for establishing a model nation, for starting over from scratch, for beginning again. "From out of this absolute absence of features," the voice resonates, "this flat, empty tabula rasa, this blank slate of nothingness, can come anything at all, anything that a majority of folks agrees to put here."

There follows a comical, mugging, home-movie sequence of three men in gas masks, helmets, fatigues, rubber-sealed gloves, and, for some inscrutable reason, frogman flippers, wheeling on-camera a cylindrical lead canister. They prop the tube upright and motion to it with Chaplinesque jabs. Then one of the frogmen does a double take, realizing that the explanatory gestures mean nothing because the tube is turned around. The three reverse the cylinder with self-defeating efforts, revealing an amateurishly lettered sign reading FAIRY DUST.

After another round of ringmaster hand waves, the inmates stand back while the central figure removes the canister's top with exaggerated caution. He double checks his gas mask and dramatically unscrews what becomes the tube's lid within a lid within a lid. As he breaks through the *final seal, a host of animated sprites shoot out of the opened flask startling everyone, including Disney, a thousand miles and several weeks away. The spirit squadron buzzes the canister a few times, then disperses across empty fields. The camera cranes up and over the lid of the container. Inside is an earthen metal powder, which a second team of animators makes sparkle yellow-purple, an iridiscent glow carrying all the colors of the rainbow. The lens gives a quick glimpse before the gas-masked trio closes the flask gingerly.*

The corny voice-over elaborates: "What you have just seen is almost half a kilogram of Fairy Dust, squirreled away in precious allotments obtained from private, international channels, kept under the most stringent safeguards and security, saved for the most urgent occasion. That occasion is now, with the whole globe pitched in a battle where everything of value is at stake. This potent substance can turn a lump of pasty papier-mâché into a terraced garden." *Proving the claim, the next shot shows one of the masked soldiers, fingers glowing with a pinch of the invisible stuff, standing in the middle of emptiness. He opens his hand with a colored flourish and, following a perfect jump cut, the fields around him transform into a bustling downtown. The sequence repeats in another open space: a sprinkling of powder, and up springs a mountain range. Three times in succession the protectively clothed creature creates,* ex nihilo, *factories, scenic gorges, and quiet residential streets.*

The narrator explains, "This is no ordinary element. The dust derives its power by acting as the mind's prism. It is, in essence, imagination reified." *The unaccented voice claims that if used sparingly,* "and a mere fingernailful packs a punch capable of amazing things," *the stuff will bleed goodwill across their condensed country's borders, spilling over enchantment into the finished film.*

Disney is stunned. While much of the trailer is done with paint and models, he is nevertheless impressed by the work already accomplished by his pickup team. He watches the staff rally their talent for one final, curtain-closing tour de force. The narration spells out the theory of Fairy Dust more clearly, slowly losing its parodic quality and taking on something of the promise of the metallic glow itself. "Can this powder really turn a rock pile into the Rockies? Can it in fact turn a miniature model of a sleepy town into a living, breathing replica, as convincing as the original? Can it explain us to ourselves, show us why we must win this one or die trying? Can we be standing in the presence of the substance that will not only crack the back of the Axis and blow this war wide open but also blow the very desire to wage war loose from the face of this forgetting earth? We dare not believe. But think of what we lose if we are wrong, if we fail to give the stuff a proper chance?"

The final shot, mirroring the first, pans daringly over the synthetic mountains and simulated cities that now tower over the prairies, dwarfing the surrounding cow towns. World World. Nothing on this scale has been attempted since D. W. Griffith's Babylon set for Intolerance soared above the flypaper shacks on Sunset Boulevard back in 1915. The scope of the set suggests we fight another war this time, one that makes the first one look like 8 mm. The camera pulls all the way back, revealing the carpenters still extending the edges of the set, the voice-over urging the viewer to suspend judgment until hope casts its ballot.

The film flicks through the projector and flaps loosely against the take-up reel. The screen in Disney's private viewing room goes white and he sits motionless in the dark, making no move to shut off the machine. The crew has cast the footage as a bit of camp strictly for his own amusement. But under the burlesque of flag-waving, he hears his crew's own genuine hope in the restorative power of Never-never Land, calamine for a tortured and diseased world intent on betraying itself. He hears his ten thousand fellow internees ask how much a band of visionaries, armed with Fairy Dust, can do to correct history.

He feels the cast flexing its new freedom, gauging the odds against good intentions rising up irresistibly on the day the canister is finally uncorked. The final image of the comic short is so powerful that it undercuts its own irony. Real death, global snuffing out of people, slaughter for borders, economics, colored charts, and ideology, the glacial drift of perennially mucked-up national bickering: the whole bloody mess will fall away, the trailer insists, despite knowing better, if we can just tell the story of one person, tell the particular case fully and urgently and honestly, show how all that this fellow ever wanted is to get along and assist in the harvest of Goodwill. How can conflagration come of that?

If they can tell the Bud Middleton story convincingly and universally, the way to mutual trust might at last become clear. A life-size portrait of a fellow prisoner will reduce temptation to shoot before asking. Future dictators and demagogues will be laughed out of the beer hall. When they try to incite fear of the perfidious enemy, saying get the Jew, the Slav, the Asian, before he can get you, the crowd, having seen You Are the War, will say, "Who? Bud Middleton? You must be joking." The secret subtext of the project, which must convince even the wartime censors, is: We man the trenches opposite ourselves. The twelve-minute film spoofs itself for believing make-believe. But its makers can no more not believe than they can stop their own circulation.

Nevertheless, however technically impressive the World World set, The Furious Phase demonstrates to Disney that neither steering committee nor cast of thousands really knows whether "Wishing might make it so" has any empirical validity to it whatsoever. In the darkened preview room, celluloid flapping loosely around the reel, the attempt to remedy a world gone madder than a galloping cancer through any medium as silly as documentary cartoon seems ludicrous. This war is the largest coordinated endeavor ever undertaken by man. Brooklyn Bridge, Boulder Dam, and the Great Wall of China combined are weekend excursions in comparison. Every person on the earth is in on the activity, inspired by it. We make love to this employment. Nothing in the entire thread of human endeavor—not cathedrals, not astronomy, not high finance—comes close to our expertise in mutual destruction.

The real game, pieces stretching over Normandy, the North Sea, Suez, the Urals, the Caucasus, the Low Countries, Burma, Singapore, Saipan, Guam, and everywhere in between, is by far the greatest testament to human engineering and ingenuity, to what collective effort can put together. Beginning with vestiges of horse cavalry, it has already graduated to rockets and soon jets. And this war will be dwarfed by the next one, the quiet, extended chessboard stretching out over decades in unthinkable complexity of move and countermove, working up to its silent denouement. While technically true, it is certainly numerically insouciant for Disney to point out that all vegetation begins in the Bud.

For a moment, on the painfully white screen, Disney sees how immense, amorphous, and undeniably real the war is compared to what he means to do. For a moment, the war seems so ubiquitous and undirected as to make the definite article seem ridiculous. The scope and obscene speed of the unstoppable undertaking all around him splinters its monolithic façade and becomes a bouquet of operations: Overlord, Citadel, Greif, Punishment, Market-Garden, Barbarossa, Sledgehammer, Torch. Each involves millions of Middletons, but Bud, whether buck private or bird colonel, no longer has any real choice in the matter.

Disney sees, years before the demure textbooks point it out, that this is the first round of a permanent People's War. The accounts in the morning papers, with their line drawings and casualty counts, are so many box scores of mass suicide, the first universal violence that will take more civilian lives than soldiers'. Death will never again surprise us, coming in clean packets out of the sky, from underwater, across the sterilized earth, out of ovens and showers. The only weapon Disney has to fight the People's War is the People's Art Form. The madness of the human pageant got you down? See a Show. Out with the houselights. Break forth the Fairy Dust. Magic powder, absorbed into the lungs and capillaries of the audience, reduces Stalingrad, Dresden, and Buchenwald to you and the you you share the armrest with.

All he has to offer the lost cause of embraced carnage is a good cartoon. All he can do is show Bud Middleton in all his details, convince the audience that his story is their story. Within the confines of the darkened theater, the public's capacity to feel must seem crucial to the entire outcome of the collapsing planet. The caretaking of seasons, the survival of midwinter, is in small hands, the heart's private bonfire.

He shuts off the dead projector. He must pull off the task in a two-hour slice of everyday life with the ugly spots edited out. A stirring soundtrack, slick set, and pretty leads, Disney has long ago discovered, can convince just about anybody of anything. His movie can manipulate by cropping out, selectively deciding what not to show. World World, that prison-built set in the empty Midwest, must be his lever and his place to stand. He is insane even to consider going through with the idea. But the alternative is to send his staff back to the concentration camp.

The sheer enormity of the project makes Disney long for the far easier task of selling the war. Victory Through Air Power was child's play. Agitprop could come effortlessly: a little piece about the boys at Anzio getting nostalgic for the old neighborhood around Grauman's Chinese Theatre. He dredges up a dusty old bottle of Moxie from the inner recesses of his makeshift desk. He drinks it recalcitrantly, with no idea of how long it has been there. He considers the wartime dispersal of his colleagues—the *old Hollywood and Vine gang. He envies them; just about anything else he might have ended up doing for the war effort would have been unspeakably easier than what he is now considering.*

Walt rubs his ears for hours, wondering if Huston and Capra, at this very minute making documentaries and cheer films for the army, are having half as much difficulty overcoming the technical obstacles to believability as he. Capra's making Why We Fight. *Disney must make the far more problematic and unpopular* Why We Shouldn't Have To. *It occurs to him that Capra is a first-generation Italian.* We're at war with the Eye-ties too, right? What are THEY doing walking around free while we're locked up? *The suggestion is clear: national security is not separable from budding hatred.*

All the other big directors and producers are off making straightforward propaganda documentaries, nothing tormented about them. All they have to do is keep the camera vertical and the cameraman alive under fire. Major George Stevens, of Swing Time *fame, in the Atlantic with his "Hollywood Irregulars," heads up the Special Coverage Unit of the U.S. Army Signal Corps, directly attached to SHAEF. And there's John Ford in the Pacific, working for Wild Bill Donovan's OSS on his most spectacular and convincing western of them all. Ford wins both an Oscar and a Purple Heart for* The Battle of Midway, *while his buddy and genius cameraman Gregg Toland makes a feature on what Disney's blood relations did to the Pacific Fleet on the day of infamy.*

On the Home Front, the private morale-boosting business enjoys nothing short of a creative renaissance. The glossy war epic is the greatest carnivore to come to Tinsel Town since Rin Tin Tin. As a genre, the War Film runs the gamut from Casablanca *and* Watch on the Rhine *to* Four Jills in a Jeep. *Even Sherlock Holmes enlists in stemming the Nazi threat. The torrent of films following Hitler's invasion of Poland already leads to a Senate investigation of Hollywood warmongering and profiteering. The movie industry, emptied of 30 percent of its males, continues churning out celluloid wars as diversion from the real thing, all on the same topic from the same point of view. The sole task of these films—and Walt, in his professional capacity, has seen his share of them—as well as their chief source of revenue is to mythologize the fighting as if it took place somewhere in the distant past. While Huston and Capra and John Ford shoot real war footage on location with the original cast, countless*

Hollywood hacks throw together monthly remakes of The Prisoner of Zenda, *only in battle fatigues with interminable stock slaughter footage, all the love scenes taking place on South Pacific islands between the noncoms and their men. "Sarge, are you sc-scared?" "I'm always scared, son."*

What alarms Disney is not the relation between fiction and catastrophe, the profit and pleasure motives. *He considers how* Guadalcanal Diary, *opening even as he measures his next step, must have gone into production within a week of the outbreak of fighting on that island. Similarly,* The Mortal Storm, Waterloo Bridge, *and Fritz Lang's great* Man Hunt, *not to mention Abbott and Costello's* Buck Privates, *each released before we were even in the fray, either showed remarkable foresight or were privy to advance information.*

At this moment, it hits Disney with the force of religious revelation: We have done this. *We filmmakers. The world is in flames because we told people that they could cross the line into Anything Goes and get away with it. Leni Riefenstahl put that painter bastard in the hearts and minds of his people. She and Hans Steinhoff and Harlan. And our films, the Gold Diggers and Broadway Melodies: that's how we wandered into this mess, let it get out of hand. Films that said that Don Winslow and Doug MacArthur are the same guy, that nothing could get so fouled up it couldn't get extricated in the fifth reel.*

Now that the unreal has lured us into it, the war can only be *comprehended through the same portal. The war no longer has anything to do with the Casablanca conference. It is Rick and Ilsa. "You wore blue. The Germans wore gray." That is the only color scheme a captive audience can understand. Paulus versus Chuikov means absolutely nothing. Disney and company are guilty of entrenching the real fight, in most minds, between Münchhausen and Sergeant York.*

Well, he thinks: *if film launched us on the trip into the inferno, then the world's most famous film mouse must gnaw our way back out. But Disney knows the return trip will be far harder.* You Are the War *must tap into the same spirit of invention that led the pack into wholesale catastrophe in the first place. What happens on the World World set will be his most crucial work ever, far exceeding the routine war-bond drives. The project's particulars take on so overwhelming an importance that Disney resorts to the most potent source of creative inspiration of this era: plagiarism. The* stakes are so great, so much hangs in the balance, that nothing less than pinching from the old masters will do. About some things they are never wrong.

The technique he means to pinch is that view of Middle Americana going about its ordinary, small-town dance of courtship and romance that he has glimpsed two weeks before and still cannot shake. Disney has in mind to create on the World World set a full-size mock-up along the lines of the town in It's a Wonderful Life. Disney, a member of the inner circle, has had a privileged early look at the project, and finds it a masterpiece. Capra has shown him the working script, but because of his involvement with Why We Fight, the country's other Italian Navigator won't be able to start it until after we win. Disney's idea is to place that haunting scene between the youthful romantic leads, sweetly and greenly crooning a "Buffalo Gals" duet, against the backdrop of a world gone wholly and irrevocably insane. Then the audience, turning from their cozy, ordinary lanes down a back alley where bodies hang like piñatas, sliding from Second Street to Second Army, an encirclement too big to fit onto the atlas page, strolling from Bedford Falls into global Pottersville without noticing, will realize that the fate of their own town truly relies on two billion sets of single votes, the sum of uncountable and inconsequential Middleton middlemen.

For the sake of the future, he decides to steal that love duet that everything depends on: the hidden chain of connections inherent in George Bailey's saving his brother from the sledding accident. Only this time, the script will run: if Bud isn't here doing his part, he will trigger a series of cataclysms that won't stop short of the ignition of the earth's atmosphere. For the film to work, the layout must not tip off where the cultivated atrium of Bud's life leaves off and the genuine garden-at-large begins. You Are the War must have no border, no chalk seam proclaiming "Fairyland Ends Here. Now Entering the Real Thing." The two must gradate smoothly into each other. The audience must believe, for two hours, that Bud's decision will determine what awaits them outside the theater.

For in truth, everything depends on the successful application of Tinker Bell's delivering powder. Neither Anzio nor Peenemünde nor indiscriminate civilian carnage renders World World's cause so desperate. Something else has been let loose, something the Dwarves know little about, something Disney himself has only briefly glimpsed. George Stevens drops

Disney a quick note about it in the winter of '43, from his toehold in Britain: "There's something on the continent, deep inland, something immense and terrible, awful beyond considering. . . . Rumors of it are everywhere. . . . I'm bringing the cameras when we at last get ashore, but I don't know if we dare look on it, let alone film it."

He cannot name it, but Disney knows that the terror deep in Central Europe already spreads outward. His own country, in the cold light of necessity, considers sending against the Japs incendiary bombs tied to the legs of bats. The idea is sponsored by the United States Navy and the Army Chemical Warfare Department. Is the charter of Disney's film, then, any more fantastic? It is no more desperate, no more urgent, no more surreal, no more irrational, no more hopeless, no more unrealistic, no more misplaced, than the world it hopes to save by simulating. He sees clearly, as definitive and cleanly lettered as that flask the keystone frogmen uncorked: history conspires toward what we decide to rescue from the pyre. Out of the rubble of Central Europe, in what will instantly become the polarized battlefield for the next showdown, a German will put the idea perfectly: "World History is the World's Fair."

Disney determines to escape that fair, deny the grip of necessity. He sets down the dusty bottle of Moxie, gives the same idea another twist: he will deny that reality exists. He will live only for escape. Put that way, all the evil he means to outdistance comes creeping back. Which is it? So much depends on whether the other hostage, the audience, dares to make the break along with him. Perhaps no crime was ever righted except through retaliation, reprisal. But he will try another angle just this once, before the light fails.

Already his crew has built a place, a little place, where little can trickle into big. They will man it with a mouse whom everyone recognizes and a boy whom everybody knows. Can it serve, for two hours, to improve upon the source? The answer to that ancient question, a reply from mid-century, will come to be called the Turing Test, after Alan Turing, the man who conceived and expressed it most succinctly. Turing's conclusion, before the Wicked Witch disperses it completely and expediently, is that a perfect simulation of a thing serves very nicely for that thing. Big can grow out of sufficient, collected littles.

The issue is moot. Whatever the prospect for success, Disney and company are already committed to the cash and carry. The nisei have no choice but to portray an ideal world and pray that the matinee crowd can chart their private route to it. They can only believe that belief is the only ticket out. They can only hope that the price of living can be paid by hope.

Disney fiddles with his dictaphone, brought along from coast to coast for just this purpose. He starts the recording and says:

My colleagues in Hollywood have an old saying: "If it looks like a duck, and sounds like a duck, and acts like a duck . . . then call it Donald."

He shuts off the machine and knocks out a telegram.

TEASER IS BRILLIANT. LAUGHED AND CRIED. PLEASE ADD TO SETS SHOWN ONE INTERIOR DRUGSTORE ONE JERSEY LOWER MIDDLE HOME ONE SHOWBOAT RESTAURANT ONE AIR FORCE BASE EMPHASIS REPAIR. BAD NEWS BUD MIDDLETON MORT AU GUADALCANAL. GOOD NEWS HAVE FOUND PERFECT REPLACEMENT.

He looks over what he has written and nods, convinced. He adds:

KEEP UP FIRST CLASS WORK. BACK SOON. REMEMBER THIS IS AMERICA.

He stops and reads the message. Something is missing but he does not know what. Finally, he supplies, with a perverse grin, the refrain from that old war-bond tune:

THIS IS WORTH FIGHTING FOR.

13

Dad stood in the Loop, anchored at Clark and Randolph, two weekends before Christmas, on the busiest shopping day in the most populous year in Chicago's history. More people than at any other moment in time wanted possession of the precise spot outside the bus station where Eddie Sr. now stood and were willing to be ugly, even violent, if need be, to achieve that holiday end.

At that exact moment, the world's population stood at four and a half billion, a fifth of a million being added a day. Eddie Sr. read those figures out loud from a magazine to wife, daughter, and son on the bus ride in. "A billion here, a billion there. Pretty soon we'll be talking *real people*. It's enough to make one suspect the sanity of the species." He proceeded to repeat the figures to a pretty woman of procreative age in the seat in front of them, asking if she would forego having children for the sake of the human race. When the woman reeled around in alarm, Lily flashed her a desperate look: *Please don't make a scene. The man is not well. We just have to get him through today.* To her infinite relief, the woman sassed back, saying that if the numbers he had just read out loud were true, she didn't see why another half-dozen babies made any difference.

And when the barbed-wire contingent disembarked in the terminal belonging to the line Rach affectionately branded "The Dog," they struggled up to street level to find themselves smack in the middle of five of those millions, a crowd of cognizant packages wandering aimlessly between porno theaters, dingy retail outlets, and monolithic civic art. Wedged into these few square miles by the lake were more people than had been alive in the entire country at the beginning of the last century. They gathered like grunion by moonlight, buying gifts for one another. And at their still hub stood Dad, breaking up pedestrian traffic, panning over the abstract multitude of strangers as if just now becoming aware of the awful miracle of fecundity.

Little Eddie, Ailene, and Lily stood on one corner of the Civic Center Plaza, trying to edge him on, anywhere, before his standing there doing nothing started a Christmas fistfight. But amid all the obstructing structures—the rows of Mies van der Rohe boxes blocking all views except the trough immediately in front of them—they could not answer that perennial Chicago question: which way to the lake? Mom and kids tried desperately to get their bearings, while Dad seemed perfectly content with staring at the immense Picasso sculpture on the plaza. He cornered Eddie Jr. Pointing at the famous ambiguity, he said, "My boy, I've finally figured out who this is."

Eddie Jr. did not want to hear his father's conclusion. "Looks like a pimple with a parachute on, don't it?" the kid diverted. Underneath his unexpected misanthropy, Eddie Jr. wanted only to avert the man until they could sign him over to the professionals. He could feel Pop flashing the seven warning signals. He could feel the man aching to try something as certainly as any mother can feel her five-year-old flexing to throw a good-night fit. But he could not head it off without provoking it. That was what belonging to a family meant.

Dad brushed off his son's aside and insisted, "No. Really. Look closely: think funny nose. Think big ears. Think bigger than life."

One or two seasoned Chicagoans stopped to look in the direction of the cubist commotion, which they had not glanced at for years. Finding no local celeb, no nut with submachine gun hiding in the rusting structure, they passed on. Little Eddie looked from Picasso to Pop and back again. Across the packed and desolate open place, a euphonium choir managed to make "Joy to the World" sound like "Smile Though Your Heart Is Breaking."

Unable to dislodge Pop from the spot, Little Eddie crossed a street at random and attempted to lose himself in front of a window-front elephant graveyard of consumer electronic goods bearing red fire-sale price tags. Let the man have his last wraps, he told himself. They were only downtown, after all, as a delaying action, simply to meet one of Pop's preconditions—a last look at the State Street Christmas windows—before putting the man in the hands of the Veterans Administration.

Not far away, Lily wandered over to the mundane protest rally that spread itself homogeneously across the plaza like a flock of birds under a winter feeder. She strained to read the bobbing pickets and placards. The issue seemed to be human rights in one of those subtropical countries where they extracted loyalty with cattle prods. Thirty people forming a fairy ring in Chicago to ward off a thing so distant and unstoppable so distressed her with its pathetic urgency that she returned quickly to the reconciled part of the world, that great majority to whom everything was all right so long as they were allowed to shop.

She returned just in time to rescue Mom from a lunatic fringe religious zealot of indesignate denomination who had just given Ailene a copy of holy scripture for free and now angrily demanded payment. "How come I always have to be the one who does the rescue work?" Lily asked, grabbing her mother by the elbow. "If I had been looking the other way, you'd be a Hare Krishna by now." She jabbed not so much at her mother as at Artie and Rach, conspicuous in their absence. Two weeks back they had promised, per Dad's request, to show up for the holiday meal, but both, out of what Lily knew to be premeditated cowardice, had reneged. Instead, begging off Thanksgiving dinner, they had arranged to meet the family when they came downtown.

Lily, persistent grassy-knollist that she was, considered their absence a mutually calculated conspiracy, and she held it against them. But all she could do now to retaliate was make sure that Hobson West kept its part of the appointment. Gathering Dad from the Picasso, Mom from the robed evangelist, and Little Brother from the seductive clutches of consumer electronics, she piloted her family through downtown disturbances toward their appointed meeting place.

Rachel and Artie at that very instant emerged from the underground Grant Park parking garage. Artie accused Rachel, "I would have gone if I had gotten any sort of encouragement from you."

Without letting him finish, Rach answered over top, "Don't blame *me* for making up *your* mind."

They paused for the obligatory book-gawking in front of Kroch's on Wabash. Glimpsing himself reflected in the bookstore's picture window, Artie sickened with a surge of self-revelation. Reflected there was the first telltale indication of what a genuine *nebbish* he had become: he'd managed to go the entire morning without realizing that his shirt was one button out of line.

The giggles of a passing pack of teenage girls convinced him: his ineptitude had gone public. For a long time, his terror of ending up alone had driven him into semiseclusion, a you-can't-fire-me, preemptive quitting. His deep need for conversation led him into increasing bouts of silence. But he had not until that moment suspected the broadcast signal clear enough for all except himself to hear. Hiding within the pristine button-down Oxford lay this declaration of secret slovenliness, a deliberate act of self-sabotage, a plea to the outside world for charity, like those plaintiff requests of "Wash Me!" written into the dust of neglected cars.

Witnessing his distress, Rach laughed out loud. She had noticed her brother's oversight an hour earlier when she picked him up. She had waited on edge the entire drive downtown, wondering how long the fastidious fellow would take to discover it. Savoring the slapstick inherent in his disaster, she squeezed his arm and wheedled, "Artie make a fox paw?"

The misbuttoning at once became his sister's fault. Artie filled with the urge to take retribution on her. He could hardly enjoy the instant justice of a lynching, even in the lawless Loop. So he contented himself with an unbelievably vile and colorful string of verbal abuse, a surge of potty-mouthing invective that stunned even himself the moment he put the finishing touches on it. He at once regretted having overreacted; his lack of restraint was, like his inability to dress himself, one more dead giveaway of his dissolution.

Far from taking offense, Rach greeted his creative profanity with astonished delight. She caught her breath and gasped, "I'll get you, my pretty, and your little dog too." She leapt at him, chasing him through the holiday-shopping crowd. Artie took off, hooking west on Madison toward the designated rendezvous spot on State Street, that Great Street. He dug into the icy pavement for traction, dispersing a flock of pigeons— little more in his estimation than rats with wings—all the while repeating to himself, under his breath, "I've become a self-parody."

Rounding the corner onto State, Artie once more felt that shopping, more than any other activity, was now the only thing everyone had in common. It had become our entertainment, work, social life, and culture, the only thing that got people outside anymore. A study in Brownian motion, Artie bounced from parcel to parcel, keeping a pretty good clip until he saw the family loom up out of the nine-shopping-days-to-Christmas crowd.

Swiss Family Hobson stood marooned outside Woolworth's, the folks looking nonchalant, Eddie Jr. trying to look jive, and Lily managing to look a little like Joan of Arc *after* the stake-out. Only here, as the dense exercise in human-population dynamics split into countless Markov chains and eddied about his familiar domestic group, did Artie finally see: they were lost, truly lost, as lost as that world in Pop's famous supposition. The Christmas crowd cut a circular bypass around them. They were clearly in quarantine, written off as injured, fair game to the herd's trimming predators.

Just as suddenly, the insight slid away from Artie as he noticed a side effect to Pop's problem, a symptom less dramatic than the lesions and visions and passing out and bloody toothbrushes. But it was no less shocking for being relatively benign: Dad was clearly *smaller* than Artie remembered him. The man had begun to shrink prematurely.

Artie, still eluding Rachel, easily could have checked his speed in time. Instead he slammed festively into the family group, grabbing hold of the big guy, intending to use him as an anchor to bring himself into orbit. But Dad's new weight wasn't up to the task. Lighter than of old, too, the man swung off-balance on Artie's impact. Only Artie's adept recovery kept them from crashing to the pavement.

"Ya gotta protect me. Pop. Yer daughter's after me and she's gonna . . ."

But Rachel was upon them already, adding her own momentum to the human pileup. Forgetting her original target at her first glance at Dad, she released her hold on Artie and grabbed the other man's body. She wrapped her thumb and little finger around Pop's wrist. Their tips joined easily. Her astonished face rose up, scolding, "Biafra!"

Dad laughed. His hat—a farmer's visor cap bearing De Kalb insignia, a winged, flying ear of corn for which he had frequently delivered Freudian interpretations—jarred loose in the collision. Rach reached up to right it, but Pop drew back and fixed it himself with a speed and severity that surprised the whole group. The little borrowed piece of pavement outside Woolworth's filled with mutual knowledge: each knew what that hat failed to cover up. Rach and Artie saw their suspicions ratified in their mother's eyes. All they could do was chalk up another symptom on the list. Somehow, overnight, the man had begun to lose his thick shock of black hair. Pop's parts began to shed in a waterfall in front of them. Unable to dam the flow, each picked a spot on their gloves to inspect. At last, the man who had created the moment of shared shame broke it. "Proceed directly to Christmas windows. Do not pass Go, do not address outstanding business."

Artie heard the voice of reason insist: *Good Christ, how can we be going through with this?* But he had no confidence in the practical support he would get from the others if he objected. Besides: what could another hour hurt? So Dad got away again, for one last afternoon. As this was his baby—the Platonic ghost of a child's remembered Christmas on Fifth Avenue a half-century ago—Eddie Sr. took charge, towing Ailene and the haplotypes along in his wake. They formed, against their separate wills, an All-Hobsons-in-Single-File parade through the indifferent, purchasing crowd.

Eddie Jr. brought up the rear guard, whining, "Guys. Guys. It's thirty degrees below, counting windchill. We gotta stop this Christmas noise and get indoors." The mid-December temperature had taken a perverse turn downward toward bleak midwinter. But in Eddie's begging was also that old romance of the dangerous cold. He beat his hands together and laughed, unable to feel his fingers. He gave in to giddiness, wondering if he would make it to the next shelter. He found himself agreeing with the bearish thermometer: something remarkable was about to happen.

Artie dropped back into step next to his kid brother, wondering what to say to a guy like Little Eddie. "So, kid. How was T-Day?" Artie's unsponsored memory offered: *T-1, T-2, T-3. When did you hit the beach? On T plus 3.* "Sorry I, uh, crapped out on you," he added, taking up the slack.

"Thanksgiving? S'allright. Hey! Remember that guy on . . . what the hell show was that? 'All right?' 'S'allright.' "

"What do you know about that? That show had been canned for years by the time you were conscious. I tell you: *my* generation might have its brains stuffed with half-hour scripts, but at least they're the *real thing* and not reruns."

"Hey. Blow, all right?"

"S'allright."

"Anyway, Thanksgiving was okay. White meat a little dry. Some calamity over Mom dropping a mincemeat pie on the kitchen floor. Can't remember. Seems like such a long time ago." Eddie let his voice trail off in Gothic parody.

"Dig for it, buddy. It's all there. You can tell me. You're blocking."

"Well . . . your father had an interesting story or two, as you can imagine. Guy reads too much. Wouldn't have half the problems he does if he'd just lay off the capital-L literature." Eddie borrowed a nervous habit from his brother and pinched the bridge of his nose. He unconsciously tried to make whomever he was talking to more comfortable by copying one of their physical mannerisms. With Dad, he winced. "Everything was fine. The Cowboys won. The usual. And your mother's bird stuffing . . ."

". . . makes up for a multitude of sins," Artie supplied.

"Yeah." At a commanding glance from the ringleader, the two of them brought themselves back into the column. They exchanged a quick, quizzical, unseen, misunderstood look. The slight tightening about one another's mouths triggered both boys to recall, in differing versions, that old favorite pedagogical chestnut of Pop's: Sometimes we need coaxing to act on our own.

Marshall Field's, traditionally the most extravagant of the window dressers, was the family's first stop. Field's theme this year was "Christmas Through the Decades," an elaborate, multiwindow display dug out of mothballs and restored to the splendor of all its elaborate moving parts. Each box of plate glass became a diorama devoted to its own ten-year period: Christmas from the 1880s to the present.

"How convenient," Rach commented. "They just pull it out every ten years, drop the oldest number, add a new one at the other end, and bingo. Ready-made nostalgia."

An unlikely assortment of decidedly contemporary people milled about history's windows. One exhibit was mobbed by a local television-news crew documenting the antique display as viewed by the contemporary audience. The crowd formed that magic toadstool ring that invariably collects around any video camera and microphone, the mere presence of broadcast electronics turning the banal into news. The TV team roared with satisfaction as kids with bits of crap around their mouths stopped in front of the older decades, saying, "What's with the funny hats?" or, "Why are all the streetlights on fire?"

The windows followed chronological order, south to north. Artie suggested under his breath to his brother, "Notice the layout? Up from the slums toward the Gold Coast. Every day in every way, things are getting better and better." His sardonic reading was in the next minute duplicated without the irony. A gang of materially blessed kids from Lincolnwood skipped from time portal to time portal, stopping to enumerate the milestones of progress each one marked: "Now they've got cars. Now they're getting *fun* presents, with batteries."

The double edge of the time line cut Artie until he could no longer stand it. Here they were, kept alive by the sight of their own past artificially preserved behind plate glass, waiting for the eternally improving future to bail them out of an obviously untenable present. For the first time since age twelve, he ran to his parents' side, although their protective spell had long ago deserted them.

At the sight of the moving parts—the butcher raising the killed goose by its neck, the man tipping his stovepipe hat to the pretty woman curtsying in cummerbund, the rocking horse, the sledders in stocking caps—Mom and Dad departed together into memory. "I remember my mother telling me about those kind of stoves. They were supposedly quite dangerous."

"The very first house I lived in, in Teaneck, had a fireplace exactly like that." Artie, calmed by the catalog of inconsequences, dropped back to take the decades at his own pace.

In front of 1900, an intimate interior of a living room with candle-trimmed tree as yet untouched by Ludlow, Lowell, Lawrence, or the Triangle Shirt Factory Fire, where a handlebar-mustachioed father read to several wide-eyed children decked out by the fire while mother sneaked about behind their backs, planting presents, Rach accosted Lily. "Admit it," she said.

"Admit what?" Lily demurred.

"Don't give me that. Just admit it."

"I don't have the foggiest idea what you're talking about. Admit what?"

In answer, Young Sister simply pointed to the porcelain-modeled mother, toy-bedecked, coming from the pantry with its icebox, grinder, and spices hanging from the ceiling. "That's you, isn't it? Taking our time with this decade, aren't we? Poor girl isn't getting dreamy-eyed, is she?"

Lily tried to brush her tormentor off, but refused to use her hands. Instead, she shoved her hips against her antagonist's hips and slammed her shoulders against Rach's, but kept her hands folded over in front of her, the chance of leprosy too great to risk pushing away persecution with bare skin. Rach persisted, "That's you. Admit it," while Lily, self-straight-jacketed, struggled against her, voicing vowels. A small altercation in the greater conflict all around them.

Artie came to the rescue. "What seems to be the trouble here, ladies?" Lily came and snuggled against him, turning her back against Rachel, closing her sister out. She kept her arms crossed, but pressed her head and winter-coated torso against him. She reminded Artie of one of those Raggedy Ann dolls whose arms are permanently sewn together. Her posture—armadillo ball—irritated him, one of those affectations of posture that he hated most about his sister, that drove him away from her. But he suffered her body contact in silence, neither recoiling nor reciprocating.

Her face still pressing her brother's heavy coat, Lily asked, "Artie, how much do you know about the project?"

"What project is that, Mrs. Leeds? The TVA?"

"You know what I mean." Her voiced flashed a sudden undercurrent of violence. "Pop's project. Hobstown." Artie nodded, but said nothing. "For some reason," she continued unnecessarily, "I picture it like this." She stretched her neck out toward Christmas in 1900, still in her protective posture-ball.

Banned from the club, Rach hovered behind them. She leveled her own opinion of Hobstown. "It *cain't* be anythin' lahk this. That's just wishful thinkin', honey-chile."

Lily defended herself without turning around to acknowledge. "Not like this *one*. Like the whole series. All the windows at once. Taken as an entirety." Neither sib said anything, and Lily added, "He is a history teacher, after all."

"Was," corrected Artie, and instantly hated himself. Here, in the unforgiving minute, the woman put herself on the line and all he could do was play the discriminating prig. "Now he's just another . . ." The attempted quick change to comedy didn't come off, so he abandoned the predicate.

Rach delighted in the wound her sister was widening. She thrust her head between the others, announcing, "I know exactly what Hobstown is." This disclosure produced two alarmed looks of disbelief. She waited the full dramatic measure, then began to sing in an uncanny reproduction of the famous bass: "Stalag by Starlight." Lily at last uncrossed her hands to hit her. All three laughed a little nervously.

Artie thought there would be only one way to find out for certain about the project Pop had occupied himself with all these years: espionage. He pictured himself breaking into Dad's archives and listening to the interminable monologues the man was always plotting. The very idea was as blasphemous as chewing on the Host. Just thinking of it made Artie look furtively toward his folks.

The others were several decades north, Eddie Jr. with a parent under either arm. Ailene was saying, "Isn't it clever how they've done the music? A bouquet of Christmas tunes. Each window has a carol from its own slice of time. Listen!" The three of them drew up to the 1940s, a snowy street at night, just outside a well-lit and now obviously suburban home. A young man in dress uniform stood poised on the snowy steps, his hands reaching for the knocker. About to make his presence known, the figure looked into the window of the protecting home, seeing an older couple poised anxiously around an ancient walnut-cabinet radio. The tune accompanying this window was "I'll Be Home for Christmas." If only in my dreams.

Eddie Jr. looked at his dad. As though the diorama glass were a funhouse mirror, the boy became a copy of those anxious parents, waiting for his child-father soldier to come home. For some reason, he expected his old man to respond horribly to the scene. Pop did nothing. Instead, old Eddie looked over at Ailene, who returned his look of complicity with another. They turned choreographically toward each other, took one another's waist, and, each submitting to the other, walked from the window into the below-freezing, mid-December, State Street traffic stream.

Dad started to sing, "I saw a man who danced with his wife in Chicago, Chicago," Sinatra style, and tried to waltz his woman. Mom resisted, laughing, self-conscious in the anonymous crowd. Eddie Jr. marveled. He had never before thought of his parents as a *couple*, bound together contractually and emotionally for all time. The unashamed little dance, now attracting grins from strangers, struck the boy as a miracle of defiance in the face of all that had happened and would continue to happen.

Only then, at that minute, did Dad start to go down. Eddie Jr., still tagging close by, grabbed his father by both elbows and held him up. "Easy, big guy. I've got you." He pretended calm.

The other kids, near enough to see what had happened, ran to lend their assistance. Ailene braced herself for the worst, turning her body into a contact block against the human current. Brittle distress pressed in on her. All she could think was: *Whistle. Where is the whistle to call the swimmers in, retrieve them from the surf and undertow?*

But just as Artie closed ranks and drew up to Dad's other side, ready to fight off five million to keep this one alive, big Eddie surfaced again. He pulled himself up, turned on them, and said brightly, "Berghoff's for lunch. Beat you there." He set off toward the restaurant, bouncing, leaving the others frozen in the lurch.

His five appendages stood riveted in place, shocked by Dad's sudden recovery from major incident. They had traveled the length of the decade dioramas, the quaint Christmas scenes, only to find themselves catapulted back into 1978. They stood paralyzed by the man's abrupt return to the present. Their brief nostalgic look backward dissolved, and they crashed back into now, the year that 4 prominent Soviet human-rights activists were sent to the gulag, the year that 917 religious cultists practiced mass ritual suicide in South America, the year that Pop disappeared from under them as State Street spread its simulated good cheer in all directions.

At last Rachel broke the stunned silence. "Berghoff's?" she asked incredulously. "Did he say *Berghoff's*? Mr. Antidisestablishedeatinghouse, Mr. Never-a-Sit-Down-Meal himself? Must be he wants to take us out for something other than pizza at least once before he kicks off." The joke's incredible bad taste straightened the group with a second shock wave. Mother and children stared at the felon, who made no attempt to defend her gag. Ailene had raised her offspring never to call long-lost friends out of fear of hearing of the loved ones who had died in the meantime. The very word itself was taboo, as if it could cause what it stood for. Now one of their own had spoken it. Lent had reared its ugly head, here in Advent.

But in the next minute, Artie laughed. Eddie Jr. followed him, quickly infected. With the horror of the immediate moment shattered, even Lily and Ailene saw the obvious, and the edges of their mouths curled up against their will. *Something other than pizza before he kicks*: only one other person in the world could have made that joke. And this was Rach's eulogy for him.

Dad took them to the restaurant via Carson's windows. This year, Field's major competitor had gone with the sugar plum, gingerbread, toy soldiers, and giant rats of *The Nutcracker*. The family caught up with Dad underneath the Louis Sullivan grillwork. He was teaching the descant of "God Rest Ye Merry, Gentlemen" to a street drunk, promising the man a dollar in change if they could get through two verses and a chorus. "Here come the inner lines now," Pop said, seeing them. Rach threw herself into the counterpoint with the necessary glee. Eddie Jr. and Artie harmonized more grudgingly. Lily wanted to run and hide behind the giant two-hundred-dollar box of Frango mints in Field's. Ailene tugged at her husband's arm, hissing, "Ed, Ed," as if at any minute the police might round them up for teasing indigents in G minor, without a permit.

They dispersed just before the local camera crew could break from prearranged script and pick up on their ad lib. In this, too, the family tagged along behind Pop's aesthetic: always stay one step ahead of written-out plans. They arrived in troupe at the promised restaurant, but Dad did not turn in. Rather, he carried on to a far shabbier place a half-block away.

"I knew it," Rach wailed bitterly. "A trick. He never really meant Berghoff's. We've been had." As they filed into the alternate selection, the reason for the change became clear. The Miller Tiller had led Dad here. Over the loudspeaker system, just loud enough to be danceable, a bank of brass did their Big Band bit. "Moonlight Serenade."

Resisting the urge to give funny answers to the hostess when she asked them how many they were, the Hobsons settled in and ordered. Dad echoed that Depression-era Eleventh Commandment, "Take all that you want, but eat all that you take." They ate leisurely, aware that it might be their last meal all assembled for a while. They talked of current events, Christmas plans, spectator sports. For a few astonishing minutes, the Hobsons actually found themselves enjoying each other in public. As the meal wound down, Dad challenged Rachel to put her wallet on the table in sight of everyone.

"Forget it, buddy. If you're too cheap to take us to Berghoff's, then I'm not going to bail you out of this dive."

"No, no. New game. Here. Here's my wallet. Put yours out too. Come on. Now. Neither of us knows how much is in the other's, right? Whoever has *less* money in theirs gets the whole pot. Is it a good bet?"

Rach put her magic actuarial powers to use before responding. "Well, the most I can lose is what's in my wallet. But if I win, it will be a sum greater than twice what I have. And it's even odds, right? So if I have a one-in-two chance of more than doubling my money, the situation favors me."

"I reason the same way," said Dad, simply.

In silence, the paradox grew to full flower. Lily groaned. She put a paper napkin over her head. "Why do you do this to us?" Under her question was a more serious one, unasked: *Is this how you want us to remember you?*

Eddie Jr. tried to back them out of the wallet game by saying that the contest was no contest, since Dad had had plenty of time to empty his billfold in advance. He knew it had nothing to do with the point in question, but it kept the last moments relatively seamless.

Pulling his fork from out of a playground of cold mashed potatoes, Artie was next to recover. "My turn. I've got another one. Not a paradox, exactly. Not logic. More along the lines of experiment. But pretty interesting, all the same." He paused, giving an emcee's look around the table. The audience was his, providing he did not try to hold it too long.

"I know you guys think all I read is law, law, law." He paused again, distracted by an aural association: "Jaw, Jaw is better than War, War." He tried to place the quote; it had to be some Brit, probably Churchill, in order to make the rhyme work out. Artie suddenly realized something about himself, who he was. He himself had been formed by that 1940s window at Field's that had given Dad so much trouble. But the revelation would have to wait for its full working out until the crisis ran its course. For now, he had to deliver his magic act.

"Just the other day, I was in the U. of C. library and I happened across something apropos. Seems there's this fellow, a Doctor Wolff, at some Ivy League place. Cornell . . ." He shot a glance at Eddie Sr. to catch the reaction take. Dad registered only a slightly pleased look: *You found it. I knew you would. Good researcher.* "Brain man," Artie continued. "I mean, he studies neurology. Anyway, he hypnotized several experimental subjects and, while they were under, told them he was going to brand them with a red-hot iron. Then he touched them with a pencil. That's science for you, huh?" His audience only motioned impatiently for him to get on with the story. "When the subjects came out of the trance, most of them developed a red, tender area where the pencil had touched them. A few developed badly seared blisters." As usual, Artie left the last link unspoken.

But the import was clear. Everyone understood, but nobody seemed too anxious to follow up on the implication. Ailene straightened her dirty dishes; Lil excused herself and went to the WC. Pop, however, looked around animatedly and asked, "So what are you saying?"

"Isn't it obvious? This physical reaction of cells, these pencil burns: well, the brain did it. The subjects *believed* themselves into a burn. Suggestion burned them."

"Wild," said old Eddie. "So what can and can't it do, then? The brain, I mean."

"How do I know? The point is, certain inarguably physical responses needing, so we think, physical causes, can be created, if you will, by sufficiently powerful imagination." Dad pulled his lower lip in and nodded. He looked for all the world like one of those little plastic dogs with spring necks that one puts in the rear windows of cars. Artie followed up his point, unnecessarily. "In the familiar phrase of a man who will remain nameless, 'Wishing might make it so.' "

By the look on his face, Pop might have been feeling anything: hurt, angered, pleased, indifferent. Rach and Eddie Jr. sank into the booth vinyl, stunned that Artie had dared stray so close to the real issue. Finally, Ailene spat at him, sharply: "Have a little respect."

Artie, confused, looked from one parent to the other. "Respect? Respect? You've got to be kidding. What are you talking about?" He pointed an accusing finger at Pop. "*He's* the one who put me on to the man."

Nothing more was said about suggestion, or any other matter. When lunch broke up, they brought Dad out to Maywood and committed him to the Old Soldiers' Home.

IF YOU CAN FILL THE
UNFORGIVING MINUTE

I have in front of me a folder of documents, all that remains of my father. Photos, letters, government forms: the stuff that carries our weight through the fact-demanding world. Most of it is the printed matter we must constantly show to prove our existence. Incredible to me, in some my father is my age or even younger.

I cannot adjust to this switch, even in the teeth of the evidence. My father always seemed to have stepped out of the infants' ward fully blown. For a long time, the best I can do is paste the fifty-two-year-old soul onto the twenty-year-old wrestler's body. The man stubbornly remains who he was when I waved good-bye to him. I tear apart the folder all afternoon. But my father changes more slowly than glaciers.

I rearrange the sheaf of papers. I squint at the pictures, trying to forget what I know. Still no good. I spread them around me in an orchestra. He remains Dad, black-humored, baroque, evasive Dad, with a different waist, different skin tone, different circumstances, but destined to disappear all the same. As I am about to put them away, a single, hand-written, blue-lined sheet of school notebook paper separates itself from the others. In the top right, in the scrawl of a boy forced to write in unnatural cursive, he has written the teacher's name, his own name, and the date: September 1, 1939.

My Favorite Poem

My favorite poem is Rudyard Kipling's "If." In particular, the lines "If you can fill the unforgiving minute/ with sixty seconds' worth of distance run." This paper is about what those lines mean, and how to fill those sixty seconds.

All at once he is no longer the quizmaster, the great doublethinker, the distanced ironist who had me second-guessed and checked at every step of the game. He is no longer the man imprisoned by all the wrong answers at the end of his interrupted life. All at once my father is a child, as uncertain, terrified, and abandoned to the terrible abundance of being alive as I am. He is no longer the man who, reciting the poem at high speed, used to deny that the old colonialist's idealism could still save him. He is defenseless, thirteen, struggling with a composition, holding on to the lines for all he is worth, as I hold on to his.

What could that grade-school teacher possibly have been thinking, giving out the hackneyed assignment on the day that the whole globe set itself in flames? I wonder what possessed Dad's mother to keep this page, what possessed him, and finally my mother in turn. What is it doing here, with the birth certificate and insurance forms? No reason on earth why it should have been saved.

I read the lines again. It strikes me for the first time that wherever we find ourselves in the unforgiving minute, we had somehow to get there. Dad's manila folder proves it: he is no more than a work in progress. He takes the first tentative step out of his racing block, running headlong into a world bursting apart in cataclysm, a world that has nothing to do with him, one that will tear him apart if he ever stops. And it is at once clear to me that the very thing he hoped would keep the violent beauty outside the classroom from killing him instead sent him out alone into the hopeless contest: this schoolboy's belief that he had some say in the distance run.

More: I begin to suspect, for the first time, that he did have that say. And still does.

All at once, the random file of documents reads like a story. I trace his way, island to island, no longer afraid to make up the missing material between. The pediatric nurse at the Teaneck Lying-in Hospital commemorates his birth by sticking two inky baby footprints against a state form. She gives him his first form of ID, flourishing his name across the top in twenties nub-pen italics, as if the world will mark it, in time. I see my grandmother, years later, after winning her first gold star, holding on to the paper as if it were him.

I follow him through his school days in a steady stream of report cards and evaluations: the C's in handwriting, the A's in music. He attends the senior prom with a spookily beautiful utter stranger. I read, over his *shoulder, the letter from the government about his brother. He pounds on the door of his neighborhood draft board but is kept home, two inches too many in the height box.*

In uniform, he swings through the south, closing up air bases, bringing down the curtain on what his separation papers poetically call the "American Theater of Operations." We both know that his locale qualifies as a Theater only charitably. It cannot match the Pacific, the European, or even the African Theaters for the raw expiation he is after. I read the Theater programs from the Shelby-Amarillo circuit: definitely Off-Off-Broadway. My father, in the supporting cast, hangs out in the stage wings, "examining them for evidence of wear, correcting such defects by appropriate maintenance."

To earn his rations, he lies on his back on a dolly underneath a fuselage of a B-29 that has liberated who knows how many square miles by dropping who knows how many tons of bombs on who knows how many people like himself. Convinced that the chain of command mocks him bitterly, he composes mental letters to his mother, tragic, if routine. "Dear Mom: We lost seven thousand men in the South Pacific yesterday. I adjusted carburetors."

She writes back weekly, grateful that her remaining boy is out of the line of fire. "Hope you are well, and PLEASE take care." Each word tortures him to find some way to emerge from this world conflagration a casualty. My father, fixing fuselages, mouths his magic charm: "If you can wait, and not be tired by waiting."

The official papers say he fills his every hour "manipulating cockpit controls and making required adjustments." But home leaves, inescapable, drag him back to a house papered with certificates, triumphs, and cum laudes of a dead older brother. My father boxes against an unbeatable ghost. He cannot hope to improve on his brother's fluke disaster at Brownsville, captured in a prize-winning photo, clipped from a popular magazine for the family archives.

His father is conspicuously silent. The man has forfeited the voting franchise. What Granddad thinks of the son-ruining world goes unrecorded. He achieves reconciliation flat on his back on the sofa, clinically uninteresting and unheralded, except in family legends: the tale of a drippy faucet that, fist-smashed, dried him out for good.

The official papers go on to describe another home leave. Dad marries my mother, to my relief. In a lightning honeymoon, they dine at a place whose preserved menu warns: "Cela exige le temps de sa preparation." These things take time to make. He tells her it is pizzas from here on, and she laughs, agreeing.

He writes her funny and fitful letters. "Dear lady from the matinee." He dares to talk about that historical incongruity: their life together, after the war. He types imperative plans for what will happen in their shared life after his "duration and six." Duration and six! The favorite phrase applied a hundred times a month when I turned draftable age. Here it is for real, in the original sense.

Most urgent among these scenarios he paints for Mom is the agreed-upon need to fall to work, at once or sooner, in surrounding themselves with at least a dozen kids. He sustains himself in these letters on the thought of the next, better generation. Meaning their daughters, their sons, me. Mom readily concurs with this plan of battle. She writes back methodically to this stranger, her husband, telling him all the Stateside news, the scrap drives and community campaigns, forgetting that loose lips sink ships and that deep South air bases are not, after all, another country. "Children," she always adds in the closing paragraphs, blushing visibly through her pen, "and lots of them." She harvests his letters and preserves them, more certain of their substance than of his. She does not dare hope that the fighting will ever wind down.

But soon the last hot shot is fired, the last B-29 maintained. My father comes home in June of '46, his date of separation and honorable discharge, after "honest and faithful service to this country." But sometime before the end of his tour, something makes him begin to walk away from the world, and for good reason. Somewhere in the Southwest, while he recites, "If you can meet with Triumph and Disaster/ And treat those two impostors just the same." Looking carefully, I find the account in the folder: just where, when, and how everything begins to change.

Aimless in a world that has pushed through to its destiny, Dad goes back to school on the GI Bill of Rights. He takes night classes, earning a whirlwind degree. Days he devotes to an assembly line. Mom keeps her job after the war, leaving little time to begin producing the hoped-for dozen babies. They pass a nervous interlude of years. Each sees respective specialists, but both check out A-OK.

They obey the doctor's orders to the letter. They time their intimacy, waiting for the opportune moments. They throw themselves to the task at hand with all the industry of postwar recovery. I imagine my mother, who during the entire four years of war could not rouse herself to feel hatred toward the impersonal enemy, hating her own familiar but blameless body with a deepening fury. As the situation becomes increasingly grim, my father's famous black humor makes the first of its many appearances. The countless cruel and unusual jokes about renting a furnished womb never make it into the final records. But I can hear each one of them, and their prolific offspring.

In the sterile time, Dad earns another degree. He responds to a growing need for teachers to meet the spike in the nation's children graph. He drifts into a certificate in history for entirely private reasons. He wants to undo what was done to him out in the desert, during his tour of duty. He wants to understand the incomprehensible climax of the present, the cathedral of justifiable injustice he has only read about, never felt. Already people talk about the last necessary evil as if it is fairy tale. He wants to see if big is the sum of little, or if the two belong to unjoinable worlds. He wants to see if he can keep his head while all about him are losing theirs and blaming it on him.

I follow the terms of their first mortgage. I proofread their payments. I assume the pride and curse of ownership. I witness my father in his first teaching job. And then, miraculously, when they have both resigned themselves to vanishing from the face of the earth without a trace, after they go back to coupling for its own sake, my mother returns from a checkup with a wild look and astonishing news. The law of averages has at long last earned out in their favor. The new round of inky infant footprints begin another folder. My father insists on the christening. "It is a good name," he tells his wife. "And it's time somebody brought it back into circulation." They resurrect my uncle's name, a casualty in the global war.

Encouraged, the couple, once more in love, return to their dreams of an infant production line. In three years, they knock out a few more. Whatever they had been doing wrong, this quick turnaround corrects: But a quarter of the way into the long-dreamed-of army of offspring, they hit a dry spell, pause for a breather, or realize that they no longer have enough time remaining to make it all the way to an even dozen, the wall of fresh souls they had hoped to surround themselves with.

Photos describe the life of the diminished tribe. Life together alters my *parents slowly beyond recognition. They dissolve into parental roles, gradually become those outside interveners in science fairs, paper routes, music lessons, white glue, and home bread molds. Once or twice, every few years, they stumble into an aha, the evidence of older, untouched civilizations. Their parents die; the world shifts alliances. They learn by reading, decades later, just what upheaval they have lived through. Through a series of partial differentials—infinitesimal, incremental, and interlocked decisions—they become the two people I knew.*

Mother works, gets out from time to time. But she lives for the children, their daily and remarkable differentiation. Dad discharges his half of the upbringing. A few keepsakes document his life outside the home. Mere years before, he had known no more serious an occupation than kicking around the Palisades with the singing-waiter routine. Now he throws himself into the crucial work of teaching children who know nothing except how to explicate their favorite poems something about history.

He begins like every other teacher: well meaning but inept. Then, a handful of semesters into his career, while standing up in front of thirty-two at best indifferent pubescent teenagers, lecturing about the importance of the X Y Z Affair, he has a revelation. Dad suddenly sees that every one of these fifteen-year-olds has reached this classroom and will leave it for places unknown through a series of small and unnoticed decisions—thousands of them a day. More often than not, those incremental decisions are made in complete ignorance of the Big Picture. All at once, the traditional teaching of history as assorted facts means nothing. The only thing that matters is to reveal to that pasty boy in the second row that he is the inheritor and future of the world.

From that moment, the cartoon tales about silver dollars thrown across the Potomac disappear. My father sweats in the classroom to create History, that single, linked quilt connecting the school principal's handling of a recent varsity blackballing to Ike's refusing to pardon the Rosenbergs. He shows how Perry's words on Lake Erie mutate, in startlingly short time span, into words such as Finger Ridge, Heartbreak Ridge, and Panmunjom. Everything becomes fair game in the search for the connective tissue: the quiz-show scandals, the Oppenheimer case, the shady doings behind selecting this year's homecoming queen.

He becomes a stickler for the overlooked, the reinterpreted, the taken-for-granted. His specialty is superimpositions: he takes his classes on field trips to an imaginary Hudson River Valley of words. From the banks, he conjures up a series of vertical scenes—from the trapper cleaning pelts to the manufacturer dumping sulfate sludge: the passage of events, including the current diorama, becomes not so much successive solutions as branched alternatives, some harmonious, some tragic. But none inevitable. None without our say.

Everything becomes an excuse for drawing relations between things. My father grows notorious in small circles. For a stretch of years, he is an annual shoo-in for the Most Influential Teacher plaque. The documents are all here: the teaching awards, the spotlights in local newspapers. One high school journalist writes, "He is one of the few adults whose opinion teenagers actively seek out." But his opinion is nowhere written down. My father's opinion has vanished into world history, the world's fair.

I don't need printed material to animate this era of the man. I was there. I cannot build a simple soapbox-derby entry without bringing on a bout with the Golden Book: Automobiles Through the Ages. My sister cannot excuse herself from the table without first checking for a quorum, securing a second to the motion, and following Robert's Rules all the way to the parliamentary vote. Even choosing sides for a game of cards leads to a debate on the Cuban missile crisis. We cannot simply take our immunizations like other children; we have to hear the whole, horrifying tale, from rats' viruses in medieval Europe to the iron lung of a few summers before.

Where you are depends on how you got there: that is the man's whole point. Just underneath the late-breaking headlines, just inside the international trends, everything pops with consequences. He uses no textbook except the one we are plunged into, the one American life was designed to ignore. Things happen. Things matter. We are the present's war.

I now see the danger in such a stance. The demon in the machine must stay hidden, and curse the one who wakes it. Each year our ability to feel the dangerous abundance on all sides of us slips away. We stay inside, sampling in half-hour slots the myths and rumors of the outdoors. When we do get out, the first, nervous titter of things bigger than us sends us screaming to the theater exits to beat the stampede. We cannot survive the head-on look, because we have lost our practice at it. We forgive everything except experience.

My dad stands naïvely at the head of his classroom, asking, "What happened today, too far away to feel? What will you do about it?" He himself receives far more history secondhand than he has seen. But the modest bits that he has lived through he shares openly: Flushing Meadow, B-29 school in Amarillo. These are his tools for teaching the current urgency.

But somewhere, he oversteps himself. Someplace along the way, he goes to the well of private biography too often, and history flashes alive in front of unsuspecting students' eyes. It is no great surprise when his critique of school policies on historical principles forces local politics to put him in the criminal box. He comes away from the incident quietly stripped, scarred, with nothing between himself and the brink but his black humor.

I did not learn until years later about my father's run-in with community. But here is the thumbnail sketch of the event in front of me: a summons from the school board, asking him to appear for questioning. Dad called it his "bout with the Tribunal," although it is in fact just an inquiry by de facto committee.

The trouble begins when one of his seniors complains that the man is preaching communism. Dad appears in front of the informal session to answer the charge. In five minutes, he has the whole board laughing at a hypothetical teacher trying to describe the modern world without going into the Russian revolution. The punchline is his equating Superintendent Vance's recent handling of the cafeteria crisis with the battleship Potemkin. He makes the country's love/hatred with individualism jump off the page.

Another board member asks about the rumor that Dad has proclaimed the existence of more than one American revolution. Dad reels off four populist revolts—Shays's Uprising, the Whiskey Rebellion, Nat Turner, the Southern secession—before they acquiesce in admiration. He is the history teacher more than one of them might have wished for.

My father understands how every now and then, organized groups feel the need to defend themselves from their inner parts. He knows that the present is in love with interrogation, as it has been in the past and will be again. Self-policing is, by common consent, the only way for individual interests to get along. Knowing this is after all his stock in trade. He has seen it before, about once every ten years. Why shouldn't their own local nation on the Jersey shore have a home version, a HUAC of their own? He has long planned what he would do when his moment in front of the *committee came. Not too rational, not too polemical. Don't infuriate. Entertain.*

And he almost gets away without a reprimand. The group discards any idea of recommending disciplinary action. Nor do they ask him to name names. It is not, as Dad, still playing for the laugh, will characterize it for us a decade later, simply another case of Hiss and Tell. But having survived the burden of disproof, he must still survive their compliments and congratulations. I imagine, as he is almost out of the room, someone asking how he has come to have such an immediate and vigorous sense of what is going on. And I see Dad start in glibly about what happened to him in The War, about his private brush with history. And that is when the man's magnetic poles shift for all time. There, as he tells his instructional life story.

Nothing in the documents my family has saved makes any mention about my father's first illness. I do not imagine anything so dramatic as a fit on his examiners' floor. But I am sure he comes out of that first examination an enemy of the people. What he has seen firsthand, and has tried to tell about in lessons and riddles, will by nature cut him off from the protection of others. Soon it cuts him off for real, starting with a party of friends who stand in horror over the cocktail dip as Dad makes his first public swan dive.

It's to the man's great credit that he does not, right then, roll over and die. I survey the family archives, and tick off the strikes against him. A man with dependent family who loses his job. Whose savings might tide them over for a few months. Who tears himself up from the only place he has ever lived and moves into the blank spot on the map. Whose disease prevents him from ever again working steadily. Who knows, from the beginning, what the disease is and where it will lead. Who is stripped of membership, told that he can no more expect society's safety net. Who knows that that society has reached a point where it cannot save itself from cultivated catastrophe without taking its own members hostage. Who is told that his outlook, the only undeceived look, a look he has stumbled on by historical accident and cannot shake from in front of his eyes, is unacceptable and wrong.

So dangerous to others that they must cut him loose, he is many times more dangerous to himself. My father, in front of the class, seeing through the agreed-on fantasy, cannot himself make the alternative jibe. The

247

theory remains at best an If. The single figure simply does not, cannot fit into the greater landscape. The world becomes too runaway-abundant to yield any but an abstract connection.

He insists, through logical proof and moral imperative, that ours is the earth and everything that's in it. He spends his breath telling of the mysterious and required link, but he cannot show it. Ought and Can tear him up between them. The danger of the search drives him, pointless and alone, into a place of no recovery.

Dad remains condemned to his solo nation. For all his formal and continuing education, he carries with him his place and time: immigrant parents, needy upbringing, the Lord's Prayer crocheted to the kitchen wall. He acquires enough worldliness to be sardonic when he recites the Kipling credo. But inside I can see the perpetual schoolboy scribbling over his writing desk, working on a schoolboy theme: All we need do is keep our head and give the world our best shot, ignore that it is godforsaken, hellish, and forever damned.

For all his insistence that we look full face into the evil of the day, he never gives up his love of the escapist film. Without Orchestra Wives to live in, he would have died in 1951. The American black and white Hollywood Canteen gives him a kingdom to rule during his long exile. Achieving the impossible, poking his head through the walls of prison, gazing up close at the murderous truth of where we really are, he has no language to tell what he sees except the only tongue he is native in: Boy meets Girl; Boy goes to War; Boy fights War to Irving Berlin; Boy returns to Girl, to Betty Grable.

If is now and forever his only weapon against brute realism. He must give in to brute realism in order to turn it around. But to turn it around, to move the pragmatic world, he must create a somewhere else to wedge the lever. I can hear his famous bass: "And it wouldn't be make believe if you believe in me." And he has trapped me just as hopelessly between these irreconcilables. In the early sixties, when the first films from Indochina come across the television and the whole nation changes the channel, he stands me, a little boy, in front of the tube and says, "Don't look the other way. We are going to have our day in the trenches after all." But this time, he is wrong. Event will skirt us again. I have already learned from him that this is a movie. I slip past experience by the slimmest margin.

It is heroic that, after his first sign of sickness, Dad not only stays alive for another fifteen years but he even begins to shift around for some way to rehabilitate himself. A proof-of-personal-loyalty project. A project doomed from inception. Another handful of documents for the archives. I see my father setting off on this endeavor, starting the hobby that he will never abandon, giving it increasing doses of time and attention until it replaces all other activities, including the motions of everyday life. I see my mother, one afternoon, in one of the blamelessly median houses where they raised their blamelessly median family, earned the advanced degree, received the promotions, paid the utilities, garnered the accolades, destroyed the credit cards, and suffered the jury of peers, walking in on him in his makeshift study. He is sprawled over a pile of papers and forms— army insurance vouchers, mortgage tables, letters from since-sacrificed friends. He couches his chin in the inside of his bent arm. Mother's immediate impression is that he has again passed out, for hours, with no one to attend him.

As she comes near him, however, he shifts position. She gasps and jerks back, not expecting the corpse to move. He takes no notice of her alarm, makes no effort to soothe it. He says, instead, eyes not focused on her but off somewhere, opaque, "I have an idea." A matinee production, definitely Off-Off Broadway. That first, vast operation the army had started him on. The name his separation papers poetically gives it. "An American Theater."

I have a picture of the man in front of me, taken during those last few weeks. He sits at a table, facing the camera front on. My sister stands behind him to one side, head next to his, arms around his neck in a joking, exasperated choke. She is grinning. He is on the edge of death. He is grinning too.

I can't believe that I did not see before what was so patently clear to the camera. Because he was a man who threw everything back to me in the abstract, I abstracted his real suffering. Dad had a burst appendix once, and was still walking around. He didn't check in to a hospital for two days. And that was the only time I remember him entering a hospital. The only time until the last. As a result, it was easy, in those winter months of 1978, for me to overlook the chaos of pain in his still-joking face. He masked it convincingly, in character. But I have no excuse for not seeing it.

The photo makes it obvious: Dad wants to go down. It has nothing to do with his legendary distrust of doctors. It isn't a religious thing, God knows. The man is a lapsed Lutheran at best, whose faith can only charitably be called private and eclectic. He simply wants the sharp, stabbing pain, and will sooner die of it than mask it with analgesics. He demands to feel the genuine and valuable signal of something gone wrong that needs correcting. He wants death by loneliness to add to his vita. It is not too auspicious a biography, as biographies go. But with the right death, it could become the corrective biography for his time, an era when the unexperienced life has at last gotten the uncontested upper hand.

For he has had one small brush with real *history. And he wants to experience, to go* through, *just this once, once in this one life, what he has seen, the outside's killing abundance and the inside's incapacity to know. That is the disease so obvious in the photograph. The one I failed to see.*

My father, as should have been obvious to us for a long time, was a very sick man. Real sickness, although all we saw were the symptoms. We worried most about the irrelevant name of the disease. The problem, only now obvious, is that we never sat down and asked him *what was wrong until he was jaundiced beyond recall. We should have tended to the illness, not the evasion. When I think of him retching in the bathroom, a sound I simply didn't hear as it happened, I realize we should have remedied the unforgiving minute, and not left him to his solo distance run.*

In the end, my father's sickness was his need to love people without knowing whether they deserved it. His madness came from never giving up on a place that had embraced the escalating and retaliatory threat. He lived through the specific moment of modern history when, in order to free ourselves, we locked ourselves away. And oddly, irrationally, he held to the boy's hypothetical: if you, being hated, do not give way to hating . . . My father is lost, cut off from mankind, doomed to an idea. But, strange to say, the idea is compassion.

I sit in the middle of a folder of papers. From a couple of incisors, I reconstruct the whole skeleton in all its dips and sways. Blind to the fact that nothing more can be said on the matter, the world keeps minting new sons and fathers. I forgive the misguided grade-school teacher: there are only hackneyed *themes.*

Now I must find in his surviving records—the photos, letters, government forms—a way to forgive myself for not seeing how sick my father really was. I must find, in his life, the proof that history is not the big, which will never reform, nor the little, which will never know where it is.

I must be coaxed to act on my own. Tell me how free I am, Dad. Tell me how free I am. Here, in the tracks and tapes of his having once lived and breathed and moved and changed other people, what counts is not the past or the future but the Standing Now, a thirteen-year-old explicating, as if all history depended on it, unwitting of what waits for him:

> If you can fill the unforgiving minute
> With sixty seconds' worth of distance run,
> Yours is the Earth and everything that's in it,
> And—which is more—

The child at the school desk writes to me, long after his death, from the morning of the very day that starts to rip his life apart, "you'll be a Man, my son!"

14

"The VA sure can pick 'em," Ailene said brightly, by way of making conversation. She had honed, after three decades of practice, the art of cheerful inanity, speaking nonsense simply because anything she might say, however fatuous or misplaced or filled with hollow cheer, was better than silence.

Lily, from the backseat of the rented sedan, returned Mom's inanity, stripped of the redeeming well-meaning. "The outbound Ike is a dismal expressway, Maywood is a dismal suburb, and *this place*," she gestured as they pulled into the hospital lot, "is a particularly dismal hotbed of sepsis." She lit a cigarette over the objections of Eddie Jr., trapped in the seat next to her.

Artie was still arguing how inefficient the folks had been in leaving their car in De Kalb, abandoning Rach's too-small Pinto in Grant Park, and renting a car to go a dozen blocks to the southwest suburbs. Only Rach paid him any attention. "It's unpatriotic to be efficient, chump."

Dad was the only happy one of the whole group. He had blossomed into the African Adventurer returning to the London Explorers' Club. He evidently hoped to compare notes with the only group on earth— wounded veterans—who could understand or empathize with him. He had packed lightly for the occasion in the same beaten-up khaki duffle bag stenciled "PFC Hobson" that had taken him through his two-year tour of duty across the American Campaign. But when the rental pulled in to the Hines parking lot and the family bailed out, Pop hadn't the strength to hoist the bag out of the trunk let alone haul it into the building. He signaled Artie: "Cover for me, before your mother finds out."

Artie passed the task along the chain of command. "You take it," Artie told Eddie Jr. He added, under his breath, "Private."

Little Eddie grinned and saluted, poking himself in the eye for additional effect. The whole Hobson parade followed the flag into the hospital lobby, single file, as all families walked. Eddie Jr. further entertained his older brother by launching into a virtuoso Mack Sennett routine, spinning around and waving the bag precariously at every passing hospital employee, raising a finger and saying, just out of earshot, "Front! Front! What kind of establishment is this? Get me the manager."

Artie, against his better judgment, laughed out loud. But when Dad, on the far side of the entrance from the little vaudeville act, independently invented a variant on the Hotel Hines joke by approaching the registration desk and saying, "I have a reservation for one. Indefinite stay," both boys registered disgust on the roofs of their mouths. The old man's breaches of taste seemed stripped of their last shred of good humor.

"I'm sorry we ever decided to take your father out in public," Artie said. "We should have let him simmer in his own gangrene."

"What? And give him what he wanted?" Eddie Jr. recovered his saving, crooked smile.

The check-in staff directed Pop to an invisible upper floor typically reserved for basket cases. Because the initial history and physical wasn't for a couple hours, everybody tagged along. Rach brought up the rear, humming, "I Love a Parade." The halls of the place looked, to quote vintage Ailene, like a bomb had struck. Trays of pills, strings of plastic tubes, and carts loaded with listless fluid sacks littered the halls. In the crowded rooms, Artie caught a glimpse of patients cabled to masses of chrome and dials, the pale flicker of electroluminescent reds that, like miniature marching bands, arranged themselves into high-tech readouts. The numbers delivered the final judgment, the quantitative evaluation that told the professionals at a glance everything they needed to know about how near the attached body was to deliverance.

And at a glance, Artie saw what the centuries-long drive for eternal progress had led to. Death used to be a horrible, demanding, agonizing, nauseating ordeal, the closing experience. But his era had at last taken care of it, turned it into a level spot on a graph, a rounded decimal. Artie imagined the hospital suite as the final State Street window: Christmas in the seventies. The moving parts were all silicon and semiconductor. The anxious family huddled in the shared sickroom, looking not at the mass they were related to but at the Christmas lights on the life-support machine, happy with the glorious temporary uptick of the LED.

People filled the halls too, in a manner of speaking. The white outfits walked crisply and tried not to touch anything, while the drab-green seersucker robes slouched, slumped, or shuffled about uncaringly in their hospital-issue tissue slippers. They traded the horrible for the anesthetized at a hideous rate of exchange. In short, the place was a grotesque clearinghouse and convention center for the jaundiced, tumored, and forsaken. The advantages of bringing together into one place such a supersaturation of the sick eluded Artie as he threaded his way toward Dad's appointed ward. Wasn't that a sure way of making the sick get sicker, by power of association if not contamination?

Rachel finished her perfidious tune and started in on "St. James Infirmary." She sang, bluesy, "My God, why couldn't it be me?" a line Artie did not recall from the original, but which he couldn't imagine Rach interpolating. His sister had never been in better voice, and he liked the way the antiseptic corridor echoed with the smoky key.

Dad marched cheerfully down the hall to his sentence, saluting left and right, stating his rites of passage by calling out divisional numbers from the Big One, on the outside chance of finding a distant regimental buddy. Those wounded vets who weren't engaged in reconnoitering the halls sat in stunned silence in scattered lounges, shuffling dog-eared fifty-one-card decks of Armed Forces complimentary playing cards and picking over obsolete *Sports Illustrateds*. Some huddled around sets blaring afternoon soaps, not really watching. Some just sat, eyes closed, hands clasped to the armrests of their chairs.

Dad beat the rest of the family to his suite by a hundred steps. But by the time everybody else got there, he introduced his roommates as if they were old friends. Mr. Banks, Army, '54–'56, a big, stately black man from down by Blue Island, was eager to discuss and analyze his symptoms with all newcomers. Mr. Menkis, or just Menkis, as Dad already presumed to call him, Marines, '41–'46, a pasty, frightened fellow from Cicero, shrank back into the corner by his bed. At the family's onslaught, he asked in a pathetic, reedy voice, "Is *everybody* moving in, or . . . ?"

While mother reassured Menkis that there was only one new tenant, Pop experimented with the green shower curtain that could be pulled on a runner around his bed, sealing it off in a parody of a private room. He then hopped into the bed and jacked with the hydraulics. Rach, by this time, had shifted to "Puttin' on the Ritz." Lily listened to Mr. Banks's symptoms, told him that it sounded to her like diabetes, that millions of people had it, that it could be maintained, and that the sufferer could still lead a full life.

An officious teenager in short white smock and clipboard came in to get Pop's dog tags. Between questions, Pop stage-whispered to Artie, "Tell him about Dr. Wolff." Artie rolled his eyes, pretending not to hear anything. When the kid finished fact-gathering and left, Dad wheeled on his eldest and demanded, "Why didn't you say anything? Aiding and abetting? Trying to withhold evidence?"

"Pop, he's just an orderly. He hasn't a thought in his brain." Artie became inexplicably depressed. Experience was a cruel joke; no wonder most people shut it off long before getting to it.

"Well, when the *real* doctors come, make sure that you tell them what you've discovered."

"Tell them yourself, man. You're the one who discovered the son of a bitch."

"I can't tell them," Pop said, still smiling.

"Why the hell not?"

"I'm the patient. That makes me the last person in the world that the doctors are going to believe about anything." He gave his son a look at once soulful, long-suffering, and sardonic: *How can I prove my loyalty, when the very attempt to do so draws suspicion to itself?*

"I'm sure that the doctors know all about Dr. Wolff's work without my . . ." Artie trickled off, unable to complete the thought. The whole exchange was ludicrous. Pop suckered him into irrelevant places one last time.

"Without your throwing them for a *lupus?*"

"Exactly." Artie grinned, unable to help himself. The man would never reform; but suddenly, that was all right. Everything was all right, worthwhile, because everything was already lost. The pressure was off. All he really had to do was live. Pop's triple pun suddenly seemed very funny.

The first doctor showed for a cursory prep. He verified the work-up so far and made sure Pop knew when to go where for what tests. Ailene intercepted the physician diagonally on his way out. With an economy of words she said: "He's weak and he's bleeding and he's blacking out. That's cancer, isn't it? You can tell us. We want to know the worst. We're not your typical family."

The doctor put on his professional counselor's demeanor. "Differential diagnosis is a subtle thing, Mrs. Hobson. There is often no telling, *from symptoms alone*, just what is wrong with a patient. *That* can only be gotten through observation and more observation. The best thing you can do now is head home and dwell as little as possible on the matter. I personally will call you when we have a lead on anything."

"They want us to leave, Ma," translated Eddie Jr. after the physician had gone. Setting a good precedent, he went to the bed where Pop was changing into hospital gown for the first battery of tests, and shook his hand. "So long, big guy. We're outta here."

Dad looked up. "I know this is going to be hard for either of us to believe I'm really saying," he said offhandedly. "But try to do what your mother says."

"Within reason," said Eddie Jr., grinning. Everybody followed suit, saying good-bye and good luck as well to Mr. Menkis and Mr. Banks. Rach was last.

"Know what?" she asked, leaning over and jabbing at the terminally sick man.

"No. What?" A comeback from way back, one that used to send her into howls of laughter when she was little. At eight, she could have played that same question-and-answer game all day long, and probably still could.

"I think you're schizo." Dad returned his polite smile: *Is that a fact?* "And I hope the both of you will be very happy here," she added, kissing him with impeccable sweetness.

Mom was crying softly when they dropped off the rental car. The De Kalb contingent walked Rach and Art back to the Grant Park garage. Her two departing children could give the woman no comfort short of lying, so Artie simply said, "We'll be out soon. Call us as soon as you hear anything. Anything at all."

Mom demanded that Artie or Rach go out to Hines the following day. No objection of impracticality or irrationality would dissuade her, so they promised to make the visit. Artie pointed mother, sister, and brother in the direction of the bus station and watched them disappear down the way—however temporary and vulnerable—back home.

Rach and Artie had no coin to flip to designate visiting duty. Rach decided they should stop a policeman and ask his opinion. "Officer, which of us do you think should visit our pop tomorrow? He's extremely sick in the veterans' hospital, and probably dying." Artie watched his sister go quietly off the deep end of grief, discharging one more infected joke, the sick humor their father had sentenced them to. He was powerless to keep her from falling apart in giggles here in the middle of the city crowd. The officer would run them in for snickering at the word *dying* in public. "I've got the car, and my brother is busy with law school. But on the other hand, he's older and Dad likes him a lot better." To Artie's astonishment, the policeman didn't even blink. Instead, he replied parentally in a Polish-American drawl that he thought that kind of thing was more of a son's responsibility. Rach concurred. She made Artie take her home and lent him the Pinto for twenty-four hours, taking his watch as collateral.

Artie couldn't afford any more time away from the books. But then, for the last two decades and more, he had not really been able to afford the family he had. He allotted an hour for the visit, an unrealistic estimate, he knew, but one that made him feel disciplined. Arriving at the room the next evening, he found Pop teaching Mr. Banks and Mr. Menkis how to play pinochle, which the man had long declared the best activity people can engage in without a fourth. Seeing Artie, Pop excused himself from the game, moved to his own bunk, and pulled the flimsy green curtain shut, more for the joke effect than for the illusion of privacy.

"Sorry about checking up on you so soon," Artie began. "Your mother made me come out."

"I figured. Don't worry about it."

"So what's up? What'd they find?"

"You think they'd tell me, wouldn't you?"

"Christ. They must have said *something*."

"Oh, sure. The proctologist said, 'Hold still.' "

Artie shook his head, said, "Not funny, Pop," and burst out laughing. But in truth, Dad had no news. Artie offered to go down to the ward nurse's station and ask around. But Eddie surprisingly waved him off. The gesture indicated that Pop considered the step unnecessary.

For want of a conversational topic, Eddie whispered, "My colleague Mr. Menkis over in the corner must, the day after tomorrow, submit to what is euphemistically referred to in these parts as elective surgery. Last night, he dreamt they did the deed with an acetylene torch, burnt out the offending tissue, and sewed him back up. Later, they came and said they'd accidentally left a few ashes in him and had to go back in after them. Eye has not heard, nor ear seen, nor . . ." He caught Artie's eye and his voice changed. "Nor heart report, what Menkis's dream meant." Father and son fell silent, thinking of the doomed third party. "Guess what I've been doing?" Pop at last segued a key change.

Artie held out his hand for a moment's pause. "Wait a minute. . . . Let me guess. You've been lecturing in the TV lounge about the long-term effects of the Kefauver Committee on American media."

"Close. I've been reading poetry."

"Oh, Jesus. You insist on living long enough to embarrass me. Well, I had better know the worst." He wanted to say that grown men, particularly sick grown men, had no business playing with lyrics. But he could not suppress his curiosity about what rhymes his father could possibly find consolation in, here at Hines. Dad did not respond right away. Instead, he gazed at his son with misplaced sorrow. Artie felt, with all the force of the old distress, the upheaval a few years back, when he had told his father that he intended to study literature. Dad had many times told him to study whatever he needed. But Artie had felt the man's disapproval on pragmatic grounds. After several agonized months, Artie switched to prelaw on his own volition, without again asking his father how free he was. Now he could almost swear that the old guy was begging his forgiveness. Acutely uncomfortable, almost to the point of shame, Artie mumbled, "What has it been, big guy? Kipling?"

"Close."

"Robert Service? 'The Cremation of Sam McGee'?" Artie felt horror-struck as he heard himself pronounce the words. He hadn't even thought of the implications, but was just pulling the title out of the air. He knew of no way out of the humiliation except to pretend he had meant what he said and did not think it embarrassing.

Dad at last came to his rescue. "What might have been and what has been/ Point to one end . . ."

In a rush of affection, Artie completed, "which is always present." He felt suddenly flushed, limitless, as if his father had just confessed to loving him. "*Eliot*, Dad? You going highbrow on me in your old age?"

"Somehow I knew you'd come through on that couplet. I used to hate that poem. Know why?" Artie shook his head. "Here's the leading poetic figure of the twentieth century. An air-raid warden during the Blitz. He's going to write the definitive literary statement on the world apocalypse. Comes out in '42. And he doesn't once mention the *real shooting*."

"Oh, but he does," Artie objected.

"That's what I have only now seen," Dad agreed.

For more minutes than Artie had allotted, the two of them sat together and played Complete the Quotation. Dad began. "Nor law, nor duty bade me fight," and Artie completed, "Nor public men, nor cheering crowds." Dad did the third: "A lonely impulse of delight," and Artie wrapped up, "Drove to this tumult in the clouds."

Dad challenged, "I have a rendezvous with Death," and Artie supplied, "At some disputed barricade." They wandered from Frost to Auden to Rupert Brooke. Years later, Artie remembered the few minutes as the only time he had ever spent with his father on equal terms, with no invasion or distrust between them. He had never enjoyed his time with the man so much, and would never match the moment again.

At length, they returned to *Four Quartets*. Dad demanded, "The end of all our exploring/ Will be to arrive where we started . . ."

"And know the place for the first time."

Dad expressed his admiration for his son's unexpected reservoir of trivial knowledge. "Unstumpable," he declared. Finally, he deadpanned, "If you can keep your head while all about you are losing theirs . . ." and Artie, at last the man's equal, answered, "You call that poetry?"

They lapsed into one of those silent holes that swallows surrounding noise. Artie listened until he could not stand another second. He looked at the enclosing curtain and said, "I understand from Little Eddie that you pointed out to him the problems with 'An eye for an eye' as an extended strategy?"

Dad needed no gloss. "It might work," he answered softly, "if we could be sure of getting more than one time through the showdown."

"What about unilateral disarmament?" Artie said, still to no one in particular.

"What do you mean?"

"I mean, 'I refuse to defect, no matter what you decide to do.' "

Dad did not answer at first. When he did, Artie could hear mucus welling up in the man's vocal cords. "You see where that strategy has landed me."

A circuit breaker flipped inside him, and Artie jumped up. "Hey, call your family, all right?" he said. But already he knew his father's answer. Neither of his folks would ever acclimate to long distance. They kept a stopwatch by the phone and turned every toll call into a three-minute mile. After twice the time he had allotted for the visit, Artie made the obligatory "Don't touch the nurses" joke and said he'd give Pop a call the next morning, when the first lab results were supposed to be ready. They shook hands and the visit was history. Or almost. Dad stopped him in the doorway.

"Don't forget, kid. Calamine. The Sea will provide."

"Right, Pop. Many brave hearts. Talk to you soon."

Artie forgot to make his promised call. Two days later, on Thursday morning, the phone rang in Barbed-Wire City. Ailene was in the middle of the extended cosmetic ritual that Rach liked to call "putting on a happy face." Lily still slept, having gone for a late walk the night before. Eddie Jr. engaged in the robust pastime of singing the alphabet song along with kiddie TV while waiting for the bus that would take him to high school. Ailene yelled at him to get the phone at the same instant he yelled at her that he was getting it.

"Yo!"

"Edward Hobson, please."

"This is he." Both Eddie and the party of the second part missed beats. The ensuing silence spread from the center of the line to both ends. Then both started speaking at once, like the stuck two-step people on the pavement make in failing to get around one another. Eddie kicked back and let the other guy have a go.

"I guess I mean your father. Is he there, please?"

"Big Ed is at the hospital for a few tests. He'll be sprung by the weekend. This is . . ." For the first time in years, he remembered the title Pop had plagued him with while the kids were growing up. In yet another frequently repeated, quasi-pedagogic game Pop marshaled the kids around, Artie became the Heir Apparent, Lil the Crown Princess, Rach the Arch Duchess, and Eddie Jr., always near tears at the gag, suffered as the Pretender to the Throne. "This is the Pretender to the Throne. May I ask who's calling?"

"This *is* the hospital." Another silence, as both ends did some quick calculating. "It seems your dad has sprung himself ahead of schedule."

1944

The boy is perfect: Walt knows it from the first set of the singing waiter's act. Disney snatches teenaged Eddie Hobson from the jaws of current events and whisks his lead-to-be back to the safe haven of World World. He snares the boy just in time, before he is touched by outside developments. The nisei pilots scrape the belly of their DC-3 while bringing it down in the cornfields, but the director and his discovery reach the hidden kingdom intact. As young Eddie steps down onto the simulated Tarmac, his eyes open in astonishment. For spreading in front of him is a miniature, picture-perfect Lost Domain.

The insignificant swatch of cornbelt has transformed beyond recognition into a panorama of steep mountains, dismal swamps, forbidding tundra, mysterious forests, and meandering rivers. It fills with great cities that start, peak, and drop off again within a few yards. Traffic clogs the congested arteries of a hundred towns, turns the corner at shimmering intersections, and just as suddenly disappears. Villages and farms dot nearby rolling meadows in an optical illusion of plenitude and miles. Animals from every niche of the food chain graze the layout, side by side.

And the people: the most miraculous of all, they pass back and forth in constant industry, building and refining the outskirts of their still-growing creation. Eddie cannot tell how many they are. They swell to millions and in the next minute shrink down to a dozen. It seems only moderately strange, then, that they are all black-haired, umber-skinned beings of another country.

"Where are we?" asks the boy, although he recognizes the place better than his own home. He has spent whole years here, lifetimes. He grew up in this place's shadow, the magnificent portal of Perhaps that has always run just alongside his own life, hidden a few steps behind or ahead, to the *right or left. The Maybe his movies have always hinted at. The one place necessity cannot touch.*

Up close, he sees that the Shangri-La is only a pasteboard nation. But that hardly matters. All Eddie has ever known of moonlight anyway is the little bit that sifts into his chamber. Nips and tucks by the busy countrymen produce so strong a suggestion that the resulting castles and countryside serve nicely for the real thing. The boy Hobson is still young enough to believe that a hole is a well if he can drink the resulting water. Halfway down the airplane steps, he promises Disney full allegiance. "I'll do anything. Just let me be a part of this."

The world's most popular artist explains to the boy that he already is a part, and more. He is the crucial ingredient, the guest of honor, the moral and motive force. He is the one the sovereign state has been built for. Disney fills the kid in as they tour the shooting set. Every person they pass, he explains to the uncomprehending child, would be in jail if not for this project. "You locked up your own neighbors in order to win the current fight," he tells young Hobson, "a sin you didn't even know was on your hands. How would you like to make a little compensation?" The boy gives a stunned and furious nod of his head.

Together, they explore the live-in models and locations. A sweep of Disney's hand indicates the size of his support staff, its magnitude. "Of course we didn't need ten thousand pairs of hands to pull this off. We could have brought the project in with twenty dozen." But from the beginning, he says, the point has been the same as that animating his most modest cartoon: to set free as many as possible, to coax them into acting on their own. Now these folks are free. "But we still live in a world that needs to jail them."

They walk in silence along a line of A-frame houses, flat movie props, piecing things together. "Life as we live it," Disney says, "is about to become a free-for-all. Completely up for grabs." The anger and the beet-red violence that comes into his protégé's face forces Disney to laugh and quickly add, "Don't worry. The Nazis and Nips haven't a prayer. The good guys will win this one."

"What danger, then . . ?" As bright as he obviously is, Eddie has bought into the same morale-raising that Disney himself has hawked since Pearl Harbor: the sucker's hope that the fighting will be over when the fighting's over. Slowly and succinctly, Disney explains it to him. We have

reached the point where we imprison ourselves by the hundred thousand, commonly agreed to be in the best collective interest. We must, because the Other Guy is even less scrupulous about playing by the rules. Such a moment never fades. The world is now so treacherous and immense that the private citizen in the postwar world will lock himself up rather than face the prospect of prison.

"I don't mean chaos or collapsing buildings. The explosions and insurgencies will all disappear, except for livable doses, far away. But our lives a few decades from now will be a closet hell: each person passive, static, too terrorized to leave the apartment. The standard of living will keep creeping upward, but everyone will be dead bankrupt. Life will be endlessly entertaining, with nothing to dig into. Trust will have flown, and we will all know it. Each for himself, and the group against all."

Disney listens to himself speak. He stares full face into the scene he is painting. For a moment, he despairs of taking arms against it, he, the national spokesman against Despair. He takes a breath, and is ready again. "It's up to the two of us to fend that off. To convince the world to keep trusting. You with me, buddy?"

"But how will we ever do that?" the child asks.

According to Walt, nothing could be easier in the whole of creation. "We will tell a fable. We'll rewrite your life, spin it from the top all over again." He describes the long and revered tradition they will extend. "A creature of another order will come to show you what you otherwise could not suspect: where you fit in, what difference you make." He speaks of Dante's Beatrice; Scrooge's Ghosts; and George Bailey's Clarence, AS2, Angel Second Class. "Your job is the easiest of all. All you have to do is live. Wait for everything to come clear. Go through what the shooting script asks you to. Keep your eyes open, and believe."

A scowl passes over the seventeen-year-old face, and Disney fears for a moment that the boy is already too old. The scowl shows the knowledge of howitzers and political upheavals, strategic power plays spreading over seven continents. But he gives the boy a chance to speak. "How will telling my story do anything?"

"Easy," reveals Disney. That silent and well-mannered free-for-all is not inevitable. The world is not millions; it is one and one and one. It does not become an impasse until those ones start to renounce it. And they will have no cause to, if they stay tied to the good faith of others. "That's where

2 6 5

we come in," the cartoonist croons. "We show them how one life, yours, changes all the others it touches on. How the game remains worth the candle, so long as one walks by faith and not by sight."

Young Eddie still cannot see it. "Who will believe that what happens to me makes any difference whatsoever?"

"They will if you will," Disney corrects him. "Don't worry about the global tie-in. That's my job. Our artists will paint that in. Look at it this way. If we can make forty million people weep over a cartoon woman, we should be able to swing it with flesh and blood. If our Duck can take on the Nazis, surely you can chip in. These things have ways of propagating. The audience will think they matter, if you believe you do," he says again. "And if everyone thinks they matter, then they do." Disney again falls silent, darkly so. "But the minute you lose faith, down comes the whole house of cards. Everybody might just as well run for cover."

"So who's my guardian angel?" Eddie asks with a grin.

"Haven't you guessed?" replies the high-pitched voice that Walt himself has always supplied for his most powerful creation. The voice heard around the world.

They begin shooting the following week. Eddie meets his parents-to-be, Samuel Hinds and Beulah Bondi. Jimmy Lydon is the older brother. The boyhood home shifts from Teaneck to Hell's Kitchen. The nisei carpenters create a family apartment more rustic and more comfortable than any Eddie has ever seen. The first few weeks of shooting cover domestic scenes, with everyone except the lead speaking in delightful immigrants' accents that Eddie can barely understand.

Disney's elegant and simple scheme is to shoot all of the Eddie Hobson story in black and white. At critical points, he will set the little man afoul of periodic crises, small showdowns with history. Then Mickey will appear and pull child Hobson out of the celluloid frame into another world, a place of unsuspected connections and living color. There, the mouse will explain enough of the ineffable to get the boy through his next segment of gray scales and halftones.

The story starts in Flushing Meadow in September of '39. Eddie is there, with cameras rolling, when they sink the time capsule. The seventeen-year-old gives a stunning portrayal of himself at thirteen. The camera catches the dream of Progress in his eye as the model future unfolds at the fair. Through the time-honored device of time compression, Disney *has the first news of total war flash over the fair's loudspeakers. Eddie has his first moment of doubt, his first confrontation with the other sphere.*

"Who'll be around to open the capsule?" he asks his dad. An ashen Sammy Hinds is too terrified to answer. Then a nose peaks out from around the pavilion corner, and the unmistakable ears. The twentieth century's spokesman for kindness appears.

"Your children will," the mouse assures him. Mickey takes Eddie by the hand and the two of them disappear. The cameras stop, and Disney explains that this entire segment will be colored in later, by artists at drafting tables in distant studios. He briefly blocks the segment in: Mickey lifts the boy straight up from New York until the contours of the coastline smooth away. Mouse and man sit in a magical aerie in the stratosphere, watching the map change colors below. Mickey explains the necessity of the moral war, how many will die, how most of what is beautiful will be forever lost, but how we must and ought to throw our strength into the fray and clear away the rotting parts of the ancient and corrupted world.

Explaining the interpolated scenes, Disney delineates the dark edge between political science and fairy tale. "The special effects will knock the viewers out." The living, shifting atlas, from above, will be like nothing ever seen before. But Eddie has to take his word for it. To shoot these scenes, they put him on an empty sound stage in front of a neutral scrim. Tom Ishi, off-camera, reads the rough draft of Mickey's lines for the boy to act against. Eddie must respond in character: "Oh, I see. I've never thought of it that way before."

These scenes are extremely difficult. Hobson has to deliver a thousand looks of astonishment, gazing at the empty sound stage as if it were filled with wonder. "It will be," Disney promises. It will be. When Mickey rushes him on a rainbow back into the black-and-white belly of his family, nobody, to Eddie's amazement, even suspects he was away.

After the sweet burst of success in filming the scenes from '39 to Pearl, the next black-and-white sessions seem dismally forced and strained. The Hobson family goes wooden, and nobody knows why. Then, during especially wretched multiple takes of the scene where older brother Art tells of his enlistment, walking out of the apartment vowing to "teach those fanatical Japs to keep their hands off," the entire camera crew breaks out laughing. The problem dawns on them. The segment director, Ralph Sato, Disney's right-hand man, fixes everything. "Try not to worry about our feelings," he tells the embarrassed cast. "We are as American as the rest of you Germans." Lydon performs his bit with flying colors and is gone.

Next comes the pivotal Drugstore scene. The set crew creates a brilliant replica of a soda fountain and druggist's, down to the last magazine rack and candy bar. They populate it with extras including two nisei and a beautiful, young, since-forgotten ingenue whose career will end with this film. Sato tells Eddie there's no script for this one. "Just go over to the right side of the magazine rack and browse the photo weeklies."

Eddie does, and discovers the poison image planted there. In shock, he forgets the cameras, forgets entirely where he is, and breaks down like a child for a family that cannot be kept from loss. His face flashes hot and bitter at the shopgirl's attempted consolation. He tenses himself to charge off the set, to run out of the project altogether.

"Believe, son," yells Disney from off-camera. "Only believe."

"Keep rolling," Sato yells at the reticent cameramen who want to turn away in shame from this hot grief they capture. "Don't you dare stop. This is what we are after."

After the take, Hobson pushes his way through restraining hands and locks himself in his trailer, refusing all entreaties to come out. Shooting stops for three days. When Eddie at last emerges, emaciated, he storms Disney's office. "Is the magazine for real? Is it really Artie? My brother?" Disney says nothing. The mouse must speak for him.

Back on the empty stage, Eddie, in front of a curtain, pretends revelation. The mouse meets the grieving boy outside the soda shop, tears in his own mammalian eyes. He takes Eddie to a vantage point from which they see how even the sacrificed life, seemingly wasted, contributes in mysterious ways we cannot understand. The magazine photo of the meaningless tragedy at Brownsville becomes an inspiration and rallying point for countless American pilots. Mickey shows how big brother Artie's death trickles outward and, by putting boys on their cautionary mettle, saves lives.

Even with guiding synopsis, Eddie finds this scene the most difficult in the movie's production. In loss and suffering, he must conjure up from imagination alone what the studio animators will add only months later. He must see the mouse, and his face must radiate full understanding. Somehow the boy does it, hallucinating his reconciliation *with the meaningless accident, inventing acceptance from the shoals of sorrow.*

The hope of screen enlistment sees him through. They shoot the draft-board scene next, Eddie camping out in bedroll on his eighteenth birthday, waiting to make his private petition. But in the Disney version, he is too tall. He receives the crippling news of assignment to a noncombatant's role. Stern Sato keeps his cameras turning. Eddie goes to purgatory, hell; Aircraft Training School, Amarillo. Sweet Mickey comes like Virgil to steady him in his darkest hour.

"You see," says the rodent, wise beyond his species, "your every action furthers a thousand others. Take that carburetor you cleaned this morning. It doesn't seem like much, but . . ." And the two of them are off, following the elaborate chain reaction put into motion by Eddie's simple act of good faith. Eddie sees, under Mickey's tutelage, the force his contribution accumulates. "If it weren't for that one clean carburetor, then that one plane . . . and if not for that one plane, then this one raid . . . and if not this one raid, then this campaign . . ." And campaign to theater to war. And war, as Hobson has already learned in the first color segment, is the only way to a clean world of mutual goodwill. No such thing as the single vote, the single defection. Persuasion cascades, tipping the scale.

Eddie returns to black and white, awakened and purified. When the defection, the loss of faith, finally does come, it's from an unexpected quarter. Ralph Sato, the film's director of the real-world, black-and-white segments, one morning arrives at Disney's office and lets himself in. He surprises Disney in the act of talking into a black metal bullhorn attached to a mechanical dictaphone. He hears just a fragment.

We shall not cease from exploration . . .

Disney snaps the machine off and slides it out of sight. He asks Sato the question. Sato, who has succeeded in capturing the boy's urgency beyond any expectation, cannot quite say what causes his nonspecific malaise. Is he sick? Disney recalls the opening of that great Capra script he has, through friendship, been allowed to see. No, worse, comes the answer out of the cosmos. Discouraged. Disney has a brainstorm about casting:

Colonel Jimmy Stewart, now flying his twentieth mission over Germany, is perfect for the homebound George Bailey of Bedford Falls. He must tell Capra.

Sato, still inarticulate, stumbles over to an old Baldwin upright sitting in the corner of Disney's remarkably unremarkable workroom. He strokes a few keys aimlessly, launching into a "Turkey in the Straw" faintly reminiscent of Charles Ives. But the tune soon crumbles into malicious and dissonant burlesque. He starts again with a Glenn Miller favorite, but in a few bars it becomes, despite Sato's best intentions, a send-up of the "Marines' Hymn." Ralph breaks down and sobs silently. He puts his head against the music stand and says, softly, "Outside, Walt. What's happening to us outside?" Disney touches the man's shoulder, giving no consolation. Sato springs back up on the bench, launches into an animated, perfect Shirley Temple impression. The Good Ship Lollipop: "While bonbons play, on the sunny beach of Peppermint Bay."

Disney recognizes the danger at once. The man suffers from the late stages of the Stockholm Syndrome, where long-held hostages fall in love with their jailers. The entire infrastructure of the project, the culmination of Disney's life work, is in imminent peril of disintegration. For the creator of modern animation, the father of separate-cel technique, the man who has built his life on challenging reality, knows that if Sato breaks down, a ripple of domino defections will tear World World apart. "Easy, Ralph," he says gently. He says they are doing everything in their power to remedy the spreading evil Outside. Their fable must be their weapon. Any more direct opposition risks making things worse.

Sato listens to the explanation, shaking. He tickles the ivories again, slower now, in the melodious minor, something bluesy and wistful, Gershwin, music to walk over the Brooklyn Bridge and into the fiery South Pacific by. Calm descends on his frantic face. Sato's eyebrows arch slightly. His eyes examine a scene some several thousand miles away. The corners of his mouth flicker up and down, like the ticker on a brisk, mixed day on Wall Street. The tune underneath his fingers grows increasingly strange: Bird Parker jumps around in there, and Copeland, and W. C. Handy, and snippets of Protestant hymnody and patriotic marches by William Billings. He migrates to the black keys, a parody of Oriental pentatonic, before returning back home to Ives, and Tin Pan Alley.

Finally, Sato stops playing and closes the keyboard lid. He looks up at Disney, who is about to fall through the floor. All trace of anxiety, the desperation of too many headlines, washes clean from the man. He looks straight at Disney, his black Asian eyes wet with Lethean waters. He opens his mouth. "I see." *Emphasis on the I. Disney, trying to appear wise, motions him to go on.* "I see now. What the fuss is all about." *He stands and walks around the room. He stops to pick up bric-a-brac—a book, an afghan, a plaster statue of Goofy that a six-year-old sent to Disney. He holds these junk items as if he cannot make out their purpose, as if they are the last commodities on earth.*

He walks as if he had just learned how that morning. He arrives back where Disney is standing. He stretches out both arms and grabs Disney by the shoulders, either affectionately or to keep himself from falling. "Walt." *Sato shakes his mentor.* "Walt." *His first familiarity with the boss beyond Disney-san. Sato smiles and shakes his head. He laughs the worldly, incredulous, liberated, but exhausted laugh of a returning exile who never thought he would touch foot on home soil again.* "Walt. Walt, oh Walt, oh Walt." *By the look of things, the fellow has come back from the dead, from abject pragmatism, with tidings of how all manner of things will be well. But the next words out of Sato's mouth make Disney's blood stop in its capillaries.* "Walt, my boy, you lied to us." *Sato, the image of one who has gone beyond good and bad will to arrive at the islands of indifference, smiles at the word* lie, *as if to say,* But of course, you couldn't have known.

"What do you mean, Ralph? What did I lie about?" *Disney's conscience is clear. He still, at this minute, believes not only in the internal consistency and purity but also in the absolute urgency of World World, of You Are the War.*

Sato smiles at him beatifically, forgiving. "You said it was either the concentration camps or this. But there's a third place. Another way out." *He paces again, returning to the vengeful disappointment we are all born into.* "We could have been out in late '42."

"How, Ralph?"

Sato walks to the window without slackening his pace. He looks one direction, clear to the mountains of Colorado. He looks the other, and sees the rolling, older hills of Pennsylvania. Everything is there, written small on the set, to be gathered up in one sweep of the rolling cameras.

He gestures to Disney to look at what they have made with their blank slate. "Walt, we are trying to rescue a world that is currently burning forty thousand casualties every day. You can't beat those kind of numbers except with numbers. We are trying to cure an entire planet, the only inhabitable place anyone has ever seen, one that has gone completely, out-the-window, stark, raving insane. And with what? The story of a snot-nosed kid whose brother is killed. Wishful thinking. Toy trains!"

With the easy grace of those born into a country not their own, Sato glides back to the piano where Disney still stands frozen. In one smooth motion, he removes the watch from his wrist. Disney thinks for a moment that Sato means to fasten the timepiece around his fist and use it as a brass knuckle. Instead, Sato places the instrument face up on the piano keys, Mickey's hands still waving imperceptibly in the winds of time. The action is unmistakable: Ralph has turned in his ears. He says nothing further, just spins on the ball of his foot and heads toward the door. It's a heroic gesture, otherworldly. The timing is not lost on the great producer. Disney has the first, frightened, but hopeful flickerings of suspicion that he might really have overlooked all the possibilities: how does Sato expect to make it out that door and keep going, past the military guard, past the Congress, past the political system that strands them here, past the protectors of national security? Is there another way out of this camp without being rounded up and boxcarred immediately into the other? Disney has to ask, at least. "Where you headed, Ralph?"

Sato glides around in the doorway. He looks at Disney with compassionate eyes, eyes that have looked at something beyond human retribution. He gazes at the author of The Führer's Face, the inventor and principal executor of the World World breakout, and spells out his departure from the good-intentions pavement company. "We belong out there, Walt. Nothing can be fixed, except from inside." Strange to say, he still wears that transcendent smile, as if the conflagration out there were not only livable but more remarkable, more newsworthy, luckier, than anyone supposes. "It is wonderful, out there, Walt. Something remarkable is about to happen. We've got to go meet it. Tell them, if anyone asks, that I've gone for a Burton."

Ralph disappears, leaving the project forever. Gone for a Burton: Disney recognizes the slang. It started a couple of years back in the RAF, then gradually caught on in all the British services, and has by now crept into all branches of Allied fighting men. A Burton, a beer, a brew. Gone for a drink. Gone into the drink. Deep-sixed; six-packed. Gone to see a man about a dog. Departed, DOA, deceased.

Of course, Disney realizes. He decodes the message without any help from the code-cracking staffs over at Signal Corps or Bletchley Park. There is another way out for any of the male staff, if they want it. Perhaps he is guilty for not encouraging this option, pushing it with the dwarves. Enlistment: the draft board's offer of freedom.

Weeks later, Disney traces Sato's path through official channels. He has joined the 442nd, the national nisei outfit. By this point, the 442nd is one of the most heavily decorated units in the war and among the highest in per capita casualties. The former prisoners of war compile a magnificent record for combat performance and bravery. At one especially hard-fought battle in Europe, an astonished German prisoner of war asks where all the Japanese had come from. "Didn't you know they were on our side?" says an American lieutenant. "Or do you believe all that stuff Goebbels tells you?"

But Sato joins at a tricky time for the nisei battalions. The war in Europe is sure to end in a few months. People begin to ask what to do with the 442nd after V-E day. Send them against the Japanese? The American High Command is uncomfortable with the idea. Jokes abound about how to tell who is on which side. Funny; that was never an issue when the American Germans were shipped to Europe.

Sato's departure hits Disney hard. Disney is sure he will be killed in the world's catastrophe, or worse. The man walked through the door wanting it. If Ralph cannot find it with the 442nd in active combat, he will run into it somewhere Stateside, in some fluke accident in the American Theater. And the resulting blood will be on Disney's hands. Worse, Sato's departure puts a new tint on the project. Far from springing themselves and providing a springboard for imagination's triumph over brutality, Disney and the High-Ho ten thousand may have, in constructing World World and shooting the rushes for You Are the War, flown from all responsibility and left the global cancer to fester.

All this happens just before the final and most difficult hurdle. Young Hobson has not yet come face to face with his biggest test, his real scrape with contemporary history. All that Disney has to preserve the teenager's crucial faith is a handful of Fairy Dust. He has no choice: the mouse must take the boy to see the future.

15

All Little Eddie could do was stand, clutch the phone, and wait, as family life had trained him, for the punchline. No punchline came, meaning it *was* the hospital at the other end. Mom was downstairs in an instant, buzzing him with that unfailing sense of things going wrong she had developed through years of conditioning.

"Who is it? What do they want?" As answer, Eddie rolled the receiver off his shoulder into her waiting hands. He went into the living room, powered down the TV tube, and tried to think. But he could not think. He could either listen to the rest of the call, or he could concentrate on not listening. Both prevented his concentrating on anything else. He chose the first, piecing back the unheard conversant on the other end through Ailene's cues. The hospital assured Ailene that Pop was indeed a sick fellow. *Point one for the obvious*, thought Eddie, toughing it out. The diagnosis, however, was still outstanding. More tests were required. *Weren't they always?* The problem, the health professional patiently explained, was that the testee had flown, leaving no forwarding address.

"No,"Ailene assured the fellow. "We haven't heard from him since . . ." The thought jerked the eavesdropping son: *Since Artie, earlier that week.* No evidence to the contrary, he assumed the most comforting solution to Dad's disappearance: Artie had allowed Pop to break the rules and come home with him for the night. Eddie imagined the two boys plotting the secret abduction, relieved.

As long as he was listening in, he decided to go all the way. He tore upstairs to the other extension in the folks' bedroom. But when he picked up the receiver the Hines man was wrapping things up, saying he was familiar with Mr. Hobson's case but it wouldn't be a good thing to discuss it until they knew what it *was*, which required getting the runaway back into the ward to complete the tests. The man rang off. Mother and son let receivers lapse back into respective cradles. When Eddie got back down to the kitchen, Sister Lily, still asleep, was propped up at the table in her nightgown, mumbling, "What . . . ? Who . . . ?"

"I can't stay any longer," Ailene answered, lingering. "I'm going to be late for work if I don't leave this minute." Since she had never once been late for work in her entire professional life, she could not afford, at this late a date, to set a precedent. So she hurriedly drank an aspirin and coffee compote, making her usual, startled swallowing noises. Eddie grew irritated that she could not swallow silently just this once, given the emergency and his need to think. Ailene dictated a faked-calm series of noninstructions to her children that made absolutely no sense. Then, realizing that what she had just said was gibberish, she countermanded herself by saying, "Don't either of you do anything until I call you from work."

She fluttered out, further alarming stunned offspring by kissing them both gravely. The December air, taking another sharp turn downward, gusted the door open at her touch. It took her ten minutes of idling time to get the Olds warmed up and drivable, minutes that Eddie might have spent outside, talking over options with her. But by the time that possibility occurred to him, she was finally hitting on all cylinders and disappearing down the driveway. A voice from the table called Eddie Jr. back from the land of failed concentration. "Will someone kindly fill me in? I haven't the foggiest notion of what in the world is coming down."

"Your father," Eddie began, but his voice would let him get no further. All they had to go through rose up and wedged in his throat, like a crowd plugging an escalator. And yet, he was surprised to find that what blocked his windpipe was not, as he first thought, a lump of vocal distress but the similar cord constriction of joy. He delighted in speaking the two words that prevented him from going on. The old man was still alive, unpredictable, capable of the liberating caper. There was more to him than anybody suspected. Eddie turned to face his sister, flushed with fullness. "I mean *yer* father. Yer father has—how shall I put this delicately?—jumped bail."

Lily groaned slowly and deliberately. She put the tip of her nose down on the table and made suffering sounds. The gesture—another of Big Sis's contrivances—ordinarily offensive to Eddie, now was simply one of the things his sister had to do. Eddie accepted this collection of mannerisms as Lily's way of making her way, as Lily. She would never reform. She was simply the person who could be counted on to put her nose on the table when crisis came. Lily without Lilyisms meant nothing. Nothing stood underneath her but her.

"That'll teach you to care what happens to the man," he said, not needing to strain much to bring off an uncannily good Eddie Sr. impression. He had to turn toward the kitchen window to keep her from noticing the broad smile of rapprochement he could not keep off his face. Outside, the pretty next-door-neighbor girl, Gina Weatherby, two years younger than he, looked up from smoothing her clothes and balancing her school books, and noticed his grin. She thought his smile was for her and returned it, one ingenue to another, waving the innocent wave of one whom catastrophe cannot touch.

He waved back as the school bus pulled up. Gina pointed a pretty digit in its direction and tilted her head, inquiring: *You gonna deign . . . ?* He pulled the skin around his lower lip into a disapproving fatness and shook his head: *Wouldn't catch me climbing onto that deathtrap.* She shrugged, and waved once more as she boarded. Sixteen, with a wave that created its own white elbow gloves: Eddie's heart filled with an odd, warm, protective affection for the clear-faced sandy-haired kid. He caught her eye again as the bus pulled away and smiled sadly back at her, a smile that indicated she would have to find someone else. He couldn't possibly marry her: there was insanity in his family. Besides, he was already pledged to another. Then he grew conscious of his thoughts and yelled at himself for bogging down in the everyday while there was a disaster at hand.

"So what do we do now?" That most familiar of questions, coming from that unmistakably Hobsonian voice, called Little Eddie back to the things of this world. What *do* we do? If she had nothing else to recommend, Lily had a way of reducing the outstanding issues to their bare-boned essentials. Pop was on the loose; what could *we* do to reverse the situation? Eddie had no immediate answer, except to pace out to the front porch to verify that the big guy had not somehow slipped back to his traditional place on the kapok while everyone was looking the other way.

When he paced back in, Lily pulled herself together, removing the cereal box from the shelf and stalking a milk gallon and a bowl. She grabbed a second bowl and tossed it to him without preparation. He caught it athletically and set to work on his second breakfast of the morning. The situation called for another 25 percent of the U.S. RDA of everything. Between mouthfuls, he managed, "We wait for Mom to call. Right? She said she would call when she got to work. So we wait. Am I right?" So this was what adulthood, achieving one's majority, was all about. He far preferred your basic puerile irresponsibility. "She's gonna call. We can't do anything until then."

"What did the hospital say?"

He spoke between spoonfuls. "Sick. Tests bad. More tests needed. Gone."

Lily pushed the cereal bits around in her bowl, studying their effects on the milk's surface tension. "Did he just leave his stuff? His books and his change of clothes and all?" Eddie shrugged at the pointless question and kept shoveling. Lily moved from irrelevance to irrelevance, concerned with the logistics of the escape. "How can you get past the front desk of a hospital without anyone noticing?"

"Easy. Make a noise like you're healthy." Lily cried out in pain. That was their last real transaction, aside from Eddie's adding, every few spoonfuls, "So what do we do now?" If either formulated any plans for action, they both had the good sense to keep mum.

When the refrigerator hum and the tick of the stove clock grew too much for her, Lily walked around the table and yanked Little Bro up by the arm socket. "I know how we can get her to call." Above his protests, without explanations, she led him to the downstairs bathroom off her room. Before he could figure out what she was doing, Lil forced Eddie into the dry tub, fully clothed. Instantly, the phone rang. He looked up at her, startled. In the most matter-of-fact voice Eddie had ever heard her level, Lily explained, "*She* can't tell there's no water in it from across town," and skipped to answer the ringing line.

The call was brief. "Call Artie."

"Call Artie," said Lily, disconnecting.

"Of course. Call Artie," echoed Eddie. "Why didn't *we* think of that?"

Artie didn't know anything. He'd seen Pop a couple of days ago. "But we didn't really talk about anything. Something about his roommate's dream. Surgery. Oh, yeah. We talked silliness. Played Name That Poem."

"Jeezuz," said Eddie. Verse was his least favorite thing in the world. "What poetry?"

"Oh, Eliot, Yeats, Kipling. All the big guys. But it didn't mean anything," said Artie. "At least not to me. Also, he rejected one more solution to the prisoner problem. But he gave no hint that he was thinking of *this.*" Eddie rang off, making his older brother promise to call Rach at work and get back to them collect if she had any word.

Lily was right at his elbow when Eddie hung up. "Tell, tell, tell."

Affectation again. Eddie forgot about these quirks being her, and before he could check himself he said, "Artie's been in touch with Pop, who says he'll come home as soon as you get a job." Although she didn't even flex a lip muscle, he at once came as close to hating himself as his nature allowed. He blamed the outburst on Artie, whom he always tried to imitate immediately after talking to.

Eddie called Mom back at work, and for once she didn't reprimand him for doing so. They reassured one another that there was nothing to get alarmed about. Dad had simply taken a walk or something equally ludicrous. He was no doubt trying to prove a point about patients' rights. He would show up by noon. After ringing off, Eddie conveyed this new party philosophy to Lil, who snorted, went back to her room, and shut the door. Eddie hitched the two miles to school, explaining to the detention-hall proctor that his mother had given him express permission to skip homeroom, seeing as how Christmas was just a few days away. He got four hours, with no appeal.

Noon became evening, and still they had no word. Rach checked in after five, as did Artie, neither with any contributions. The hospital called back, needing to know if the family wanted them to alert the Cook County sheriff's office. Outwardly optimistic, Ailene told them not to bother.

Ailene, Lily, and Ed Jr. gathered for perfunctory dinner, a sorry affair all around. Despite the looming cataclysm, Mom saw to it that the four basic food groups were amply represented. She carefully rinsed an array of vegetables under the tap, exchanging insecticides for lead. The nuclear three had spent the previous few evenings alone, but this was their first night ever without a sponsor. For lack of a better way to grind up time after the meal, they dealt the cards. Three-handed pinochle.

Aside from Lily solicitously fixing everybody drinks and Ailene bidding rather more ambitiously than usual, the cards fell out pretty much as expected. Occasionally, one of the three would go out on a limb and predict: "I have a hunch we'll be hearing something in the next couple of minutes. Just a feeling." But all forecasts came to nothing, except to make everyone lose track of trumps. Psychological warfare coupled with a roundhouse led Lily to win two consecutive matches. Eddie declined a third, saying he had to go lie down and toss around for a while.

He left the women to their low conversation and headed upstairs. At the top of the flight, the phone rang. He dove the three yards into the folks' bedroom, grabbing the upstairs extension with the grace of an on-base leadoff man performing his end of a hit-and-run. He cornered the receiver and for a moment forgot the standard invocation. Then he gathered himself and got out something close to "Hollow." His "low" collided with a *lo* of another persuasion all together.

From the other end came that unmistakable bass singing the foundation line of the old favorite chorale. How a Rose E'er Blooming, from tender stem hath sprung. Eddie Jr. stood transfixed, unable to cut in on the tune, noticing only how truly beautiful that voice was, how the throat alone on the man remained untouched by any outward destruction of disease. By all appearances, the old guy still had a good deal of singing waiter left in him, despite his unfortunate, long-standing mix-up with History.

The kid's hesitation proved fatal. The faint static of long-distance-relayed lines indicated anything from the sixty miles to Chicago all the way up to the ends of the earth. Dad would not quit singing, although the bass line, stripped of the family's upper voices, seemed more like that sultry, minor, old favorite of his, "Don't Get Around Much Anymore." As he headed home toward that remarkable deceptive cadence in the next to the last strain, another voice, female, joined in on the crystalline melody: Amid the snows of winter, when half spent was the night. Eddie Jr. could not figure out what he was hearing. He couldn't believe the evidence, or get the voices to cohere. Pop had run away with a woman; it was as simple and insane as that. Then the son realized that the soprano, sounding as far away as the bass, actually came from as close as downstairs.

Pop pointed that out to him. "Thanks, girl. I might have been at that all night before *certain* unnamed parties would have condescended to lend a tenor."

Eddie Jr. took the cue. " 'Lo, Pop. Listen, you're a sick man. You gotta get back to the hospital."

"No credit for stating the obvious," Dad said, his voice combating the static. "How's your mother?"

"How are *you*?" Lily inserted. Little Eddie hated three-way conversations. They were impossible to synchronize, even in the best of circumstances. He could not yell at his sister to shut up without violating the special delicacy of this connection. Besides, she seemed to be doing much better with the third wheel than he.

"Not bad, hon. Want to know where I am?"

"Where are you?" Eddie Jr. blurted out, instantly feeling more than routinely stupid.

"Just a second, I'll check." The distant handset tumbled to the ground with a clunk. Eddie and Lil had only a few seconds to work out a strategy, and they wasted them. Before they could say anything to one another, Dad was back. "Man behind the cash register says this is Neosho. I believe him. Funny name. Probably an Indian thing. What do *you* think?"

"What *state*, Dad?" asked Eddie, trying not to sound testy.

"State? Why, I'm perfectly sober, I assure you." The utter noncooperation of this predictable gag sent Eddie scrambling for the reference shelf that the man kept near his bedstead. Eddie cursed himself for his cultivated illiteracy, not knowing which of the thick books was the best prospect for locating the town. Reduced to repeating "Are you . . . ? Are you . . ." he scrounged for and eventually located an atlas.

Lily cut in again, with a question he could not quite make out. Distracted, he could hear Mom in the background downstairs, demanding the phone. He blessed his sister silently for not transferring the call. He found the unlikely name in the atlas index, followed by an inscrutable look-up code of numbers. Flipping to the designated map, he heard Dad reply, "By hitchhiking, of course." Eddie gathered enough presence of mind to warn his parent about the dangers of that means of travel, hypocritically making no mention of his jaunt to school that morning.

Dad ignored him, instead giving a condensed travelogue of his last eighteen hours. "I really made pretty good time. Lost a little edge around St. Louis, though."

Good time to where? And at that moment, he put his finger on the spot. Neosho was an entirely overlookable rat's eyelash just south of Joplin, Missouri. It fell right on the crossover of two highways, but that was about it. His eyes scanned the immediate environs for an appeal to motive but found nothing even remotely interesting anywhere in the area. Eddie's eyes flicked down as Dad jabbered on about nothing. A familiar name jumped out due south of Neosho: De Kalb. De Kalb, Texas.

For a minute, the strangest, half-formed possibilities presented themselves. The man had gotten confused. Turned around. Alternate universe, like in the comics, where everything is the same, only different, or like that church logic where alpha and omega constantly turn up as one another. Dad was finding his way back to a place he had never been. Eddie cleared his head enough to ask, "Where you headed, Pop?"

But the blunt route also got nowhere, except to launch the old man into "Goin' home, goin' home, I'ma goin' home." Dad quit after the chorus, adding, "Those folk-song writers have a lot of nerve, ripping off Dvořák like that."

Eddie could feel Dad winding up the conversation. He felt like screaming, singing, whispering, begging, pleading, reciting the Gettysburg Address at high speed—anything to delay the inevitable severance. He was more alarmed, more in the dark, than he had been that morning upon hearing of the prison break. Eddie Jr. had always known that his fundamental inability to get a straight answer out of his namesake, no matter how forthright he played it, would eventually spell trouble. And right now was fast becoming eventually. Trying to think like the fellow in question, he employed one more tactic, one he hated to stoop to: allusion. He cut in on Lily, who was saying something inane about how the hospital needed him back for tests. "Hey, Dad-o. Lemme ask you something."

"Yes, Eddie?" Pure high-school-teacher intonation.

"Do those two guys in the bind ever get it together?"

For a brief silence, it seemed as if Pop might suddenly come across, surrender something of substance. At last he answered. "Do they ever break out of the matrix? Do they stop murdering themselves over the long haul? Too many maybes. First, they have to get a second chance. Second, they have to ignore the fact that evolution favors the nasty and brutish, that success is always at the other guy's expense. Third, even if the game stabilizes with two players, it's certainly hopeless at four billion."

Pop was back in the saddle, in the land of allegory and evasive metaphor. Eddie Jr. ran out of countering resources. He was about ready to tell Lily to put Mom on when Big Sis fell back, way back, to a level of questioning he'd totally overlooked. "You must have been on the road most of last night," she said, making it sound as if the trip were your basic, planned-out summer vacation. "How long have you been awake?"

Dad, jovial again, answered, "Oh, about thirty years or so." Then, over both children's accelerating, crescendoed, and panicked protests, he told them he'd call again soon and ordered them to wish the rest of the family well. "Keep them honest for me, will you?"

16

In her dream, Lily rose in the cold, green water, emptying her lungs as she shot upward. But at the surface, a sheet of ice blocked her way. Airless, she hammered at the crust, but her blows had no force. She felt her way along the seamless and solid sheet for miles, about to black out for good. At last she found a crumbled edge and, scrambling for life, she widened the passage and surfaced. Instantly, a hand crashed through the blowhole and forced her back into the cold water. She woke in total terror, tried to sit up and scream, but the same hand held her against her pillow. Someone was in the room with her. Lily let out a deep, sleep-drugged wail, pitchless and spectral in her vocal cords. Then she woke enough to recognize her mother. Ailene had come into her room to sit on the edge of her bed and pet her hair. And that pathetic, secret gesture created Lily's nightmare.

"It's all right. It's only me. My God, I'm sorry, child." Ailene put her arms around her dazed daughter and kissed her, the most forsaken kiss Lily had ever received. A kiss that probed for comfort and came up dry. "Forgive me." Lily's neck muscles, still straining to bolt upright, relaxed, and she sank back against the pillow. Her mother, forgetting the year let alone the hour, returned to stroking her hair abstractedly. "You were so young, once. You were all so young."

Lily reached out from under the linen and took her mother's hand. Tensing slightly, she stilled Ailene's rocking. She could comfort her parent in the middle of the night without panic. But comforting her *rocking parent*: she would have better luck trapped under the ice. "When were we young, Mother?"

Ailene heard the sedative gentleness in her daughter's voice. She freed her hand and said, disgusted, "Oh, I'm all right." They sat in silence, each hating the other. "I wish to heaven you had let me talk to him."

Too furious to answer, Lily at length got control of her hands and voice. It was stupid to fight, she knew. Neither of them wanted to. Their anger was with awkward kindness in an unkind place. "So what would you have said?"

"I don't *know* what I would have said," Mother answered, testiness draining from her in mid-sentence. "I would have found words as soon as I heard his voice." After a long silence, she said, "You let him shake your composure."

Lily fired back, angered again. "You were as shook as we were."

"I was *not*. You didn't even give me a chance." Her mouth crumpled, and Lily reached out to guide the woman's hand back into her hair. Stroking awhile in darkness, Ailene at last said, "I've lived with the man for thirty years. I signed the papers. I could have said things to him that might have brought him around. Things that I never told any of *you*."

"Secrets, Mom?" Lily said, softly skeptical. Ailene laughed silently at the absurdity.

"I would have told him that we needed a fourth to make a table."

Lily smiled, unseen in the dark. "Mother, what's wrong with him?"

Ailene shrugged. Lily felt her bony shoulders erupt. "Your father never made it a habit of telling me anything. I suppose if I had gone to college on a scholarship things might have been different. But the way they turned out . . ." She shrugged again, cutting Lily's heart. " 'Just the facts, ma'am.' "

Ailene opened, spoke her thoughts out loud as if Lily had at last become that other part of herself that blood made her. "Not that he doesn't talk to me when we're alone. My God, you know nobody can shut the man up sometimes. He carries on about things I couldn't follow even *with* a college degree. But Ed never says how *he* feels about anything. Just some instructive example from the fifties or the twenties. That and his stupid fear of doctors. He wasn't so bad when we were young. He didn't have half so many ideas. But a little farther away every year. Life with your father has not been . . . simple." Suddenly hearing what she confessed, Ailene added hastily, "Of course, I could have done far worse."

Lily sank deeper under the petting hand. Her mother knew no more than she did. The answer would disappear with Pop. But just as she had almost given in to the comforting hand, she sat bolt upright, with the force of her original fright. She kept her eyes lowered, focused on an idea. "Mother, what do you know about Hobstown?"

The mention of the word startled Ailene. Her face became a mix of reticence and eagerness to talk about an awful topic. "The first time I walked in on him, in the late 1950s, it scared the living daylights out of me. His mind was in another place. His eyes were smoked over. I don't think he even recognized me. I thought he had had a fit. It came just weeks after he had first fallen sick."

Lily, by reflex, shook a finger and said, *"Post hoc, ergo propter hoc,"* the old schoolteacher's admonition. Both women smiled weakly, but lowered their heads in shame.

"No, Lil. Really. I have a sneaking suspicion . . ." But she would not say what her suspicion was. Instead, she returned to the facts. "When he first started recording the tapes, he used an ancient machine. We couldn't play the first ones now, even if we wanted to. I can't tell you how many times I passed closed doors and heard the monologue on the other side. I even listened in a few times. I never understood anything I heard. The things he dictated into the tape machine were like chunks of a dream, melting into each other, changing shape without any connection. It spooked me, like discovering, after thirty years, that your husband's Thursday night jaunts to supposed Elks meetings were really trips to an anarchist's bomb factory."

Ailene began to rock again. This time Lily let her. The hour was so late, the story so strange, that the annoying motion now seemed better than the alternative. "He invented such strange stuff, speaking it right off of the top of his head, in perfect sentences. I can't piece it back together now. Full sentences. Spooky. I . . ." Ailene paused a long time. "I didn't *want* to know what he was saying.

"I thought the passing out—you know how stroke victims become different people? I thought that whatever change in blood vessels made him pass out must also have changed him enough to make him want to . . . tape his journey. In the early years, Hobstown filled him with excitement and enthusiasm. He spent days at the library, returning with maps, charts, and plans. He used to come down from a half-hour session rubbing his hands and kiss me. I thought he was working on a book or a movie script. I'd ask when I was going to be able to hear it. He'd say, 'You hear it already. Everybody does.' " She looked at her child across the pitch-dark inches. Her face asked for some sign of agreement. Lily nodded, wanting her to go on.

"For a long while, wherever we moved, he hung photos above his desk in the corner of his workroom. The pictures would change every few months. Sometimes they were well-known personalities—a famous scientist, a politician, an actress, an inventor, a revolutionary. Sometimes they were stills, landscapes, or famous events: the Statue of Liberty from out at sea, or a labor-strike riot early in the century. I imagined he was writing a great history text, that when it at last came out, he would get an offer from a college back East and we could go home." She spoke bitterly at her own willingness to hope.

"What picture did he have up most recently?" Lily asked, less for information than to distract the woman.

"About six months ago, he hung a photo from a thirties magazine. Walt Disney sitting at a desk, dictating into a black horn microphone, recording an idea for a Silly Symphony. You kids wouldn't know what those were. They were cartoons, but not like any cartoon anyone had seen up until then. All back and forth, three dimensions, with everything moving, even the background. As a child, I could feel myself falling into the frame. They were long shorts, shown before the feature. No words: all set to a classical piece, image fitting music. Three days before we took him to Hines, he took the picture down."

The bedroom shrunk, became a little girl's room, far too small for two full-grown people. For a brief instant, both women looked like cornered rabbits, gauging the danger the other represented before preparing to dart. When Ailene spoke again, her words would have passed for free association to anyone except her daughter.

"Your father was already pretty sick when we first moved to Ohio. I didn't let on to you at the time, but it was touch and go. He was all jaundiced, as bad as last week, and sullen, too, which he never is. He was between jobs, like now, and all I could think about was, 'There's just the army life insurance between us and disaster.' I never told you kids that he was so much worse than you saw."

"For God's sake, Mother. You think you have to tell *me?*"

"You were all so young. There was no need to put you through it, too. The unemployment was murder on him. You know how he always says, 'Whatever work your hands can do, do now.' One day he came down to breakfast with that newspaper article about—remember?" Lily nodded, motionless, knowing what was coming. "About how that famous entertainer cured himself of self-destructive behavior and substance abuse, just by talking into a tape recorder. By holding a dialogue between his healthy personality and his ill one.

"The tapes came back out, for the hardest work he ever put in on them. He took a surprise turn for the better. His mind cleared up. He grew kinder again. We moved to Illinois, into this house. He got the job at the high school. He didn't work on Hobstown then. He hardly went to it at all. The tapes stayed in the back of the closet. He was totally clean for I don't know how long. It seemed like Hobstown had done its job, cured him, made itself useless. I thought he would retire the place, put the hobby out to pasture, for good."

"But he didn't."

"No, he didn't. He started up again, on the sly. I didn't even notice at first. I'd be in the kitchen and think he was talking to me from upstairs. I'd call back to him, and when he didn't say anything in return, I'd let it slide. Then it was back to full-length sessions, all over again. Adding tapes to that neat library in the closet: ink-labeled, always in order. He got ill again. My heart hit low-water mark. When he lost this latest job soon after, it was cause and effect. A replay of the old days.

"I felt like a woman I once read about who'd lost one hundred and thirty pounds. When she started to gain it back, four pounds, then ten, she went into the bathroom one day and killed herself. She left a note saying she knew the weight would all come back and that she just couldn't stand having to surrender all that hard-won ground."

Lily saw her mother's cheeks wetting in the dark. She said nothing, and Mother carried on alone. "Maybe he tapes what he hears and sees when he goes down. Maybe it's the record of those cells going bad." Ailene's voice spilled. "The worst part is hope. I think every change will be a change for the better. His small kindnesses, his annual resolutions. I cannot help it. What's the alternative? When he agreed to go to the hospital for the first time in twenty years, I thought, 'Now, at last.' A few days later, this."

"Mother," Lily said, heading off the worst. "You are too good."

"You think I'm a saint? I'm not even close. I've tried any number of things they don't recommend in heaven."

2 8 9

Lily could not help smiling at the vintage-Ailene phrase. "Like what?"

"That time I ran away? Lil, you're old enough to remember. He passed out in his room, while working on the project. He'd locked his door, and I couldn't get in to help him. Twenty minutes is a long time to sit in front of a locked door, smashing it with your fist, calling out, not knowing what is on the other side. The next day I packed, explaining to you and Art and little Rachel that I was only leaving your father for his own good, to try to bring him around.

"Artie must have been ten. But he was so old already. He helped me carry my bags out to the car, saying he understood and approved of my actions. I looked at that little boy—he was wearing a pair of chinos and a paisley shirt; he hated paisley, and only wore it because I gave it to him for Christmas. All of a sudden, I couldn't do it. If that child hadn't been so accommodating, things might have worked out differently. For one, your father might still be around today. And in good health."

Ailene got up suddenly and walked out of the room. Lily sat up, threw on a robe, and wearily followed her out into the kitchen. "The problem," her mother said to herself, "is that the alternative to foolish hope is even worse."

Lily toyed with the playing cards and score pad, still on the table, as her mother paced the kitchen straightening things and boiling water.

"If you're tired, you should sleep. You don't have to keep me company."

"I'm not tired, Mom."

"I don't want to keep you up."

"It's no bother."

"I know it's no bother. I just don't want to, well, *trouble* you."

"Mom, just quit." When Lily felt it safe to talk again, she asked, "What's your guess?" Getting a blank look from her mother, she glossed, "Your guess where."

"Where he's going? He has a definite destination all worked out. We'll know soon enough."

The answer didn't satisfy. " 'Man is the animal that surprises.' Remember that old favorite? Like 'single-file Indians,' or 'Sometimes we need coaxing.' He wants to keep each of us guessing. Mother, I know where he's going."

Ailene froze her pointless shuffling and held still.

"Do you remember the Whistle Man?" Ailene's baffled eyes showed she did not. "The lifeguard, the protector of all swimmers? I think it's Aptos he's after. He's headed back to Back When. He's a little south now, but he could turn."

"What on earth for?"

Lily swelled with the anger of rejection. "You have to remember it: that summer, our rented beach cottage. You on the porch, with your handiwork, humming. Dad pulling medicine from out of the surf. Mother, weren't we happy then? Wasn't he? I always thought so. I always thought he might try for a return visit."

Ailene stared at her, defiantly, a look that could only have come to her this far into night. "We were never happier than we were last week."

Silence fell across the room. The two women dutifully kissed each other good-night, knowing they could no longer help one another. Lily went to her own room and prepared for bed. In this, she was guilty of the same foolish optimism her mother had just described. After lying under the covers for twenty minutes, she got up and turned the light back on. She went to the bookshelf that housed those volumes she had preserved from childhood. She removed and read one of her favorite bits of juvenilia, a book titled *This Is What Would Happen If Everybody Did.* "Do you like to squeeze the cat?" she read out loud. She turned the page to reveal a feline squashed into an hourglass. "This is what would happen if everybody did."

17

"Okay, campers. Let's play What's Your Favorite? You start. What's your favoriiite . . . make of automobile?" Rachel, in the driver's seat, cheered stoically while stroking the metal seam joining the windshield to the door. She kept her chin up, pretending to bring off today's game as nonchalantly as all the others. Artie, passenger side, pushed up the corners of his mouth at these heroics. He dropped his head and scratched a nonexistent itch on his scalp. He heard in Sis's routine her homage to the man who taught them all that a running irreverence was *always* more appropriate than distress.

Winter fastened down the North, stronger than seasonal. Route 5 lay well-drifted in. Snow controlled the stray fields to either side of the road, with more on the way. Stubble of last fall's corn poked through the white crust, indigent prairie dogs killed and frozen vertical by the cold. Farmhouses lost their resolute look and hid scattered, white on white, waiting for the Arctic visitation to pass over. They glided through a landscape of grays and halftones, a world out of the old newsreels. Above them, a sky steepening with clouds unbaled its white freight on an already repentant ground. The land rolled underneath its cover of cold and fell lifeless.

Except for the salt trucks, Artie thought, with their mundane amber lights and pragmatic plows, the scene might be that Brueghel painting, "Hunters Returning in Snow," that he so loved. Everything waited for the old, tired, miraculous, often-repeated, but never quite sufficient midwinter birth, a birth made more desperate during the long delay. Everything waited except the two of them, forced to work out their own salvation.

Artie thought: *This road again.* They stuck to thirty, feeling their way along the shoulder. Rach denied him the wheel, saying she didn't trust intellectuals on slippery roads. Visibility fell off steeply with each mile west. They had not yet passed the Aurora exit, with nothing in front of them except white. An hour before noon, Rachel had to revert to lights. Flakes spread an opaque curtain over the dash, tucked them in for the duration and six. Every ten minutes Rach laughed maniacally at the danger, fish-tailed, crept back into the lane, and tried to keep the car pointed in the approximate direction of home on intuition alone.

She seemed completely unafraid of a crack-up. The prospect of a stall or a spinout, the odds of becoming stuck, stranded on the obscured road with only a feather tick in the backseat to keep them alive until spring, did not frighten her. Exposure to cold seemed glorious about now. It would freeze those uninvited hypotheticals into holding still. "Answer me, buddy," she said, doing her favorite gag of clenching her jaw until her head began to quiver on her neck. "Favorite car. Or we're going sledding."

Artie smiled wider. From somewhere, a surprise infusion of calm came over him. He grabbed his sister's neck between his fingers and thumb and rubbed, comforting her, settling the runaway strain of imagination. "My favorite car," he said in the demi-recitation voice of a sixth-grader rehearsing an oral report the evening before, "is the Lincoln Cadillac."

Her cheeks blew apart with the violent laughter reserved for sheer idiocy. The burst of air released viral spit spores against the steering wheel and window. "Lincoln Caddy," she exclaimed. "*Lin*-coln *Caddy*-yak. Dig this guy, will ya?"

Artie, pretending incomprehension, fish-gaped. "What? What?" He curled his nose, defensively.

"What kind of . . . ? You are a disgrace, my friend. You're lucky the voting public lets you stay in this country. No wonder your dad disowned you. He just couldn't face having a firstborn who . . . Lincoln Caddyack. I can't believe you're related to me."

"What's yours?"

"Porsche." Just then the car moved laterally across the ice sheet and required a few full oscillations of the steering wheel to correct it. Rach at once patted the dashboard, cooing at the car, assuring Mr. Nader, "I mean Pinto. What's your favoriiite . . . meal? Quick. No fair thinking."

At a loss to remember anything edible aside from his daily regimen of open-face peanut butter on balloon bread, Artie fumbled for and retrieved the traditional holiday menu that Ailene even now spread for them this Christmas Eve Day. "Uh, roast turkey with Mom's stuffing, with the cranberries and mashies and gravy and everything. And you?"

She shot him a glance: "You really wanna know, or are you just asking to be polite?" Artie scowled. She said, "Meatball sub."

"Nonsense. There is no such thing."

Sis took offense, and her driving showed it. "Is too. I can get one up on Division Street." She threatened to wheel the car around and prove it until he conceded.

The nonsense conversation shut off abruptly so she could concentrate on a particularly iced, obliterated patch of road. For fifty yards they slid out of control, their safety decided by inches either way. In the proprietary, respectful moment after near-tragedy, they launched back into the avoidance game with doubled urgency. They did movies, books, former teachers, states of the Union, flowers, ice cream flavors, and popular songs. Considering how long they had known one another— "You're almost like a brother to me," as she was fond of saying—both were surprised at how little they knew about each other.

After exhausting all other topics, Artie knew there was no more point in hiding. "Favorite moment with Dad?"

Rach's mouth wavered in insurrection. She hesitated, tried to answer, then shook her head. Artie covered for her. "I was just a kid. Twelve, maybe. Dad was teaching; we still lived out East. He took me into school on a Saturday. Remember how he used to do that? Made you feel a little vulnerable, sneaking behind enemy lines. He took me into a classroom and hooked up a tape recorder. He gave me a set of headphones and took one himself. Fun. Like we were pilots, or something. We listened to a tape of a man with an astonishing voice, recorded outdoors, over a PA system. I had never heard such a voice, and at first I couldn't make out the speech. A dream of mountains being leveled and valleys lifted. All very strange to me. I looked over at Pop, and he was crying like a little child. Free at last. It frightened me. But I've thought of it every day since."

Rach tried to ask him why, if it had been so frightening then, the moment was now his favorite. But she could not get the question out.

After an unbearably long silence during which they made only three quarters of a mile, she asked hoarsely, "How's about poems? Or did we do that one already?"

Artie looked off south where the snow seemed to be lifting. A farm dog wandered lost near the snow fence just over the shoulder. It lifted one leg at a time, spewing powder with each move, pistoning back into the drifts without making progress. Flakes dusted its face, a skinless skull on body. Artie watched the animal pick itself up and plunge back in, scraping its belly against a white tide that left its limbs useless. Favorite poetry: he thought of Pop's discovery of Eliot, "Quick now, here, now, always," the war poem. And the Irish Airman, and the Unforgiving Minute: all of them war poems. He thought of his own love for the rhythmic line, sacrificed to a career in practical reading. He thought of the few moments he had spent with Dad, their truce of mutual enjoyment, and he knew there would be no more like them.

"No favorite poem? How about favorite line?" Artie looked over, his lip pinched up. The same idea occurred to them both—old spell of atavism—and they rushed each other to the punchline: "Hey, baby, whatcha doin' tonight?" They laughed and fell silent. Rach did not pursue.

They pulled into the driveway an hour later than planned. Artie guided Rach in with Lily's old joke: "It's the white one, with the pitched roof." So were they all, on this street, and on the next, and in the next town over. Eddie Jr., out in the yard, an overbundled blob in knit stocking cap, was attempting something with a snow shovel, although by the look of the driveway it could not possibly have been shoveling.

The kid looked up as his elders and wisers pulled in. "Finey desie to show up for Chrisyma?" Mealymouthed, chill-blained, he was past being aware of having been out too long. Artie and Rach exchanged quick looks. Older brother relieved the boy of the shovel while Sis wrapped a warm arm around him, led him up the walk, and shepherded him indoors. Inside, she helped him off with his boots.

Mother made a show of bravely waving them in. She had dressed festively, gussied up with odds and ends from out of the long-unused wardrobe. She looked wonderful except for the incongruous oven mitt she waved at them. The oversized hand made her look like a fiddler crab.

Greeting was brief; she immediately retreated to the kitchen, where some item was just due up and needed attending.

Lily, on the front couch, the one that folded out into a sleeper which Rach called the hide-a-backache, waved lazily and said, "Yo yo yo." Art flopped down beside her and thrust his boots into her lap for removing. She protested, "You're getting me all yucky." But she was visibly pleased at being included in the activity.

Rach took Eddie upstairs and ran lukewarm water over his toes. On the way, her stage whisper filled the house. "So what did he say, what did he say?" Eddie summarized the call from Neosho. Rach would have nothing to do with synopsis: "Tell me eggs-*actly*. Whad-you-say, whad-he-say, whad-you-say, whad-he-say." She swung her head back and forth, tennis-match–style. Eddie told all the details he could remember, which were by then spotty and largely made up.

Eddie flexed what was left of his whitened toes under the thawing water and said, "Lil thinks he's on his way to Aptos, but that's crazy." A moment later, he added, "Isn't it?"

In the front room, Lily, extricating her brother from his boots, returned to toying with the diversion she had invented to pass time until his arrival. Now that Art and Rach had gotten in safely, she kept to the time killer that had gotten her this far. Her invention involved the TV remote control, a late, reluctant Hobson concession to gadgetry. Mom bought it after Pop almost fell through the picture tube while passing out on the way to changing channels. Lily found a way of using the device for creative editing, splicing together assorted network Christmas Eve fare into a mélange. The more Lily segued, the more the hybrid creation took on a life all its own. She switched channels, timing each crosscut so perfectly that Artie watched the dial roulette in fascination. She achieved a perfect graphic match between a fighting-fundy-from-spiritus-mundi pulpit-pounder and Reginald Owen in 1938's A *Christmas Carol*. Scrooge's knees knocked together at the grave as the ghost of Christmas Future made him push aside the moldy leaves and read the inscription. Then the preacher described how this could happen to *you*. A few deft, rapid-fire switches back and forth between these two had Artie in stitches.

She made a quick jump to a perfect sound match on Channel 7 where a retired jock called bowl-game play-by-plays from up in the booth: "He ran for that tiny sliver of possibility, but They were waiting for him." Then she shot back to Owen's "Spirit, spirit," and then the fundy, "One says, over and over and over," and then the sportscaster's "but it gets you nowhere." She introduced a fourth party, a man seated in armchair in front of a fake library, saying, "You've probably seen me on TV." The crosscut dialogue tightened. Lily managed to keep all the conversants speaking relevantly to one another, as if more concerned with what the competition on the other networks were saying than with what viewers might think of the private conversation.

The game ground to a halt with the crash of pans hitting the floor in the kitchen. Lil and Art jumped to their feet and raced to the scene of the accident. Mother stood breathing heavily over the catastrophe, an overturned mince pie shattered on the floor. She shot an accusing look at the two of them. "*Now* you come running, when it's too late to help matters any." She sat down in a folding chair and sobbed openly.

Lily fell to the floor and began collecting bits of broken crockery. She took a cookie sheet and scooped up the pie, speaking brightly about how much of it was salvageable. "Mother's floors are cleaner than most people's mouths."

Artie sat down near Mom and let her heave a little. Then he reached out and stroked her upper arm. "I'll guarantee he'll call us today." Mom caught her breath, wiped her face with a hanky, and nodded obediently. She cast about for an apology, but Artie overrode her. "He knows we're all here. He'll want to . . ." But Artie could not say what, if anything, the old man would want to do. Her son's failure to finish again unnerved Ailene. She set off on another series of wet gasps, somewhat softer this time.

The crash and ensuing silence brought the last two children down. Witnesses after the fact, Rach and Eddie pieced events back together from the evidence. Eddie looked at his sister scraping food off the floor. He concluded that the problem that had reduced Ailene to tears had to do with food and said, "Good God, Mom. Give us some soggy sandwiches on a tray and we'll be fine."

Rach went over to Artie, stuck her lip out, and said, "Why don'tcha pick on somebody yer own size for a change? Knockin' pies outta old women's hands."

Mom at last cleared her throat enough to laugh. She looked up, swallowed, and said, "Merry Christmas, you guys."

To undo the disaster, they agreed to reverse the normal sequence of holiday events. They would trim the tree before dinner, an undertaking normally delayed each year for as long as possible by the tormenting and gleefully sadistic fugitive in question. "In my day, when I was a boy, we didn't get to open our presents until Washington's Birthday." Or: "Trim the tree in the middle of December? What do you think this is, some kind of pagan fertility ritual?" From Jersey to Penn to Ohio to Ill, he remained unmoved by his children's pleas, secure in the knowledge that they got a bigger kick out of the season for all the delay and begging.

But not this year. They would get the better of the ghost, gone so recently from the house. In the man's absence, they at last found the courage to stand up to him, to cheat him by an hour or two of a long-withheld delight. Lily ran into the cellar to dig up the ornament box. Artie and Eddie hauled in the tree from where it stood propped against the frozen back porch. Rach administered. Mom neither interfered nor approved. They exhumed the forgotten bangles. Everyone put on good cheer as each ornament came out of its paper wrappings. "Oh, God. Remember this one? I made this in Mrs. Shellenberger's class. Third grade."

"Wait a minute. Didn't we have a *golden* one like this? I was sure this one was golden."

By the time the angel went up on the top bough, they had achieved a reasonable facsimile of glad tidings and good cheer. They had gotten up a beautiful amalgam of green and artifice, and had done it a few hours early, against the house rules. Each felt a secret, childhood joy in breaking the schedule, as they had always for years felt in following it. And the missing man was none the wiser.

As soon as they mounted the last ornament, Mom was ready with the turkey. She had one that could have fed twenty. Rach made up the linen to resemble flowers. Eddie, the only manually adept one among them, did the carving honors. Lil put music on, a hilarious potboiler record of twelve contemporary celebrities swimming against the tide of traditional Christmas tunes. Each kid added a unique, sweeping tremolo.

When they were all seated, it fell to Artie to handle the dinner blessing.

Long out of practice, praying only pro forma, he could not find the words. He found himself wanting to pray for experience, believing for a minute that no better cure existed for a world where so many were unwell. Instead, he settled for phrasing the usual petitions: health, well-being, peace, and more such gatherings. He veered away decorously from prosperity and wound up, discreetly making no mention of the missing party. His self-possession guttered, however, when Mom tacked on an envoi, to herself but audible: "And it goes without saying, protect the husband, too."

Artie cast a last look at the foodstuffs, then gave the go-ahead for their ruin by lifting an eyebrow. At once, platters and gravy boats swung into disciplined orbits around the oval table, years of childhood training coordinating the clockwise motion. After Mom's coda, no one alluded to Dad until Rach, scraping her tooth enamel with a spoon, grabbed her mouth, muttered in pain, and said, "I've got an idea. Drive-up dentistry."

Form and content were perfect and uncanny imitations of the old New Dealer—his perennial, crackpot, back-door solutions passed off as sure-fire, overlooked money-makers. The room fell silent, as if visited. Rach looked as surprised as any of them: "Now where did *that* come from?" Ailene seemed ready to launch into tears or violent reprimand when Rach was saved by the telephone bell. She excused herself with a squeaky falsetto "I'll get it," sounding like Margaret Dumont setting up Groucho for a put-down.

"Tell them we're having our goddamn holiday dinner," said Eddie Jr., suddenly proprietary about the old traditions. Mom shot him a look that both rewarded his newfound traditionalism and chastised his diction. Artie stacked dishes in orderly piles while Lily retrieved what was salvaged of the pies.

Snapping up the kitchen extension, Rach said, "Yellow. You're *where*? Just outside Amar. . . ? Jesus, Dad. Every time I hitch, it takes me days to go ten miles. How do you make such good time?"

As one, the remaining family broke from pleasantries to the upstairs extension. This time Ailene had the better jump; she beat her children to the receiver, picking it up in time to hear Eddie Sr. demanding to know why he had never heard about Rach's hitchhiking before this. Mom heard her daughter say, "Don't you think the lecture's just a tad hypocritical, Popski? I mean, I am an adult, and *I* always tell *my* family *before* I make any extended trips."

"Who's lecturing? I'm looking for tips." And a half-second later, acknowledging the new party, "Hello, love." After three decades of shared days, he knew his wife's breathing, even over wires, even at great distance.

Eddie Jr., second in the dash upstairs, fell on the atlas and scanned the A-M-A-R's. He eliminated the only other contender as too remote and far afield. That left Amarillo, Texas. Taught from birth never to deface a book with anything indelible, he grabbed two colored pins from out of the pin cushion his mother always kept within reach of her bed. He placed one in Neosho and the other in Amarillo. Although the exercise made him feel a little like a vestige of High Command, it did the trick. He now had a good sense of Pop's route.

Artie reached the top of the stairs and entered the folks' bedroom just as Mom began pleading. "Ed. Ed, listen to me. Don't you dare joke, damn it." Artie drew up short; it was the first time he had ever heard his mother swear, and the sound seemed a violation of physical law. He turned around and headed back down to the kitchen, where he methodically pulled the downstairs phone out of Rachel's protesting hands. He held her at bay with a straight arm.

Mom was still begging. She was so distressed that she hadn't any notion of how little good begging could possibly do. Artie was clearheaded enough to realize that the thing had gotten out of hand. The situation was already lost unless he took to power tactics immediately. "Pop," he commanded, trying to give the word an extra couple of decades. The sound of his adult voice gave him the oddest insight: he was now his father's contemporary.

"Hey, son. You know where the papers are, don't you? I mean, the GI and teachers' life insurance, and all."

Mother wailed spectrally from the other line. "Don't talk to me about papers." Artie held the phone away from his ear.

"Have a look at them, huh? Help out a little. Put that legal training of yours to use. What do they teach you at that school anyway?"

Artie wanted to tell the man that he was still stuck in Contracts, that he hadn't a clue about Claims, that the only thing law school had taught him was to short sell just before litigation and buy back in just before settlement. He wanted to tell Dad how just that week, his senior adviser had exulted in having bought puts in a pharmaceuticals firm being sued for producing birth defects. He wanted to tell Pop that it was time to study poetry. But it didn't seem the appropriate moment to talk about education.

"They're in the attic cubby, right?" Artie sounded proud of the old memory. "Why do you want me to look over the papers, Pop? Where are you? Where are you headed?"

Mom was still vocalizing upstairs. The three-way conversation and the spookiness of what Dad had just asked edged Artie from his strong-arm resolution. Time took on that underwater, alternative quality of car wrecks, of disaster. Things happened far too slowly to be real, yet they had that sense of being one step ahead of experience, hypothetical, yet far too awful to be anything but fact. He barely comprehended what was happening.

Pop chuckled. "Where am I headed? You're kidding, aren't you? Figure it out. I should have made this trip years ago." Mom pleaded some more, as if the case were not already decided. Artie stumbled fatally, grew meek, and gave Dad time to say, "Don't worry. I've never felt better in my life. Merry Christmas. I love you all." Artie felt his own failure rush toward him as the line to the Southwest, to the past, went dead. Cruelly, he gave the receiver to Rachel, still scrapping for it. She spoke a few hellos into the mouthpiece before realizing the man was gone.

Throughout the call Lil remained a study in indifference, the only member of the household whom calamity could not touch. She kept at the dinner dishes, a one-woman portage from table to soapy sink. She raised her ears politely, but said only, "Dad, is it? Say hello from me." When Artie finally dropped into a kitchen chair, he looked up and saw her gazing out the window, arms plunged into warm dishwater, running a lazy experiment with the lemon-scented dish detergent.

"What do you know?" he accused her.

She swung on her heels, looked on him with a smile. "You resent me for making peace with the matter?" Lily did not wait for an answer. She addressed Rachel: "He's all right, then? Good for him. There's nothing a doctor can do for him that a road trip can't."

Rach flew at the woman in disgust. Artie stepped between them. Before the three knew they were fighting, Eddie Jr. entered the kitchen triumphantly. He held the open atlas in one hand, their mother in the other. He pressed the book's binding to the tabletop, spread open to the southern Great Plains. He looked around the group, unable to suppress a desire to imitate the great conjurer. Silently, he challenged each of them to come up with what he'd discovered.

When they made no motion toward the map, he put a fingernail to a spot 150 miles southwest of the newest pin. There, in boldface, but several typeface points smaller than the Amarillo-Lubock class, lighter, even, than the Abilene-San Angelo persuasion, in a font darker than your basic Ropesville-Shallowater mirage town, was a filled bull's-eye labeled Hobbs. The family stared at the name, uncomprehending. Rach, the first to assimilate to the idea, said, "Not possible. It's got two *b*'s."

An hour later, the only thing the family knew for certain was that Pop's metaphorical mind might lead him anywhere. They could do nothing now but live. Artie and Rach retrieved their presents from the trunk of Mr. Nader and planted them alongside the gifts of the other three, under the prematurely trimmed tree. Yet they could not bring themselves to act on the bright wrappings. Opening presents, giving in to acquiring, seemed the grossest impertinence. Rach rustled up some carols, but they were halfhearted and top-heavy because Artie could not hit the lowest notes in the bass. Mom kept the mugs full of cocoa, no task at all since no one was drinking. They slipped into a ridiculous Christmas where everyone was too stupid or cowardly to quit faking bravery.

Out of the shared silence, Eddie Jr. said, "What have I been thinking? I have no school until past New Year's. No obligations at all." This observation evolved into a notion that evolved into a full-fledged idea, despite Artie's vocal objections and attempts to sidetrack it.

Eddie would not be derailed. He roused himself and went to call the car-rental place. "*The* car-rental place," Rach reminded everyone, a backhanded barb at the size of Barb City.

"They've still got one on the lot," Eddie reported. "But they can't make any promises about it still being around tomorrow. Big day for the car-rental business, Christ's nativity." The family, circumspect, was split on a decision. Eddie called back and reserved the vehicle, borrowing the magic numbers from Rachel's credit card. Mom looked on dazed at the cashless transaction, incredulous that her own daughter could have grown up to use the same cards forbidden her.

Eddie went up to his bedroom to pack his things. Artie followed, aware of the burden of being the Sensible One. The Home-Fronter. While Little Bro transferred his worldly goods into a suitcase, Artie lectured him on how unfeasible the plan was. "The odds are impossible. You'll never find him."

"You're probably right," Eddie agreed pleasantly, and continued packing. He felt exhilarated, just fitting everything he needed into a three-day rucksack. "Where do you think the corduroys should go? How you supposed to get shirts in this thing without wrinkling?" Liberation washed over him as he discovered that his newly bleached underwear perfectly filled an odd spot at the edge of the bag, taking up almost no room at all. Packing a bag revealed his freedom.

"Completely impractical," Artie objected. "It'll cost you a hundred to rent a car. And then the motels and all. Even if you're only out a week, it'll run you your life savings."

"Yer sister's putting it on her plastic. And I'm going to hit yer mother up for a couple of C-notes." The kid was importunate, but as charming as ever.

"You know how unlikely it is that you can track the guy past Amarillo? What leads do you have?"

"Aw, how big can things be out there? It all fits on two atlas pages, right? He's got to be somewhere between Dallas and L.A." Baiting Big Brother, Eddie remembered, had a lot of basic entertainment value.

"You're throwing your time away, you know. It's impossible. Stupid. Can't be done."

"Look," said Eddie, at last giving Artie the gratification of anger. "Let me just do it first, okay? We can figure out the probabilities afterwards."

The kid took a shower, thinking ahead to the grime of driving. He came downstairs, combed and groomed and packed. Mother tried to hide her evident approval of the plan, or rather, the nonplan: "He cleans up pretty well, doesn't he?" Rach laughed and scratched, for the same reason she always did: not just sadism or incongruity or tension, although these were all there, but for the escape of the punchline, somebody poking through the far side, breaking through the barrier.

She addressed Mom's compliment: "That's the most hyperbolic thing anyone's ever said about the boy."

Lily sat placidly on the sofa. Failing to attract attention through inattention, she announced, "Dad said he was happy, didn't he? Why don't we just leave him be?" She did have something beatific about her. Something reconciled.

Mom slipped Eddie Jr. the expected bank wad and made him promise to call the next evening. Rach said, "It'll be just like Houston Control. We'll be your navigation beacon. Over." Mom voiced her reservations about his starting out at night. But Eddie said it was best to get a jump on it, since the old guy had such a big head start.

"I'm not tired, anyway. You certainly don't expect me to sleep, do you? Besides," he added quietly, "if I don't do this on a lark, I'll talk myself out of it."

They exchanged kisses all around. Artie grabbed his brother at the door, looking for some way to renounce his previous pragmatism as simply a test of good faith. "Keep us posted. Holler if you need help. And don't be afraid to break off. Win your winners and lose your losers, as the man says."

Eddie pinched his brother on the shoulder awkwardly, intending to make a more encompassing gesture but missing. It was okay. All manner of things were okay. He gave Artie a transcendental grin, opened the door on an unnaturally cold midwinter, and repeated, for the one who now couldn't, the old Hobson warhorse: "We sometimes need coaxing to act on our own."

1945

Thus Disney conceives the great fifth reel of You Are the War. Following a rapid courtship as shy, fetching, and painful as any the screen has ever assembled, Eddie Hobson marries the beautiful Joan Leslie. They discuss, in a few days of hurried home leave, the hope of their mutual futures: children. They plan for enough offspring to surround themselves with a sustaining fortress of goodwill. In montage, Eddie kisses his war bride good-bye and returns to his tour of duty, sweeping up and closing down the American Theater, Southwest. He floats from base to base like a bad penny, closing them down in his wake. He gets transferred to the remotest reaches of endless gypsum deserts near the Tularosa Valley. Late one summer night, taking a cigarette break from a barracks card game, Eddie receives another visit from the mouse, who appears suddenly from out of his cartoon dimension.

The visit takes PFC Hobson by surprise. On each previous encounter, Mickey has arrived just in time to rescue the boy from personal crisis. But tonight Eddie feels better than fine. In fact, he has just been imagining the life he and Miss Leslie will share come the end of his duration and six. He has taken Mickey's previous color-segment pep talks to heart. He now sees how even he is necessary in the wider effort, and he feels ready for anything history might put in his way. Seeing his old friend pop out of nowhere, he assumes this must be just a social call. Perhaps the little guy has come to say adieu, for PFC Hobson feels he no longer needs him.

"What's up, Governor?" he jokes with the mouse. "What can I bail you out of this time?"

But Mickey only smiles weakly. "Something is about to happen, Eddie," he squeaks. "Something I need to prepare you for." Hobson tries to laugh the greeting off, but Mickey remains adamant, increasingly grave. He takes the rapidly aging child lead's hand and the neighborhood *flashes rainbow and polychrome one last time. They set off on the trail of denouement, one that puts to the test every set that World World has to offer.*

First they soar out to the marble monuments of Washington, D.C., arriving in the blink of a shutter. There, the Supreme Court has just decided that the mass imprisonment of Japanese is constitutionally justified on the grounds of military emergency. An overwhelming sickness at heart comes over Eddie. He watches in secret as the justices reach their decision. He witnesses the final triumph of self-defeating realism, a last, mass surrender to dreadful practicality, the dying spark of his age, the Age of Utility, the beginning of what will be a long and spasmodic end. Eddie calls out to the justices to stop. But, as always in this genre, they cannot hear him. "Those people are innocent," he shouts. "Don't they know what they are doing?"

"Wait and see," says Mickey. Wait and see. He reaches his white kid gloves into the pockets of his patented red shorts and pulls forth two small handfuls of iridescent ore. A brilliant animator's pen gives the precious metallic dust all the colors of the rainbow.

"What is it?" asks Eddie, wide-eyed in astonishment. He cannot conceal his childish delight.

"Close your eyes." Mickey commands him, "Concentrate for all you are worth on the future."

The cartoon creature stretches on tiptoe and sprinkles the stuff in Eddie Hobson's hair. A violent burst of color and deep brass tremolos announce an astounding host of images that rush forward from all four corners of the screen. The glittering instant is the high-water mark of forties animation, of animation in this century. The images pour forth in terrifying fecundity, foretelling the faces and icons of things still decades off with amazing prescience and specificity. How Disney's artists do it remains one of the trade secrets of the industry.

"What is all this?" Eddie shouts, taking cover behind his guide. "What's happening?"

A spooky moment, the scene easily surpasses the Wicked Witch wreaking her holy terror, its closest rival in sheer fright. It surpasses the mouse's cameo as Sorcerer's Apprentice: every broom for itself, and each with a mind of its own. Only this time the images are far more threatening. Eddie's heart ices and extinguishes as these amorphous phantoms take shape and fly out of the frame. They grow to unbelievable size and infest whole continents while he hides, powerless to intervene. He considers lunging at one, but Mickey holds him back. For to touch the shapes is surely to disappear.

When the animation settles and the terrible flux subsides, the first thing they see is jubilation. Far off in space, they hear the nations celebrating. The mouse produces a magnifying glass, and they peek in on New York, Paris, Peking. A Victory Parade such as the world has never before mounted snakes its way through streets thronged with people. Strangers grab one another and embrace. Victory in Europe, in the Pacific. V-E, V-J. The death of the world by water and fire has been postponed.

Eddie smiles at his guardian from ear to ear. "So you were just testing me."

But Mickey returns the most chilling look of pity in the history of cinema: there is more to current events than anyone suspects. They watch in time lapse as the globe's population, only slightly nicked during five years of wholesale slaughter, doubles and redoubles in one lifetime. They see the place expand beyond all reckoning. They watch the four-color map splinter into infinitesimal factions, unmendable, a perpetual seesaw of provincial suspicions.

Heart cannot say just what Eddie sees. Only the cartoon cave shadow, drawn in after the fact, remains. But whatever Eddie looks on, his face confirms a first full grasp of the worst. Mouse and man, from distant vantage, follow the trail of Operation Paper Clip: the butchers of Dora, those same Nazi scientists Eddie thought the war was against, get clean tickets to help fuel the victors' ever more exotic competition. He sees the ideal cause, the one that took Artie, the one he would have laid down his life for, go cynical, sacrificed to contested postwar claims.

For all the hoopla of Victory, Eddie now sees that the war has decided nothing. It continues: that much is obvious, even in Silly Symphony. It simply changes from massive stroke to slow cancer. It spreads from titanic fronts to steady brush fires smoldering everywhere he looks across the earth's fragile crust. "Does it never end?" he asks sotto voce, unable to look Mickey between the ears. "Who in their right mind could possibly have wished this?"

"Nobody," comes the soft rodent reply.

"If nobody . . . then how . . . ?"

Another Fairy Dusting, and they fly on. The fitful flowering of group will, the advantage of ganging together, withers and disintegrates. Constitutions take over their constituency. Defense becomes a transitive verb. Alarms create the nightmare emergencies they warn against. Each does unto the other before the other can do first.

Eddie follows the aerial view through to all its bitter ironies: decades of exposures and counterexposures. Landscapes of hysteria and accusation. Mandates for mutual escalation. A rift tears open between big and little. Headlines no longer mesh with experience. A nineteen-year-old from another time watches the ascent of unbeatable efficacy plunge human need into the dark.

The sole, flukish warm spot in all the frozen universe defaces itself, graffitied beyond recognition. Species strip away. Forests unacre and are lost. Humankind proudly peels off even the protective atmosphere. Hobson does not comprehend it, not for a minute. But he needs no guide to spell out how badly things have gone wrong. In ten minutes of artist's conception, he reaches the same unavoidable conclusion of anyone paying attention. "Get me out of here."

"That's what they all say," Mickey says sadly. But unlike Scrooge or George Bailey, they have no place to get out to. A wave of the white glove indicates they can reach any location in front of them. "Where would you like to go?"

"Teaneck," the frightened kid says, desperate to get down to eye level. "I want to go home."

Mickey warns him that his parents will be gone, his own generation grown up and dispersed. Eddie, hysterical, persists. He needs to shrink to a scale he can understand. He needs to return to a size he can put together.

But once they are there, he sees that that scale, even from the ground, is forever blown away. Something has happened: a spider's web, an invasive forest, a spell of narcolepsy, falls over the entire town. People in the street cannot see each other. Everyone he passes is undone, eyes forward, trading feeling for the freedom to be left alone. The average tenant lives in cinder blocks, buying water in containers. They spend their days in endless litigation, suits against enormous institutions that have no people at the switch. They surrender all event, all involvement in the common project of being alive.

The stakes of the world outside them grow too abstract to consider; they trade sense for sensation, frantic to enjoy. Entertainment is plusher than ever. Slick, quick, and perfectly produced music strapped to the head replaces singing. All threat, all chance, all achievement, all breakthrough, all the horrible danger of tying one's life to the fortunes of others, takes place only in electronic tales, in little films, for a tiny screen, not like any motion picture Eddie has ever thrilled to, not so much fables as pacifications. Rotating itches replace the grand passion; car chases fill in for the awful moment of fragility. No one needs go through things anymore, or risk arriving at the unforgiving minute alone.

Mickey and his charge rest on a rotting park bench, next to a wall of pathetic, urgent initials. Near them a silent scrawl screams: SHUT UP AND BUY, BUY, BUY. *"What has happened to them?" Eddie's face races through a hundred calculations, all of them flawed.*

"Ask me one I can answer." The mouse shakes his head and takes the human's hand. He gives his reading of the derailment. It's really very simple: two men are put in separate rooms. They can play it safe or they can put their fate in the hands of another. Lack of trust begets lack of trust. The fear of being undercut trickles into the garden, as irreversible as falling. The choice of those first two people filters into four, the four eight, and the eight several billion. "That last step's a doozy," Mickey explains.

"How did it start? How did suspicion get in?" But Hobson already knows at least one port of entry, and then some.

In reply, Mickey takes him to the government vaults of late century. Thieves in the night, they uncover the final evidence in the AJAn case, papers proving that government lawyers knew of no military emergency. They manufactured one for the Supreme Court hearing. Mickey explains that this evidence will be discovered again, late in the century. But by then, a federal court will deem it too expensive to make reparations.

The last color trip is all but over. Eddie feels the mouse summoning strength to bring him back to the air base, circa 1945. He needs additional answers, and fast. "What will happen to me?" he shouts. "Will I at least find enough room to love my family?" The mouse reveals everything in store for the Hobsons-to-be. He traces the fate of the sons and daughters, describing the way Eddie's great moment makes over their lives without their ever knowing.

But Eddie cannot hear him. His face tips off how he is stranded on a deserted set in front of blank scrim, talking to emptiness, waiting for the delivering animation. He can no longer sustain the extended conversation with something not there. No matter how often Walt shoots it, they cannot get a decent take. On repeated viewings, the minuscule slip of the boy's features becomes apparent: the small price Disney pays for using an amateur.

The mouse fades before Eddie's eyes into airy insubstance. Eddie yells for more answers. Everything he has just seen hangs in the balance. "Is it inevitable? What do you expect me to do?" But he is alone, pacing the desert by himself, back on cigarette break. "Tell me how free I am, Hobson," he says silently, holding back the jitters. "You tell me."

As with each visit in the first four reels, no one knows he has been gone. His friends call him back to the game. He turns to join them, throws his cigarette out onto the desert floor. He is greeted in mid-turn by the glorious light of day. Only brighter. In that last, classic hesitation, Hobson cannot tell what is happening. "Fairy Dust," he says to himself. "Only believe."

The light increases. For the first time, Hobson's black-and-white surroundings go color without getting whisked off anywhere himself. It is the high-water mark of forties realism. "Who is going to open the time capsule?" he asks the evacuated sound stage. Except for the silent, off-camera command—keep rolling; this is what we're after—his only answer is the beating of insect wings.

18

Suddenly, in the middle of the night, Artie awoke and shot bolt upright. He snapped awake on a thought, one that forced into his head even through sleep. He instantly saw, in the pitch-black room, a way to break Dad's prisoner's matrix. Only the way was terrible.

He froze stock-still, as if the idea were in the room and would destroy him if he gave away his location. He checked the solution again in his mind, proving it was not one of those products of sleep that seem so brilliant until they dissolve in light and sanity. This one held firm all the way across the board. Artie had discovered the only and awful way back to We.

He knew the idea was true, even at this impossible hour, because of its complete simplicity. If guarding one's self-interests condemned both player and antagonist to the perpetual worst case, then self-interest was not in the self's best interest. The only logic was the logic of the combined payoff. The only reasonable choice was not the choice of reason but the choice that kept both out of the hole.

Artie felt his arms and legs under the blanket, paralyzed just inches from the thing that stalked it. Everything charged with danger: the bed linen, the outline of his hanging clothes, the promise of translucent windows against the far wall, the chill of the air. Afraid that he would never get out of the dark room to speak of it, Artie named his answer: Crackpot Realism.

The only way out was to release the us-and-us that was trapped inside the you-versus-he. Lying very still, Artie saw that Dad had known the outcome from the beginning. Artie felt himself collapse under the man's infected past, his symptoms, his insufferable evasion, his misguided and misunderstood themes. Crackpot Realism meant that he and his remaining fellow genes, if they hoped to survive the man's disappearance, had to will, for everything they were worth, that he not disappear. They had to tie their hopes to Little Brother, who, even if he located Pop against all odds, alive and forsaken in the Great Western Basin, would never be able to bring the guy back home.

They had to demand that Dad not go away, even though he was already gone. They had to love the man so fiercely and unconditionally that when he was at last lost, they would be lost too, wandering confused through the one thing the universe did better than any other. The only path out was to stray at random around their lamppost, with no hope of returning to him. That was what crackpot empathy freed them, forced them to do.

Artie tried to swing his feet down onto the cold floorboards, but he could not. He could do nothing but lie still, the only thing awake in the drafty house, the only spark anywhere at this hour. He heard his own breathing, his own blood sloshing through the capillaries in his ears. As slowly and incalculably as a Devonian tree becoming mineral, Artie became his father: a minute, statistically insignificant coward who could not live if it meant losing things. How could people go on? Yet they went, even as headlines accumulated beyond all capacity to understand them. Artie lay frozen in an alarm of nerves set off by the unlivable crisis of beauty.

But nerves, he gradually remembered, always settled—settled into the old, local routines of work and sleep, of dishes and laundry. Settled at the sound of someone in the next room breathing, whose presence, only moments before, had seemed too beautiful to bear. Nerves settled and died, and he had only a minute or two to use them.

He could not hope to go back to sleep. But Artie was not ready to keep himself company during all the hours of darkness still ahead. Getting up in the middle of the night changed the rules beyond recognition, all the terror of a new game. Then it struck him, exactly where he might begin testing the idea that had awakened him. Artie forced his pink feet to the floor and instantly became free. He could do anything he wanted. The house was ready and was his. For a moment, as he felt the flannel of his winter robe, abundance again ran wild and became terrible. But moving around—crackpot moving—was the only choice he had. And he took it.

The house was different, the layout strange. He could not remember, in the light of his insight, which rooms connected and led where. The strangest sensation came over him in the dark: life was like one of Pop's costume dramas—Norma Shearer in *Marie Antoinette*—only without the costumes and without the drama. A sleeping house, a town that time forgot, a ridiculously narrow sliver on the time line.

Artie climbed the stairs slowly, lifting his weight onto the bannister so as not to creak the eternally settling stair boards. He let the women in the house keep whatever light sleep they'd managed to win. He paced the front room for a few minutes, where his sister slept unsuspecting on the sofa bed. Then he camped out in the kitchen, working up the courage to go put his hands directly on the hard facts he was after. This very house hid period-piece evidence about where Dad had gone. And Artie knew where to get it. He had only to convince himself, in the greater costume drama, in the rush of possibility opened at this hour, that he really wanted to know.

He did. He climbed back upstairs, once more avoiding the sound mines. At the top landing, he hung a hard left and opened the cubbyhole crawl space that the folks used for long-term storage. He pulled the aged light string gingerly, craned to reach the highest shelf, and with both hands removed the quarry: two dozen reels of recording tape.

He heard his mother groan slightly from her adjoining bedroom, and he redoubled his attempts at silence. He had no desire to add to her nightmare in progress. He grabbed the neatly penned, neatly arranged library of tapes. He swung his free hand back and forth along the distant back wall of the closet until he brushed against and grabbed the tape machine. He pulled the light string off with his teeth, pushed the door shut with his hip, and retreated to the front bedroom.

In the safety of that closed place, Artie counted the tapes: a little over two dozen reels. The speculative and speculated-about Project spread all around him on a few hours of spools. He could absorb the whole thing in a couple of days of solid listening. His father had worked conscientiously for a quarter of a century, adding, revising, rethinking, editing out the gaps and blank pauses, to produce whatever story these reels contained.

His father's years-long work on this secret and alien project filled Artie with the horror hidden in the commonplace. The box of tape might have been anything—a house built by hand, a family album of children and children's children, the idea for a better mousetrap, or the careful, perennial records of a well-tended garden. Artie looked at the box and understood that whatever it contained, it further proved that the attempt to speak the connection behind things was as unavoidable and as oppressive as breathing.

Although the tapes were all neatly named and dated, Artie saw at once that the dates were not the dates they were made. He pulled out one bearing the earliest date, titled "The Cecilia Colony: 1890." Without knowing what to expect, he threaded the first reel. He listened for a minute, and then another. Nothing. He fast-forwarded the story, becoming anxious. Still nothing. The tape had been erased. Artie removed the reel and replaced it with one called "The Peace Ship: 1915." Whatever story Pop had told into the microphone he had once more carefully removed. Expecting the worst, Artie tried a third: "The Hollywood Ten: 1947." Once more, the evidence had been destroyed, the trail of footprints smoothed. The man had deliberately headed to oblivion, removing all traces of his ever having been there.

Defeated, Artie began to pack the machine back up. But wedged into the lid, apart from all the other tapes, unboxed and unnamed, was a loose reel. Rethreading the spool with shaking hands, Artie put on the tape that he knew to be Dad's last, the one the man had been working on at the end, the one Artie was after. Slowly, incredulously, he heard the completely foreign, wholly familiar singing waiter's bass fill up the empty room.

Everything we are at that moment goes into the capsule: a camera, a wall switch, a safety pin. The task, a tough one, is to fit inside a ten-foot, streamlined missile a complete picture of us Americans, circa 1939.

By accident or design, the tale had escaped erasure. Either Pop had taken off before he could kill it, or he found he could not kill it and therefore took off. Artie listened, with only partial comprehension, to the unfolding fable of incarceration and adaptation. He soon determined that the picture therein was not of "us Americans," but of one American, the one Artie himself hoped to find.

He stopped often, rewound, and reviewed selected spots in order to take the story in. Soon, Artie hit the pause button and crept back into his parents' room, where he snared the massive single-volume encyclopedia

Pop always kept close to the bed. He brought it back into the front room. To his surprise, he located a reference to the tape's central event. The mass imprisoning of more than a hundred thousand American citizens had really happened. He stopped several times, going to his thick volume to verify the details or differentiate between fact and phantasm.

The Disney in the reference books bore only slight relation to the one in the tapes. Disney *had* suffered and survived a labor strike at his outfit, in '41, brought on by his dictatorial management practices. But the Disney on official record, an American not of Japanese ancestry, had been at liberty all during the war. While he had made the government propaganda cartoons Pop mentioned, the magnum opus seemed to be all Pop's own.

But soon Artie gave up on checking his dad's world against the official tally. Pop's land, it became increasingly clear, however rooted in fact, branched into a web of bewildering invention designed for its curative power alone. The story of Hobstown, so far as Artie could make it out from the Byzantine and baffling shifts of events, traced out Dad's favorite hobby horse of all: how we are invariably trapped by immediate concerns into missing the long run, the big picture. By now it had the ring of an old and familiar friend, and as Artie listened, he could hear Pop stopping the motor, rewinding, reviewing, rerecording his tale countless times, until the results satisfied the famous perfectionist. The famous prisoner.

The man was fighting for his life: that much was obvious. And more than his life. Somehow, Dad had fixed on the crazy notion that he was caretaker for the entire tribe, assuming personal responsibility and guilt for all the imprisoning of innocents the group continually commits. His story was the attempt to answer the question, unbearable, of how he could go on living while another suffered even the smallest indignity of distrust. Dad was trying, in the tape, to cure the permanent condition of mistrust the world fast embraced by creating a domain where escalating suspicion had no place. Hobstown. World World. And each time he released the pause button, Artie felt more certain that such a place could never survive the light of day.

Artie never got to the end, to Pop's end. For as the fable went on, it slowly changed from being about the disease of history to being the story of his father, sick with that disease. All at once, he knew where the story would double back on: Dad's brief rub with the cataclysmic. Artie swore out loud at himself for not seeing the destination all along. So obvious: he had heard the account a hundred times, from the man himself. *Figure it out*, Pop had told him. *I should have made this trip long ago.* Now the tape had taken Artie there too.

With a few minutes of the story still remaining, he reached out and hit the stop button. Leaving his father's life work scattered across his bedroom floor, he went back downstairs. This time he let the wood creak all it could. He paced in the kitchen until he lost track of time. He was sitting calmly at the table when his mother came down that morning. "Merry Christmas," he said quietly. "I know where Pop has gone."

BREAKING THE MATRIX

Late on a slow Sunday evening in mid-July 1945, *my father and his bunkmates gather around the fold-out barracks table for their week-ending session of cards. A string of closed-down bases in his wake, Dad finds himself in what must be the most desolate spot in this hemisphere: an immense, blasted plain the original Spanish explorers named the Jornada del Muerto—the Journey of Death. His base lies about 250 miles southwest of his old B-29 school in Amarillo. Pop isn't sure why he has been transferred here. For that matter, he isn't sure what an army air field is doing out in the middle of so much emptiness. On the day he arrived, in answer to his unspoken questions, Dad's new bunkmates told him that the only things certain out here in the Jornada were that work was slow and it never rained.*

They are right on the first account. But since the previous Friday, it has showered continuously, raining like there will be no tomorrow. Dad, after three days of soaking, concludes that rain in the desert is a strange thing. Gorged, purple blood vessels of clouds anvil up within minutes, as in time-lapse photography. The thunderheads rip open, dousing everything in a mix of water and whipped-up dust. He tastes ionized slate in his cheeks and feels it in the linings of his nostrils. The rain doesn't dampen anything, although the scattered succulents swell visibly and show a spot of waxy pink here and there. The ground swallows the flood instantly, channels it away in walls of running water that fill the chiseled arroyos, feet deep. After each violent baptism the Jornada returns within minutes to zero humidity. The sun returns to full, skin-parching power.

Rules at the isolated base have relaxed since the capitulation of the Germans. Fewer planes come in for servicing; fewer need to return to service. Sooner or later, everyone knows, the Japs too will have to throw in the towel. As a result, discipline in the rank and file is not what it had been back in '43. The card-table quorum know they can get away with a couple of extra hours after lights-out. And so the hands keep coming.

By my father's standards, his companions play neither subtly nor well. They play a bastard hybrid of Acey Deucey, a game that, even in the original, demands nowhere near the concentration or skill of bridge or even pinochle. For their part, his companions have no reason to tolerate the newcomer or take him into their table. But a three-pound can of peanuts—a gift from my mother back in Jersey—provides a plentiful and perfect table stake, earning my father all the hands he wants.

A bunkmate from the Bronx with an idiot savant's way with electrical devices hooks up an illicit FM radio link, providing the card table with Big Band music as they bid each other up into peanut heaven. Since the card session is not studious, the table swarms with kibitzing. Everybody has something to say about everything: how long the Japs can hold out; how many men Operation Olympic will cost us; what the world will be like after the war; what the army is cooking up on the other side of the mountains; whose wife is doing what dirty deeds with what members of trade occupations.

The new PFC pitches in with the best of them. But every few hands he devotes his forensic skills to trying to talk the others into a decent game of Hearts, or even Rummy. Getting nowhere, he concentrates on the radio, Hoagy Carmichael stuff—the man behind "I'm a Cranky Old Yank in a Clanky Old Tank on the Streets of Yokohama with My Honolulu Mama Singin' Those Beat-o, Beat-o, Flat on My Seat-o Hirohito Blues." Dad listens to some Big Band play a show tune from Thanks for the Memory or Every Day's a Holiday. I can't remember which. He plays the most intelligent game of high-low possible, given the house rules.

The boys keep on playing into the wee hours of Monday morning. Nobody shows any signs of slackening. They keep right on gambling at that idiot Acey Deucey game, literally for goobers, finding some intrinsic fascination to the payoff. A little after five A.M., Pop gives up in disgust. The others won't let him quit if it means his taking the peanut can away, so he leaves it with the table, reminding himself to write his wife to send peanut butter next time.

He goes to the barracks screen door, lights up a Lucky, and thinks up *new phrases for the L.S./M.F.T. acronym. Still a half hour or so before sunrise, the desert is dark, repentantly cool, clicking with the activity of unseen nocturnals. A brace of quail, attracted to the camp's water supply, grieves as it comes awake.*

This is the sole half hour of the day when my father finds the desert livable. With the terrain charged with peace, he thinks out his next letter to his yet unknown wife, a letter filled with precious little news. Precious little happens to him these days, under the fuselage. His tour will be over just after the war, and he still has no real sense of how the two of them might best proceed when he gets his walking papers.

Dad thinks about hitting the sack but knows that the card party won't accommodate. That skinny Sinatra kid is on the FM link; Pop can't see what the girls go crazy over as far as that guy is concerned. His back to the bunks, smoke trickling out the screen, he listens to the song—sinners kissing angels—as it mingles with the card-game arguments. For a second, it dawns on him—the draw, the appeal of a game like Acey Deucey. Whatever its failings as an exercise in strategy, it gives a bunch of pent-up, confused, shiftless grease monkeys working a thankless job for the State a chance to bicker harmlessly, even socially. He listens to the early-morning dark—that sweet, social sound of Acey—takes a last pull on the butt, and flicks it into the air.

At the instant the Lucky hits the sand, the sun comes up. Too fast, too sharply, too bright, it grows into a light more luminous than noon. The desert blooms. For a fraction of a second, Dad chalks up the glare to sleeplessness, fatigue. But when the first tracers fail to fade, he knows that this sunrise will not yield easily to theory.

Years later, he frequently read that what he had seen had not lasted more than half a dozen seconds. But Dad forever maintained otherwise. The light, three times brighter than midday, simply persists. At the moment that Oppenheimer, a few miles west, speaks to himself those often-quoted words from the Bhagavad Gita, "I am become Death, the destroyer of worlds," my father hears, at his back, the unchanged chatter of card players, Sinatra's sinners still smooching angels, in an early and unexplainable sun-shower.

The light effuses a bright, warm matrix of desire. Dad decides he might as well call this premature sunrise the actual one, that he might as well turn back into the barracks, wash, go to work, get a jump on the now longer-than-usual day. Everything has changed except my father's power to make any difference. This fireball just hangs in the air, a glow, a desert heat against his face. For my father, the brightness hangs on like this forever. For my dad, it stays bright for good.

19

Ailene, startled, stopped halfway to the coffeepot. The shortest path between bed and breakfast brewer, beaten out in so many houses over the family's long exodus, a habit as certain as the measured course of daylight or the law of conservation of energy, vanished in the face of Artie's extraordinary announcement. She went to the table and sat down, curlered and afraid. Artie addressed her with a quizzical look. Ailene returned one of nonplussed bewilderment, the expression she wore when playing Three No Trump and losing count. Artie was shocked to notice the first shafts of dead hair speckling her head. Ailene dropped her jaw to speak. She halted, overcome by how curious and unfortunate a thing being alive was.

At last Artie delivered. "This is Dad's second sweep through Amarillo, isn't it?" Mom lowered her head and nodded, as if Artie had just detected *her* secret sin. But she volunteered nothing further. Art let her collect herself and then shouted at her. "Mom, Mom. Don't leave me hanging. What else do you know about all this?"

"What do you mean, what do *I* know? *You're* the one who he's always so keen on talking war with." Winning back a little self-esteem, she reminded him, in a small voice, of what he had all along known but had chosen to forget until his night session with what remained of Dad's tape library. She repeated those details of the past—Dad's youthful swing through the American Theater, closing down the War—that they had all gotten in countless historical and illustrative exercises over the years.

Artie groaned. "Oh, Mother. It's worse than I thought. We have to go look at the papers."

Just then, Lily came into the room. She could barely mask her desire to rush out into the front room and see the Christmas tree, an old prohibition that still inhabited the Eddie-less house. She had dressed circumspectly, putting on a knit vest for the occasion, a dapperness that betrayed her. She never dressed up for the man when he was still around. She stole down the hallway from her room, hoping against hope that she was the first one up. When she saw Mother and Brother sitting at the table, she knew something had happened.

She sat down defeated at the table, giving up on Christmas-tree renewal, resigning herself to the old burden of family. There was no way around them to a covert celebration of tinsel. Family, as much as she would do without it if she could, was the only celebration she would ever have. The others filled her in on the connection they had drawn. Then the detachment of three crept upstairs to the lockbox, keeping one another from turning around and backing down.

The relevant sheaf of documents only confirmed what they had already received firsthand from the source himself, long ago. Separation papers, Camp Shelby, Mississippi. Honorable discharge. Mass-produced letter of thanks from Harry Truman and Henry "Hap" Arnold, Commanding General of the Army Air Forces, Pop's name typed in on the receiving line. A diploma from Training Command, B-29 school, Amarillo.

"Didn't Uncle Art crash in Brownsville, Texas?" Lily asked, her finger on the named spot in the atlas. Mom nodded and tried to elaborate. But she could not get past the first words. The three sprawled across the folks' bed, passing the records to one another, scouring them in turn for whatever clues they could extract. All of a sudden Ailene put her sheaf down carelessly, looked over at her daughter and son, and tried to hug both of them at once. Artie shouted out, embarrassed by the effusion, and fought free. At that moment he caught sight of the document they sought, one that drew him up vertically: a transfer order to a remote base in the wastelands of New Mexico.

Ailene looked at the paper and nodded. Artie was almost white, as close to bloodless as he could come without stroking. "Alamogordo, Mom. He was really there." Ailene made no answer, an opaque look about her sockets and cheekbones. "The A-bomb, Mom," Artie said, with the exasperation of a high school history teacher giving away to his class that the answer was, after all that, just old, familiar B.

"Did you think he was lying?" Mother spat, violently. Her son had neither thought nor said as much. But the place name and the device had never been more than an abstraction to him, despite his father's frequent stories. Artie recalled Pop giving them the whole White Sands high drama over dinner, in his best *Movietone/March of Time* newsreel voice. As to Pop's details, Artie could recall nothing specific except the man's preserved amazement, after more than thirty years, at the night sky of the desert suddenly shooting up several times brighter than noon and staying that way for some time.

Until that instant, the invention had seemed to all of them no more tangent to their own experience than the numeric payoff game Pop forced on them. Lily shook her head and said, "All that happened thirty years ago. Of course, *we* wouldn't remember. To our generation, that's prehistory."

It came to all of them at once that Dad's sickness, from day one, came from his being the last man in the Northern Hemisphere who refused to think of the past as *over*. He had never followed the universal, self-protecting practice of flattening out the past, abstracting it, rendering it neuter and quaint. He had spent twenty years of dinners trying to point out that the whole program of civilization had not arrived *ex nihilo*, out of nothing. Dad's problem was simply that he saw the destination.

Ailene said, "One never wants to make matters worse by assuming the worst. But here we are."

Pop was bound for Alamogordo. All the facts bore that out. Eddie Jr.'s colored map pins led to it. The path Dad had taken and the time he spent in each place fit the curve. It obeyed Pop's trademark sense of historical irony. Most important, the destination explained the course and nature of Dad's disease itself. Under pressure of the self-evident, Artie pointed out something everybody had frequently noticed since Pop began relapsing: just before the man went down for the count, he would screw up his eyes and wince, as if fending off a very bright light.

Rach was in the kitchen when they came back down. She was setting another capricious table for holiday breakfast. Little Sister made linen angels and archangels out of Mother's starched napkins, standing them at attention to adorn each setting. For halos, she used the ubiquitous multivitamin. On hearing them enter, she rolled her eyes, shook her jowls, and said, in tremulous bass, "Let's . . . open . . . the . . . presents!" giving a game-show host's pregnant pause between each word, doing her unsuccessful best to deliver Dad's annual taunt. When no one replied, she turned to them to say "Bah, Humbug," when she saw that something was very wrong. The one-woman kitchen patrol came to a standstill.

Artie looked at her and said, "White Sands." Then he slumped into a chair, picked up one of the folded napkins, and said, "I like these. Angels, are they?"

That morning, Eddie Jr. called collect. Rachel answered. Eddie said, "Tell me *everything* that's happening over there. Slowly. Don't race. It's holiday rates. Discount." Momentarily confused over which Eddie she was speaking to, Rachel asked him where he was and how he felt. "Seems to have been Missouri at one time," he said. "And I'm just fine, thanks. I was highway-hallucinating for a while there a few miles back, but I pulled up in a rest area and did forty."

For once, the family's joker refused to trade him banter for banter. "Ever hear of a place called Alamogordo?" The kid, despite his having no sense of history aside from which came first, the Chicken McNugget or the Egg McMuffin, caught on quickly. The two of them worked out a new itinerary on and around the spot.

When Rachel rang off, Artie placed a call of his own. He reached Hines Hospital, and after suffering considerable bureaucratic shuffle, he got through to the resident who had worked up Dad's charts and now spent his Christmas on call, keeping watch over flocks by night. Artie did not mince preliminaries. He identified himself and the case in question and said, simply, "Radiation poisoning."

"Astonishing you should mention that," said the resident. "Many of the symptoms put me in mind of it." The physician went on to demand to know why exposure to radiation wasn't mentioned at all during the history and physical.

"If he ever took a real dose of any size, which is debatable, it was over thirty years ago." The doctor assured Artie that the disease could not possibly drag on malignant that way, so long after exposure. Even if some of the symptoms matched, the etiology was all wrong. Artie assured the physician, "I'm sure you're right. Unfortunately, I'm not the one that needs convincing."

He had done everything he could possibly do. Emptied, Artie climbed slowly back to his bedroom. He found the tape player where he had left it, interrupted near the end, a few minutes left on the reel. He had come up to hear the rest of the tale but now found he could not summon the courage to start the machine in motion. He sat staring out the iced-over window, wondering what he was supposed to learn from this last and most emphatic of Dad's riddles, his resignation from all games. He thought of his family's complete inability to see where Pop had been heading all these years. Artie wanted to know how they all could have messed up so badly.

None of them, despite personalities as varied as an unplanned garden, saw what was coming until it had already passed. Despite Pop's daily admonitions over breakfast eggs or dishwashing, they had all let the immediate past become *history*, that most abstract, detached, impersonal, and curatorial of disciplines. Artie lost track of how many minutes had passed when a soft knock came at his door.

Lil entered the room quietly. "So *you* have it. I was about to steal it myself." Artie looked up at her, his eyes for the first time in years asking for her help. Lily sat down next to him on the floor. "Look what else I found. The last thing he was reading." She showed him a beaten-up, old paperback copy of *The Decameron*. Artie smiled to see the old standard. One of Pop's favorites: a handful of people escape the Black Death and keep themselves alive and entertained in their exile by telling one another fantastic stories. Pop pulled it out and read it, sometimes out loud to one or more of the family, every five years or so.

They sat together, touching lightly, saying nothing. In another few minutes, Rach came in and settled down without a sound. The sisters said nothing to each other, but in time fell silently to braiding each other's hair, the way they had always done when they were girls. Rachel spoke first. "Now we're *all* guilty, huh, guys? We might as well listen from the top."

They did. Artie rewound the tape, and let them in from the beginning. As the story unfolded, each felt how their lives had been written out by 1946, years before their birth. But they hadn't any real *experience* of the time or place with which to apprehend it. Their parents were their jailers, building their fate and their children's fate. Somewhere in the layers of sedimented ground the releasing key, the cathartic, firsthand knowledge of where they came from, lay buried.

They listened to Dad's last riddle in silence, with nothing to protect themselves from its conclusion except one another. They reached the point in the story where Artie had broken off. Artie thought: *He has one last chance to get us out. The master of escapism must pull off a political miracle.* But what weapon could save them from his return to the self-opposing world? What could a cartoon biopic work, or whistling on stars?

This time, he let the tape run all the way to its magnetic end.

V-J

When the miniature, simulated sun at last dies out, Eddie Hobson walks off of the vacant sound stage into a World World he does not recognize. The sets are still there, still the same. The blank midwestern fields still play host to the most remarkable geographical variety ever concentrated into so small a space. But the industrious cast of thousands has disappeared.

"They have been freed," Disney explains, "by the magic, iridescent powder." Eddie discovers the man sitting on the stoop of World World's world headquarters in De Kalb's Elwood Mansion. The director grips an old newspaper, The Chicago Daily News, whose headlines scream, ROOSEVELT DEAD—DIES AT 63 OF HEMORRHAGE IN GEORGIA. But Disney is not mourning the death of the man who signed the nisei into prison. His attention is held by a sidebar from the same front page reading, REDS OPEN DRIVE ON BERLIN. Near page bottom, almost an afterthought, next to the box that gives the pages for Bridge, Comics, and Crossword, adjacent to a human-interest teaser titled "What Shall We Do with Japan?" a reporter announces casually that

Two Russian armies were closing in on the last two districts of burning Vienna still in German hands. The Leopoldstadt commercial district, including the 2,000-acre Prater Amusement Park, was cleared yesterday by troops that forced the Danube River canal.

The Reds have the Prater. Disney explains to the bewildered boy that the place is the most famous amusement park in what was the most beautiful capital city in what was once the West. And one can bet that they will attempt to hold on to the prize, no matter how much talk goes on after the war. He interprets the sidebar for Eddie. "The only country that will make

329

it through this conflagration with enough raw entertainment resources to rival our own has a two-thousand-acre leg up on us.

"The time for movie dreams has passed," Disney concludes. "We need something more substantial if we are to survive. We need to go beyond animation. It's no longer enough to breathe spirit back into an exhausted world." The Communists have the Big One. There's only one thing to do. Tit for Tat. Park Warfare. Build a place that's twenty-five hundred.

Disney retreats to his office and locks himself in, dictating plans for his new undertaking into his machine. Eddie is left to wander the deserted set of the abandoned masterpiece You Are the War. *He is stranded here in the forsaken fields, alone. The next morning, by the time-honored technique of time compression, the* Daily News *appears again on their stoop, as if by magic. Its headline reads,* ATOM RUIN STUNS JAPS. *"What Just One Bomb Did." Page one contains three graphics. The first explains, "How an uranium atom splits." The second shows two craters, one being the largest previously produced by any explosive, and this new one, an order of magnitude larger. The third shows a map of Japan with five black circles and a finned silhouette reading, "5,000 Atomic Bombs." Its caption reads: "What Might Happen—Map shows how atomic bombs, 1,000 dropped in each circle, might destroy everything on the home islands of Japan."*

Disney comes out of his room and addresses his last recruit, his lost child lead. He says that the war is effectively over, that Eddie is free to go. Condemned to go. Go ye therefore and do whatever work your hands can find to do. Disney shakes the boy's hand and is gone. He buys up a huge tract of land in Anaheim and paces out the boundaries for a magic kingdom, documentary cameras rolling all the while. His paces are those of a zoo animal released into the wild, still running the loop defined by its old cage. On the far side of the apocalypse the man continues to suffer the Stockholm Syndrome, in love with the jailers of this new landscape, this small world.

C-47's buzz the deserted camp. They release from the sky ten thousand letters, each bearing the national seal and the White House return address. Eddie stands in the falling snow of paper and rips one open to find a page headed by a star-entrapped e pluribus *eagle. Underneath, the sheet bears the name of one of the vanished dwarves, followed by the message:*

To you who answered the call of your country and served in its Armed Forces to bring about the total defeat of the enemy, I extend the heartfelt thanks of a grateful Nation. As one of the Nation's finest, you undertook the most severe task one can be called upon to perform. Because you demonstrated the fortitude, resourcefulness and calm judgment necessary to carry out that task, we now look to you for leadership and example in further exalting our country in peace.

The epistle is signed, "Harry Truman, the White House."

The captured nisei are no longer prisoners of war, no longer dangerous foreign nationals, because their foreign nation no longer exists. Eddie invents fates for the seven founders. Tom Ishi is free to go to Korea six years later and donate his life to foreign affairs. Billy Sasaki is free to return to Santa Monica and prove his patriotism by acquiring a bigger mortgage, an uglier house, a more demeaning job, and more assimilated children than any of his Scandinavian neighbors. Basho Mitsushi is free to repatriate to Japan and spend the rest of his days in a Shinto monastery while the country around him devotes itself to producing cars, consumer electronics, and baseball. Paul Okira is free to resume his law practice and suffer for years under a vague sense of wrong, until one day in the late seventies he joins a San Diego committee for redress and reparations for those citizens imprisoned illegally in World War II. Steve Ushima turns his incredible engineering skills over to the government, on the Oak Ridge–Hanford, Washington–Los Alamos circuit. Dr. Tamagami Simms retires a venerable academic, and late in life, his mind slipping, becomes one of those 11 percent of Americans who respond to a survey that America has never used a nuclear weapon in anger. Sato, of course, is safe where all safety's lost, safest of all.

In short, they are all free to struggle with the same, entrapping question of what, if anything, one private citizen can do to make the shared scenario less horrible. Eddie walks into the white wood A-frame that Disney lived in when the project was in its heyday. He goes to the dusty upright piano still standing in the corner and strokes a few ivories— Gershwin, or Charles Ives. He goes upstairs to the man's office and searches around until he finds what he is after. From the back closet of a long-forgotten room, he pulls out an antique dictaphone, replete with black metal bullhorn.

He sets the machine up in the middle of the room and begins to play the tape still threaded on it, at the ready position. The unmistakable sound of Disney, the man who himself dubbed in the voice of the world's most famous rodent, comes out of the machine and fills the room.

You must often have heard, as I have, that to make a sensible use of one's reason harms nobody. It is natural for everybody to aid, preserve and defend his life as far as possible. And this is so far admitted that to save their own lives men often kill others who have done no harm. If this is permitted by the laws which are concerned with the general good, it must certainly be lawful for us to take any reasonable means for the preservation of our lives. . . .

In my opinion we remain here for no other purpose than to witness how many bodies are buried. . . . On every side we hear nothing but "So-and-so is dead" or "So-and-so is dying." And if there were anyone left to weep we should hear nothing but piteous lamentations. . . .

If this is so (and we may plainly see it is) what are we doing here? What are we waiting for? What are we dreaming about? . . . I do not know if you think as I do, but in my opinion if we, through carelessness, do not want to fall into this calamity when we can escape it, I think we should do well to leave this town, just as many others have done and are doing. Let us avoid the wicked examples of others like death itself, and go and live virtuously in our country houses. . . . There let us take what happiness and pleasure we can, without ever breaking the rules of reason in any manner.

There we shall hear the birds sing, we shall see the green hills and valleys, the wheat fields rolling like a sea, and all kinds of trees. We shall see the open Heavens which, although now angered against man, do not withhold from us their eternal beauties that are so much fairer to look upon than the empty walls of our city. . . . On the other hand I believe we are not abandoning anybody here. Indeed we can truthfully say that we are abandoned, since our relatives have either died or fled from death and have left us alone in this calamity as if we were nothing to them.

. . . Let us live in this way (unless death comes upon us) until we see what end Heaven decrees to this plague. And remember that going away virtuously will not harm us so much as staying here in wickedness will harm others.

Eddie shakes his head sadly when the tape runs out. He has seen men go away virtuously. He knows where going away virtuously will lead. And he suspects that in no time at all, there will be no place to go away virtuously to.

Carefully, deliberately, in full knowledge of what he is about, Eddie rethreads the machine and tapes over the old message. As he does so, the astonishing sets of World World—the mountains and rivers and magically foreshortened cities—dissolve back into the empty and level cornfields.

Let's start again, from scratch. Let us make a small world, a miniature of a miniature, say an even half-dozen, since we screw up everything larger. Let's model the daily workings of an unremarkable, mid-sized family, and see if we can't get it right. A family of six, who had one halfway happy summer vacation on the Pacific a decade and a half back.

As Eddie speaks, metallic greens and purples emanate from the machine, and the house fills up with his description. A house in a small, white wood town, like any other. He adds detail to detail, until the family itself takes over—the stunned, bewildered trauma victims of this new landscape. He sets them on their way, marooned in the unforgiving place, finishing what he has started by saying:

It's one of those unrepeatable days in mid-May, and all those who are still at home sit down to dinner.

20

To Eddie Jr.'s way of seeing, the former American frontier from the Great Lakes westward had become a giant tourist trap, swelling with a thousand and one diversions both amazing and edifying. Every third exit along the interstate.bore a brown Park Service sign announcing some natural wonder, scenic vista, historic battlesite, landmark achievement, or birthplace of some president or inventor. If not a subdued Park Service brown, the exit sign sported the gaudy reds and yellows of free enterprise proclaiming a scenic wonder just over the embankment: Crystal Cave, the Moon Gardens, the Town that Time Forgot, or Eddie Jr.'s favorite, Massacre Mesa. "Visit the actual spot where they filmed the classic western *The Tribe That Wouldn't Die.*"

Traveling a few hundred miles, Eddie got the distinct impression that the whole country was a giant theme park, a series of scenic vistas where one could drive from Residence World along Driver's World to Mark Twain's Boyhood Home World, then split for lunch to Food World, the historic concession stand that invariably waited nearby. By the end of the Great Plains, even the occasional, solitary Bingo sign—$10,000 NIGHTLY!—isolated come-ons springing up in the most desolate places, made Eddie Jr. want to stop at one of these shrines and at least case the joint for the Old Historian's sake.

But after trying a couple of such Must Sees and feeling more than guilty over the delay, Eddie generalized that the interminable hot spots were all of a piece. A centrally located, WPA-vintage tar-shingle shack manned by college kids in badges and soggy khaki scout outfits served as Information Center and Orientation Museum. After a brief lecture with slides delivered every hour starting at twenty minutes after, the guide took the collected band of pilgrims out to see the blessed birthplace. The fee for the whole shooting match was always three dollars and fifty cents for adults, which Eddie now was. That pretty much summed them all up. Or at least the one that concerned him. At least the one he saw.

Eddie Jr. arrived at the Science Hall and Museum of Los Alamos National Laboratory early in the morning of the last visiting day of the year. A small place, very understated, it contained the bones of Indians, their pottery and weapons. It preserved Oppenheimer's chair and his formal requisition to the government for a nail on which to hang his hat. It included a lump of melted Nagasaki glass and one of "trinitite," the glassy substance the sand had become under the tower of the first explosion. On its walls hung beautiful mounted pictures of fireballs and mushroom clouds. But it contained no Pop nor any sign of him.

Eddie proceeded to Kirtland Air Force Base, Albuquerque, arriving two hours later. He drove the rental to the security checkpoint at the front gate and was duly assured that if the base had received a visit from the person described, he would have been routed through the Visitor Information Center at the National Atomic Museum, the only part of the base open to the public. The crewcut guard gave him a permit, saying, "Drive directly to the museum. No stopping."

Eddie dutifully checked in to the Center, took the tour, and learned much about the history of atomic weaponry, from Little Boy and Fat Man to Davy Crockett, a bomb two feet long and twelve inches wide. He read a copy of the Albuquerque *Tribune* of July 16, 1945:

MUNITIONS EXPLODE AT ALAMO DUMP

An ammunition magazine exploded early today in a remote area of the Alamogordo Air Base reservation, producing a brilliant flash and blast, which were reported to have been observed as far away as Gallup, two hundred and thirty-five miles northwest.

But he discovered no sign of his disappeared Dad. Filing out of the diorama-laden exhibit hall, he collared one of the khaki curators, looking to Eddie a little like Joseph Cotten just before his shell-shock relapse in *I'll Be Seeing You*. "Is this all there is to see? I've been up at the lab, and down here, and I'm wondering if there's anything else." The fellow pointed out that another, tiny exhibit, one much closer to Trinity Site, sat two hours south of here, in the White Sands National Monument, on the southern tip of the missile range. Eddie thanked the officer. He silently agreed that ground zero or as close as possible was as likely a place as any to find a missing man of his father's persuasion.

After a brief stop at Snack World and Rest Room World, Little Eddie got back in the rented car. To his eyes, the northernmost region of the Chihuahuan Desert was, even without the historical overtones, a place unlike any other on this earth. The landscape was perfect, endless, and unmitigated: even emptier than De Kalb. The ground underneath, if it could be called ground, seemed synthetic, newly prepared, comparable only to the seamless, starched linen on a fastidious nurse. The unlikely parfait of colors and outcroppings, the otherworldly scrub and vegetation—occasional creosote, yucca, bizarre cactus varieties—the scope of a horizon with so little on it that was human, made him more susceptible to highway hypnosis than usual. He strayed off the last fifteen miles of road a dozen times.

The missile range was understandably immense. A human could not see from one side to the other, even across the narrowest dimension. The earth's curve prevented that. The range completely enclosed the National Monument, a mere 150,000 acres, established in 1933 because the land was cheap, uninhabited, and contained some truly staggering dunes and wind sculptures of white gypsum sands. As he made his approach Eddie Jr. wondered: how many people die in the desert annually? How many individuals each year, looking for an illegal passage into the country or, as in the case that concerned him, an equally illegal way out, end up waylaid, drifted over in sand dunes, dehydrated, baked, burned, or, like that by now clichéd cow-skull icon, bleached into works of abstract art? Eddie hadn't even a guess as to the order of magnitude.

To his surprise, the Tour Center at White Sands Monument was devoted almost exclusively to the geological curiosities of the park, dealing very little with the detonation of the device Pop had inadvertently witnessed. The tourist hacienda had as its focus a detailed papier-mâché model of the lay of the land, pointing out the park highlights in miniature: Lake Lucero, the crystallized marsh, the Alkali Flats. Several photos about the walls documented the most truly dazzling and ghostly gypsum dunes, some more than fifty feet high.

The composite scenic wonders would ordinarily have appealed to Eddie Jr. But now they seemed beside the point. He put in a few minutes buzzing the displays so as not to seem rude. Then he gravitated to the Information Desk, where he could not help but notice that the local variation on the uniformed guide nicely filled out hers. He read the tag sidelong as he spoke. "Hi, uh, Ms. Henderson. Could you tell me if I've come to the right place? I was told this was roughly where the atomic bomb . . ." He let the clause dangle, having said enough.

Ms. Henderson looked around the room furtively and rolled her eyes: another Bomb nut. The Center, so soon after Christmas, was having a slow day, with only one or two geriatric couples browsing the paste-ups and exclaiming. In a low but official voice she said, "Yes. Trinity Site is about fifty miles north and west of where you now stand." Eddie looked quickly at the floor to find the tape marks. "It's on the missile range. You can't actually go see the actual location at present. But if you want to travel around the rest of the park for a bit and come back here at twenty minutes after the hour, we've got a great presentation about the blast in the auditorium."

Eddie told her charmingly that he didn't care a hoot about gypsum drifts and never had. "I'll just wait, and chat here with you, if you don't mind." The prospect did not thrill Ms. Henderson, whom he found terrifically charming in spite or perhaps because of a half-centimeter gap between her front incisors. After engaging her in discussions about every professional sport and several currently popular television shows, Eddie exhausted his conversational repertoire and fell silent. At fifteen minutes past, seeing that he was now the sole visitor in the Center, Ms. Henderson took his three dollars and fifty cents and said she'd go see about getting the show under way.

As she slipped the money into the cash drawer, Eddie caught sight of something remarkable. "What's that?" he shouted, startling both of them with the force of his words. She reopened the drawer reluctantly and withdrew a pair of mouse ears marked with the name "Ed."

"Now how did those get in there?" she asked, equal parts irritated and shocked. She took them out gingerly between thumb and forefinger and carried them into a back room as if they were still attached to a plague-dosed rat. When she returned, Eddie barraged her with questions about the ears, several times repeating a description of Dad and refusing to believe that no man answering to it had been seen around the premises in the last two days.

After the tour guide's repeated denials, he let her go and followed her into the auditorium, a little room with a little white screen for showing a little film about the Bomb. Although Eddie was the only audience in sight, Ms. Henderson nevertheless delivered her canned speech about what had happened just outside this building and down the road less than forty years ago. She had countless intriguing facts at her disposal: how Trinity Site got its name (Oppenheimer had been reading a John Donne sonnet beginning "Batter my heart, three-person'd God"); how a large circle of surrounding sand had been turned to glass; how the physicists formed a betting pool on the size of the blast; how Enrico Fermi calculated it precisely by sprinkling bits of paper at impact; how others ran calculations on the possibility of igniting the atmosphere.

Eddie, isolated in the closed auditorium, had the eerie sense of being alone in an amusement park, listening to the spiel of a carnival barker spouting rehearsed lines for his benefit only. Such an archaic, sideshow delivery, like the perpetuation and nurturing of the delivery systems being described, struck Eddie as a clear-cut case of Dad's Loser's Auction, in which a two-dollar door prize is auctioned off for ten bucks because none of the bidders can afford to let the prize go to another. He sat on his hands and listened. Mercifully completing her lecture, Ms. Henderson fired up the projector. But instead of the promised *March of Time* newsreel, the screen lit up with a cartoon leader, a short subject introducing Our Feature Attraction.

Ms. Henderson reacted faster than he did. She killed the projector; the screen went dim and the sound drooped to a ghastly halt. But in the instant before she could stop the cartoon, Eddie was sure he had seen Donald Duck, of all people, in a Nazi uniform. Ms. Henderson reappeared, apologizing profusely, saying that things had been very strange around here for the last couple of days. She claimed that a co-worker, recently fired, had returned to play pranks of revenge on her. She promised to find the proper reel of documentary film and thread it up for him ASAP.

Eddie knew better. So the old guy *had* been here. Or still was. Eddie walked slowly out of the darkened theater into the desert daylight. He stood in front of the modest building, looked out on that ungaugeable expanse of sand. Pop had decided to fight noncooperation with noncooperation: he was refusing to go along with refusing to go along. The strategy seemed less polemical than Tit for Tat, but more pragmatic than attacking missile silos with hatchets. Pop had exploded out of the old payoff matrix and was now in some other domain altogether, one that subscribed to another order of numeric and physical law.

Eddie walked out into the plantless sand and lay down in it. The sand was close enough to white, he decided, for sake of nomenclature. In a few minutes, Ms. Henderson came out to tell him that the real film was now ready. But as she poked her head out of the Tour Center, another voice cut her off. A familiar bass came over the PA system, singing "The Prisoner's Song," an old Broadway version of that traditional American tune "New Jail":

> *I'm going to my new jail tomorrow*
> *A place where I've never been before*
> *With those cold prison bars all around me*
> *And my head on a pillow of stone.*

Ms. Henderson gave Eddie a long and uncomprehending look. "Do you hear that?" she asked. "It's not possible." He shut her up, stilled her with a violent glance.

> *Meet me tonight in the moonlight*
> *Meet me out in the moonlight alone*
> *For I have a sad secret to tell you*
> *Must be told in the moonlight alone.*

The park guide, in all her starched, uniformed glory, ran back inside her exhibit hall to find out the source of the impossible intrusion and try to stop it. Eddie simply flopped down on his back farther into the sand and listened out the last stanza:

> *I wish I had someone to love me*
> *Someone to call my own*
> *I wish I had someone to trust in*
> *For I'm tired of living alone.*

It was finally clear to Eddie, here, at White Sands, just a little to the north of epicenter, what had become of his dad. The man had at last completed his own longed-for cremation, half-begun some forty years before. It only remained for a member of the family to make it a decent sacrament by distributing the ashes. The kid rolled over, his face almost touching the sand grains. He reached out and pinched a handful of the unworldly crystals between his fingers. They vibrated, gave off a pure musical pitch, almost all fundamental, without partials or overtones. He whispered something into them and threw the ashes straight up into the air.

The white sand whipped directly upward at an astounding rate, entered the trade winds, and instantly spread around the earth three times in a girdle of imperceptible thinness. As they fell back to earth, the grains, countless now, entered the eyes of the people of the sleeping kingdom, dislodging the spell that had hung there for hundreds of years. Some say it was at that moment that folks finally began to sit up and see things with some measure of sense.

21

The tape ran out. The fairy tale came to its end. Disney, the world of *You Are the War*, grew seamlessly into the world of NORAD and underground hardened silos. Brother and sisters sat stilled in the stilled room. Outside, shadows lengthened as the day disappeared into December afternoon. Snow thickened, wrapped them in the childhood mystery of winter.

For some reason, Artie felt himself grow strangely exhilarated. Listening to the tape all the way through with his sisters in the room gave him, for the first time ever, the sense of his father actually having *lived*. The taped story, with his own surprise cameo at the very end, made him feel, for the first time, how he lived at the most crucial and momentous instant in history. He felt how not one of us can be allowed to abdicate, to give up what little we matter. Dad would have to be the last person to go under.

Somehow, the few moments they had just spent in the Never-never Land Dad had felt compelled to destroy had given Artie an idea as clear as the cold clarity of the late day: *What we can't bring about in no way releases us from what we must.* The top, the big picture, would never reform. The world was, as Pop so fondly put it, already lost, making it all the more urgent that the five of them remaining perfect their own corner. If *they* couldn't get along, what else mattered? But these thoughts came apart when Lily spoke out in bitterness. "Do you mean to tell me that that . . . son of a bitch *kills* himself, and drags all of us down with him, because of a fluke posting to Alamogordo?"

Artie, yanked back to this place, remembered how difficult, how all but impossible, getting along with even the remaining few would always be. "Not because of the posting, Lil," he said quietly, conviction disappearing. "Because he thought, wrongly, that he had been posted there *alone*."

---

3 4 3

Rach burst out, "Ha! It had nothing to do with the posting. He'd have ended up there anyway." And the moment she spoke, the other two knew she was right.

Artie tried to rally the idea that was fast getting away from him. He was shaking, and his voice came out in short halts. "Tell me, you two. Shit aside. Tell me just *one* thing. Do you love the man? Do you love being here?"

For the longest time, neither sister answered. Then Rach replied, giggling, "That's two things, Artie."

"Rachel. Lily." Just saying their names out loud, so hard upon their loss, seemed a miracle. "Don't you see? Pop's deliberately left the door open." It was true. For Hobstown, evolving as it had through endless new jails, had come full circle, back to that old imprisoner: do what you can while you can before you cannot. Having listened in, they were now each of them condemned to do something about the ending.

Artie looked over at his sisters and smiled. They could clearly make out his teeth in the first winter dusk. Slowly, deliberately, with the last reel still in position on the machine, in full and mutual knowledge of what they were about to do, Artie rewound the tape, reached forward, and hit record.

Somewhere, my father is teaching us the names of the constellations.

When he had spoken some, he passed the device to another, who did her turn and passed it to the other. Around they went, all in single file.

CALAMINE

It's one of those unrepeatable days in mid-May, and all those who are still at home sit down to dinner. A house in a small, white wood town: De Kalb, Illinois. My mother knocks herself out to prepare a meal that each of us might find remarkable. My two sisters are upstairs, one with her child, bickering good-naturedly over how to redesign the master bedroom. We boys, all three of us, are in the front yard, playing an out-of-season round of pigskin. My older brother is just in town for the weekend, home from medical school. My younger asks us whether he should attend the local junior college.

Dad has just died, of cancer, the previous winter. No one is sure what caused the disease. Some of us blame his assignment at Alamogordo, thirty-three years before. Others think a more likely culprit to be the style of life he chose in response to a long and unrequited love affair with the world.

I, the middle son, going out into the flats on a long post, a deep pass, a bomb, stop short in mid-pattern. I have had an idea for how I might begin to make some sense of the loss. The plans for a place to hide out in long enough to learn how to come back. Call it Powers World.

It's one of those unrepeatable days in mid-May, and all those who are still at home sit down to dinner. Rach and Artie drive into town for the weekend. She has somehow nursed Mr. Nader through a severe midwestern winter, one that has left the machine unsafe at any speed. Eddie Jr. cools out in front of the tube; acceptance at a notorious, four-year, public, party university downstate means he can now nurse a senior slump of truly monumental proportions. Lily teaches him how to play the segue game with the remote control.

Artie can't really afford the weekend away from law studies. He has more booking to do than he can hope to get through in the remaining time allotted. But rather than get to it, he stalls in the kitchen, offering to shuck corn, engaging Mom in trivial talk. She responds, wrestling over the range. "Art, why don't we talk about this after dinner?"

To Rach falls the assignment of fixing the dining-room table. She tries to invent a napkin variation that has not been done, a place-setting possibility she has not exhausted, one that will delight her family into just this once thinking that surprises still hang about the island, untamed. But a table napkin will only fold into so many finite shapes. So she takes the entire stack of linen and piles it up into a Vesuvius cone in the middle of the red maple. That much will at least get a rise out of Mom.

The four food groups served up, they sit down at their understood places. The kids suffer Mom her little spate of benediction, two adding an amen, two abstaining. Artie tries to think up some amusing or edifying anecdote, some brain teaser that will go well with fish. "Has anybody here ever noticed how all families eat in single file?" Those mouths not full of food take a moment to flash him some teeth.

When everyone has had a genteel sufficiency, Ailene heads into the kitchen to retrieve a pie she has put together expressly for the occasion. But *as she carries it back in, it slips from her hands to the floor. And good cause: there, through the front-porch window, peers a face she has seen somewhere before.*

The apparition lets himself in. He stands in the foyer and inspects the domestic scene, breathing lightly, as if he has just returned from carrying the trash cans out to the street. "Deal the cards," he says. When no one responds, no one dares move, he adds, "What? You haven't set a place for your poor old father?"

"You! But you're . . ." That's all that Ailene can manage.

"What?" the specter demands. "What am I?" The trademark, sardonic, challenging smile. It occurs to them all that there is more to any of them than any of them suspects. But sometimes we need coaxing to act on our own accord. At last Artie masters the apparition. "Tell us how free we are, Pop," he says, through the side of his mouth. Tell me how free I am.

ABOUT THE AUTHOR

Richard Powers is the author of the highly acclaimed first novel *Three Farmers on Their Way to a Dance*. It was a finalist for the 1985 National Book Critics Circle Award and was the recipient of the 1986 Richard and Hinda Rosenthal Foundation Award of the American Academy and Institute of Arts and Letters and a PEN/Hemingway Foundation Award Special Citation. He is currently living in the Netherlands.

COLLIER FICTION

Ballard, J. G. *The Day of Creation.*	ISBN 0-02-041514-1
Barthelme, Frederick. *Two Against One.*	ISBN 0-02-030445-5
Beattie, Ann. *Where You'll Find Me.*	ISBN 0-02-016560-9
Cantor, Jay. *Krazy Kat.*	ISBN 0-02-042081-1
Carrère, Emmanuel. *The Mustache.*	ISBN 0-02-018870-6
Coover, Robert. *A Night at the Movies.*	ISBN 0-02-019120-0
Coover, Robert. *Whatever Happened to Gloomy Gus of the Chicago Bears?*	ISBN 0-02-042781-6
Dickinson, Charles. *With or Without.*	ISBN 0-02-019560-5
Handke, Peter. *Across.*	ISBN 0-02-051540-5
Handke, Peter. *Repetition.*	ISBN 0-02-020762-X
Handke, Peter. *Slow Homecoming.*	ISBN 0-02-051530-8
Handke, Peter. *3 X Handke.*	ISBN 0-02-020761-1
Handke, Peter. *2 X Handke.*	ISBN 0-02-051520-0
Havazelet, Ehud. *What Is It Then Between Us?*	ISBN 0-02-051750-5
Hawkes, John. *Whistlejacket.*	ISBN 0-02-043591-6
Hemingway, Ernest. *The Garden of Eden.*	ISBN 0-684-18871-6
Mathews, Harry. *Cigarettes.*	ISBN 0-02-013971-3
McIlvoy, Kevin. *The Fifth Station.*	ISBN 0-02-034622-0
Miller, John (Ed.). *Hot Type.*	ISBN 0-02-044701-9
Morrow, Bradford. *Come Sunday.*	ISBN 0-02-023001-X
Olson, Toby. *The Woman Who Escaped from Shame.*	ISBN 0-02-023231-4
Olson, Toby. *Utah.*	ISBN 0-02-098410-3
Pelletier, Cathie. *The Funeral Makers.*	ISBN 0-02-023610-7
Phillips, Caryl. *A State of Independence.*	ISBN 0-02-015080-6
Powers, Richard. *Prisoner's Dilemma.*	ISBN 0-02-036055-X
Pritchard, Melissa. *Spirit Seizures.*	ISBN 0-02-036070-3
Robison, Mary. *Believe Them.*	ISBN 0-02-036380-X
Rush, Norman. *Whites.*	ISBN 0-02-023841-X
Tallent, Elizabeth. *Time with Children.*	ISBN 0-02-045540-2
Theroux, Alexander. *An Adultery.*	ISBN 0-02-008821-3
Vargas Llosa, Mario. *Who Killed Palomino Molero?*	ISBN 0-02-022570-9
West, Paul. *Rat Man of Paris.*	ISBN 0-02-026250-7
West, Paul. *The Place in Flowers Where Pollen Rests.*	ISBN 0-02-038260-X

Available from your local bookstore, or from Macmillan Publishing Company, 100K Brown Street, Riverside, New Jersey 08370